The Taoiseach

PETER CUNNINGHAM

The Taoiseach

Hodder & Stoughton

First published in Ireland in 2003 by Hodder Headline Ireland
First published in paperback in 2004 by Hodder Headline Ireland
A division of Hodder Headline

A LIR Hardback

1 3 5 7 9 10 8 6 4 2

A CIP catalogue record for this title is available from the
British Library

ISBN 0 340 83266 5

Typeset in Plantin light by Palimpsest Book Production Limited,
Polmont, Stirlingshire

Printed and bound by
Clays Ltd, St Ives plc

Hodder Headline's policy is to use papers that are natural,
renewable and recyclable products and made from wood
grown in sustainable forests. The logging and manufacturing
processes are expected to conform to the environmental
regulations of the country of origin

Hodder Headline Ireland
8 Castlecourt Centre, Castleknock
Dublin 15, Ireland

A division of Hodder Headline
338 Euston Road
London NW1 3BH

Carol

Taoiseach
(ti:s'əx m. chief, ruler,
man of substance,
prime minister of Ireland)

This story is about people and power, and about the forces that bring them together. The people are works of fiction. But the passions, the fears, the pressures and the emotions are real.

Foreword

I have much to tell and little time in which to tell it. But tell I will, because I am the only one who will ever do so. Others will try, of course, but unlike me, none of them were there, none of them saw the thousand tiny cuts that made us what we are.

I stepped aside some time back from all my other commitments, relocated my computer from my office to my new study at home and began, as I promised I would. Every hour or so I take a break, walking out into my garden beneath my sycamores, or occasionally down onto the Clontarf Road and along the sea wall where I can see Howth in the distance.

You see, so many things happened then in Ireland and I was part of them. Things you could never have imagined. Good and bad. How bad were the bad? Very, I'm afraid. People died or were otherwise taken care of. *Murdered*? you ask. Well, murder is a difficult word; even in law it is mentioned in varying degrees, reflecting the fact that there are many ways to kill someone, some less heinous than others – at least, that is how I understand the position. But yes, yes, people died, people killed them, yes. And grand theft took place too, and crimes against humanity. Pillage. Despoliation. Lies in their legions, betrayal, breath-taking deception. Trickery. Cozenage on an epic scale. Grim balance sheet, you think?

It wasn't all bad. A lot of people were very happy, despite everything, and led prosperous, contented lives. Living standards rose. More houses were built, more children educated. Fewer went hungry. And although this may be hard to believe, however bad things were *they could have been much worse.*

This, then, is the story of our Ireland as it emerged to me over that one, long and never-to-be-forgotten day. Everything I know about, or felt, is in here: I've left nothing out, however sordid or painful. I was always at the centre and saw history being created. But such creation requires intense heat. No one involved survives it, in the end. Yet my hope is that I will be remembered as a man who did his best for his family and his country, and finally, when it was all but too late, for himself. As someone who, in the tender and precious moments in which he eventually found true love, discovered the seeds of his personal redemption.

PART I

1

Dublin, March 1992

Dublin bubbled. Heat swept up from the south in a big balloon with H stamped on it and settled over the grateful city. I was late as I crossed the top of Grafton Street. I hate being late. Hot, incommoded from having hurried, I paused, breathing deeply, a process that made me dizzy. My back hurt. I resumed course, briefly checking my appearance in the Joke Shop on South King Street. It was not even ten fifteen by the time I reached the uppermost floor of the office building. A good omen, I thought. We worry mostly about nothing. The royal-blue carpet of the reception area sank agreeably beneath my feet, the black leather chairs seemed deep and all-possessing. At her reception desk, the woman now whispering my arrival was more bookkeeper than receptionist, a dogged ticker-and-totter type, not preoccupied with nail varnish. It happens with a change of regime, a swathe is cut and all the lovely heads fall. A year before, when I had last come up here, I had been met by a leggy beauty, if memory served, a moody queen who portioned out her smiles like trinkets and who had flirted with me. Beside this one, leaning against her desk, was a large, glossy cardboard rectangle of artwork proclaiming:

FOY'S GENUINE CASHMERE SWEATERS
NOW ONLY £19.99!

On a glass table brochures were laid out showing spring and summer clothes collections, I could see as I got my breath back. Quality stuff, by the look of it. Had to be nowadays, people demanded quality and choice. Annual turnover £800 million at the last estimate, huge, everything funded by cash flow.

The father, Dennis, had been in his late fifties when I had first met him, a small-set, broad-shouldered little bull of few words, forever watching – which had come from the very early days in Henry Street where you'd have been robbed blind without eyes in the back of your head. Ground away down there for nearly thirty years, Mrs Foy in a corner of the back office, writing up the books and making the tea. And all for what? Dennis Foy had died in a three-star hotel out in Bray when he could have bought the Shelbourne. Was that what life amounted to? Cash in the hundreds of millions but death in a hotel in Bray?

–Mr Gardener?

A young man in a lightweight, double-breasted grey suit had appeared. The lower part of his rather oblong face was almost black south of the shaving line and the knot of his tie was no bigger than a thumbnail.

–Miss Foy will see you now.

Framed copies of various Foy's advertisements were displayed above small, gold plaques awarded for excellence, all along a corridor.

–Sorry to have kept you, but she's just seen the last presentation of winter fashions, he said.

We had entered a room about half the size of a tennis-court.

A number of functions were still accommodated within this space: a sitting-room area with sofa, armchairs, standard lamps, a coffee table and a television set; a workout area, with a treadmill and a weights bench; and the office itself all in one corner, a big kidney-shaped desk, filing cabinets and a communications console stacked with screens, telephones and other gadgetry. At the desk sat a woman in her early forties. She was speaking softly but urgently on a phone. Her black hair was square-cut across her forehead and fell in two pleasing curtains either side of her face. Standing behind the desk, between it and another door, were two men and a woman. Their attention was all for the woman on the phone and they seemed unsure as to whether or not their ongoing presence was required. The seated woman continued to speak in tight, concentrated sentences. Face still pretty; any thinner it would have been called sharp. I was shown over to the sitting-room area.

–Coffee, Mr Gardener, or tea?

–Tea, please.

The young man brought over a tea set – Wedgwood, I believe – and a plate of chocolate biscuits. He went to another area of the room and returned with a teapot. He looked over to the desk. –Miss Foy?

A slicing motion of her flattened hand made gold blur. This seemed to be the signal the group behind the desk had been waiting for: they hastened out, as if now to delay another second might result in censure. The young man, too, had seized his moment. I was left with the drawing teapot.

I tried not to listen to what was being said, nor to examine her too obviously and see how she was coping. None the less, as the seconds went by, I was drawn to the slim, almost boyish figure in the V-necked T-shirt that allowed the bones going from her chest to her shoulders and the shape of her small breasts to be seen and discerned. Although in her forties, she still looked younger to me. She was married to a dentist and they had three children. Up to recently she had been in charge only of the clothes and fashions end of the business. A member of the board of directors, granted, but in reality, little more than an employee. No more.

As I leaned forward to pour the tea, I became aware that she had finished her telephone conversation. She came out from behind the desk. I stood up. –Chris.

She allowed me to kiss her on both cheeks, then flopped into the couch.

–You're looking very well, I said, which was quite untrue since now, in the light, I could see that Chris Foy looked as if she had not slept for a week.

–I feel gutted, Bunny, she said and shuddered. –I actually thought last week I was going to die.

Very far outside, as if across the border of another country, I could hear buses' brakes and then church bells. Clarendon Street. Sometimes, when I'd been in Bewley's, I'd nip in to Clarendon Street church, dip my fingers in the font, then briefly on my knees say a prayer for all the fond faces in the past. Ask them to see me right.

–Can you *imagine* it? Chris was shaking her head, her elfin face tight, her eyes sharp and venomous. She said, –I was physically sick, actually sick. Can you imagine the effect it's having on his children? Their father's face plastered like that over every newspaper? Can you even begin to think how his wife feels? It's beyond words.

–It's unimaginable.

–And then that – that prostitute giving interviews to the papers. It's a nightmare, a total nightmare, Bunny.

–He's back home, I understand.

–Filled with remorse, pouring his heart out. My brother – the laughing stock of the country. What do you think our customers must imagine? Or the girls on the shop floor?

–It's appalling.

–Do you know something? I never thought I'd get down on my knees and thank God that my own father is dead. Can you imagine him picking up the newspaper these last few days?

–He was a fine man.

–He would have died.

–He was good to me.

–It would be like someone stuck a knife in his back.

–He proposed me for the yacht club, you know.

–What?

–The yacht club – Dennis proposed me for membership.

–Did he? I never knew that.

–When I was only starting out. There was no way I wasn't going to get in with Mr Foy behind me.

–I don't think he was ever even on a yacht.

–They used to come down there once or twice a month and have their supper. When he proposed me, I thought it was the kind of thing he did for young fellows starting out, but I found out years later I was the only person he'd ever proposed.

In the club they'd smirked at him behind his back, at his coarse wealth.

Chris smiled. –He must have liked you.

–I certainly liked him.

He was balm to her. As if by magic the lines lifted from her face and she was the pretty girl from years ago, her eyes bright and admiring, and I was sure she could feel the warmth of a man's hand on the back of her slim neck. As we sat there, the purpose of the building – her father's dream – its reach and centrality seemed to throb and resonate around us.

–What are you going to do?

–Do? She snapped back into the present. –I told Barry I wanted him out. Off the board. That he was finished here. That he must sell me his share-holding. Initially he agreed – he'd have agreed to anything – but now that he's home and isn't stuffed full of cocaine, he's digging in. Actually refusing to take my calls. So I'm going to force the issue. I'm calling in a firm of independent auditors to go through everything. You won't like this, and I'm sorry, but when they report I'm going to go public with all Barry's been up to over the last ten years. You know what I'm talking about. It has to be made quite clear to everyone that he's not a fit person to be involved in this business.

–There's an old saying in the country – make sure when you open the door to hunt out one rat that three don't come in.

Chris sat absolutely still, looking into my face with almost surgical interest. –Are you threatening me?

–Of course not. All I'm saying is that there are consequences to your proposed course of action. Big consequences. Way beyond your business. We're talking about the stability of this country.

–Fuck you, Bunny, what has that got to do with me?

–I just don't want to see you get badly hurt.

–You're threatening me. I don't believe it. You're sitting here in my office and fucking threatening me.

I put both hands up. –Chris, hold on. This is me, remember?

She eyeballed me for another few seconds, then the wind went out of her. She sighed. –I told Barry a hundred times, I told him, this has got to stop. He ignored me. He told me I didn't understand how politics and business interrelate – but now I know, don't I? Now I know that you have to be found bollock naked outside your room in a hotel in Florida with a prostitute in tow, out of your mind on drugs, threatening to throw yourself over the balcony and screaming for your dead father, in order to grasp completely how business and politics interrelate.

–Don't let Barry's behaviour dictate to you.

Chris shook her head slowly from side to side. –I've spent years hoping that one day he would grow up, that he'd no longer be standing there in awe, his mouth open, wondering how much more money he had to spend in order to buy the respect of men who were not fit to wipe his father's shoes. But he never did grow up and now it's all over. Everything has to come out. After all, no matter what happens we can't be more humiliated than we are at the moment.

We sat without speaking for almost half a minute. We could do that, she and I.

Chris said, –Do you know one thing I've never been able to understand? I've never been able to understand what a man like you saw in Harry Messenger.

Longchamps Racecourse, Paris, October 1987

I stood alone on the balcony and breathed in the autumn air. The private dining room behind me was spacious and wood-panelled and was hung with oils of famous French racehorses. Chrome-framed glass double doors led from the dining room out on to the covered balcony, which was appointed in three descending tiers of leather seats. From the balcony one looked down on the winning post, and up the wide finishing straight, and across the racecourse and over the Bois de Boulogne into Paris. It was just before three thirty on a Sunday afternoon and dancing horses were being led down the centre of the course below me and in under the stands to the stables where they were to be saddled.

–Whoever would have thought?

I hadn't heard him coming out. He was standing just behind me. He reached out and put his hand on my shoulder.

–Not bad for two St Peter's boys. He chuckled.

Inside, I could see the French secret service people, sinister-looking men with dark glasses and ear implants, whispering into their radio sets; and I could see the way those at the table we had left were following his every move, the way one does when one's attention is consumed by the fabulous, or the very dangerous.

–If Mr Murphy could see us now, I said.

–Little bastard, the Taoiseach said, his eyes on the people far below us. –Did he ever give you any trouble after?

–Never. I followed your advice.

–What was that?

–To remind him from time to time that what he'd been given was just a loan.

The Taoiseach laughed. –That was vital. He'd have turned on you otherwise.

In the enclosure far below us two girls in immense hats were having their photographs taken.

The Taoiseach said, –I know you've been looking for me at home.

–It's not important.

–It's the banks, isn't it?

–Yes. But I can keep them off you.

–I don't know what I'd do without you, Bunny, and that's the truth, the Taoiseach said, and his hooded eyes scanned back into the dining room where just at the moment Larry Maher, the newly created Minister for Home Affairs, was knocking over a bottle of red wine and sending those seated either side of him skittling back from their places.

The Taoiseach's eyes briefly closed. –You know how Napoleon built this city? He made a hundred thousand people homeless to create the Champs-Elysées. A hundred thousand people. He didn't have to worry about some little fucker of a bank manager whining about his overdraft. Vision is something that has to be nurtured.

In the dining room, the Irish ambassador to France was being attended to, or her cream suit was, by waiters with linen napkins and water from a champagne bucket.

–This is October, the Taoiseach was saying. –Get me six months' breathing space, until next April. I'll have it sorted by then. They should run with that, but if they don't, remind them that I can be a very troublesome adversary. Do you understand me?

–Yes, I do.

–Six months should do the trick. You have my word, Harry said as we made our way back inside. –The main thing is, I don't want you worrying. I've too much regard for you to let you worry on my behalf about something as banal as money.

Mass had been said at eight that morning in the drawing room of Oakwood, Harry's residence, then we'd taken an Air Corps helicopter to Dublin Airport and flown from there in the government jet to Paris: the Taoiseach, myself, home-affairs minister Larry Maher, George Trout from Solinberg's Bank, Bermuda, and Harry's press secretary, a man known as Big Mac. The Taoiseach had spent most of the flight reading the Sunday newspapers, but Larry Maher had his first vodka tonic in hand before we cleared Lambay Island. Keg-chested and overweight, in his mid-fifties, he could be relied upon, whatever the issues, to show blind loyalty and allegiance, and always to bad-mouth the Taoiseach's opponents. These assets of Larry's had outweighed some of his personal failings, such as his heavy drinking. Many said he had been given this brand-new portfolio only because the Taoiseach himself wanted to keep a tight hold on domestic politics. Half an hour out from Paris the Taoiseach had crooked his index finger, and spent the remainder of the airborne time in discussion with his minister.

We'd landed at a military airfield somewhere north of Paris where we'd been met by Imelda Knowles, the Irish ambassador to France, an appointee of the Taoiseach. In a convoy of black Mercedes Benzes, followed by Peugeots full of French secret-service officials, we had barrelled in along the motorways at rarely less than ninety, arriving at Longchamps just before noon. Imelda gave the appearance of being austere and impregnable, but a persistent rumour – which I cannot even now confirm – had long suggested a romantic side to her relationship with Taoiseach Harry Messenger.

Everyone stood up as we came back in. The Taoiseach made little patting motions with his hands, a waiter ran forward to pull out his chair and another stood by to pour him wine. As Harry sat, the young Frenchwoman next to him leaned across and whispered something. Harry laughed. He was ever radiant for women, and they shone for him, drawn into his never less than charming ambit, bedazzled by the legends that preceded him, by the risks he was forever taking, whether in politics or in matters of the heart.

Her first name was Chantal, as I remember, her husband was a French trainer of racehorses and one of his principal patrons was Dr Brendan Broe, the Irish industrialist, who had a horse running that afternoon. Wisps of Chantal's blonde hair fell almost to her high cheekbones and across her neon-bright blue eyes. She was absorbed in Harry, listening to him intently, or frowning, or doing the French thing with her lips, or leaning back in amusement.

Dr Broe spoke across the table. –I was just telling them about the first time I gave big money for a horse, Taoiseach, he began.

The Taoiseach patted Chantal's hand, then turned his attention benignly to Broe. The Irish industrialist was diminutive and broad but his surprisingly large hands, as well as his accent, still spoke of his west Clare origins where he had mixed cement on building sites from the age of twelve.

–I'd never given more than five or six grand for a horse before. Agent who bought him for me said, 'Dr Broe, if this horse doesn't win the Derby I'll eat me wife and children.' Cost me eighty grand.

Larry Maher peered with bemusement into his wine glass. –Eighty grand, he said.

Brendan Broe had been one of the first modern Irishmen to equip himself with all the symbols of great wealth: a yacht and crew, a private jet, racehorses in five countries, houses and villas scattered like decorations on a cake. Dr Broe – the honorary degree in law had been conferred five years before; there was now a Dr Broe stadium outside Ennis for hurling and Gaelic football – had made his fortune buying and selling companies, beginning in the UK, where he had been described as a 'people-crusher', a man whose genius lay in his ability to strip large corporations of human beings in their thousands.

–Anyway, he never ran as a two-year-old, kept going lame, I kept paying the bills, Broe said. –Training bills, vets' bills, you name it, I paid it.

Dr Broe's personal lifestyle had become the fixation of a small but insatiable section of Irish society. It was said that he now slept only between his personal sheets, which were always alpine white and made of a patented mixture of silk and linen by a firm in Bedfordshire. These items had to be FedExed ahead to wherever Broe was bound. The used sheets were then FedExed back from wheresoever they had been employed to a laundry outside Mullingar where one full-time job had apparently been created to deal with Dr Broe's used bed linen.

–So a year went by and one day we all went up to the Phoenix Park to see the horse run in his first race, myself, the wife and kids, the agent who'd bought him for me. The trainer said, 'Dr Broe, if this fella doesn't win here today, I'll emigrate.'

I knew from the look on Harry's face that, although he appeared to be following every word, his mind was elsewhere.

–I had five grand on him, Dr Broe continued. –The horse went down to the start six-to-four-on favourite. As he was being loaded into the starting stalls, he whipped around, lashed out with his hind legs and broke his hock into smithereens. They shot him out on the track at about the same time as the winner – a thirty-three-to-one shot – was being led in. My fella wasn't insured because he'd been lame so often no one would touch him. The agent and the trainer went the colour of the tablecloth. I said to them, 'It's only money to me, lads, but I know it's much more serious for you. One of you has to emigrate, the other has to kill his family and eat them.' I said it dead-pan, like, and you should have seen their faces. 'Jesus, Dr Broe, that was all just a bit of harmless fun,' they said. 'Oh, I'm glad to know that, lads,' I said. 'I thought for a minute this business was serious.'

Led by the Taoiseach, everyone guffawed at this tale of barely concealed menace. Harry had always been drawn to wealthy individuals, and they to him, but sometimes I woke with a start from a dream in which Harry's mouth was cavernously open, as if he was about to eat; then, from the back of his throat, emerged the head of a snake.

–That's the best one I ever heard! Larry Maher guffawed as he reached behind him and grasped the neck of a champagne bottle from its ice bucket.

Waiters began to serve coffee. On television, beautiful colts cantered on green turf, their hoofs flirting with the ground.

–Taoiseach. The Irish ambassador was on her feet. –We must do our duty for the big race, she said.

Harry looked up at her, his expression reluctant.

–RTÉ are covering it live, Taoiseach, said Big Mac.

–Well, then, we must give the punters at home value for money, the Taoiseach said, and stood up.

So did everyone then, including Larry Maher. –Best foot forward, he said.

–You stay here, Harry growled, and the Minister for Home Affairs sat down again as if chopped at the ankles.

George Trout still chain-smoked and his voice was even hoarser and more furred than it had been and his tanned scalp now lacked even wisps of his black hair; but he was still the unfailingly courteous banker I'd first met in Bermuda nearly twenty years before. Solinberg's, the bank George managed, was, like Lipman Brothers Bank in Dublin, of which I was chairman, the subsidiary of a merchant bank in London.

George loved to gamble. When he began coming to Ireland, I had brought him out to Leopardstown where my firm had reserved seats – not that it had mattered, since George spent most of his time down among the bookies. It was in Leopardstown that I introduced him to Harry, on a sunny afternoon on which a horse of Harry's cantered home in a big race and Harry led it in to the cheers of the stands. On this trip, George had been in Dublin to see me and had rerouted his homeward flight in order to come to the races in Paris. Now he and I sat out on the balcony and watched the jockeys' silks streaming below us in a great exotic shoal.

–It's your call. I'll support any decision you make, he said at last.

–We may get another year out of it, maybe two. We've had a great run. Neither of us is on the bread line. But my judgement is that we should get out while we're ahead. Before something happens and we can't.

George leaned back, sun on his face. –Of course

you're right. And the charm of it is that if we wind it up over a couple of years and go quietly away, no one will ever know it happened. No one. That is what makes it so beautiful.

–Exactly.

–You're a genius, Bunny, George said.

I thought back to the time when we had first met, of how little I had known then compared to what I knew now, of the turbulence of those long-ago years, but also of their intermittent sweetness. Wondrous how the mind, even at such a remove, can effortlessly pluck a memory and allow you to suck it as if it had only just been picked. As I looked at George I saw his face darken. I followed his gaze into the dining room. Larry Maher had hauled himself to his feet and was walking backwards. An auctioneer from Raheny whose father, Jim Maher, had served briefly as a junior minister before keeling over at the moment he had cut the tape of a new bridge spanning some southern river and in the process propelling his son into politics, Larry was notoriously accidentprone. Once, on a live television programme devoted to famine in Africa, he had burst into tears, a performance undermined by the fact that he had been drunk. On another occasion, down the country to help fight a by-election, he had, believing himself to be off-mike, described a renowned female media figure in terms of unapproachable filth. Now as I watched he righted himself and tilted in our direction.

–Is he always like this? George asked.

I didn't have time to reply, for the Irish Minister for Home Affairs was within three strides of us, his face round and wet and the shade of pea soup. Jaw a-sag, hands groping, his frantic eyes told us exactly what would happen next. He hit each of the three steps down to the front of the box with a deadweight tread. Then he lurched to the parapet, folded over it with his upper body and puked magnificently into the public enclosure.

–Good God, George murmured.

I prayed that what had taken place might be dispersed, as happens when you flush the toilet in an aeroplane. –He's under a bit of pressure, I said.

–I'm going to bet some horses, George said.

Over heads I could see Harry in the parade ring, surrounded by a group of Arab-looking men. I loved the sense of excitement and intrigue down here and the way the French crowd harangued their politicians and their aristocracy and hurled obscenities at the jockeys. I turned away from the horses and strolled across lawns and over to a spot removed from the excitement, to a wooden seat beneath a big chestnut tree. Conkers shone from the grass. Years ago they had been like currency: we'd stuffed our pockets with them and threaded them with twine.

The Taoiseach's remarks had stirred deep memories within me. I will tell you in time what they meant to me, how the past suddenly felt so vital and close, how clearly here in Paris I could now hear the voices from both yards in St Peter's School. But for the moment believe me when I say that I was content to sit beneath the bounteous chestnut tree, hidden by its shadow from the world and happy in the knowledge that the past is never more than a moment away.

At home we still talked about it, the majesty, the feeling for the first time of being ten feet tall.

–A whole sea a people, Da would say, and he'd do this with his hands to show how big the sea was. –A million people on their knees.

–The colours, Mam would say, and smile, although she hadn't been there at all: Gran Gardener had been sick that week and Mam had stayed at home to mind her.

–They say you could only find the likes of it in St Peter's, Da would say, matter-of-fact. –St Peter's in Rome.

–I was there! Rosemary would shout. –I was there for the Children's Mass!

Da would reach out his hand and Rosemary would snuggle into his knees. Then Dick, or maybe Da's brother, Father John, if he was home, would say, –And was Bunny there?

And everyone would say, –How could Bunny have been there? He was too young!

And I'd jump up, shouting, –I was there! I was!

–How could you a been there and you only a baby? Dick'd say.

I'd catch him winking at Da when he said this, or at Mam. –Da carried me! I'd say. –Didn't you, Da? Didn't you?

Da'd look very serious then and he'd frown and tap his ash into the packet and say, –I can't remember. It was years ago.

–Ah, come on! Da!

Da'd shrug like he really couldn't remember and then Rosemary or Dick would always come in with, –So how do we *know* you was there, Bunny?

I always looked to Mam then for she'd be smiling at me so warm I knew I was special. –That's right, how do we know? she'd say very soft, and she'd cross her legs, the shoe dangling from the toe of one foot.

I'd draw myself up straight. –'Cos I remember the procession.

–So tell us the procession, if you really was there, Dick'd say.

Another look to Mam; another smile. –Tell us, Bunny.

–First came a detachment of cavalry . . . I'd see her happy face and feel a king. –. . . followed by the Banner of the Blessed Sacrament . . .

Da'd be looking over at Father John with a big grin. –. . . then sixty thousand men, according to their parish, cross-bearers, acolytes, Reverend Brothers . . .

–How many?

–Stop that, Dick! Da'd snap.

–. . . Canons Regular, in the following order: Canons Regular of the Lateran, Premonstratensians, Canons Regular of the Holy Cross . . . Mam'd nod; I'd lick my lips. –. . . Monks: Benedictines, Cistercians, Basilians. Mendicant orders: Dominicans, Franciscans – Friars Minor, Conventuals, Capuchins – Augustinians, Carmelites . . .

Father John'd be laughing to himself. –Good man! And then to Da, –I couldn't remember half a them if I tried!

–He never misses one! Da'd chortle. –And he reads the paper as well – at seven years of age!

–. . . Clerics regular: Theatines, Barnabites and Jesuits. Ecclesiastical Congregations: Oratorians, Vincentians, Sulpicians, Fathers of the Society of Foreign Missions of Paris . . . Out of nowhere the smell of incense'd lick me, and for a moment too brief to hold, I could see all the people. –. . . Passionists, Redemptorists,

Fathers of the Sacred Heart, Fathers of the Holy Ghost, Oblates, Marists, Assumptionists, Fathers of the Blessed Sacrament, Salesians. Torch-bearers. The Blessed Sacrament.

At this mention everyone would dip their heads and, particularly if Father John was in the room, bless themselves. I'd count to five. One day when Mam's head was bowed I saw white hairs along the line of her parting.

–Cardinals. Archbishops. Bishops. Members of the Permanent Committee for Eucharistic Congresses . . .

It was a kind of power when I said the Eucharistic Congress because everyone, even Dick, kept quiet. I'd learned it off of Gran Gardener when she'd read it out loud from the paper. I'd say it after her and she'd give me bullseyes.

–. . . Urban district councils, Boards of Public Assistance, National University representatives, others. Distinguished and representative women. Female singers. Women.

They clapped, Da and Father John still smiling at each other.

–He has a future, whatever it is, Da'd say.

–He certainly has, Father John'd agree, with sudden and serious interest.

–Gran! Rosemary had jumped up and run upstairs. Mam went to the stove and put on Gran's beef-tea. Da and Father John'd go out for a walk along the canal as far as Baggot Street, and Dick'd skive off around the back of the gasworks. I'd bring Gran up her big cup of soup, imagining as I climbed the stairs that I was carrying the body and blood of Our Lord Jesus Christ.

I picked up a chestnut, put it in my pocket and made my way back to the stands. As I re-entered the dining-room,

Harry was in deep conversation near the balcony doors with a sallow-faced, jockey-sized Middle Eastern man. The Taoiseach saw me and beckoned me over. –Prince, this is a very old and dear friend of mine, Bunny Gardener, he said.

We shook hands. It was impossible to see any expression in the Arab's face since the bottom half of it was covered with a tight beard and the top half by enormous dark glasses.

–Mijas, the prince's colt, is hot favourite, Harry said.

–I hope he runs well for you, Your Highness, I said.

–He'll run away with it, Harry said.

–It is now for the gods to decide, the prince said.

–Bunny will say a novena for you. Harry laughed, then added, –It's a kind of Irish prayer.

–He will need it in this race, the prince said.

–His Highness and I will watch it from the balcony, Harry announced.

The shorthand of power was well understood: Harry and the Arab went outside and left the rest of us, including Broe and his wife, an active little thing with a face like a crocodile handbag, and the lady ambassador, the French trainer and Chantal, his wife, and Big Mac, Larry, myself, three Irish embassy people, four French secret-service personnel and several Arab men, presumably in the prince's entourage, in the dining room to watch the big race on television.

–Have you any idea how much that man is worth? Big Mac muttered. A broad-shouldered six-and-a-half-footer, with a shock of untidy, steel grey hair, he had once been the editor of a provincial newspaper. His real name was Dermot MacNamara. He hissed, –Over a billion US. Comes out of a hole in the ground somewhere in the Gulf. They say he owns a hundred Bentleys.

George came in and handed me a betting slip. –If it wins, we buy the girls presents, he said, so that only I could hear. –If it loses, it goes down to client account.

–What have I backed?

–Dr Broe's filly. George smiled and his gold fillings sparkled. –At sixty-six to one.

–I backed Mijas, Big Mac said. –The prince told the Taoiseach he'll piss in.

The horses were loaded, the race began. Out on the spacious balcony, Taoiseach and prince remained deeply engaged. I knew no one more single-minded than Harry in the pursuit of an objective. For he had confounded everyone, this man whose hair was still full if now grey, whose eyes still danced in his head. He had escaped Gillespie's trap seventeen years ago, had gone on to eat a thousand chicken dinners in remote towns and villages that seemed ever encased in mist, had tolerated barely literate sycophants, drunken local pols and hairy men who masticated with their jaws agape, and under the noses of his party machine had built himself the power base that had swept him back into command and left his enemies on the political sidelines for the rest of their lives.

The horses turned into the head of the straight and the Arabs began to yell and to wave their hands. The gold colours of Mijas were forging arrow-straight down the Paris turf, five lengths clear. Outside, I saw the prince take out a pair of tiny binoculars.

–Come on, you good thing! cried Big Mac.

The crowd's voice rose. I searched for Broe's filly and

found her way back and alone, on the outside. But then, even as I watched, she began her move.

–*Allez!* hissed Broe's trainer, a hairy man with multiple chins. –*Allez!*

Harry used power like a master magician used stage tricks. Audiences were bedazzled, they never quite knew what was happening, just that they loved it. And him.

On television the picture tightened on Mijas, on his shining, reaching neck, his flared, delicately curved pink nostrils. The Arabs were jumping about and screaming. Mijas needed only to stay in front for another few strides.

I saw the French trainer suck in his breath. Green flashed past like the wink of sunset. Broe leaped up. –*Yes!*

He blessed himself.

The Arabs were looking at one another in bewilderment. On the balcony, the prince sat down and Harry patted his shoulder. Inside, Chantal had her arms round Broe's neck, and her husband was trying to steady his hands as he lit a cigarette.

–In the very last stride, someone said. –Amazing.

–We must go down and lead her in, Dr Broe said.

Everyone made to leave at the same time, but at that moment the Taoiseach was standing at the door to the balcony, finger crooked. –Brendan.

They froze.

–A moment.

–But he has to lead in the filly, Taoiseach! cried Broe's wife.

Broe looked at her, as if one side of his face was warm and flushed, and the other, the one he had just shown her, made of ice. –You lead her in, he said. Then, –Of course, Taoiseach. Broe went out to the balcony.

–For fuck's sake, Big Mac muttered, and tore up his silver foil betting slip.

The gasworks was across the road behind O'Connors' house and the railway line to Howth. The air smelt of gas the whole time but no one passed any remarks – except people from other places.

–How do yous live with the smell?

–What smell? We get no smell.

–As bad as we are, we don't have a smell.

Aunt Nancy lived in Ringsend. She was Mam's younger sister, even though she looked much older. She had a sick baby that went blue when it cried and had twice nearly died. When they went home, Mam always looked sad and said, –Poor Aunt Nancy.

–If only she had a husband, said Gran.

–But she has, Granny! Mam said very loud and my heart jumped. –He just ran out on her!

–She's still young, Gran persisted. –She could find someone else.

–Who'd want a woman with a sick baby? Mam asked.

–There's some, Gran said.

–No one wants you in Ireland if you're poor and sick, Mam said.

Aunt Nancy had married a man called Mooney. She had had one child with him but then, when she had another, Mooney had run off with the first child. Aunt Nancy always put the pram beside the stove in our house because her baby was always cold. She tried to give her a bottle but the baby cried and cried.

–Oh, Jesus, she's gone blue! Aunt Nancy cried, and picked her up.

Mam took the baby from her and tried to stop her crying by making little coos. –She weighs nothing.

–Three and a half pounds.

–Mother a God.

Mam used to bring Aunt Nancy into the front room and give her a nip of whiskey, just to cheer her up. When Aunt Nancy and her baby had gone home Mam'd sit down and her face would be sad.

–Mam?

–I'm all right, Bunny. I'm just sad for Aunt Nancy.

–Might her baby die?

–Oh, God forgive you, Mam said, and blessed herself.

I snuggled up. –But might she?

–She's already nearly died twice from one of those blue fits, Mam said. –Aunt Nancy has to watch her the whole time.

–Where is Mooney?

–He went away. Please God he'll never come back.

–What did he do?

–Bad things. Come here and give me a hug.

Mooney was a shadow that I never understood; for he moved like that in fragments of conversation, as if everyone was scared of him. I heard low talk when they thought I was asleep and Mam's voice saying, 'I told her she should call the guards.' I was scared of Mooney but Mam said it was all right, there was nothing to be scared of, that he was in Liverpool. But I heard Da telling Father John that your man was mixed up in something.

Uncle Myles had a moustache as big and white as a seagull. He was retired from Clerys department store and they lived in Baldoyle. Uncle Myles was Da's uncle, the brother of Da's father who was out in Deansgrange, and Uncle Myles came over at Christmas with Aunt Mary to put flowers on the grave. Da brought home stout for Uncle Myles because Aunt Mary never let drink inside the door.

–Did you get a goose this year? asked Uncle Myles.

–We're having turkey, please God, Mam said.

–Have you never tried goose?

–Sure there's nothing on a goose, Da said.

–It depends, said Uncle Myles, on the goose.

His suit was three-piece, he wore a wing collar, and Aunt Mary's long skirt fell in deep, generous pleats, only the very best because, as Mam explained, Clerys was very good to them. As Uncle Myles sat out on the edge of the chair, knees splayed, glass tilted to receive the chugging liquid from the brown bottle mouth, I could see all the mysterious lumps and bulges ensconced between his crotch and his waistcoat.

–Ours comes up every year on the train from Castlebar, he said.

–From Castlebar? Dick said. –That's a long way for a goose to travel, Uncle Myles.

Dick was Gene Autry those days and with his friend Pat Smith and their gang used to gallop up and down the canal banks on Champion and jump the railway line. Da gave Dick a dirty look.

–D'you know that your grandfather came from Castlebar? Uncle Myles said with a big frown, as if he was worried all of a sudden. –Came up in '88 to hear Parnell speak at a rally of the Irish Land League. Never went home, not once, although he thought about the west every day. I'm the same. You keep your roots. I was fifty years in Clerys but here I am, still a country lad.

–Did you ever hear Parnell speak, Uncle Myles? asked Dick.

–No, but I heard it all from those who did, Uncle Myles said and Da handed him another bottle.

–Myles . . . warned Aunt Mary.

–I'm all right! Uncle Myles snapped. –A voice like honey, five thousand of a crowd – ten thousand! – and when the chief was on his feet you could hear a farthing fall.

–Was he better than Dev? asked Dick, and looked over at me the way Uncle Myles couldn't see and gave me a big wink.

–Better than Dev? Uncle Myles sat back, blinking, as if someone had biffed him on the nose. –D'you mean was Parnell better than that yoke who has brought this country to its knees? Are you asking me to compare a prince with a common thief?

–Myles . . .

–Are you asking me to compare Parnell with the Irish Kerensky, is that what you're asking me?

–Ah, Dev is not the worst, Da said. –We're self-sufficient because a Dev.

–Self-sufficient me hat! shouted Uncle Myles. –Half the country is unemployed, half the children in Dublin don't have enough to eat. Self-sufficient?

–Thank God we've enough, said Mam.

–You've enough because Billy has a job from Findlater's, said Uncle Myles. –Mark my words, de Valera will bring this country into the poorhouse.

–They say he's a daily communicant, said Aunt Mary.

–He's illegitimate! Uncle Myles raged. –Did you know that? His father was a Cuban itinerant, that's where 'de Valera' comes from. He's a bastard!

–*Myles!*

I could see that Aunt Mary was very vexed with Uncle Myles for having said that. They sat, looking away from each other. Mam went and put the kettle on the range.

–Is it true they're taking women on in Clerys? she asked.

–I heard something, but I'm not sure, said Aunt Mary, looking sideways at Uncle Myles. –Did you hear anything?

–No, he said, and licked his moustache. He looked at Mam. –Why? Were you thinking of . . .?

–No, but Nancy was, said Mam.

A long stream of air whistled out from Uncle Myles.

–Uncle Myles'd write her a reference, wouldn't you, Uncle Myles? said Da. –She'd walk into Clerys with a reference from you.

Uncle Myles stuck out his bottom lip until it rolled over. –You have to be very careful before you ever write a reference, he proclaimed. –It's your own character is at stake the moment you put pen to paper. And he looked meaningfully at Aunt Mary and nodded as if to say, You know what I'm talking about.

–Dick and Bunny, go out and play, Mam said.

Dick went off down towards Bolands Mills, firing shots as he went, and I drifted over towards O'Connors' to look for Mickey O. I could tell when Mam was worried, the way her face changed. It always changed when Aunt Nancy was mentioned. Only Da could take the worry off her: he'd put his arm round her and Mam'd smile the way she did when they went out to the pictures. Mickey O was the Cisco Kid, but I was Ray Corrigan on Sultan on account of Mam having brought me to see him. I sneaked back in later and heard Uncle

Myles singing 'Down by the Sally Gardens'. He sang it every Christmas. When they came out to go home his face was red and he gave me sixpence. –Divide that with your brother, he said.

I knew by the smell of him that he'd had a few half ones as well as stout and that he was boozed.

–See what you can do for her, Da was saying to him.

–Remember. It's – my – character, said Uncle Myles, stabbing Da on the chest.

–Myles!

–Happy Christmas, all!

Da and me watched them going down our path and every few steps Uncle Myles'd stagger into Aunt Mary and she'd shake him as if she was very cross and he'd say, 'I'm *all right*, for Jasus' sake!'

Later I heard Mam say to Da, –God forgive me for saying this, but poor Nancy'd be better off if that child died.

The sun had begun to slip down towards the fringe of trees. The Taoiseach with Dr Broe and his wife, Ambassador Knowles and I were sitting out on the balcony drinking champagne or, in Broe's case, tea. The Arabs had departed, as had the French trainer and his wife. George Trout was catching a flight that evening from Paris to New York and had left an hour beforehand. In the dining room, the shining race trophy stood in the centre of the table. Beside it, in an armchair, slept Larry Maher.

–We have riches that others can only imagine in their dreams, the Taoiseach was saying. –I'm talking about security, the ability to go to bed at night with the complete certainty that when you wake up in the morning, the structures on which our country is based, its democratic political system, its laws, its membership of Europe, its guarantees of personal freedom to its citizens will all be intact. Of course we have flaws, of course we are poor compared to others. But, mark my words, those others who are rich in material ways would gladly exchange places with us in order to have the certainties that we enjoy.

–The whole Gulf area is seeing an upsurge of Muslim fundamentalism, the lady ambassador remarked. –People such as Prince Abdul are looking twenty, thirty years, more, down the road to the possibilities of Iran-type situations developing in their own backyards.

–Look at what happened to the Shah, Dr Broe said. –He had, by some accounts, more than a billion, mainly in Switzerland, yet he and his family ended life like vagrants. No one would take them in.

–It's the wives and children I feel sorry for, the Taoiseach said.

–Of course, Dr Broe said, and considered the depths of his teacup. –It's the innocents who always suffer.

His wife reached over and caught his hand.

The Taoiseach said, –Generosity has always been the mark of great civilisations. The Celts were renowned for their hospitality. Agrippa himself came to Ireland to buy his horses and was given the best of wine to drink from solid gold cups. Stayed as long as he liked. Had his pick of the most beautiful Irish girls – isn't that so, Imelda?

–Without a doubt, Taoiseach. The ambassador smiled and cocked her head.

–And when we needed generosity shown to us during the Great Famine, America opened her arms and took us in. By the millions. What an example.

I could always tell when Harry was constructing an argument to justify a course of action.

He said, –Now that our turn has come round again, we mustn't be found wanting. We won't be. We won't let innocents suffer. Become vagrants. Have no homes to go to. We'll show them all how the Irish are the most civilised people on earth.

Dr Broe nodded half a dozen times as a pool of assenting silence encompassed our little group. The doors behind us opened and an embassy official came out and said, –Taoiseach, a visitor.

The Taoiseach looked up. –I don't believe it.

–I heard this was where all the winners were, said Barry Foy.

He had put on weight since I had last met him, which had been a few months before on Grafton Street. His hair was cut very short, which emphasised his somewhat bulbous head. He loomed over everyone. –Congratulations, he said to Dr Broe.

Harry introduced Imelda, then we all, except the Taoiseach, stood up. Harry had a way of conveying his wishes by mere movements of his head, or his eyes; or perhaps it was because in the presence of power everyone was extra-fine-tuned to anticipate what was required of them; which in this case, imparted by a single, iguana-like turn of the neck, was that we should leave the terrace to himself and Barry Foy.

–How are they hangin', Bunny? Barry chuckled as I went out.

It had never been entirely possible for me to shake off the impression whenever I met him that he was still a schoolboy and one from the very bottom end of the class at that. Inside, I stood with my back to the terrace door. It swung open in a little gust of wind.

–How are the family? I heard the Taoiseach ask.

–The best, Taoiseach. The wife is here with me, I left her downstairs.

–You should have brought her up.

–It wasn't worth it – I'm only here for a minute. Listen, I had a few quid on Broe's filly for you, Taoiseach.

–Good man.

–Don't lose it, for the love of Jesus.

I could not help turning round. I saw Harry shoving something into the pocket of his coat.

–Thanks, young fella.

–Never be short, Taoiseach.

–God bless you.

I was watching the television as Barry came through five minutes later. –See you at home, Bunny, he said and winked.

I went back out. Harry was looking across the dispersing crowds to the skyline. –Enjoy it, Bunny?

–Great day, Taoiseach.

–We're only beginning, d'you understand what I mean? This is only the start. Every day can be like this, a great day. He put his hand into his jacket and took out an envelope. –Here, count this for me, will you? And when you get home, give it to me in punts, he said. He got up and went in and the secret-service men spoke into their mikes to call up the cars.

I was in Raheny that night by ten; Adi was already in bed. She looked up at me and smiled. In a small china dish beside her bedside light, her slate-blue engagement ring sparkled. –I'm glad you're home.

–So am I. It was a long day.

She looked at me. Her hair, mostly grey now but with blonde dashes still gleaming through it, lay on her bare shoulders. –Did you enjoy it – without me? she asked.

–Of course not.

–I saw Harry on the television, she said, as I got in beside her. –He certainly looked as if he was enjoying himself.

–He was, I said, and turned out the light and reached for her in the darkness.

2

Dublin, 1992

Chris Foy raised her slim arm and shook her sleeve until a gold watch appeared. –I'm all right till twelve. But don't think you can change me on this one, Bunny. Whatever the consequences.

–I don't.

She smiled faintly, a sad process, a glimpse into the intense loneliness of money. –Of course you do, or else you wouldn't have asked to come here.

I didn't reply. We both knew that there are no absolutes, that just as with the price of cashmere sweaters, everything changes in the end.

–I sometimes see your picture in the papers, you and your wife, Chris said. –You look very happy together.

–We are, really. Yes.

Chris smiled and seemed to be on the point of saying something, but then changed her mind. She produced a packet of cigarettes. –When I was a little girl, the only thing Dennis really spoke to me about was education. Never business, never. Education was a woman's way to improve socially. University was the goal for Mary, my sister, and for me. We would meet someone from the professions and get married. Of course, Dennis hadn't been to a university, nor had my mother. Nor had any of their friends. They called it 'the uni'.

–Mary must have been lovely, I said.

Chris closed her eyes. –People came up to me afterwards and said, 'I'm sorry for your trouble.' I hated them for that. It was as if Mary had been trouble.

–People just don't understand.

Chris looked at me curiously, as if I'd said something unusually true. –Women used to look after the three of us. They'd often worked in one of the shops and this was a kind of promotion for them, to be in the boss's house. My mother was never there. It was as if she was sort of attached to Dennis and had no function except to be two steps behind him when he went out the door in the morning.

The father had raised them in a modest house in Clontarf. In one way, he never quite grasped the fact that he had made so much money. It wasn't for *him*. It was for the business.

–Did he want Barry to go to . . . the uni?

Chris laughed. –God, no! Barry was going to be a businessman! And who better to teach him that than Dennis Foy?

I remembered pictures, one in particular, of the small, bespectacled father with his arm protectively around the big, self-conscious son.

–I see Barry from time to time, I said.

–No doubt you do, Chris said drily. She looked away. –We're twins, you know.

–I didn't.

–It was irrelevant. Dennis ignored me, adored Barry. I got used to it. When I was in school I loved nature, biology. I read about this bird in Africa – it lives out in the desert, and every year it lays two eggs. A chick hatches from each egg. But because of the harsh environment, the bird can only rear one chick. It has to make a choice. And so off it goes, into the desert with the chosen one, leaving the other chick behind. I used to cry every time I read that story because I knew I was the left-behind chick.

Chris became locked on some faraway scene, her coffee in both hands.

–Dennis always came across to me as tough but fair, I said.

–He was hollow inside, Chris said. –Fear of poverty does that to people. The shame of it is like a disability. In some people it takes away their crucial faculties, such as the ability to see other people's points of view, or the need to show compassion. He was running not just from the poverty he'd known as a child but from generations of it.

Dennis would have added consumption, and the sight of siblings dying, and the miasma with which they all had had to do battle daily in order to survive; but poverty is a beleaguering word, it captures so much in its grip, so it will do. Once or twice, or maybe a few times, I had an impression, rather than a memory, of the kind of world he had come from. So much worse, in its way, than anything we had known, for in our case there had been a solid base in Ireland's west, Castlebar, people who had owned their own land there and who had thus bestowed on the unborn generations of Gardeners a quixotic but enduring pride. But Dennis Foy told me once that he felt 'hunted'.

The bar of the yacht club, sometime in the late sixties. Mrs Foy had gone home and I was going to drive the boss, as he was known. An evening in May or early June: the sun lay on the evening sea like a giant scarab.

–Hunted by what?

–I don't know, he had replied.

His great-grandfather had been born in a cart on the

roadside, somewhere in Galway in the summer of 1850. They'd come down that way, pushing their belongings from Sligo. Road people. The evictions of Ballygilgan, legendary brutality. The Foys, tenant farmers somewhere along the bottom of a land pyramid, grubbing. Eviction, and then with the blight, flight. Moving on. Begging from the doors of priests' houses. Moving on. Hunted.

–I suppose, he said then, –by fear.

In the late sixties Barry and Chris were just children, living in Clontarf as their father ran ahead of his fear, his shame.

Chris was saying, –It must have been desperate. No dignity. My grandfather rented a room in Cork, he was a drover, and they survived the death of two children there, didn't move again. My father remembers waiting at four in the morning outside bakeries for the dough they'd be throwing out after the main bake.

His father had seen men bleeding to death in Cork from gunshot wounds in 1922, struggling for breath. The old man swore he'd never in his life vote having seen that. Dennis grew up that way – it wasn't until later that he realised he couldn't ignore politics.

–I think he had a sneaking admiration for Dev, Chris said.

–I can understand that, I said.

Dublin, winter 1987, two months after Longchamps

Adi and I went to London for a weekend early in December. Larry Maher was the first person we saw when we boarded the plane in Dublin. We swapped seats around so that we all could sit together and he told me about the problems the government were having with the bill for extradition they were forced to try to get through the Dáil under the Anglo-Irish Agreement. Larry was on his way to meet his counterpart in Whitehall. In truth he was a man who, had he been possessed of just a scintilla more ability or sense, would have been a likely leader of Fianna Fáil and a Taoiseach in waiting; but in that tiny lack lay a gulf of awesome magnitude.

–When we were in opposition last year, we attacked extradition like fucking leprosy, Larry said. He was drinking coffee and his hands were steady. –The back benches'll eat us raw, Pat Smith especially. He'll try and roast the Taoiseach, if he gets half a chance. Bastard. You'd never think they were once inseparable, would you?

Into my mind came a face from years ago, sitting back quietly from the main discussion, observing. And before that time, his voice, deep for his age, resonating up through my bedroom floorboards.

–Myself and Primrose were out in Oakwood the other night. Larry beamed. –Just the two of us and the Taoiseach and Brigid. What a set-up! The comfort and the space. His own chef and everything brought to you by the butler – what's his name?

–Malcolm.

–Malcolm! A lovely character. And the wine, Jesus, you could drink it for breakfast. We get up after the meal and the Taoiseach says, 'Come and I'll show you something, Larry, and we puts on the coats and goes out just the two of us and walks down behind the house. Lights on everywhere. And we goes into this big barn and there's a row of stables inside in it – some set-up! – and he starts to show me his mares. Lovely, lovely horses, all of them in foal, don't ask me the names, and he opens the stable doors himself, the Taoiseach, and goes in, and pats their necks and strokes their ears. 'This is what I love, Larry,' he says to me. 'I love coming out here at this time of night when the world is asleep and just being with my mares. It puts all that old shit you and I have to put up with into perspective, doesn't it?' And I knew he was talking about the Extradition Bill and I hadn't the heart to tell him what I really think'll happen, so I said, 'We'll get there somehow, Taoiseach,' and he said, 'Good man, I knew I could depend on you.' But the fact is, Bunny, that the Fianna Fáil party is never going to let a bill go through on the nod that allows the Brits to apply by post whenever they want one of our lads sent over to them in handcuffs.

–Public opinion has a way of changing overnight, I said.

–Jesus, but it'd nearly make you pray for bad news, wouldn't it? Larry said. –A bombing or an outrage that would focus people's minds, God forgive me.

He spoke these last words in a shaking voice. I saw his eyes, somehow canine all at once, go to the stewardess and I knew that although he had vowed not to drink that day until his government business was concluded the vow in question was just about to be sundered. But then the 'Fasten Seat Belt' sign came on and the pitch of the engines announced our descent.

–Have a word with Harry, will you, Bunny? Larry said. –He listens to you more than anyone.

Adi and I shopped together in the pre-Christmas bustle of Oxford Street, took coffee at a pavement café that had novel gas heaters outside it and watched the procession of humanity, shopped at Harrods for trinkets and foods that could not be found at home. That evening we went to a theatre in the West End – Big Mac had got us tickets for a show that was booked out a year in advance but whose title I cannot now recall – had dinner on a converted Thames barge and retired to a king-size bed where we made love overlooking Green Park. Afterwards, we lay in each other's arms, the curtains slightly ajar and a half-moon hanging over London.

–Do you love me? Adi asked.

I could taste salt on her neck. –Very much.

–How much?

–If I was to live to be a hundred and fifty I wouldn't have the time to tell you how much.

She kissed my chest. –Can I ask you something?

–You can ask me anything.

–Something about someone you know very well?

–Ask me.

–Are all these stories about Harry sleeping with other women true?

I could see her profile against the night. Although she had known Harry personally for over twenty-five years, she shared with thousands of others a fascination for details about his life.

–What stories? I asked.

Adi laughed. –Come on, Bunny! You know what I'm talking about! The stories, the rumours. You know Harry like no one else does.

–That doesn't mean I would know if such rumours were true, I said.

She nestled her body closer to me. –You know everything else. You once told me that you know where all the bodies are. Does that not mean women's bodies too?

–You make me sound like a grave-robber.

–Don't you, Bunny? You can tell me.

I sat up. –This is not a conversation worthy of you, I said and immediately regretted it.

I could feel her draw back. Sometimes – and it had been happening more frequently these last six months – inky squalls erupted out of nowhere on the calm water we shared. Just a miscued word was enough, or, as now, the sudden emergence of the possibility that we were on different sides of a principle. Usually Harry was involved.

–Please don't patronise me, Bunny, Adi said quietly.

–Let's change the subject.

–You're very good at sliding out of issues that don't suit you, aren't you?

–I merely said . . .

She switched on the light. –You know far more than you ever let on to me, don't you?

–Adi . . .

–I know you do, which is very hurtful, because if you really loved me, there wouldn't be secrets between us.

–There are no secrets.

–I'm sorry, but I don't believe you. In fact, the truth is I don't trust you.

–You don't *trust* me?

–I did once, years ago. Before – before you and Harry and people like you had it made. When we were all young and it was still all to play for. There were signs, of course, but I ignored them. Signals along the way that I pretended I hadn't seen. I was foolish, because if I had followed my own instinct we mightn't be in this position today.

–You amaze me, I said. –Here we are – or were a few moments ago – happy, looking out at the moon, and out of nothing you have created a problem.

–It's not out of nothing, Adi said. –And it's true. You don't love me completely because your duty to Harry is more important than your love for me. And so it has always been.

–That's nonsense.

–It's not nonsense! she cried. –You know exactly what I mean!

I reached for her. –I know I'm not married to Harry, I said.

But Adi drew away further. –You might as well be, she said, and turned her face from me.

–Adi . . .

–Just leave it, Bunny.

–This is ridiculous, I said.

–Is it? she asked, and I could see the bones in her jaw working. –You have no idea, have you?

–What are you talking about now?

–About you, Bunny. I'm very angry with you now. And very sad.

I felt my breath shorten.

Adi said: –Has it been worth it all, Bunny? Has it? What have you really achieved, you and Harry? What will you look back on and be truly proud of?

I knew in my heart what the issue was here, but I said, –My lovely wife and family, I hope.

–Damn you, Bunny! she cried. –You've replaced one ruling class with another, that's what you've done! An illusion of freedom exists and people accept it. But the only truly free people are those at the top of the system, men like you and like Harry. Your concerns are for yourselves, your families and your cronies – but even we, your family, are secondary when it comes down to it. You call that politics. Well, I hate politics! I despise it and everyone in it!

I wondered why she had waited to come to London to say this, then realised that due to my work we had rarely met at home recently, which was one of the reasons we had come to London in the first place.

–That's . . . harsh, I said.

–I grew up in a house in which the concept of fairness was sacred, Adi said. –My parents believed passionately in the rights of ordinary people. In decency and fairness. I see what you're involved in, the banking, the strokes, and I know I can't take it much longer.

She was crying, knees up at her chin.

–What are you saying? I asked quietly.

–That you – we – need to change, she said. –We need a big change to make our marriage deep and rich again like it once was, an upheaval, maybe a loss of all that is precious to you in the material sense. But maybe it's too late.

–I still don't know what you want me to do.

She looked at me and her face was drawn and frightened. –I want you to leave him, Bunny, she said. –I want you to choose finally between Harry and me.

Next day her words remained embedded in my consciousness. We hadn't had a set-to quite like that one before, but I knew she was right and the time had come to cut; I had said as much two months before to George Trout in Paris. And yet getting out would mean leaving Harry. I had realised before how much he depended on me, but now the reality was emphasised anew. That, and the other side of the equation: that I depended on him. It was with these thoughts next afternoon on the flight home that I opened the *Irish Times* and read a report of the formation of a new semi-state body to be known as the Irish National Resources

Corporation (INRC). It would take over the function of the old Natural Resources Board and would be responsible for the development, licensing and general management of Ireland's gas, oil and mineral resources. The government had appointed, as chairman of the new body, Dr Brendan Broe.

There was a time when I would have known in advance that news like this was going to break, when I would not have had to read about it in a newspaper. For the remainder of the short flight home, as intermittent sunlight through the plane's window caught Adi's engagement ring and made it sparkle, my thoughts kept returning to the late afternoon at the races in Paris when the Taoiseach and the Arab prince had commandeered the spacious balcony and the rest of us had had to make do inside.

Waves stood on their white hind legs, then crashed with a sense of anticlimax on the long shoreline of Dollymount Strand. Gulls rose and fell in desultory arcs as airborne cones of sand spindled around my feet. There was a time when I had had a dog, a crazy red setter, and he and I had come out here and the dog had, by my conservative estimate, covered fifty times more ground in our walk than I had. I tried to remember his name. When he died a few years back, we had not replaced him. I tucked my coat tighter, lowered my head and dug into the wind. It would be behind me coming back, I thought, it would bowl me all the way back to where I had parked the car.

I was preoccupied, those Christmas mornings, with choosing the strategy to be used with the banks to which Harry owed money: £1.5 million in one case, £500,000 in another. Remembering his promise in October that he needed six months to sort the problem out, I had played for time and Christmas was a useful half-month to notch up. And yet I had absolutely no idea where Harry was planning to spring the cash from: we had not discussed the matter since Paris, and the few times that we had met his main preoccupation had been the necessities facing his government in regard to the Extradition Bill. A rump of rural Fianna Fáil deputies had made it clear in the run-up to Christmas that they were not going to be quislings for the Brits. Larry Maher had been right, I thought, as I regained my car. And Murphy! Murphy had been the name of the red setter.

Over the New Year I continued to ponder Harry's finances, knowing that when the right solution presented itself I would recognise it instinctually. I hesitated to call the usual clients of Lipman's who had helped Harry out in the recent past – when they had been approached before they had contributed with generosity. My chemistry told me to trust Harry's promise of a six-month solution and to bareface the banks in the meantime. Then, just two days into the New Year when I was back in my office, the bank manager who was owed the larger amount rang, requesting rather stiffly that I come and see him.

I arrived at eleven into the splendid room of an equally splendid building just off Dame Street. My coat was taken by the manager, who introduced me to a male colleague, identified only by name but who, I guessed, had been assigned this case by Head Office. As tea was ordered, I admired the spaciousness of the setting and how, above the plainly wrought dado, the plasterwork soared into a lofted ceiling where maidens shouldered urns, cherubs laced fingers and horses pranced through the lush pastures of Arcadia.

–Business is good with you, we hear, Mr Gardener, the manager said.

He was a tough-nosed little operator, heading for retirement age, with greying hair and hard eyes framed by gold-rimmed spectacles.

–We can't complain.

–Thank God for that at least, he said, and sat back and crossed his legs.

His colleague, younger, dark-suited, a man who probably held a business degree from an American university, was writing on a pad balanced on his knees.

I said, –I'd like to clarify before we start that anything discussed here this morning is without prejudice to my client's interests.

The bankers looked at each other. The younger one nodded, the manager said, –Very well.

The younger one put down his pad.

–Harold Messenger, said the manager, –owes this bank one million five hundred and ninety-eight thousand, seven hundred and fifty-six pounds. Interest is accruing at the rate of four hundred and thirty-eight pounds every day. That's over three thousand a week. Mr Messenger has for the last three months ignored all correspondence from the bank, does not take our telephone calls and has made no effort whatsoever to deal with his debt, except latterly to refer us to your good self. The bank, as you can imagine, is very concerned.

–Mr Messenger is an extremely busy man, I said. –The fact is that he does not have the time to deal with matters of this kind, which is why I am here.

–With a substantial lodgement, I hope, the manager said.

–Not at this point.

The manager wriggled his lower lip into an ugly shape. –Look, Bunny, the time for games is over. We want our money back.

I could see what his job had done to him, this manager, or perhaps he had always been someone who fed off aggression. Now, of course, he faced the inglorious prospect of his record being blotted with this enormous debt just as his retirement was within reach. –There will be money, I am assured of that, I said, –but you'll have to give him some time.

–Such as?

–Six months.

–No way, the manager said. –Unless we get a lodgement – and I'm talking about a serious number – within a week, we're going in.

–You're going to sue the Taoiseach of Ireland?

–It doesn't matter who he is. The bank's duty is to its shareholders. This is a major debt. The bank can't make exceptions.

–When you're dealing with the prime minister of a country, everyone has to make exceptions.

–For Christ's sake, Gardener, the bank is being made a monkey of here, said the younger man, his first utterance. –The dogs in the street know the rate Messenger lives at. The wines, the yacht, the racehorses in training. He has his shoes specially made by a firm in Milan and they cost fifteen hundred quid a pair. For fucking shoes! A man flies over and measures his feet. He has forty or fifty pairs. It's obscene.

–I don't think what the Taoiseach chooses to spend his money on is relevant to this discussion.

–What he chooses to spend *our* money on is.

–Unless we get a lodgement, we're going in, Bunny,

said the manager doggedly. –We have security, as you know. His house, all his land out there. Remember, he came to the bank and asked for the money. We didn't force him to take it.

A door opened and a porter in uniform appeared bearing a handsome, silver-plated tray, which he placed down on a side table and began to unload. This operation, conducted in silence, took about four minutes. I took a bite from a fluffy biscuit and drank tea from a cup with a gold rim.

–Thanks, Charlie, said the manager, and the porter withdrew.

–I don't mean to be discourteous, Mr Gardener, said the other man, –but I don't see much point in the circumstances in continuing this discussion.

The branch manager nodded grimly that he was forced to agree. He said, –We've done nothing wrong here. We are the aggrieved party. We did not choose to get into this adversarial situation.

–Is that how you would like me to report back the situation to my client? To tell him that this bank now regards itself as an adversary of the Taoiseach of Ireland?

Both men drew in their breath.

I went on, –I am sure that, on reflection, that is not the position that the bank would like to put abroad. I mean, the Taoiseach is the elected leader of the people, he represents them at the highest level, and the people chose him to so do on their behalf. He is the chief. An attack on the chief is an attack on the tribe, isn't it?

The two men were staring at me. The younger one said, –He owes us money.

–Which I have told you will be repaid, but not for six months.

–This is outrageous. You're twisting the situation. You're making it seem as if we're the ones at fault.

–Six months is too long, the manager interjected, his voice much fainter. –Much too long.

–Five, then.

–Three.

–Four. He'll pay the money back in April.

A brief consultation of the bankers' eyes took place.

–Very well.

–On one condition.

The bank manager's hands were shaking. –Go on.

–That you freeze interest from today. He'll pay you today's sum, but no more. The clock stops now.

–Impossible, the younger man said.

–Fine. Then sue him, I said and stood up.

–We'll look at it! the manager cried, also on his feet. –We'll look at it.

–Give me a ring when you have, I said.

–April, then, said the manager.

–April it is, I said, and we shook hands.

Dublin, 1992

Chris wasn't looking at me, she was sitting sideways and her attention was on the middle of the three windows. As once before, it took me time to reconcile her toughness with her neediness, for they alternated like shadows crossing the sun. I doubt if she was aware of this, of how mercurial she appeared to me. Sometimes her brown eyes were deep and giving enough to dive into, and at other times they were shell-hard and cold.

–My father never mentioned Mary at home, she said. –Her name was never uttered.

The sun was shining in directly now and the line of her face was illuminated, not unkindly.

–What did my parents think they were doing? she asked. –How did they think they could just . . . deal with something like that by pretending to ignore it?

–It's the way they did things back then.

–It must have been. After two months Dennis was working twice as hard. He expanded into Northern Ireland.

Dublin, November 1963

No one speaks of anything else. The whole house is full of it. People drop in, their faces aghast, some of them crying. They can't believe it, no one can. Teachers, the girls in the shops, John, the taxi man, who drives Mr Dennis Foy. How it happened, when it happened. Everyone relates what they were doing when they heard, and how they reacted. The unthinkable. The sudden death of someone so young and full of hope. Big black newspaper headlines and pictures, every morning, of the thatched cottage in New Ross. So cruel, not just for him and his family, but for all of Ireland. And then the man who did it: all you see everywhere is the picture of him screwing up his eyes as he himself takes a bullet.

–Why isn't Mary down? asks the stout woman who comes in when the parents leave in the morning. Her name is also Mary and she was on the clothes counter in Phibsboro before she came out here to work for the boss. She gets Mary, Chris and Barry up for school, and out, and then she does the housework.

–She's sick, Chris says.

–Sick, says Mary, and throws her eyes to heaven. –She should be gone to school. Go on, you two, away with you or you'll miss the bus. Barry, where's your lunch?

Barry mutters that his lunch is in his schoolbag where she put it.

–Mary! Mary from Phibsboro shouts, going out to the hall. –Mary Foy, get up out of that bed or I'll come up after you! Watching that television last night, I'd swear, Mary says, and begins her heavy climb of the stairs.

Chris and Barry leave the house. The mornings are dark now. Television is a new thing that they're only meant to watch for an hour a night. 'It ruins the eyes,' someone told the boss, and the boss as a result never watched it – until last week when he couldn't be got away from it. Chris and Barry take the same bus, but get off at different stops: Barry first for St Joseph's in Fairview, then Chris at the Convent of the Holy Faith. Barry doesn't talk much. One of his teachers wrote a letter at Hallowe'en saying that Barry was cheeky and never had his homework done. The boss brought Barry in to tear a strip off him, but later Chris could hear the old man laughing.

Chris is fine-boned and small for thirteen. She wants to look like Mary – tall, with long legs and breasts that have suddenly appeared. Mary is sixteen and she and the boss joke together in a way that the boss and her mother never do. Everyone describes Mary as 'lovely'. Her dark eyes have lashes half an inch long that some girls at school used to think were fake, and her hair is long and gleams and she wears it in a plait with a ribbon on the end – a different colour for every day of the week: Mary goes down to the shop in Henry Street and brings home all the ribbons she likes.

Chris is not yet allowed do that, to go into town or to the shops on her own, and even though she's thirteen, a teenager, the boss has said that it's not until you're sixteen that you can go out alone, or go places. Even Mary isn't allowed go to dances, not until she's eighteen, the boss says, and their mother agrees. 'If you do it all now, what will be left?' the boss asks. 'I was nineteen before I went to my first dance,' their mother says.

Chris thinks of her mother now and then throughout that November day, as she does on many other days. Mam goes out to work with the boss every morning and comes home with him that evening. She's been doing the same thing since the week after they got married. The boss always says he'd be bankrupt if Mam walked under a bus, that he wouldn't last one day without her because Kitty Foy knows where all the shillings are.

When the boss and Mam come home it's often late and Mary from Phibsboro always stays until they come in. Then John drives Mary home and they all kneel down and say the rosary. Over the years, it's the one thing they have all done together. Not so much in recent times, but when she was eight or nine Chris used to hope it wouldn't be time for bed before her parents came home and the boss came in and said, 'Rosary, everyone,' and the five of them would have to go into the front room and kneel. Everyone had a set of good rosary beads: Mam had brought them home from Lourdes in the Marian year. When the rosary was over, Chris's parents and Mary said the 'Hail Holy Queen' and Chris and Barry stumbled along.

If ever the doorbell rang and someone called in, the visitor either sat in the kitchen and waited or came into the front room and joined in. Chris likes the rosary, not so much the prayers, which are all the same and which she never thinks about or even knows where they are in the cycle of prayer at any given time, but the fact of being together, of all kneeling down and doing something as a family. Like the Holy Family, she thinks. They all lived and worked together and the rosary is a bit like that. She likes to kneel beside the boss when he is head into an armchair, and smell him, her father's smells that lie in the bathroom behind him, and see the texture of his neck and the heels of his socks the way he likes to slip his shoes off – no one in the shops ever sees that, the boss's heels and the way the fabric has thinned there.

Now that the business has grown and the parents often come home later, the saying of the rosary has become less. But during the widespread shock of the week before, the boss had come in and said, 'God help poor Jackie,' and then when he had at last finished watching television he said, 'We'll say a rosary for him, God rest his soul.' And no one minded, least of all Chris, kneeling down in the front room, and when it came to her Sorrowful Mystery she gave it out with meaning, for that evening in the general atmosphere of grief she had seen for the first time a deep sadness in her father and mother, something she had never seen in them before and which scared her.

She and Barry sometimes come home on the same bus, but often not. A senior girl told Chris at break that her father had been down in New Ross that summer and that the president had autographed his newspaper. He has it at home, she said. It seems an impossible thing to Chris that this can be, that someone so God-like and now so dead could have written his name on a newspaper and that this is now in a house in Clontarf. She gets off the bus and walks the remaining fifty yards to the house and sees John the taxi man's car outside.

John is in the kitchen with Mary from Phibsboro

drinking tea and smoking when Chris walks in. They both look up and stare at her. Chris actually has a glance behind her to see if it's someone else they're looking at, but no, it's her, as if she was not expected, or as if they had done something wrong. And then Chris sees Mary's red eyes. She thinks, The dead president, because Mary cried the week before too. Or maybe Jackie has died from a broken heart, although they would have heard that in school, news travels so fast these days, as the boss says.

–Where's Barry? Mary asks.

–In school, Chris says, but whatever it is about the way the question was asked, whatever primal inflections it contained or atavistic shorthand was involved – and for years after Chris will reflect on this matter – she knows immediately that there's much more amiss here than the death of the President of the United States.

–What's wrong? What are you doing here, John? Where's the boss?

–It's all right, love, it's all right, Mary says, in a way that definitely means that it's not. She begins to cry and so, out of sheer, sudden terror, does Chris.

–Sit down and I'll make you a hot drink, you poor child.

Dublin, January 1988

Seizing the illusion that winter was over, people had shed their top coats as I walked up from Westland Row by way of the National Gallery. Lipman Brothers Bank operated from the headquarters of a construction and building-materials company called FXD of which I was also chairman, in this case for twenty years. FXD had acquired a building halfway along the south side of Upper Mount Street – genuine untouched Georgian with a church at one end in the shape of a pepper-pot and at the other a portal on to Merrion Square – four floors over a basement as were all the others in the row, with railings at footpath level and five granite steps up to a quite remarkably handsome panelled front door, which retained its original fanlight, a rising-sun-with-rays motif, a testament to the craftsmanship of another era. A brass plate affixed to the wall at the left of the door was engraved 'FXD Ltd'. Beneath that plaque was another: 'Lipman Brothers Bankers Limited'. Understated class still went down well in Dublin in those days.

No conflict had ever arisen between my chairmanship of FXD and that of Lipman's, nor had the fact that much of the bank's business was carried out from FXD's boardroom – from my office, in other words – led to objection from either organisation. My life-long secretary, Violet, operated seamlessly between the obligations arising from my joint roles. A newly installed computer system in which we had both been trained, and to whose inner sanctums only Violet and I had access, segregated and arranged the affairs of both businesses with mandarin-like efficiency. Sometimes clients arrived in Upper Mount Street with holdalls stuffed with cash and Violet would not so much complain as simply remark to me later that her fingernails were cracked from counting so much money.

A two-paragraph item I had read on the DART in that morning's *Irish Times* was occupying my mind. The newly formed Irish National Resources Corporation had secured a twenty-five-year lease on a building near O'Connell Street as its headquarters. This building up to recently had been a hospital, called Dr Tobin's

Hospital, and had been closed down five months before by the government in circumstances of high controversy – the Minister for Health had been branded a sadist in the Dáil. Now, in a deal hailed as a vote of confidence in central Dublin, the INRC had signed up to pay nearly £350,000 a year rent – the highest ever then paid in Dublin – and the old hospital was to be given a £1 million makeover. The article was thin on detail, deliberately so, I suspected. Perhaps it was my knowledge that Dr Broe was the newly appointed chairman of the INRC that heightened my interest and led me to try to fill in the spaces. Or maybe with the years I had just become incorrigibly suspicious.

Despite the unseasonal weather, a coal fire was burning in the boardroom grate. Oak panels, leather armchairs and generous rugs were all infinitely reassuring to people who came here to entrust the bank with their savings. Violet whispered that my first appointment had already arrived and was in the adjoining room, drinking tea.

I took a moment for reflection. I had been feeling elated since the turn of the year, ever since, in fact, the meeting with the bank when the problems around Harry's debt had been kicked out to April. Harry, when I had spoken to him, had not referred directly to his personal financial situation, but neither had he given me any reason to believe that his self-imposed April deadline would not be met. Rather, he had grumbled on about our relationship with Britain, how they treated us with barely concealed disdain at inter-governmental meetings and how they had no idea of the very real difficulties he faced in the Dáil with his Extradition Bill.

My first appointment that morning was a direct result of my buoyant outlook. The journalist I had agreed to allow interview me had persisted in his requests over six months, and had made it his business to bump into me at several business functions, and had been charming in his assurances that I had nothing to fear from his interest. A young man with degrees in business and journalism, he worked for a Dublin-based business magazine distinguished only for the banality of its content. I had seen an opportunity to illustrate to other sections of the media when they came on to me – as they did from time to time – that I had already given one interview and thus saw no reason to elaborate on what I had said.

–Thank you for seeing me, Mr Gardener, he said, as he came in. He was dressed in a dark suit for the occasion. His brown hair concealed the upper halves of his ears and ended in bounteous curls on his shirt collar. We sat either side of the fire.

–I have another meeting at eleven, if that's all right with you, I said.

–I expect it'll have to be, he said, and took out a notebook.

–Before we start, though, there are just two conditions.

The reporter raised his eyebrows.

–The first is that I see this interview before you publish it.

The young man bit his lip. Then, rather regretfully, I thought, he put away his notebook. –I'm sorry, Mr Gardener, but that condition is unacceptable. We may as well call it a day now.

I had reckoned that his eagerness for the interview would have made him amenable, but I had been wrong; at the same time I admired him for his principled attitude. –Think about it. Maybe we can do it some other time, I said, and walked him out to the hall.

–I doubt it, if that is still your prerequisite, he said. Then he turned to me, a bemused expression on his boyish face. –As a matter of interest, what was your second condition?

–That we didn't discuss Bermuda, I said.

As soon as I said it, I cursed myself. For his part, the young man just stood there, staring at me, as I went about opening the door and standing back, and shaking hands again, all of these actions performed mechanically because my ears sang and I had sunk my back teeth into the side of my tongue so deep that I tasted blood.

I closed the door behind him and lay against it, dizzy and out of breath. My back hurt. My words, unplanned and unintended, hatched from the deep recesses of my unconscious, had turned a lovely, upbeat morning into a harbinger of everything I feared. Back in my office, awash with perspiration, the fact that my indiscretion lacked rationality was what made it so unbearable, for I had always seen myself as the incarnation of a balance sheet, inherently symmetrical in terms of logic and presentation. It did not matter that in all probability nothing would arise from what I had said: it was the fact that I had said it at all that so distressed me. I had unleashed something I had never known lay within me and that made me shake with fear.

Dublin, November 1963

Chris takes off her schoolbag, and her coat and scarf, and sits with her head spinning and tears spilling. She doesn't want to ask further questions because she has this crazy idea that if she says nothing then nothing more will be told her and everyone will be safe. But

John has got up and gone to stand at the sink and, questions or not, Mary's words begin, soon a torrent in which Chris thinks she's going to drown. –Mary, Mary keeps saying. –Mary is so lovely. And all the years, she has known her from the beginning, how she was always such a lovely little thing, the boss's pride and joy.

–Always was, says John from the sink, his eyes worried, and Mary starts to sniffle and says, –I remember her taking her first steps out there in that hall, I couldn't wait to tell the boss and the missus when they came home.

And still Chris does not dare to ask. She is frozen, it's like a different language being spoken in a world where all the people she knows have changed; and if John is here, where are her parents?

–Where's the boss? she asks again.

–They're down in the Mater, John says, and nods once and looks at her in a way that makes her want to let fresh tears burst.

But if she listens to Mary's babble, that's the easiest, because Mary is now saying how when she went up after Chris left this morning Mary was lying there in a pool of sweat and said to her, 'Oh, Mary, my head,' and Mary went down to get her a hot drink, but when she came back up ten minutes later the poor child was asleep. So she left her. –Oh, God forgive me, I should not have left her, she says, and squeezes up her plump face, which makes Chris cry even more, and they share a handkerchief.

I checked her at ten and at eleven, Mary says, and when I checked her at eleven there was something noisy about her breathing I didn't like, I thought she was having a nightmare, so I woke her. And it took her about a minute to wake up and Mary looked at her but she was sure she was some place else, that she was sick because of her eyes, and her colour too, so she went straight down as she had been told to do – as she did before when Barry had the measles, Chris would remember, d'you remember Barry's measles, Chris? – and rang Dr Flanagan. And he was up inside half an hour, a lovely man, and he says to Mary from Phibsboro, 'Where's the phone?' And Mary's heart went across her when she heard him in the hall ordering an ambulance, but it was the way he went back upstairs – he's no spring chicken and he took them in twos – that made Mary realise even more than the ambulance that this was very bad.

She went into the room and Mary's eyes were closed, he'd given her an injection, and the child's colour was gone to chalk and she said, 'Oh, Jesus, Doctor, what's wrong with her?' and the doctor said grimly, 'Meningitis. Get me the boss.' So Mary went downstairs and although she knew it by heart, she could not think of the number in Henry Street, her mind was empty, or at least it was full of noises, and she had to find the phone book, which she couldn't, and she began to cry and all she could think of was to go out and go next door and her hands were shaking when she rang the bell, but when the woman, Mrs Doyle, came out and said, 'What's the matter, Mary?', at that moment Mary remembered the number of the shop and ran back round and into the house and dialled it out before she forgot.

And she was on to the shop when the ambulance arrived, and she couldn't talk, she couldn't bring herself to say what was happening, so she called the doctor downstairs and he spoke to the boss, Mary heard him saying, 'The Mater, yes.' And then he said, 'I'm afraid so. Come immediately.' And he did, they both did, they've been up in the Mater since one, what time is it now? –Four, John says, –just gone four.

–And we've no news, but we've been praying, haven't we, John?

And John nods, yes, we have, and he says, –It's in the hands of the man upstairs now.

It's too much, the events that have taken place between the time Chris left here and returned are too much. She would have thought that if something like this had really happened you'd see it – but no. It's like a joke.

–Is this a joke?

Mary bursts into more sobs and in the hall the telephone rings. John goes out and answers it. –Come on, he says, and his lips are drawn back and he's biting his tongue. –I'm to bring you and Barry down.

–But Barry's not here! Mary cries.

–I'll find him, John says. –Come on, Chris.

–Oh, Jesus, Mary and Holy St Joseph, please take me instead! cries Mary, and falls down heavily on her knees and raises her giving face to the ceiling.

They trace the route of the bus to the school, but they don't find Barry, of course, because this day of all days he has decided to go back to Duggans', that's the name of one of the boys he shares a desk with, and although he's not meant to do so without asking, although he's been in trouble before over this, that's what he's done; but no one knows this until much later that evening.

The terror of it is not something that will ever go away: not of death itself – in fact death, if this can be believed, is still quite an abstract thing even though it is your own sister you are not allowed to see, down the corridor, laid out – but of her parents' fragmentation. They have always been private people, so for Chris to see her mother in a place like the waiting room of the Mater Hospital screaming wide-eyed was very shocking. Equally so to see the boss, a man who epitomised control, who employed hundreds of people, tough but fair, they said, to see him now, this powerful man, bent double with grief, crying unstoppably, his glasses missing – he'd mislaid them; the whole hospital had been sent looking – and allowing a nun or a Sister or someone with a badge and a headdress to sit there with her arms around him, that was incredibly shocking to see.

Dr Flanagan appears and gives Chris's mam an injection. Then the waiting room is suddenly full of people Chris knows but has not seen, in some cases, for years: two aunts, sisters of her mother, a senior manager from the shop in Henry Street, and then her uncle Stephen who works in the office, her father's brother, a tall, blinking man whose wife, he keeps saying, as if this is important information, will be here any minute.

The house, too, when Chris comes home, is crammed, everyone talking in low voices and looking strangely at Chris, and at Barry too, but he wants just to go up to his room, which he does, although Mary from Phibsboro – the distinction from now on can be left aside – keeps coming up and saying she wants to check that he has clean shirts for the church and the funeral.

The scene from the waiting room in the Mater is never repeated. Tears, of course, yes, but never the screaming and never again strange women with their arms round the boss, saying, 'Sssh, there, love, she's with the angels.' But the risk of it is never far away, Chris knows, and this knowledge governs all. So many questions she wants to ask about Mary, whose absence is incomprehensible, whose room has not been touched, nor will it be for two years; questions she might have put to Mary herself once, for with Mam at work there were things they talked about that Chris would never dream of bringing up with an employee. Like breasts and the curse and babies: Mary used to sit on the bed and cross her legs, green school socks to just below the knee, and as she polished her nails tell Chris quietly the girls' things, most of which Chris had guessed anyway, but it was a comfort to hear them confirmed so calmly, although she did in fairness take a bit of time to get over the thought of the boss and Mam doing it.

Death would have been, had it ever arisen, a subject for Mary's room, to be discussed quietly, resolved. When she thinks of the empty room now, Chris frowns. So many questions, like how much did it hurt, or where are you now, and the sudden ambushes of tears, so dangerous when Mam is in the house, as she is more often now, for tears are like sneezes, you start and suddenly everyone is at them. Mam deserves to be spared that, so Chris keeps it all to herself.

With Barry it's as if the boss has suddenly rediscovered him, for they're everywhere together now: if the boss goes on a trip to England in a plane Barry goes with him, even though this means missing class, 'This is education,' the boss says, and Chris gets on the school bus alone. And the boss seems different, both softer and harder, the way he cuddles Chris to him, the way his eyes are distant and you'd think he is looking at you but he isn't. He never mentions Mary – maybe it's for the same reason Chris doesn't, for fear of upsetting Mam; but six months later, the night before Mary's birthday when, for a change, the boss and Mam are home early and the four of them are sitting down to supper, when Chris says, 'Tomorrow's Mary's birthday,' no one speaks. Her father closes his eyes briefly, looks down at the table, Mam looks ahead of her, staring, her eyes on Barry, and Chris goes red, for she's said what she shouldn't and her father is disappointed with her for making such a mistake.

Mary eases away over the years, especially when they move to Castleknock, you can't say any more, even if you wanted to, 'This or that was Mary's': she'd been left behind in Clontarf. Chris sometimes wonders whether the new owners of the house have any idea whose room it was at the top of the stairs, or if whoever is sleeping there now might wake up one night and become conscious somehow of whose place she or he is taking.

She would love to go back there and lie on Mary's bed. She did it in the weeks after the funeral when you could still smell Mary in the room, and imagined if she lay still enough that her sister out there somewhere would become aware of her and make some sign; Chris always went to sleep.

She becomes the angry one. Hard to remember now if there was a clear transition to being angry. Probably not, it just formed in her. She is the one who goes out most to Glasnevin to the grave, and plants bulbs, and weeds; and on a personal level her body is developing, her breasts have formed, she has come into womanhood and she is now older than Mary was when Mary died. And as for the boss, he seems possessed of energy unending, but all for his shops. He has in the last five years taken his business into every town in Ireland, and into the North too. It could no longer all be kept in a little book by Mam: she could not, even if she bothered to try, know where all the shillings are.

It takes Chris another fifteen years to find out why she is so angry.

She should have seen her, she realises. On the day when John drove her to the Mater, on that awful day that memory both enshrines and stubbornly ignores, she should have been let in to see her sister. Mary would have been warm. The thought guts Chris. Her still-warm sister was laid out in a bed in a nearby room, but she, Chris, could not go to see her because her mother was going mad in the waiting room.

During the following two days, too, when Mary was in the premises of an undertaker in Drumcondra and when the boss was taken down there to have the coffin opened on the morning of the funeral Mass, Chris had wanted to go with him, to see what he was going to see, but she had not dared leave her mother, or mention it to her father. Instead she had spent the day holding her breath and walking around as if the ground was made of dynamite.

Nor in the months that follow, or indeed the leaden years, does the framework established and laid down in that waiting room of the Mater Misericordia Hospital change: it is as if Chris is the only one who is always thinking about Mary, but she can never speak. She is gagged. It frustrates her. She becomes angry. For over twenty years she carries this shadow for all of them, to school and home, up the stairs to bed, to college, into her marriage, into her life.

It helps to talk, especially when the pressure is immense, and instead of thinking of all the immediate and huge problems, of the fact that the whole country is sniggering at you behind your back, or that you, Chris

Foy, so recently a girl going to school on a bus, are now head of a business that next year will exceed a billion in turnover; no. That's not what comes to mind; what comes to mind is the morning in November nearly thirty years before, when all anyone could talk about was a place called Dallas and when your sister did not come downstairs to go to school because she was sick.

3

Dublin, 1988

One mid-February morning when the spell of good weather enjoyed the month before was as distant as a dream, news broke that Dr Matty Waters, a leading Dublin gynaecologist, had been abducted from his residence in Baldoyle by the Provisional IRA. Matty Waters had delivered all our children as well as those of the Messengers – Adi had first attended him on Brigid Messenger's recommendation. The terrorists had seized him in his bedroom and, when he resisted, beaten him and dragged him away from his screaming wife in his pyjamas and dressing-gown, the reports said. Seventy years of age, benign and rather bemused of expression, venerated by his patients, Matty did regular night duty in Dublin's inner city for the St Vincent de Paul. For many years he had been raking in fees and was one of Lipman's very early offshore clients.

The government declared that it would permit no ransom to be paid to terrorists and the evening papers all supported this stance. A photograph of Mrs Waters at her front door was especially moving, the anguish in her generous and normally jolly face, her small fists clenched in fear.

I had to smile, albeit briefly, at the official position given the history of similar cases in recent years. But then I recalled Larry Maher's words on the plane to London before Christmas and realised the wisdom of the axiom that no situation, however dire, is entirely devoid of merit.

At home that evening, Adi was in the kitchen. I kissed her. –What's for supper?

She stared at me, then turned her head away. –I don't know.

–Everything all right?

Since London, we had begun to take long walks on Dollymount Strand where we discussed ourselves and our futures, and I had assured her that my plans for change were well under way, which was largely true, since I had spent a lot of time thinking of the future.

–Have you not heard about Matty Waters? she asked.

–Of course I have. I meant to ring you. I've been in meetings all day. It's terrible.

–I've never heard anything so disgusting.

–Apparently he even put up a good fight.

–An old man who has given his life in the service of others, a doctor whose career has been devoted to women and their babies!

–The family may find a way to pay the ransom. They usually do.

–The government has said that under no circumstances will a ransom be paid. Harry himself has just been on television. 'Under no circumstances, whatever the outcome,' he said.

I sensed a primed bomb. –He has to say such things.

–He meant even if Matty's life is on the line.

–I can understand that, tough though it sounds.

Adi drew in her breath. –I beg your pardon?

–Harry's main problem at the moment is his Extradition Bill. Hard as it may seem, and awful though it is, this kidnap may be a gift.

–I don't believe you said that.

–I'm not condoning what's happened, I'm just telling you how these things work in the real world. Events like this change public opinion. The government could fall over extradition.

Adi put her hands to her head and caught at her hair. –Am I married to some sort of machine? Do you have no heart? I owe my children to Matty Waters!

I pulled up short of saying that her debt was not exclusively to Matty. –I didn't mean to sound heartless, I said. –I think it's appalling.

Adi was smouldering. –So, what are you going to do?

–Me?

–Yes, you, Bunny. Bunny the great fixer.

–I don't see what I can do. What are you going to do?

–Well, I'm not going to just stand here and say, 'Oh dear, what a terrible tragedy, what's for supper?' I'm horrified that Harry is taking such a stance. I've spoken to Brigid. She agrees. She said that even though she never interferes, this time she's going to give Harry a piece of her mind.

She turned her back to me and began to clatter pots and saucepans around the sink.

–I'm not saying I disagree with you, I said.

–You're not saying anything, that's the problem, she replied.

–One day you want me to end my association with Harry, the next day you want me to use that association to influence a matter that you have an interest in. You can't have it both ways.

–Now you're twisting the situation! she cried, and plunged a saucepan into the water.

–You're angry with me because the IRA have kidnapped your gynaecologist and the government have decided to take a tough line against terrorists, is that it?

She swung round. –I'm angry with the fact that you never get angry! I'm angry that you didn't come in here this evening raging that the man who delivered your children is being held by thugs somewhere with a gun to his head. Or that maybe he's dead. I'm angry because you coast along just far enough behind Harry not to be seen, or heard, and yet all you have to do is pick up the phone and you could probably have any government decision suspended or delayed. You people control this bloody country, for God's sake! You control the money, the judiciary, the guards, the army. You work hand in glove with the Church. You can do what you want, yet the last thing you'll do now is phone Harry Messenger and tell him to let the Waters family pay whatever they want so that Matty won't be killed.

I realised then that what I had counted as progress since London stood for nothing. –It's not as simple as that, I said.

–That's what's so maddening about you! It's very simple – it's life or death! Adi cried.

Much the same way as people in politics see the difference between holding power and losing it, I might have added. –D'you think that every time an issue arises in which I have a personal interest I should pick up the phone and give Harry an earful? D'you think that our relationship would have lasted all these years on that basis?

–This is a man's life!

–The question remains.

–Everything you do for Harry is personal! Without you he'd sink! How personal does it have to be? What do *you* feel about this? Do you have an opinion?

Does this incident not sicken your heart? Are there not times when whether the government falls or not is a secondary issue?

She would never understand, any more than would the great majority of humankind, that the retention or seizure of power is never a secondary issue.

I said, –I'm sorry. I hate to see you upset.

Adi dabbed her eyes. –I thought we had left all this behind us. I've spent years wishing that we had no money and that you had a straightforward job like a bus driver or a school teacher. That your job ended every day when the bell went.

–I'm sorry, I said. –Of course I'll see what I can do.

But she had not heard me. –Harry takes advantage of you, she said. –He always has for as long as I can remember. I saw it years ago and it nearly killed me. It's so obvious and yet you seem so powerless. You tell me that you're going to change everything, that you're going to break free. I'd say you have no intention of ever doing so, because even if you really wanted to, which I doubt you do, you're incapable of changing.

I could find no words even as I could admire her insight.

Adi sniffled and looked at her watch. –I must get ready. Brigid Messenger is calling for me any minute. We're going out to Baldoyle to see Mrs Waters.

Next morning's broadsheets all editorialised at length on the perils facing our society from subversives, thundering about the threat to our democracy and about the way we were now perceived by the rest of the world as a country with Latin-American-type politics. The IRA had plunged to fresh depths, a new era had dawned and the need for strong government had never been so urgent, every commentator agreed.

In the context of these nationally galvanising events, I almost missed a piece in that day's *Irish Times*. It was written by Mary Mates, a blunt-spoken, raw-boned political hack who had frequently been outspoken over the years in her views of Harry's governments and who had herself been courted by more than one political party to run for a Dáil seat. The piece on an inside page was typical Mates: low-key, factual, flinty and asking more questions than it answered. It concerned the granting of Irish passports to an Arab, Prince Abdul Alman, and his extended family, a total of eleven persons. The conditions for the bestowal of Irish citizenship on any non-national included the need for substantial inward investment in Ireland by the non-national concerned, Mates wrote. Detailed investigation by the *Irish Times* had failed to discover any such investment in this case. In addition, the normal requirement of an oath of fidelity to Ireland had apparently been waived. The Department of Foreign Affairs said that it never commented on individual cases. Mates had endeavoured over a period of weeks to make contact with Prince Abdul Alman with a view to clarifying the position. Neither the prince nor his office had returned her calls. The present whereabouts of Prince Abdul Alman could not be established, the paper said.

Two days later the Taoiseach rang me during an evening Dáil division to say that he had just been served a High Court summons for half a million pounds. He sounded upset and implied that he considered such matters my responsibility. The loan in question, as I already knew, had been taken out years before to fund the purchase of cattle and horses; the agreed repayment schedule had been ignored and the bank's letters had grown ever more threatening. To the best of my knowledge the bank knew nothing of Harry's financial arrangements elsewhere, although they must have suspected that their client had other debts.

I drove out next morning to Oakwood. From a negotiating point of view, this move by the bank put them in a far stronger position than their colleagues', whose threatening actions I had already forestalled. If the events that had now been set in motion took their course, the Taoiseach's debt would be confirmed by the courts and a stampede of his other creditors would ensue as they fought for access to his assets. One week was left in February and then all of March remained to be got through before April arrived, the month promised by Harry in which his liberating funds would materialise.

Cars drove with headlights on and people huddled at bus stops in the crepuscular conditions. The hedgerows on the approach to Oakwood dripped with rain and as I neared the gates a fox sloped across the road. The guard on duty recognised me and waved me through. Fresh tarmac had recently been put down on the front avenue, either side of which broad strips of mowed grass lay like green baize. I glided under giant trees and by way of stud-railed parkland where cattle grazed alongside horses, some of them with tall-legged foals in tow. I wondered if these animals formed part of the collateral of the bank whose actions I had come here to discuss.

Oakwood was an imposing, multi-chimneyed, beautifully proportioned late-eighteenth-century house, the seat in former times of an aristocratic landowner who, when in residence, had presided over thousands of acres and who could scarcely have imagined, even in his most lurid cups, that his house would one day be home not just to a Catholic politician but to the Prime Minister of an Irish republic. To one side of the hall door stood a truck, down whose ramp a horse was at that moment being led by a girl with a ponytail. Beside the truck, sheltering under the eaves, stood four leather-booted Garda motorcyclists chatting to uniformed Gardaí whose two patrol cars were parked near Harry's black Mercedes. I found the Taoiseach in his drawing room, still in jodhpurs and tweed jacket with tucked waist, standing with his back to a crackling fire, his face grey as undercoat.

He began without preamble: –I got up this morning at seven, and although it was pissing with rain, I said to Brigid, 'I'm not going to let the fact that it's raining get me down, I'm going riding on Dollymount Strand as arranged.' And I did. It was fantastic, exhilarating. I cantered in the tide and I might have been a dolphin. The rain didn't matter, I was elevated beyond caring about a bit of rain. Pompidou once told me he used to ride every morning before breakfast in the Bois de Boulogne to lift his spirits and keep them up there for the whole day. Some fucking chance I have of doing that.

Harry nodded to the stool beside him where lay that morning's *Irish Times*.

–I came back here five minutes ago and this is what I met.

I picked up the paper. Although the headline – HOPE DIMS FOR DR WATERS – dominated the front page, it was a piece by Mary Mates near the foot of the page that Harry was pointing to. It stated that in September of the previous year, at the bloodstock sales in Goff's, County Kildare, Prince Abdul Alman had purchased a yearling horse for £75,000, the property of Taoiseach Harry Messenger. The article went into considerable detail about the transaction and concluded by restating the information in Mates's previous article regarding the granting of eleven passports to Alman and his family, a transaction that seemed to have taken place without the normal requirement for substantial inward investment in Ireland being met.

–The bitch is as good as saying that I gave him the passports because he bought my horse, Harry said, jawbones popping, fists clenched. –It's fucking outrageous.

I remembered the two men in Paris, Taoiseach and Arab prince, out on the balcony watching the big race as the rest of us had made do inside with television. –Did the prince in fact buy a horse from you? I asked.

Harry looked at me sideways, his face a knife, the look captured in a thousand photographs. –I wasn't there, Bunny. I have no idea who buys my livestock. He picked up a telephone. –Get me the Minister for Home Affairs.

At that moment, the door opened and Malcolm entered bearing a morning suit on its hanger in one arm and in the other a wooden tray with a shirt and tie and assorted items. –Good morning, Mr Gardener.

–Malcolm.

–No, I don't want him to ring me back, I want to speak to him now, Harry was saying. –Now, this minute.

–We have a reception in the Aras at ten, Malcolm told me. –The President of Pakistan.

–Larry?

Harry was reclining in an armchair and Malcolm was easing off his riding boots.

–Good, good. I'm grand, thanks, grand. Yes, she's grand, thanks. How's Primrose? Good, good. Yes, I'm grand, I was just out for a ride. You should take it up yourself, Larry, you're right beside Sutton beach over there. What? Hah-hah, you're an awful bloody man! Harry said, and rolled his eyes for my benefit.

Malcolm had the knack of pushing the Taoiseach's toe back towards the instep, a manoeuvre that released the heel and allowed the boot to pop off into the crouching servant's grasp.

–Look, I wanted to get you before the rest of the morning got swallowed up, I've got to go and meet some old Indian bollocks. You probably haven't seen the paper this morning. You have? What do you think?

Malcolm, on both knees, had a grip on the hem of one leg of the jodhpurs and as the Taoiseach arched his buttocks in what was, I could see, a well-rehearsed routine, the manservant gingerly coaxed the twill garment downwards in a series of little tugs.

–Of course she's at it again, she's a bitch from hell. But this is outrageous, it's a scandal. I don't know, Larry, I'll have to get advice, but it's clear to me that she's poking her nose where she has no business.

The jodhpurs removed, Harry now stood up and, transferring the phone from one hand to another, allowed Malcolm to help in the removal of his jacket, then his polo-neck, the way one helps a child to undress.

– . . . at a very sensitive time as well. I mean, this country is in the midst of an unprecedented security crisis, all the law-enforcement agencies of the state are trying to find Matty Waters, we're being likened on foreign television to those countries that export bananas, for Jesus' sake. Meanwhile never a day goes by without the Brits turning up the pressure for us to deliver the Bill. It's not on to have a bird out there, like a loose cannon, printing shit and trying to undermine my office and the authority of the state. You agree?

The Taoiseach took a spray can of antiperspirant from Malcolm and squirted it into both armpits, then tossed the can back to Malcolm, who fielded it with his left hand, his right being committed to Harry's starched shirt.

–We still need to find out where she's getting all this filth from, Larry. I want her line tapped.

Harry transferred the phone from one hand to the other as the shirt was fitted; then he crooked it beneath his ear and began to button, at the same time stepping into dark, striped trousers of rigid crease. As Harry gave Malcolm access to his bare feet, I saw his face darken. –Look, Larry, this is not something that can be let get out of hand. This woman is a seditious bitch. How does she know the details of how I was paid for my horse? Has she access to my bank accounts? Isn't that something that the elected leader should know? That someone has access to his personal records? I would have thought so. You can't run a country if there's an enemy spy living in your house – she could be passing on all sorts of information. About my movements. Security arrangements. What would happen if she was abducted, say by a loyalist faction, and gave them information as to where I was going and when, or my appointments schedule? What might happen then? I'll tell you what, I might end up like Airey fucking Neave, that's what might happen.

As the Taoiseach's socks were rolled up over each ankle, I could see his eyes roam left and right with dangerous rapidity. –Fuck precedent! You have the power. Just sign an order!

Malcolm smoothed up the top of each sock with a well-practised flourish.

–Then do it retrospectively! Harry shouted, and jumped to his feet.

Malcolm pivoted skilfully. Harry was at the fireplace, his breath rapid, the veins at his temples standing out and throbbing. I could hear Larry Maher's tinny, wheedling voice, as if he was conducting an auction with one person.

–You're dead right I'm very angry with you, Larry.

Malcolm was presenting the shoes, highly polished, laces loose and tongues protruding.

–I'll save myself from myself, thank you very much. No, I do not. No.

Harry threw the phone down on the table and Malcolm reunited receiver with cradle.

–Stupid, drunken bastard! You should hear the tone of him, as if he was defending some high moral cause, for fuck's sake, when all I'm asking him to do is to put a stop to the run of a vindictive bitch. 'I really don't think I can do that, Taoiseach.' He'll live to regret this morning, I guarantee you that. I'll bury the fucker if this thing goes any further.

In the same way that, years before, children had cut out cardboard costumes and changed soldiers and nurses into cowboys and milkmaids, a complete transformation had taken place in Harry's appearance. In place of the squire in riding clothes stood a statesman in morning dress. The expression, of course, remained one of unconcealed venom.

–What are you doing out here at this hour anyway, Bunny? Harry glowered as Malcolm brushed his hair.

I had thought to slip in a word for Matty Waters, but decided that Dr Waters' fate deserved better than to be aired at this precise moment. –To discuss what you rang me about last night, I said, and checked in Malcolm's direction. Whereas it seemed acceptable to disparage one's Minister for Home Affairs or indeed the President of Pakistan in the presence of a valet, one's personal finances might well fall into a different category. Not so, it seemed.

–Ah-hah, Harry said, and worked his tongue back and forth along his bottom lip. –Now you tell those cunts to get off my back, you hear? This is a political ambush, it has nothing to do with a Mickey Mouse few quid. You tell them that they'll get their money in April, like I said, but tell them from me that if they don't withdraw their High Court summons, I'll make it my personal mission to destroy their organisation. I have a lot on my mind at the moment, but if they don't pull back and give me some breathing space, I swear to God I'll put them out on the side of the street. I'll cripple them and I'll take pleasure in doing it, understand? That'll do, Malcolm, thank you. Sorry I have to rush off, Bunny. How's Adi? And the lads? We must get together. Down on the island. Easter, maybe. You know, it's funny, but when I'm down there, all the shit I get up here just floats away.

He walked straight out and got into his car. The cops on the bikes roared out ahead of him. He would be in the Phoenix Park in fifteen minutes. I drove into town slowly, managing to catch the worst of the traffic and listening on the radio to the grim voices of analysts, preparing the nation for the imminent news, they said, of Dr Matty Waters's murder.

Dublin, 1992

Chris swung her legs out, got up and went over to the coffee machine, poured a cup. Between her hardness and her vulnerability lay a little untouched place of giving that dared me to approach it.

–Broe used to give me the creeps. She shivered. –I haven't seen him for years.

–He lives in Andorra.

–Thank God.

–He still flies in for any big hurling match that Clare are playing in.

–I was put beside him one night for dinner. Some charity event in Kilmainham. He had to have his own special chair – something to do with his back, he said, although it seemed fine – and a fucking footstool. But what really got to me was his special tea. Comes from some place in China, follows him around everywhere like the ashes of Muhammad. And *has* to be made with bloody Evian water, he informed me. When I burst out laughing he turned to the person on his other side and never spoke to me again all evening. Prick.

I laughed. –Tea was a big deal in our house years ago, during the war. My da worked for Findlater's and used to bring home tea sweepings wrapped in a twist of brown paper and my mother used to hide it in a tea caddy under the stairs. Dick, my brother, and my sister Rosemary and I were told that if we ever spoke about it in school, we'd have to drink dandelion.

–Was it at school that you first met Messenger?

–Yes.

I could see her all-consuming interest in Harry, even though she disliked him. But that made her no different from half the country, my wife included. As to the day I first met him, I will soon come to that. However, when I started in St Peter's in 1944, Harry Messenger had not yet arrived there.

–Andrew Gardener.

–Bunny, Brother.

–Brother to Dick.

–Yes, Brother.

–Well, we won't have to scratch far to find dirt so.

Brother Kenneth was stocky, with tight red curly hair, and red eyebrows with flecks of white in them. Eyes pale blue and angry. On the very first morning, I peed down my leg. The pee was scalding and sore and grew into a brimming pool beneath my desk. I tried to scrape it away with my feet, but the smell was dire and the boy beside me, equally small, turned his curly head with massive round eyes and screamed, 'Gardener's after pissin', Brother!'

He came down and caught me by the ear. –Are you not house-trained, Gardener? he asked, his spit flying, and he dragged me over to the door and flung me out. I sat outside until dinner and when I went home Mam burst out crying when she saw me and said she wasn't ever sending me back.

Although Dick at first pretended not to know me, and never said hello, he never had money and I always seemed to have some; so when he wanted a loan he'd ride down with his gang at break to the junior playground, and one day they found two lads picking on me and Dick's gang got them into a corner and twisted their arms behind their backs and shoved stones up their holes.

Uncle Myles believed that Ireland should have been in the war, but Da said that Dev was right, we should be neutral. Two days after the Germans bombed the North Strand, Da came home and told us that he'd met Uncle Myles in O'Connell Street but that Uncle Myles had cut him dead.

–Walked past me like I was a ghost, Da said.

–Oul' bastard, Mam said.

But Uncle Myles changed his tune when the tea ration went down to half an ounce and he was faced with drinking dandelion. Findlater's had branches all over Dublin and although every household had ration books and registration forms for tea and sugar, no one who worked for Findlater's was ever short. Sugar spills and leaks, and so does tea. It was no shame to be drinking sweepings when the whole country was recycling tea leaves, Mam said.

–Tea has the whole country brought to its knees, Gran said.

–Like the Eucharistic Congress, Granny, said Dick, and Da gave him a clip on the ear.

–No blasphemin' outa you, sir.

All anyone could speak of was rations and the lack of tea and that oul' bastard Hitler, as Mam called him. You couldn't get coffee or sugar or soap or white bread either, but it was no tea that drove the country mad.

–In An Bhlascaoid Mhóir as described in *An t-Oileánach* by Ó Criomhthain, the island women had no idea what tea was for when it was first washed ashore there, said Brother Kenneth, with some intensity. –They dyed their petticoats with it, dear Mother a God, can you imagine? Oh, the waste! Imagine all the pots and pots of tea that went into those ignorant women's petticoats!

Brother Kenneth was hard hit by the rations. He'd done almost nothing else in his spare time except drink tea – by some accounts it had been his chief form of recreation.

–The English call it cha. Does anyone know why? Because *cha* is the Chinese Mandarin word for tea and tea came first from China. Yes, Gardener?

–Is that why me da says he wouldn't wear a bowler hat for all the tea in China, Brother?

–Very witty, Gardener, very droll. The Chinese had a civilisation four thousand years ago when we were livin' on cats' fleas, and one of the reasons they had their civilisation was that they drank tea. Tea has been called the amber nectar. Nectar is the drink of the gods. One of the great blights of nature is that, although we in this little island are burstin' with spuds and milk and mutton, we can't grow tea. No nation can be expected, as we now are, to survive on a one half-ounce per week ration of such an essential commodity. Does anyone know why we are so reduced? Yes, Gardener.

–Because a that oul' bastard Hitler, Brother.

–Come out here, you little rat! he cried, and caught me by the lug and after six biffs stood me on the line. –I had you spotted from day one.

It was hard to get on Brother Kenneth's good side once you had crossed him; and when you'd crossed him he'd find fault with everything you did. Even if all your sums were right he'd give you biffs for neatness, the same with spelling: I got six biffs one day because one of my As didn't touch the top line. Although I knew Mam was keeping the tea caddy for our own emergency,

I didn't think she'd mind if I took a little once – not that I'd ever have told her that the Brother was flogging me. I put a good teaspoonful into a twist of paper, the way Da used to bring it home, and the next day after class I stayed back last and when I was going out I slipped it onto Brother Kenneth's desk.

–What's this? Come back here, Gardener, you blackguard! Some sort of jape, I'd swear!

He unrolled the brown paper and the tiny mound of glistening leaves was revealed. He couldn't believe it. He brought it up to his mouth and then shoved his pug nose into it. –Holy Mother a . . . Swinging round to stare at the open door, Brother Kenneth then jumped up, slammed the door shut and stood against it like he was expecting the Germans. –Where did you get this? he hissed.

–From someone, I said, for I knew that everything would be all right as long as it wasn't spoken of.

–Someone who?

–We're not to talk about it.

Brother Kenneth's eyes narrowed with comprehension. –Of course not. Of course not.

–I have to go home now, Brother.

–Of course you do.

He stood back and held the door for me. Mam never missed the bit of tea then, or after. But when a week or so had gone by, I'd see Brother Kenneth looking in my direction with an expression on his face that made me think he was going to cry. In fairness, he never asked for tea. I just let it go long enough until I saw that look, then the next day or the one after I'd bring in the little paper twist with its magic dried leaves.

–He's top of his class! Mam said at Christmas, red with delight.

–And the other fella's doing better as well, chuckled Da.

It was so simple, I often thought in later life. So many people made happy from the sweepings of Findlater's floor.

Dublin, 1988

One of the paradoxes of the Irish climate is that the beginning of spring often heralds what seems like the inauguration of winter – in this case, an overnight blizzard that paralysed Dublin's road traffic and closed Dublin Airport. When at last I reached my office, the first call I took was from Stan Sharkey, a property tycoon and a supporter of Harry's from the very early days. Stan had just come in to his house near Málaga from a mid-morning swim, or so he told me, and wanted to chat about some loan roll-overs in companies owned by him and on whose boards I sat. I cautiously admired Stan, a man whose ability to use other people was, I knew from personal experience, unrivalled. Stan resembled in his metabolism and continuous movements a squirrel or a rat. Most people when they spoke of him said, 'He has it made.'

When the call was concluded, I sat wondering if Adi might not after all be right, if this might not be the time at last to be thinking of leading a different kind of life. After all, I had it made just as much as Stan had, could lay my hands on money to do as much as I could ever want. Yet he could go for a swim every morning in a warm sea whereas I seemed to be forever stuck within shouting distance of Harry. That was the problem, I conceded: I thought a lot about change and did nothing. For example, the proposals I had put the previous autumn to George Trout when we were both in Paris still remained just that – proposals. I knew in theory what I should do, for my own sake, for my marriage, but never made the crucial leap of incarnation. As I reflected on such matters, Violet came in with an expression on her face that told me she was about to deliver important news. Although I don't ever recall discussing her age, Violet must have been as old as I was. Married but childless, she owned a house in flats, and her own car, and had a pension fund that I had set up for her. She loved her work and Adi said she loved me. Perhaps. She took few holidays. Were I to retire, so would Violet.

–They've found a bit of poor Dr Waters. It's on the news, she said.

I blinked. –What bit?

–His little toe.

I went out to her office and listened to her radio. A Dr Matthew Waters, son of the kidnapped man, was being interviewed. The family had demanded proof that Dr Matty was in fact in the custody of the subversives and still alive. They had that morning been directed to a church on Dublin's Thomas Street where, at the foot of a statue of the Blessed Virgin Mary, Dr Waters had found an empty cigarette packet containing the little toe from his father's left foot. Tests were being carried out to verify if the victim was alive when the digit had been severed. The brutality was beyond words, Dr Matthew Waters said.

I heard the anguish in his voice and felt pain for him, for he had come in that week to see me, a man of forty with big tanned hands reaching from spotless linen. A medical practitioner in Los Angeles, he told me he wished to withdraw all his father's cash, which came to two hundred thousand pounds. Although he had no authority to act, I had given him the money. Now he had challenged his father's abductors to show proof before he paid, and the consequence was that Matty Waters would probably never walk again.

Over the forty-eight hours that followed the delivery of Dr Matty's toe, the swell of public outrage was prodigious. The pitilessness of events seared the consciousness of the country and even hard-line republicans caught the mood and turned on those who had so brutalised an old man. In the Dáil, a queue formed of those wishing to go into the record on the side of the outraged, among them the rump of deputies who had so recently urged partisanship with, if not the members, then at least the political aspirations of the Provos. Harry caught the mood as a master yachtsman seizes the gift of a God-sent breeze. The Extradition Bill, now presented as the last remaining hope between us and the Golgotha of our civilisation, waltzed through all its stages in the Dáil and was voted into law by a substantial majority. Harry was majestic in victory. He described the new political climate as being one of unprecedented consensus, praising his own party and even those in opposition. He called for calmness, for the release of Dr Matty without further harm, and for the chance to let the country get back to addressing the problems of its economy. An opinion poll published on the following Sunday showed that Harry Messenger was the most popular Taoiseach ever to hold office.

Except, that is, with the personnel of one financial institution.

The banker wore Clark Kent-type spectacles and spoke as if his vocal cords were in permanent regression. On his desk I could see a copy of the High Court summons that he had caused to be served on the Taoiseach. A recent change of ownership at the bank had resulted in new management: this was the new chief executive, a man whose previous experience was in London and New York where he had earned a reputation as someone who delivered the bottom line. No tea or coffee here. No shake hands either. The day before I had learned with some dismay that his mother was the sister of Pat Smith, Harry's main opponent within Fianna Fáil. This information was something Harry must have known on the morning I had gone out to Oakwood, I now reflected.

–Have you brought a cheque, Mr Gardener? he whispered.

I began to outline the timescale in which our mutual problem – Harry's debt of half a million – would be solved, pitching the key date into May in order to give myself some breathing space and trying generally to infuse some humanity into the atmosphere. I had not even contemplated using Harry's threats.

–But no cheque, he said, almost inaudibly, looking at his watch.

–No . . .

He stood up. –I'm busy, you're busy, this is a waste of time.

–I'm representing the Taoiseach here, I said, with a bit of edge.

–I couldn't give a shit if you're representing Brian Boru, the bank's chief executive said, in his cellar voice. –This is a debt to the bank that has been allowed roll on for seven years for exactly the reasons that you're now trying on again.

–I'm not trying anything on, sir. What I'm actually

trying to do is to offer you some reasonable proposals.

–None of which entails cash up front, am I right? Of course I am, because how can a man on a politician's salary who drinks wine costing five hundred pounds a bottle afford to even get up in the morning, let alone address the tedious demands of his creditors?

–I don't think we should allow this discussion to become personal.

–Money is always personal. You're a banker, you know that. But you have to admit, it is a bit rich to hear him lecturing the country about tightening its belt whilst he's spending other people's money like a madman.

–I think you're making a mistake, I said, as he walked me to the corridor.

–No, I'm not, Mr Gardener, the banker responded, his eyes tiny black pinpoints. –I know exactly what I'm doing. You see, I grew up in a household that understood Messenger only too well. Understood that his word is meaningless, that his only loyalty is to himself and that he consumes things and people voraciously. He is like an infection in the blood of this country. He owes this bank a shit-load of money and up to now he has threatened and cajoled his way out of repaying it. I, however, intend to nail him to the wall, if I have to, to get it back.

–Is that why you took this job? So as to get revenge for Pat Smith?

He smiled thinly. –It won't work, Bunny. You're as smart as they come, I admire that, but now that I have the little bastard by the balls, I'm damned if I'm going to let him go.

Harry was riding high in the polls and was so exuberant about his political fortunes that I could not bring myself to worry him with the prospect of a court hearing. Such an order would not alone lead to a media sensation, but would surely provoke the bank to whom Harry owed the far larger amount to take similar action. With a week left to the court date, I arranged to have lunch in the yacht club with Barry Foy.

–Did you hear the news? was the first thing he asked.

We were seated in the dining room at the same table his father had liked, beside the window and within earshot of the boats' stays' incessant tintinnabulation.

–What news?

–Matty Waters walked into the Garda station in Dundalk about an hour ago. Walked in, take note.

–So they didn't . . . ?

–Bastards, said Barry, shaking his big head. –They sent some other poor fucker's toe down to Dublin. And, I'm told, no money changed hands.

He was like an enormous spoilt child, not just in appearance but by virtue of an underlying unpredictability that never allowed you to trust the ground that you and he were sharing. His reputation in the vast business he had assumed from his father was for taking foolish risks – many of which had, in fairness, paid off – and for treating his suppliers with a disdain and boorishness that many of them described as sadistic.

–But who am I talking to? Barry said, with no little mockery. –You and me know how it works, don't we, Bunny? Bloody sure you know what I'm talking about. Sometimes I wake up in the middle of the night and I can still hear the bastards' voices and smell their breath.

He lit up a cigarette and sucked the smoke deep, as if to smother the memory.

–Did Harry do a deal over Matty? Barry asked, and exhaled. –Course he did. Harry could teach the Jews to buy and sell. But you're not going to fucking tell me if he did, are you, Bunny? The monkey never tells on the organ-grinder.

I managed to smile. –I'd have hated anything to happen to Matty.

–I'll tell you what else I heard, although you probably know this as well. When the toe came back from the lab, the government learned that it was the toe from someone who'd been dead a month – so they knew it couldn't have been Matty's toe, right? But Harry made sure that that information never got out – not even to the family. The government actually leaked a false report saying that it was Matty's toe. In the meantime Harry's bill sailed through the Dáil. Isn't that just beautiful? Poor old Matty could have been as dead as mutton, but Harry used him to get his way.

Two steaks were brought and put in front of us, and a bottle of red wine. Barry cut into the meat aggressively, frowned, stuck a piece into his mouth and began to chew. –Do you have any brothers or sisters, Bunny?

–One sister.

–D'you want another one? Jesus, my father could never have built up the business he did if he had had his family on his back every time he wanted to make a move. Couldn't. He'd have told them to fuck off, wouldn't he? You knew him, what do you think?

–He was a tough man.

–Bloody right he was. Stood for no nonsense. I was with him a lot, saw big men in tears, on their fucking knees, begging him to pay them the money he owed them, and he'd take another ninety days and have the whole fucking lot on deposit at twelve per cent! Twelve per cent! Barry's mouth curved in distaste and he pushed aside his plate with the uneaten steak. He said, –I might get you to come on the board, Bunny. The sister always gave me the impression she had a soft spot for you.

–Really?

–'Really.' You're some fuckin' act. Can't see what she saw in you, an ugly bugger like you – only joking! But I'm serious about her. When I came back from that spot of bother years ago, I picked it up between her and the da, know what I mean? Bunny this, Bunny that. King Bunny – eh? Fair play to you, it's not everyone she likes, I can tell you. I'm not even sure if that's a compliment.

–I'll take it as one.

–Take what you can is my motto, you won't be given it, that's for certain. No, if you came onto the board you might be able to talk sense to her. Calm her down. She's off her fuckin' rocker half the time. Would you consider it?

–Thanks, but I've a lot on at the moment. Trying to cut down, actually, spend a bit more time with the family.

–Once you start thinking that kind of bollocks you're fucked, Barry said.

He looked up. The head waiter had come gingerly to our table. –Was the steak not to your satisfaction, Mr Foy?

–It was shite.

The head waiter rocked back on his heels. –Can I get you something else, sir?

–No.

–A little chicken? Or some fresh monkfish?

–Just fuck off and leave us alone, Barry said, and lit another cigarette as the man slunk away. –Business is a bit like politics, isn't it? I mean, look at the Taoiseach. No one tells Harry Messenger what to do. No one. And look where he is. The most popular Taoiseach ever. I look on that man as a second father, Bunny – and you above all others know why. Whenever I have to take an earful of bollocks from my sister, don't do this, don't do that, you'll end up bankrupt, whine fucking whine, I say to myself, 'What would Harry do now?' and then I just do it anyway.

It seemed like the appropriate moment to test his admiration. I did so. Barry screwed up his face, like a child about to cry, then ground his cigarette out on his side plate. –A hundred grand?

–I've come to you first because I know the high esteem the Taoiseach holds you in. Not that he knows anything about this, of course, he's got greater things on his mind, as we well know. This is a short-term problem. He has various income sources available to him, but they won't mature for another couple of months. Unfortunately, one particular bank is intent on going the whole way before that. My target is half a million but I'm pretty sure that with your hundred on board, the others will follow pretty quickly.

Barry helped himself from the bottle of wine. –Who are the others?

–Customers of the bank.

–When is the money needed?

–Straight away. This week.

Barry made a quick inspection of who was in the dining room. Then he leaned across the table, his index finger pointing at my chest like a pistol. –I don't want you going near anyone else, you understand? I don't want him begging, is that clear?

The small eyes were suddenly misty.

–Sure.

–That man is a great man. He has done things for this country that others only dream of. He could flatten the whole fucking lot of them with one swing of his mickey. Do you get me?

–Yes.

–I don't want you dragging your arse around to fuckers who'll try and lean on him for something if he gets a few quid from them. I'd hate that. The buck stops here. You'll have a draft in the morning for the whole lot.

I didn't dare breathe. –That's very generous, Barry.

–It's only money. I have it, he needs it. What's the problem?

–There isn't one.

–Very good, then.

He raised his arm, signalling for the bill. –It's time they changed the caterers here, he said. –It's bad enough being sick on a fucking boat, but when they start making you puke on dry land, it's time to do something about it.

4

Salmon Island (Inis Breadáin), Easter 1988

Gannets glided out from the cliffs and over the face of the ocean. True what they said, you could hear the silence, as if silence was what the island itself breathed, a quiescence that held rocks, sea and sky in its maw. Sun made it warm enough to lie in the heather in pullovers, watching water churn to froth on the black rocks, smelling new grasses pushing up, and the nests of gulls, and feeling the rinsing caress of the marine air.

–Happy? Adi made herself closer to me.

–Yes.

–You look very happy lying there. It makes me want to stop you ever leaving, she said.

We'd arrived just after noon that Good Friday, Harry and Brigid, Adi, me. Flown directly from the lawn in Oakwood in an Air Corps helicopter. Harry's Garda minders had set out ahead by car and were already on the island and on the pier of the village as we flew over.

We had not spent a weekend like this together for years, the Messengers and ourselves. Harry had married Brigid Messenger when he was twenty-seven and she twenty-three. Her father had been Mick Wall, a minister in a Fianna Fáil government in the fifties. Brigid was a taciturn, private woman whose entire life had been devoted to their four children. I always had the impression that she disapproved of me, that she somehow held me to account for failings of Harry's that I was not even aware of. Or perhaps she resented my closeness to her husband, envying me the secrets she assumed we shared, jealous of my access to him which even she herself at times did not enjoy.

–Harry is in top form, Adi said.

–He loves it here. Loves being out of reach. No telephone, no television. No newspapers.

Adi pitched a stone over the edge. –I was looking at Brigid on the way down. I was thinking, I've known Harry as long as I've known you, almost, and yet I couldn't say that I know him well – and then it struck me: he's that way with everyone, even his wife. I wouldn't say she knows him any better than you or I do, and she's slept in the same bed as him for most of her life and has had his children. I used to be able to get through to her but not any more. I blame Harry.

–So does everyone.

–I'm serious.

–Harry's himself.

–That's the Irish way of refusing to address the point. Of course he's himself, but who is that person? Who is Harry Messenger? Do you know? I certainly don't, and I'd say neither does his wife.

–Is it important to know?

–I would have thought that you above anyone would like to know since you've devoted your life to him.

I would never know all of Harry, any more than would his wife, I accepted. The letter I had received earlier that week from the bank to whom he owed one and a half million seemed to prove my point: it simply acknowledged discharge by my client, Mr Messenger, of his debt in full. I had no idea where the money had come from, nor had Harry even bothered to inform me he was paying it off. All I did know was that he had met his self-imposed April deadline.

I sat up and looked out to sea. –Harry's art is politics. In the broadest sense, beyond just power. Power is the result, but politics is what drives it. He sees everything in political terms, politics is his language. Always has been. All the sub-compartments of his life – marriage, money, constituency, the Dáil – are seen by him through different angles of a political prism. So when he borrows money from a bank, say, he doesn't think like you or I might about when he is going to pay it back, or how, he sees it simply in relation to all the other matters that are currently engaging him. Debts owed, favours due, posts to be filled, contracts to be won, nominations for the Seanad or to a marginal constituency, government grants, legislation. He is all things to all men, and also to himself. Such a man thinks literally in a different dimension from the rest of us. Such a man is unknowable. So, he is himself.

The repercussive ocean invaded my ears.

–And what about you, Bunny? she asked gently. –Have you ever stopped to analyse yourself in such detailed terms over the years? Or even lately, since we've begun to talk about the future, to wonder about the kind of person you are or where you're going?

–Yes, I said. –And I've come to a decision.

Adi cocked her head to one side. I loved it when she looked at me like that.

–So?

–Well, I know it's taken me long enough, but I've decided that the time has come to plan my departure. It won't be easy, or simple, nor can it be done overnight. But I'm going to do it.

–When?

–Straight away. I'm going to tell Harry my decision this weekend, I said.

Adi's face lit up in a smile that reminded me of the girl I had first seen in Harold's Cross over thirty years before. She reached over and folded both arms round my neck. –That's the best present I've ever got, she said. –You do mean it, don't you?

–Do you not trust me?

–If you love someone, then you trust them, she said, –and I love you and always have and always will.

There was a time in my life that I didn't know Harry, but now that seems, for reasons you will come to understand, like a time in the life of someone else entirely. Dick was my first hero. The way he rode and could shoot straight. He was Tim Holt or Wild Bill Elliot, and Pat Smith was Audie. I was Red Ryder, and Mickey O was Little Beaver, but Dick said Red Ryder was a nancy. I knew that Dick mitched school and that he got away with it by getting letters forged by Gerry Maddocks's older brother. Dick walked like a cowboy, rocking from side to side. We all rode up and down Bath Avenue and Shelbourne Road. It was a real thrill galloping down the railway line, the feel of the horse beneath you and Injuns hiding behind the bridges. When a train came, its hooter blaring, we scattered down the stony sides of the embankment and could feel the blast of air and smell the soot from the engine.

–Topper's the fastest horse in the West, said Pat Smith, who was Hopalong, as he pulled on a cigarette. –He could gallop alongside that train so's I could jump on to it.

–Trigger's the fastest in the West, then Champion, said Dick.

–Not as fast as Topper.

–Silver's the f-f-fastest, said the Lone Ranger, who had pimples and whose name was Jack O'Brien. –Hey ho, S-Silver!

–He can't be the fastest, said Art Maddocks, a dour character, –'cos Tonto keeps up with him the whole time and Tonto's horse is a real small horse.

–They're both the f-f-fastest, said Jack O'Brien.

–Maddocks is right, said Smith, –Tonto's horse is shite.

–So, if Tonto's horse can keep up with him, Silver is shite too, said Dick.

The gang laughed and puffed smoke, and myself and Mickey O just smiled with happiness, dizzy that at last we were living life on the range.

–So what does Tonto call him? Shite? asked Dick, for another laugh.

–Hey-ho, Shite! shouted Smith. He used to laugh and shout like the rest of us in those days. It was only when he got older and started going out with the likes of Rosemary, my sister, that he went all serious.

The Lone Ranger scratched a spot on his face. –Tonto doesn't c-call him anything.

–The horse must have a name. All horses have names, said Dick.

–He doesn't know the name a Tonto's horse, Maddocks said doggedly.

–Neither do you, Jack O'Brien said.

–Maybe he doesn't have a name, Smith said, and they all nodded that Smith was right.

–He does.

They looked at me, as if they hadn't seen me up to then.

–So, what's his name, then? asked Dick, his face very

anxious that I was going to let him down in front of everyone.

–Scout, I said.

–That's it! Jack O'Brien cried. –T-T-Tonto's horse is Scout!

We rode off then, down the back of the gasworks looking for Injuns. We split into two gangs and shot at each other under the wheels of the Howth train, then we had a last fag before teatime.

–Tell us some other horses' names, Smith said.

I told them about Sultan, Ray Corrigan's horse, and Koko, who belonged to Rex Allen. No one knew that Buffalo Bill's horse was called Isham, or that Annie Oakley rode Target. We moseyed down into Bath Avenue, then Dick and I and Mickey O peeled off for home because our mams were very strict about our homework.

One night there was a big commotion, people running up and down the street. Mam came in and told us that Mickey O's da was after dying.

Mr O had fought and been wounded in the battle of Mount Street Bridge and they said he'd never had a day after without pain. He used two sticks to walk with and I thought he was very old, but he was only thirty-nine. Mam had grown up beside the O'Connors in Bath Avenue and she knew the whole family. Mr O had put in a word for Mam's sister, my aunt Nancy, when she went for a corporation house in Ringsend.

The whole of the next day people dressed up in good clothes came to O'Connors'. It was in the newspapers, Da said. The government wanted a state funeral, but the family wanted it private. I saw Mickey O looking out the upstairs window like he wanted to come out but wasn't allowed. I shot at him a few times, but he just looked at me. I went around the back of O'Connors' that afternoon and climbed a tree. All these people were standing in the kitchen with cups of tea and I could see Mr O upstairs in bed, his hands joined across his pyjamas.

–You did not see him, Dick said later.

–I did. He was yella.

–You'll be yella now, Dick said, and thumped me on the arm.

They removed Mr O to Haddington Road that night and there were that many people they had to close our street. I saw the coffin being carried out and the Irish flag being put over it. Mickey O had his hand on the coffin. His mother had to be helped.

–You couldn't get into the church, Da said, when he came home. He'd been drinking in Haddington Road and his face was red. –Did you know he killed four British soldiers with a Browning revolver? They say Dev himself is coming to Deansgrange tomorrow to give the oration.

–The family don't want that, Mam said.

–Dev himself.

–He was very good to Nancy, Mam said.

–Dev and Tommy O fought shoulder to shoulder, Da said. –Imagine, I musta seen him a thousand times and he never once told me what he done.

It was exciting being close to something so important. I was asleep when Da came into the room that night and woke us. He had his finger over his lips. –Get up quick! he whispered. –Come over here!

Dick wouldn't wake up but Da caught me by the hand and brought me to the window. There were all these big black cars the length of Upper Grand Canal Street and a few guards and people at the end of the street, standing in a group, staring up in our direction.

–Dev! Da hissed in my ear. –Come to pay his respects!

I could see men in coats with slouch hats standing by the cars, their hands deep in their pockets. More guards stood on the footpath. Da's face was warm and I could feel his bristles next to my cheek. Then he sucked in his breath. –Look, Bunny!

The door of O'Connors' had opened and a tall man had emerged. He put on his hat and stood there, looking up and down the street. Then he looked straight across at us. I saw his glasses. I thought he was going to wave. Da wasn't breathing. Then Dev walked out the short path and got into a car and they all drove off. Da shook his head. He was dazed. –He knew we were here, he said. –He knew we were here.

The island ran to perhaps forty acres, most of it bare from centuries of over-grazing: sheep were brought across from the mainland in currachs, a distance of half a mile, and made to swim the final, desperate fifty yards. No roads, just sandy tracks. An area below the house on the leeward side had been cleared to allow landings by helicopters. The house, although modest, had cost a fortune to build since every nail, beam, slate and brick had had to be ferried over. The local workmen harboured a superstition, probably well founded, about remaining on the island after dark, which had meant that for six months of the year during the construction period only at best five hours a day had been worked, although full wages were paid.

On a good day it was a blessed place. One often awoke to discover the mainland disappeared, lost in sea mist.

At such moments the island seemed to be adrift on a sea of dreams. The house itself consisted of three bedrooms only and a large, central living area with a big picture window facing west. Meals were eaten at a massive, wooden table, at the head of which Harry sat on a throne-like structure that had once catered for a bishop on a high altar but which the local sycophantic Dáil member had purchased at auction, refurbished and shipped out as a means of keeping himself on the right side of the chief. No electricity or other power source existed. Tea was made with the water from a spring. No telephones, but emergency contact could be patched through on the Garda radio. Toilets were outside. The Gardaí who accompanied Harry kept in touch by radio with the mainland. Light in the evenings was provided by candles stuck in holders that had been welded to a dinner trolley; the trolley was wheeled around as required. Meals were cooked in the small kitchen on a wood-fired range. Harry was immensely proud of these unsophisticated arrangements. His diet out here was mainly fish, including salmon, presented daily by local fishermen.

–I owe you more than I can ever say, he said, and put his hand on my arm.

The women had gone outside in jackets and with rugs to sit beneath the stars. Harry had pared the Garda detail down to two men on the island – these bodyguards cooked their meals in the kitchen of the house and ate them in the small adjoining bunk room where they slept and to which they had now retired.

–I have few regrets, I said. –We did what had to be done.

–You have always seen that I have the right environment in which to do my work. That has been a priceless contribution – to me, to this country. If I hadn't had you around to fend off the begrudgers, God knows but I would never have come this far.

–I'm glad that the financial problems have been sorted out, I said, wondering if in his expansive mood I might learn how it had been done.

–Oh, they were nothing, said Harry airily and his fingers rose and fluttered their dismissal. –I told you all that was needed was six months.

We raised our glasses and touched their rims together in the candlelight. But I knew that that was as much as I was going to get, and in a way I was relieved for this absence of knowledge.

–I can tell you now, and know that you won't deride me for it, that I have never felt so confident for the future of our country, Harry said, and closed his eyes as he drew the cork from a further bottle. –Never. I feel immeasurable optimism, I feel sometimes that I can probably fly.

He sniffed the cork. –We have the Brits more on-side than they've ever been. Do you know what I believe they feel about the North? I believe they hate the place with a passion. Of course, Thatcher will never admit that, she's the daughter of a shopkeeper so she has exactly the same kind of mentality as the unionists. She'd paint her arse red, white and blue if she could. But it's obvious to anyone with a sense of history that the North is the bedridden relation of British politics. Terminally ill. It's only a matter of time before it comes back to us. Money is the key, of course. Look at France and Germany today and tell me that money doesn't mean more than blood.

The light from the flickering bank of candles rippled across the Taoiseach's face in an ever-changing configuration. –I often think of the past, he said. –The

Golden Age that every Irishman dreams of, when we ruled the land and the seas at a time when that shower beyond in Anglesey could only break wind and grunt like monkeys. You read that stuff at all, Bunny?

–A bit.

–It was food and drink to us growing up. You see, in Derry we had nothing, only dreams. You on the other hand had everything and did nothing.

–My grandfather, Richard Gardener, was a clerk in Ganly's.

–But he came from land.

–Ran from it. Some old feud with his da over in Castlebar. He was in Ganly's on Easter Monday 1916 when the Rising broke out. He went home.

–Wise man, said Harry.

–His brother Myles came in and described men lying dead in the street. He said the British Army had sent for gunboats and battleships. 'The sooner the better,' Gran Gardener is reputed to have said.

Harry chuckled.

–As this was happening, down in Bath Avenue, my other grandfather, Duffy, was digging in seed potatoes when he heard the news. He hurried inside, took off his working boots, put on his polished brogues and told my grandmother that he was going to Dublin. She asked him why he was going into town on Easter Monday. He told her he was going to join the fight for Ireland's freedom. 'You'll do nothing of the sort, you little jackanapes!' she shouted. 'Get back out there and finish those potatoes!' And he did. That was the end of his Rising.

Harry put his head back and laughed. –That's what few people realise. History is about people, but only about a few people.

Wind soughed in the big chimney.

–I've been thinking about the future lately, I said. –My own future.

–Your future and mine are the same, always have been.

–Yes, but there is a time for everything, including change, I said.

Harry frowned. –Don't tell me you're going to retire on me.

–I think there should be an exit strategy.

Harry plunged the corners of his mouth down and looked at me dubiously. –Fuck it, Bunny, I'm only fifty-nine and you're, what? Two years younger than me. Exit strategy, my arse. What's got into you?

–Take the bank, for example. The more the business has grown, the greater the interest the Central Bank are taking in it. They used to drop by every couple of years, then annually. Now it's every six months. They don't like the set-up. They're becoming more and more aggressive.

–Then I'll have the personnel removed.

–Actually, I think that would be the worst possible thing to do. I'm able to handle the problem at the moment, but what I am saying is that this is not an open-ended situation. We've had very good times for many years. A moment will come when it will be sensible to cease.

The Taoiseach sat, his face set in a contemplative expression, his eyes on the candles. –You, of course, know best, he said. –I have never concerned myself with what goes on down in the engine room, as you know. I wouldn't know how to get there. I think you accept that, Bunny?

He could sense danger from a great distance.

–Of course I accept it, I said. –You've never been involved in the details. Never. You've always had greater matters on your mind.

–Absolutely. Bank accounts, deals of any kind, details. I've never concerned myself with the details.

–That is known by everyone.

–Except when it comes to such details as foreign affairs or Ulster. Or the economy. But nothing in my personal life has ever had time for my consideration – to my own loss, no doubt.

–Agreed.

The Taoiseach was examining each layer now with forensic care.

–But are there . . . other such problems? Does the exit strategy apply elsewhere?

–I think the . . . manner in which business has been done will have to change. I'm not for a moment criticising the, if you like, symbiosis that has existed between government and certain entrepreneurs—

–You're talking about property, the Taoiseach interrupted.

–Not only property. But I had not meant to be specific.

–Go on.

–A lot of things were done over the last twenty-five years in a way that was expedient at the time. We were very poor. The last thing we wanted was for our expansive spirit to be hemmed in by petty regulations.

–Go on.

–So we all did things in a way that would produce results. We don't regret what we did and the country needed what was done. But this business tradition, if you will, cannot continue indefinitely, any more than can the banking arrangements I referred to.

The Taoiseach held up his glass and peered into its illuminated rubies. –Is there someone looking? he asked quietly.

–Not that I know of. But the changes in society also apply to the media. They're becoming increasingly hostile. Look at what's happening in the UK.

–I hate the bastards, Harry said, with feeling. –Never given me a fair crack of the whip, always want to publish bad news, never give credit where it's due. My belief in democracy is never more assailed than when I see the sheer mischief those bastards get up to.

A gust of wind from the open ocean-side door flattened the flames. I saw the women huddled, talking quietly.

–I have trusted you all my life, why would I not trust you now? Harry said. –What will you do?

–Wind down what's been built up, but that'll take time.

–But there's no catalyst, the Taoiseach insisted.

–None. Just a strategy.

–Would you like to be ambassador somewhere? You and Adi, somewhere nice? Athens? Or New Zealand? Although I don't think I'd like you that far away from me.

–Before I go anywhere, I'd like to leave the place the way I found it, I said.

–That's a good one. Harry chuckled and stood up. –That's the best one I heard for a long time.

He led the way outside. –Now, where are these girls hiding? I hope they haven't caught their death of cold.

I have an image of myself from those days before I met Harry: a thin boy in short pants, his dark hair slicked down to one side a bit like that oul' bastard Hitler's, and a Holy Communion rosette in his lapel. And then there's a jump to the next image: a thin youth with hollow cheeks looking warily out from the front door of the house on Upper Grand Canal Street. In some drawer or box lies the first image, a snapshot, but the second one was never taken, to my knowledge: it is simply how I see myself one evening in the spring of 1944.

–Where's Dick?

It was five o'clock and Mam was frying up potato cakes. Because of the times you were allowed to have the gas on, everyone had to be in on time for meals. Otherwise you risked the glimmer man.

–Did you see him? Mam asked me.

I had seen Dick as I came back after school, skiving off down the canal where he smoked his fags. But I said, –No, I didn't see him, Mam.

Mam's hair was going grey and when she was vexed it made her look fierce.

–I'll wring his neck when I find him, she said. –How am I meant to keep food warm? Go out and see if he's on the road.

–He's always late, said Rosemary.

All the talk was of the war ending. Even the Home Guard that Da had joined and went out three nights a week with on manoeuvres were talking of standing down.

–He's not there, Mam, I said. Although I hadn't bothered to go even to the gate, I knew Dick wasn't out on the road.

–I'll murder him, Mam said.

We had our tea and Mam covered Dick's plate with a saucepan lid and put it on a hot pot. It was still there an hour later. Mam put her coat on. Her face was worried.

–I'm going out to find that yoke and when I do I'll kill him, she said.

Mickey O and I kicked around a football out the back of our house. Mickey O said he was going to play for Arsenal when he left school. All at once it's seven o'clock and there's roaring outside our front door. I went out. It was Mam. Art Maddocks's mam was on one side of her and Mickey O's on the other and Mam's head was back and she was roaring. I ran back in for Rosemary. And when I went out again Mam was on her knees on the front step and I thought she'd had an attack. All these people were standing in our front garden, whispering. And then I saw Da. He came down Upper Grand Canal Street on his bike and jumped off it at the gate and the bike fell on the road. He came in the gate and the people there drew back, except one woman, Mrs Smith, who went over to him. She was crying. And Mam saw Da and she roared out and stuck her two hands up. And Da just went down there on the end of the path, he just fell down, his legs gone from under him. And Mrs Smith was trying to get him up and I could see Da's shoulders going up and down as if he was after running. And then he somehow got up and he staggered up the path. All this happened so quick. I wanted to put my hands on my ears, but something stopped me. And then Mam looked at Da and cried like she'd been stabbed, – DICK – IS – DROWNED!

5

Salmon Island (Inis Breadáin), Easter, 1988

Dawn was breaking when I awoke. I crept out from the bedroom, clothes in my arms, and dressed in the corridor, so as not to wake Adi. Along the hall, I could hear the Taoiseach's deep, even snores. Outside it was chilly and the wind had gone round, allowing the fluttering sound of the waves to be heard. I laced up a pair of boots and began to climb the hill behind the house, to where we had lain out the day before.

–All right, sir? The figure of the guard on duty slid out from the shadows.

–Fine, thanks, Guard. Just taking a walk.

–Be careful of the island in this light, the man said. –It's treacherous.

In the century gone by when this island had been inhabited by half a dozen families, children had been sent out to look for missing lambs and had never come home, swallowed up by the island, as the lore had it, but in reality lost in the deep waters beneath its cliffs. They'd fled the place just after the war when a young mother in childbirth could not be brought to shore because of the bad weather. It had taken her and her child seven days to die on this wild piece of land in the Atlantic.

I climbed cautiously but strongly, wind at my back, the coming day now a hint behind the headland I was aiming for. Unseen seabirds chuckled in the clefts and niches below me, and occasionally, when my path veered unpredictably towards the side of the precipice, the whoosh and suck of deep water roared its own warning.

We had built a fire outside the night before and had sat by its embers until two. Harry had brought out a bottle of rare Armagnac, a gift, he had explained, from the President of France. A kind of peace had enveloped our little group as we spoke, mainly, of our children, or listened to Harry describing his encounters over the years with other heads of state, or monarchs, or emperors, or cold-hearted dictators. Relaxed and with his closest and oldest friends, the power he enjoyed sat lightly on him, as if power and its discharging was his destiny. And yet I could not help feeling – and it was me alone, I knew – a sense of finality about the night, as if the matters I had raised, merely by virtue of being thus aired, had acquired a materiality they had previously lacked.

This enlargement of menace still clung to me now as I climbed. Too much wine and brandy, however good, I thought. Although I did realise, too, that Harry and I had ventured the night before, albeit tentatively, into realms which by tradition only one of us at a time attended. My instinct had ever been to protect him, and I had always seen a lack of knowledge on his part as paramount in that pursuit. I breasted the rise and beheld the glory of dawn in a clear sky. Perspiring from the climb, now that I had stopped I could feel the clamminess of my back and chest. Seabirds in their thousands were pouring out from the pit below me across the sea in the first tracks of yellow light. I removed my jacket and found my shirt saturated. With each moment, the heat on my face increased and the voice of the seabirds rose. Taking off the shirt as well, and my undershirt, I spread them on boulders, then stood, arms spread like spokes on the rising mandala. And yet even with the whole of creation to infuse me I still felt the drag of uncertainty, as if time now was but a prelude, as if this was the setting in which worlds always fragmented.

I had dressed again and was sitting on a rock watching the mainland emerge from shadow, when I heard the sound. It began like a dentist's drill, boring its way through the pith of daybreak, then rose, ever more insistent, its timbre carried before it on the vast plain of water until no other possibility of what it was remained. I saw the hunched shape, nose slightly dipped, skim the ridge of headland to the east. It hurtled straight for me over the water, consternation all around it, the din a sacrilege, then banked to my right, blades flailing, red and green belly lights flashing, before levelling out and settling beside the house like a large, omnivorous insect.

I waited thirty minutes. As I made my way back down, the nearer I got to the house the stronger was the smell of grilled rashers.

Adi, finger to her lips, caught my wrist and led me into our bedroom.

–What's wrong?

She rolled her eyes, then nodded in the direction of the bed. The *Irish Times* lay there, front page uppermost. I could read the headline without having to pick it up: PASSPORTS LINKED TO PROPERTY PURCHASE. It was, of course, written by Mary Mates, but whereas her two previous pieces had been confined to three or four paragraphs, this one was a full-blown lead story excursion into the deal in which the INRC had agreed to become the tenant of the city-centre property known as Dr Tobin's Hospital. Mates had discovered that the government had sold Dr Tobin's to an Isle of Man investment company for £3.9 million. This investment company was the same one that had, the autumn gone by, paid £75,000 to Taoiseach Harry Messenger for a horse. At the time, it had been acknowledged that the purchaser of the Taoiseach's horse was Prince Abdul Alman, a wealthy Arab who, along with his extended family, had subsequently been granted Irish citizenship. A spokesman for the prince denied that he owned Dr Tobin's, but failed either to confirm or deny that the Isle of Man investment company was in his beneficial ownership. The chairman of the INRC, Dr Brendan Broe, had not been available to comment, nor had the Taoiseach, who was believed to be spending the holiday weekend on his island retreat, Inis Breadáin.

I put the paper down. –Jesus, that's where he got the money, I said.

–What money?

–It's a long story. He owed some money, he paid it back.

–There's worse inside, Adi said.

I turned to the editorial. The newspaper was demanding that the questions raised in Mates's piece be answered satisfactorily, that full disclosure of the Dr Tobin's deal be made by the government and that the Taoiseach state what links, if any, existed between himself, his government and Prince Abdul Alman.

–Has Harry seen this?

Adi puffed her cheeks out. –He went insane, Bunny. He was drinking orange juice when they brought this in and he started screaming. He smashed the glass down on the table and cut his hand. They've radioed for a doctor to come out, just as a precaution. I've never seen anyone lose their temper like that. I was terrified.

–Where's Brigid?

–Taken to her bed.

I picked up the paper and went down to the living room. Harry was sitting in his chair, facing out to sea. He wore a fresh shirt, open at the collar, and a silk kerchief round his neck. One of his hands was wrapped in a linen table napkin. Only his eyes moved when I came in.

–I've read it, I said.

The Taoiseach said nothing. The skin around his eyes hung in pendulous folds. His lips were colourless.

I said, –It's just a series of questions, there are no conclusions.

Harry said, –I lost my temper in front of your wife. I am deeply sorry for that. I'll make it up to her.

–Adi knows you almost as long as I do, it's not a problem.

–It makes me ashamed.

–No need to be. Forget it.

He closed his eyes and his chin dropped an inch. –They had to bring the newspaper out to me, of course, I accept that. They couldn't leave me out here for Easter with the whole country talking.

–It may have already run its course. It depends on what happens now.

The Taoiseach said, –I have no intention of allowing this sort of nonsense to ruin my weekend, or of appearing to somehow ratify what has been written by cutting the weekend short and dashing back to Dublin. That's what a worried man would do. I'm not worried.

–I'm glad to hear it.

He shot me a look without turning his head. –I've

already instructed Big Mac to say that the contents of the article are beneath contempt and that I shall not be making a further statement.

–Good. I was beginning to worry that I might miss that Armagnac tonight.

Harry chewed the corner of his mouth. –I'm not worried. But someone who should be worried is Dr Broe. I haven't played hand, act or part in any of the INRC's transactions since I appointed him. He's the person who's going to have to sort this out. I don't know what company bought what or who was involved. You know my style. Details are not my strong point. I've spent the last thirty years concentrating on the dimensional. I never get involved in the nitty-gritty, you know that.

–Of course.

–This is Dr Broe's problem, not mine.

–I agree. Broe can deal with it, you've enough on your plate.

–He's a popinjay with his horses and his bed linen. If he'd been available to comment, as he should have been, he could have taken the heat out of this.

We sat, and it was hard to imagine that this same room only hours before had been the setting of such hope and ambition. The Taoiseach stood up and winced in pain.

–Want you to do a job, Bunny. I've told the chopper to wait. They'll take you up to Dublin. Go out to Larry Maher's house in Sutton, he'll be there. He's expecting me. Larry'll have read this piece, he'll know what he has to do. This can't go on, my security is at stake. Larry will know why I've sent you and the confirmation that I'm waiting for from him.

He stood and his face broke into a wintry smile. –And

just in case you have any thoughts about not coming back here afterwards, I'm keeping Adi on the island.

Mickey O was talking about the FA Cup draw during break. I was only half listening to him. I was thinking of Mam who was home in bed sick, not wanting to get up, and of Da and how he didn't talk much any more. As Mickey O was telling me how he was going to be a centre-forward for Arsenal when he left school, these big fellas came down to the lower yard, Pat Smith, Art Maddocks and Jack O'Brien, with a new lad who'd only come into the school that term, but who was already head man in their gang. I'd heard stories about this new lad whose name was Messenger, about how his da had a gun and how this new fella knew how to use it. I'd only seen him in the distance in the upper yard, but when I asked Maddocks if it was true about the gun, he just sneered and said that that was for him to know and for me to find out.

–Gardener.

They were standing around in a circle and this fella was in the middle of them. He looked big for some reason, with a beaky nose and fair hair parted down the middle. They were looking at me.

–Gardener. Come over here, Maddocks said.

My breath went short, not because they were older boys, or because I was afraid that I might get a thump from Maddocks, which I was; no, it was the eyes of the new fella that made my heart race. He was looking at me sideways, as if he knew something about me that no one else did. I wanted to turn and run over to Mickey O, but I couldn't.

–What's wrong with you, Gardener? Scared or something? jeered Maddocks when I made my way over.

–No.

–Then why is your mouth hangin' open?

–Shut up, Maddocks! said Pat Smith. –Listen, Bunny, Messenger's da's after comin' to live down here and he's not gettin' all his rations.

–He was w-w-wonderin' . . . began Jack O'Brien.

–Bunny, is it?

He was smiling now, like as if he had met me before and I didn't remember but he did.

–Yeah.

–Bunny, we're having trouble getting sugar for the tea at home, you know what I mean? The lads say you're the man to help. That you're a great man to fix things.

His voice had a funny lilt.

Maddocks said, –You know, with your da working in . . .

–F-F-Findlaters—

–He knows, the new boy cut in, his green eyes still on me. –He knows where his da works. He knows what's needed. All right?

–I'll . . . see.

–Thanks.

–You can do it, can't you, Gardener? asked Smith.

–I can try.

Messenger put his hand on my shoulder. –Thanks, he said. Then he turned, so that there were only two of us. –And sorry about the brother, he said.

They walked off then, or he did and the rest of them followed. I was left there, staring after them. Something had happened, but I had no idea what it was. All that day and all the way home I thought about him. About how he had made me feel good, about how I had wanted to please him. Nobody else had ever mentioned Dick like that. And the funny thing was that although Messenger had seemed bigger than me, the fact was that I was the taller by an inch.

The traditional glory of Ireland, her land, mountains and rivers, bloomed right across the verdant register as I clattered northwards. Sheep zigzagged ahead of dogs on pastures smooth as aprons. Women hung clothes out behind cottages and stopped to peer up, the sun picking out their faces or, in one case, a wedding ring. On the Curragh, knots of horses broke, their tails high and indignant. In a way, it was normal to be back in crisis, as if the brief peace of the day before was not something either of us had grown up with. For I was quite sure now that the sudden inrush of funds to Harry's bank had sprung directly from the events reported in the morning paper; and here I was once more, in the eye of this new crisis, delivering an ultimatum to the Minister for Home Affairs to engage the enemy. Dublin came into view on the eastern horizon. It would always be like this, I suddenly knew, we were like gamblers who would never leave the table until their last penny was gone. We could not walk away, for Harry couldn't, and so neither could I. Hard to tell Adi that, to explain that plans to get out and retire were not possible. I'd have to keep nudging her into the next year, and the next, for each year would bring a fresh crisis, as it had always done.

It was noon before I reached Larry Maher's home in Sutton, an ample, recently built detached residence, somewhat crammed into its garden. A Garda car had picked me up from the steps of the helicopter and had driven me out here, two outriders making sure we were not caught at traffic lights. Larry had been told to stay at home in order to meet the Taoiseach. He opened the door, saw me, and stood there, blinking. –Where's the Taoiseach?

–He's had an accident, Larry. He's cut himself and is waiting for the doctor. He asked me to come up.

The minister shook his head, turned and shuffled back in. From his appearance it was clear that conventional hours were of little consequence to his drinking. His clothes were rumpled and stank of tobacco. He wore carpet slippers. He had difficulty in assembling the ingredients needed to make a coffee for me – he was alone in the house – and in pouring himself a further vodka. On a low table beside an ashtray full of three-quarters-smoked cigarettes lay that morning's *Irish Times*, front page up, no less threatening than it had appeared five hours before when I had first seen it. Beside the *Times* lay half a dozen empty tonic bottles. The sequence of events as laid out in still life was self-explanatory.

–How are you, Larry?

He pointed at his chest. –Me? How do you think I am?

–I just hope you're well, that's all.

Larry screwed up one side of his face in a bitter attempt to smile. –Think I don't know why he sent you here, Bunny? Why he didn't come himself?

–Like I told you, he cut his hand.

–Cut his hand. Think I don't have pride? Think I don't know what he wants? We're all in this together, you know.

–You're tired, Larry.

–Tired? Months since I've slept three hours at one stretch. Wife is a saint. She knows what I've given to the party, to the leader. She *knows*. Has to put up with me getting up at all hours, going into the bathroom, not coming out of it again for an hour, sometimes two. Kind of life is that for a woman? What am I doing in there? You tell me.

–Don't know, Larry.

–Sitting on the toilet, looking at the wall tiles. Some sort of Turkish ceramic, she got them, light blue with veins going through them, you'd look at them and see fuck-all, but to me at two in the morning it's like watching television. See myself as a little child, my poor father . . .

Here the minister halted dead, as if he had gone flat simultaneously on all four wheels. He began to sob, a strangled business. Head back, he drew in draughts of air in recuperative balloons, then wiped the cuff of his shirt across his nose and mouth.

–'Good man, Jim,' they said, 'let her fly,' and he reached out to the ribbon with the scissors they'd given him, special gold scissors, I keep them beside the bed, and as he snipped the fucking thing he took a step back – the county manager was standing beside him, he told me the whole story fifty times – and Pa said, 'Oh! My poor Maura!' That was Mother, God rest her, and he dropped, dead before he struck the ground.

Larry covered his face with his hand and wept. I could hear children somewhere, playing in a nearby garden. Larry blew his nose and we sipped vodka and lukewarm coffee respectfully. Although Jim Maher must have died at least four decades before, here he was remembered as though it had happened just that week.

–And here's me now, Bunny, his little Lar, he called me, sitting up all night trying to read my life. Do you know how deep this goes? Do you? Do you know how long this has been going on? From the very beginning.

We had nothing, we had to get it somewhere. It's the way we are. It's our history.

–You're being too hard on yourself.

–Twenty years since I won the seat, before that for fifteen years I was on the council. Never once voted in favour of a re-zoning in Dublin North-East, never once. Didn't have to. It always went through on a majority and all I had to do was vote in favour of re-zonings everywhere else. Who invented that system? Harry, of course, and he wasn't even on the fucking county council. Never could say no to him. Jesus, I need a drink now before I can talk to him. I'm scared, Bunny. Of what? I don't know what, that's the worst part. I try to find out in the tiles, but all I see are faces of little kids, flowers, angels . . .

Larry was sweating and trembling.

–Can't do this any more. Taoiseach this, Taoiseach that. This height of extradition orders on my desk in the Green. I'm not up to it. Imagine that. Jesus Christ, there was a time I'd just fart at a problem and that'd be the end of it. D'you ever imagine yourself dead, Bunny? Laid out? I got up this morning, I hadn't had a drink in two days, and I opened the fucking newspaper. Easter Saturday today, you know. I was looking forward to the weekend with the family. Sober. I saw this. You know what I saw then? Myself dead. That's why I'm in this condition. Do the people who write these things have any idea of the misery they're causing in other people's lives? I'm finished, Bunny. So, yes, tell him, yes, Larry'll do it. I'll do it, I'll do it. I'll put on the phone tap. And it'll kill one of us, but I know damn well which one of us it'll be.

I saw my parents adrift in a grief that nothing could touch or soften. Dick surrounded my father like a swarm of flies: you could see it in the tilt of his head, the way he shook it from time to time, as if to clear it, or to see straight. He'd fix on something and a frown deep as a furrow would divide his face, making it lopsided and broken, the way one fractures with tears, so that he always looked on the verge of crying, of breaking into pieces, of his face shattering with grief and him then falling, the way I'd seen him on our path that day, sprawled with his legs at odd angles like a dog that's been run over. I feared that for ever more, seeing him like that again; which I did, or kind of did, because when he was boozed, which he was more and more, he fell about like that. I used to try ways of cheering him up, of trying to get him to think of other things. I hid all Dick's clothes and school things, but it was no good. Da'd go up to Haddington Road and when he came home his face would be all dragged down and his mouth slack and his eyes stupid and imploring.

With Mam it was a more pernicious grief, if that is possible, a possessing of her body and soul, a sucking of her away from us so that she seemed to shrink, bodily, her eyes small and seeing only inwards. She never really saw me again after Dick, I often thought.

He'd fallen into the lock at Baggot Street Bridge and he couldn't swim. No one had any way of getting him out. He drowned down in the lock with twenty people looking down and shouting at him and him splashing around and yelling up for them to help him. I never saw him dead, but Rosemary did. She told me he'd been like ice.

By late April, no one in Ireland could have been in any doubt as to what was meant by 'Dr Tobin's'.

A one-hour television documentary had probed every known aspect of the deal and come up with diagrams linking the main players: Harry, or at least his horse, was linked to Prince Abdul Alman, who in turn had sprouted a nest of links to Dr Tobin's, Dr Brendan Broe, the Department of Foreign Affairs, which issued passports, and a number of fresh and now suspect property transactions, minnows of Dr Tobin's, as it were. Another artery linked Harry, via the government, to the sale of Dr Tobin's. Every hack in town now had the same mission, it seemed, and Dr Tobin's was swelling daily like a storm that seemed certain to engulf Harry and his government. There was also a lighter side: Dr Tobin's tried, very briefly, to become a verb in smart parts of Dublin, indicating sharp practice – 'Have you been Dr Tobined?' – and if one newspaper cartoon showed a sick, downtrodden Ireland being turned away by an avaricious Dr Tobin, then so did twenty others.

Harry remained imperious and aloof, like the captain of a ship strayed into perilous waters. The media was the sole foe he lacked the weapons to engage – beyond the pursuit of them through the libel code, which he used at every opportunity.

I got a call from Big Mac in the last week of April. He had arranged a little get-together for a few friends of Harry's, to cheer the Taoiseach up, he told me. A lunch in the private room of a restaurant in Ballsbridge. Just old friends – it'll be like the old days, Big Mac said, a mysterious statement since he'd only been around for six years at the most. Wednesday, twelve thirty.

Wednesday did not begin auspiciously for the Taoiseach. Mary Mates – who was being hailed by the opposition as an Irish Joan of Arc for her diligence – had once again dominated that morning's *Irish Times*.

She was, I had to admit, an extraordinarily effective digger and would have made a top-class auditor. I had read her article on the DART, and when I met Violet in my office, I could see that she had too.

–She has some nerve, that one, Violet said.

–She's only doing her job, Violet.

–Do you never get really cross, Mr G? my secretary asked, and as she did so her two cheeks became red as apples. –I'm sorry. It's just as if nothing good has ever happened and all that people like that one want to do is pull other people down. There's nothing else on the news or in the papers. I see people who know who I am looking at me, as if to say, Look at her, she's one of them. I read the paper and I feel like a criminal. And I'm not, am I, Mr G? Any more than you are?

–This is a storm in a teacup, Violet, believe me, I said. –I promise you that in a month it will be forgotten.

The *Irish Times* piece that morning had burrowed even deeper into the Dr Tobin's labyrinth. Mates unveiled to the paper's readers her discovery that when the government had sold Dr Tobin's for £3.9 million to the Isle of Man company which was probably owned by Prince Abdul Alman, it had retained Maher & Co, auctioneers, to advise in the transaction. However, the building, which was being completely refurbished for its new tenant, the INRC, was now the property of a large British pension fund, in whose books, Mates revealed, Dr Tobin's stood at its cost price: £14 million. Moreover, the British pension fund had acquired Dr Tobin's from a company registered in Jersey, Channel Islands.

I had been told that week by Dr Ward to lose weight, so just after noon I set out on foot from Lower Mount Street to the lunch in Ballsbridge. The question asked in Mates's piece now seemed pivotal to the mystery of Dr Tobin's, I reflected, as I made my way by the cherry-blossom-strewn footpath of Northumberland Road: who owned the company in the Channel Islands that had made the killing? I knew, I felt, but did not want to be told. And yet there was a part of me, despite the unravelling under way, that had to admire the chain of events that had been set in motion the previous autumn in Paris.

I made my way as instructed through the restaurant and out into its garden, bright with daffodils, and across by way of a paved path to a mews thirty yards from the main building. A Garda minder lurked by a birch tree; he recognised me and held open the door. I heard voices and laughter. They were seated at a circular table, Harry with a woman by his side, then Big Mac, then two younger women whose provenance was a mystery, and lastly Milo Flood, a buttery-tongued, thirty-five-year-old Dublin county councillor who had been elected to the Dáil in the last six months and whom Harry had immediately elevated to the post of junior minister. A waiter was pouring Dom Pérignon.

–This is my Minister for Finance, Harry said, and they all clapped. –My very dear friend, Bunny.

–Great to see you, great, Big Mac said, and pumped my arm vigorously in an action that made the hair bob at his collar. –Doesn't the chief look great?

–Fantastic.

I shook hands with the two women, whose names I cannot recall, and with Milo Flood who ceaselessly smoked cigarettes in fierce, concentrated drags. Finally I came to the lady beside the Taoiseach. She shook my hand politely. –We've already met, I said.

She looked at me as if I'd asked a question. She wore a simple jumper of fine wool.

–In Paris, last autumn, I said.

–Of course, said Chantal, and smiled for the Taoiseach. –And this is like Paris all over again, all of you here. Except – where is your friend, the ozzer minister?

Harry frowned. –'The ozzer minister'. She means Larry, Big Mac said.

–He's not here because he's gone to the doctor's, said Milo Flood, and Harry began to shake with laughter.

–Which one does he use? Big Mac asked. –Dr Broe or Dr Tobin?

–There's no difference, because they're both Mates. Milo Flood grinned.

–Oh, I'm sorry, is he ill? asked the Frenchwoman.

–He picked up a bad infection when he was looking at a property, Milo said.

Harry's colour had turned to deep red. Milo Flood was another Larry Maher in the making, if only he knew it, a Harry creation, a big, broad-shouldered man with dark good looks and a reputation at local-government level for being insatiable when it came to monetary inducements. I wondered what I was doing there. Big Mac had established a regular routine of such lunches for Harry, but this was the first one to which I had been invited.

–Tell Bunny the Dr Broe golf story, Big Mac said to Milo.

–Ah, Jesus, Milo said.

–Go on! Big Mac urged.

Milo looked to the Taoiseach who was still speechless; Harry flapped his hands to indicate that Milo should keep it going.

–Dr Broe took up golf about a year ago, Milo said.

–Well, you know how the doctor has to not only have the best of everything, he also has to be the best in everything. So he bought all the top gear, bought his way into Portmarnock, flew in a teaching pro from the States who looks after the likes of Jack Nicklaus to get him started, had a floodlit set-up for pitching and putting installed in his back garden in Mullingar. Read every book that was ever written on golf, saw every video. Got into all the golf jargon. Spent six months flying up and down to Kerry and practising on the QT with Tony Jacklin, who used to fly in once a week just to play with the good doctor. And apparently Broe became half good at the old golf – good enough, in fact, to turn up about three weeks ago in Portmarnock for the members' weekly four-ball.

The Taoiseach had begun to shake with mirth again.

–But, of course, this is the doctor's, if you like, first trip into the real world of golf. Milo beamed. –Up to now he's been playing with hired hands, professionals who were Dr This and Dr That and, of course, you can have a free drop, Dr Broe. Portmarnock was a bit different. He turns up on the first tee with three old fellas who've been playing golf out here all their lives and who'd literally murder you for sixpence. Everyone has caddies. The players all shake hands, then pair off, and one asks Broe, 'Have you been playing much?' Broe says, 'Here and there.' 'And how is your game?' asks the one who's Broe's partner, not that he has the slightest interest beyond that he wants to take money off the other two. 'Actually,' says Dr Broe, remembering a line in one of the magazines he's read, 'I'm hitting the ball like God.'

Big Mac was grinning from ear to ear and Harry had become scarlet-faced.

–So they all tee off and Dr Broe goes last. But as often happens, out in the full heat of battle for the first time, everything he has learned goes out the window. So his tee shot scuttles along the ground about ten yards to the left and ends up in a furze bush. 'Bad luck,' the old fellows murmur, and avert their eyes. Broe's caddie has to crawl in under the bush to find the ball, which he then hands to Broe. They're still near the tee and the next four-ball have come out. Broe drops the ball, takes an eternity to pick a club, does so, then hits the ball again straight back into the bush.

–Straight back into the bush, Harry gasped.

–A small crowd has now formed back on the tee. In goes Broe's caddie again to the bush, and out he comes again with the ball. 'Drop it away over there, sir,' he suggests, but Broe gives him a withering look and drops the ball beside the bush again, and takes out another club. And hits the ball back into the bush for the third time. And the caddie turns to the other caddie and says, 'God must be some fucking golfer.'

We all laughed, Harry until he had to drink water, which then caused him to choke.

–Here, let me help you, Chantal said, and rubbed the Taoiseach's back beneath his jacket at the same time as he was being invited to taste a Montrachet.

–The Taoiseach was telling us about his horses, Bunny, said Big Mac.

–I may send some over to your dear husband to be trained, the Taoiseach wheezed, waving in the general direction of France. –I enjoy Longchamps.

–So do I, Chantal said, then I heard her add quietly, –but twice as much when you are there.

Two waiters carried in between them the biggest platter of seafood I had ever seen, and placed it in front of Harry. I could just see the top of his head over the mounds of oysters, clams and lobster tails.

–History is the only true judge of political success, Milo Flood was expanding for the benefit of the other ladies. –Look at Jefferson, derided in his time. And a hundred years ago Napoleon was regarded the same way as Hitler is today. You have to break eggs to make omelettes. People want strong leaders, they want decisions made for them. You know the worst thing a boss in a factory ever did? Everything is going fine, not a murmur from the floor, production is up, budgets are being met. What does he do? Maybe it's because he's guilty about making money or something, but the silly eegit goes down on to the shop floor and he asks, 'Is everyone all right down here?' Jesus Christ, he'll have a picket on the place within a week.

I looked over to Harry, whose eyes were unfocused. A napkin was tucked beneath his chin and he was being fed oysters by Chantal.

–You think politicians should not listen to the people? asked one of the young women, emboldened with wine.

–They can listen, but what do they hear? Milo asked. –A million people banging the table and saying, 'Me, me, me.' Where's the vision in that? He lowered his voice. –What good is it doing Ireland at this moment that the most visionary Taoiseach ever – and I mean of all time – is being thwarted from running the country properly by some fucking woman who has about as much interest in this country as Batman? Cheap sensationalism is all it is. It takes real courage to stand up and say, 'Do your worst, I'm having no part of it. I have greater things to be going on with.'

Lamb was served, and Harry's favourite red, Cheval Blanc.

–So – nothing bad happened in Dr Tobin's? the girl persisted, checking quickly across the table to where Harry was whispering something at Chantal's ear.

–Of course nothing bad happened, Milo said. –This is just political sniping that has become a full-scale war. Do you think the Taoiseach would have the time to become involved in setting up Mickey Mouse property deals? The man is exhausted. He spends ten per cent of his time in an aeroplane. Bunny, you tell her.

–The Taoiseach has spent his whole life in the service of his country, I said. –He would not claim to have given much in that period, but I can assure you that no man has given more.

–My mother says she fell in love with him when she was twenty, the other girl said, and her eyes were bright with admiration. –Now I can see why.

I remember the remainder of that luncheon on two counts. Sorry, three. First, after the cheese and a superb port, Harry excused himself and went upstairs. Five minutes later, Chantal followed. It seemed quite natural. One of the young women was explaining her thesis on multiculturalism to me when Milo was called from the room. When he came back in, he looked drawn and tense. –Is the Taoiseach still upstairs?

–And will be for the rest of the afternoon, Big Mac said. Milo had his back to the young women. He jerked his head in a dismissive gesture. Big Mac stood up. –Okay, girls, we're wrapping it up now. They want the room back, he said. He got them out by promising that we would all meet in an hour in a pub in Merrion Row.

–What's the matter? I asked.

–Pat Smith is launching a leadership challenge to Harry, Milo said.

–For fuck's sake! Big Mac said.

We went our separate ways then, but as I was leaving through the main restaurant, the owner of the place popped up beside me with a plate that had a folded bill on it. He handed me his biro. –Mr MacNamara asked would you do the honours, he murmured, referring to Big Mac.

I signed it. The lunch had cost fifteen hundred pounds. At least I now understood why I had been asked to come.

6

Dublin, 1988

Adi and I sat either side of the fire with a half-finished bottle of red wine on the table and the television on mute.

–If he goes now, he's finished for ever, she said.

–I agree with that.

–So, you think he's finished?

I said, –I didn't say that. In fact, unless some fresh dirt comes out in the ten days between now and the parliamentary party meeting, I think he'll make it.

Adi shivered. –When I saw him at Easter down on the island that morning when he'd just got the paper, I was terrified. It was horrible, Bunny. It was as if this person I was looking at was all rotten inside and at that exact moment all the rottenness was oozing out.

She smiled suddenly. –Aren't you glad now that you've made your decision to go? That you've told Harry it's all over?

–Very glad, I said.

It would have been difficult then to explain that the pace of events since Easter had left me little opportunity to take the steps she so wished for. For although few in the Fianna Fáil parliamentary party were prepared to say that they supported Pat Smith, there was enough ambivalence about for the media to propel the affair into a full-blown political crisis. I never poked my nose into such matters, or rang Harry, or tried to offer help, for

I was, and would always be, a political *ingénue* and any attempts I might make to help would be a hindrance. But two days later my caveat on fresh dirt became reality. The Mates crusade had, it seemed, reached the very walls of Harry's Jerusalem.

Sam Maher, Larry's brother, had acted for thirty years as his older brother's driver. Although on first appearances Sam came across with Larry's bluff and swagger and loud talk, beyond this very early threshold he was a man who had left school at fourteen, was barely literate, understood nothing of business, lived in awe and terror of his brother and whose principal interest in life lay in racing pigeons. This was the individual to whom Larry Maher had entrusted the chairmanship of Maher & Co, Auctioneers, albeit on a nominal basis. Sam had little to do except sign his name – a task he performed with difficulty. Larry relied on trusted clerks in the office to keep going with the business that he would one day return to. Sam occasionally came in and joked with people, or stood outside the shop and scanned the sky for overdue birds. Mary Mates went to the Companies Office, discovered that Sam Maher was chairman of Maher & Co, found out where he lived and turned up one evening on his doorstep in Killester as the chairman of Maher & Co was grooming his star performer with a toothbrush.

He seemed to have seized on the idea in his moss-laden mind that she was a pigeon fancier. Mates complimented Sam on his birds, his modest house and garden (in which they now stood), she asked him casually who owned Dr Tobin's Hospital; and Sam told her that Dr Broe did. She must, through the haze of her excitement, have felt a soft spot for Sam, for in her damning article she went out of her way to point to his commendable honesty.

Two days later the *Irish Times* ran a major two-page spread on Dr Tobin's. All the known aspects of the affair were examined in forensic detail, pinpointing the role of Maher & Co and the original government disposal of the building as the key to the mystery. There were charts and diagrams supporting the central hypothesis: a city-centre hospital had been closed and its long-term patients rehoused as far away as County Mayo in order to allow the government to sell off the hospital at a fraction of its true worth to a billionaire Arab. He had then, along with his entire family, been made an Irish citizen. As this was happening, the most recent brainchild of the Messenger government, the Irish National Resources Corporation – chairman: Irish millionaire Dr Brendan Broe – had taken a twenty-five-year lease on Dr Tobin's at a rent three times greater than had ever before been paid in Dublin. The INRC had been advised in this transaction by the redoubtable Maher & Co. Within days of this happening, Prince Abdul Alman, the so recently Hibernicised Arab, had passed on Dr Tobin's for an undisclosed sum to a Jersey-based company, allegedly the property of none other than INRC chairman, Dr Brendan Broe. And barely had the ink dried on this conveyance than the ex-hospital had again been sold, this time by its new Jersey owners to a British pension fund for a sum believed to be in excess of £14 million.

Dr Broe was first off the mark. He emphatically denied what had been printed. His solicitors announced that they had been instructed to sue Sam Maher, Maher & Co and the *Irish Times* for substantial damages.

Bookmakers were offering only even money on Harry's chances of survival.

Harry's name on the school register was Harold D. Messenger. The D was for Daniel, after Daniel O'Connell, the Liberator. The Messengers had come down from Derry and were living in one of the Dodder Cottages.

–Where do you think you're going?

I'd delivered the sugar as requested and was going back to the other side of the schoolyard. Messenger always had his gang around him: Jack O'Brien and Art Maddocks, and sometimes Pat Smith, and a lad from near Bolands called Frank Trundle whose da was a hospital porter.

–Are we not good enough for you, ay? Messenger asked.

–You can stick around with us now, Gardener, said Maddocks.

I could see Maddocks wanted to say things that Harry would approve of. –All right, I said, although I could see Mickey O looking over to know why I wasn't coming back.

It wasn't anything amazing, it just happened like that. From then on, until he left school, I was in Messenger's gang. Knocking around every day with Messenger made me feel good, it was always exciting to be near him, there was always something going on. Even the boys in sixth year looked up to him. But he had enemies, too, and if Brother Kenneth had been bad, Mr Murphy was the worst in Ireland.

–He hates me, said Harry one day.

Mr Murphy taught fifth and sixth years.

–He hated me from the moment he heard my accent.

–He's from Cork, said Trundle. –He was a Cosgrave man.

–That's what I mean.

–He's a little b-bastard, Jack O'Brien said.

–He'd love to see the likes of us swingin', Trundle said.

–He'd love to see our heels kickin' in the air.

Trundle's talk was all about politics and how his old man had been out in 1916, or so Trundle told us. Trundle's da had shot a British soldier in Holles Street, according to Trundle. Bang! –Aaah! the Tommy cried out. But as he was going down, he let off his rifle and shot Mr Trundle in the hip. But Trundle's da let off another two from his Browning pistol. Bang! Bang! This time he got the soldier between the eyes. A hole the size of a half-crown. What a shot! The Brit was dead before he knew it. I was agog. –It's true, Trundle told me solemnly. The gun is at home on the mantelpiece. One day I heard Trundle telling Maddocks that the real reason Messenger was down here at all was because his old man had had to get out of Derry in a hurry.

–He was the local IRA quartermaster, Trundle said, out of the side of his mouth.

–What's that? Maddocks asked.

–He gave out the guns, Trundle said, with some authority.

I didn't let on that Mr Murphy, the teacher, was living six doors down from us in Upper Grand Canal Street. Some evenings I'd go up the entry and down along the back of the houses and Mr Murphy'd be out in his back garden, stripped to his waist, lifting iron bars. He had tight-cut fair hair and he had muscles standing out all over him. When you met him on the street, he always went by without noticing you. Mr Murphy was around forty, but Mrs Murphy was much older. She didn't go out very much on account of their having a retarded child.

–It's very hard on them, Mam said. –She has to mind him all the time.

Sometimes I'd see Simon Murphy being led by his mam up to Mass in Haddington Road. He was as big as a man and very heavy and had hair on his face. A lot of the local kids used to shout things at him, and one Sunday when he had on a clean white shirt, they sneaked up behind him after Mass with their pens and when his mam wasn't looking pelted ink all down his back.

–Is that why Mr Murphy is always cross? I asked Mam.

–Isn't he entitled to be? Mam sighed. –Their only child.

Harry Messenger could get away with nothing with Mr Murphy, the lads told me. He'd be pulled out first on to the line and the teacher had a vicious little leather that Trundle said he'd had cut thin in a special way so's the edge of it would draw blood.

–Why don't you get your da to have him kneecapped? Trundle asked.

–B-blow his fuckin' brains out! cried Billy O'Brien.

Harry just looked at them sideways. He had a way of looking at people like that that made them shut up. But when he looked like that at Mr Murphy, I heard it used to drive Mr Murphy mad.

–Take that insolent look off your face, Messenger!

–I'm not being insolent, sir.

–And don't answer back!

Harry had been out on the line for fifteen minutes.

–All right, Maddocks, the name of Alexander the Great's father.

–Mr Alexander, sir.

Mr Murphy rushed down to Maddocks's desk. –Four for cheek! he cried, and Maddocks stuck his hand out. Mr Murphy kept the leather up the sleeve of his jacket and when he shook it down it appeared like a black tongue. He brought it up so high that the tongue curled in the air two feet above his head. Maddocks looked sideways and winked. The teacher dealt out the four slaps like a machine-gun.

–Anyone else? Blundell?

–Don't know, sir.

–Don't know because you didn't read the book. Hogan?

–Don't know, sir, sorry, sir.

Mr Murphy turned to the line. –Messenger?

Harry just looked at him.

–Are you dumb, Messenger? The name of Alexander the Great's father, if you please.

Harry remained silent. Mr Murphy's already high complexion heightened. –Messenger?

The leather appeared.

–Is there something the matter, Messenger?

–You told me not to answer back, sir.

The teacher pulled out Harry's hands and laid into them. He was trembling as he walked back up to the head of the class and his hand was unsteady as he reached for the chalk.

–Philip of Macedonia, he said, writing on the board, his voice shaking. –Alexander was his only son.

Dublin, May 1988

I love May, that trick in the calendar that seems to promise nothing but goodness, when the evenings rush out into long, blood-washed sunsets and every dawn is a show-off of creation. In school we had built altars to the Virgin Mary during May, for this was her month, and walked in processions behind her bluebell-decked statue, or preceded it, if chosen, scattering cherry blossoms on the ground.

Although a sense of siege had gripped the government, my life proceeded with seeming normality. I walked early one morning on the strand at Dollymount where Harry still rode most days at dawn and where lacquered figures in the hazy distance might well have been ghosts. I tried to clear my mind for a meeting that had been called at short notice: a man from the Central Bank named Argo had telephoned and said that he and a colleague, unnamed, required to see me urgently – I'd had to plead pressing business elsewhere to stop them coming over there and then. Of course, no connection existed between this move by the bank – I tried not to think of it as hostile – and the onslaught against Harry but, none the less, it felt so. One could not entirely dismiss theories that promoted universal confluence, or that one's enemies, however unconsciously, seized their opportunities at the moments they judged most auspicious.

I had to make a judgement call as I walked along the shell-packed foreshore: Harry would still be Taoiseach in two weeks' time and the ineffable, yet utterly real and majestic aura of power that attended and protected him, and all around him, me included, would still be intact – or not. If not, it was all over for sure, because Harry had too many miles on the clock to make another comeback, and the absence of his power would be every bit as telling as its presence now was.

At such crucial junctures, I could understand the drug

of power and how men like Harry craved it. For power, or its lack, dictated how the world beheld you and the respect you received. People's eyes shone for Taoiseach Messenger. Even those who would eat dirt rather than vote for him underwent a change in his presence. Women melted and their husbands' eyes shone. No matter that they then went home without a good word to say about Harry: they had been willingly seduced by power, many of them without even knowing it.

Perversely, the fact that Harry had all his life been surrounded by gossip and innuendo was now an asset, I calculated. People, and, crucially, Fianna Fáil deputies, would listen to each day's new allegations and say, 'What's new?' Was it worth putting their political careers at risk in an open ballot – which I was certain Harry would manage to insist on – and turn their backs on the man who had put them there in the first place? So it wasn't nostalgia or starry-eyed admiration that made up my mind for me that morning. Harry would survive, I decided. He would leave politics on his own terms. It would, I believed, take a development of nuclear proportions to alter that scenario.

–Mr Argo and Mr Kelly, said Violet, standing back and holding open the door to the boardroom.

My first reaction was: they are so young! Neither Mr Argo's thick spectacles nor his heavy shaving line could advance his age beyond the late twenties; his colleague, Mr Kelly, looked as if he should have been at school. We sat down in the leather armchairs and Violet set out cups and saucers and plates with small square linen napkins on them, and knives of silver plate. No discussion beyond the weather – disappointing for May – was undertaken as tea was poured and sandwiches and biscuits presented. Mr Kelly ate with relish, suggesting that this was his first food of the morning.

–So, is everything well with you gentlemen? I enquired.

Mr Argo tapped his mouth with a napkin and then fixed me with a dark look. –The Central Bank has grave concerns about the running of Lipman's Bank, Mr Gardener, he said.

I set my face to show puzzlement.

He said, –We have previously expressed our concern to you by way of letter and, if I am correct, over the last ten years some of my colleagues have also regularly come here to express the Central Bank's reservations.

–I have had many meetings with the Central Bank over the years, none of them ever less than cordial.

Mr Argo glanced down to a notebook. –For example, in 1976 the bank came here to express its concerns about Lipman Brothers Bank's loan book. And again in 1978. And 1982. We were concerned then not only about the loans but about the possibility of widespread tax evasion.

–Avoidance, I said gently but firmly.

–Very well, avoidance. None the less, tax issues. Major amounts involved. And very little detail available.

–We pride ourselves here above all on discretion.

–The Central Bank deals with every financial institution in Ireland, every one of them aware of the need for discretion, but the level of secrecy practised here is in our experience unique and completely out of the ordinary.

–I cannot speak for the standards prevailing in other places, I said reasonably.

The two men exchanged glances.

–These worries have escalated, pressed Mr Argo.

–Based on your latest set of returns to us, we are now looking at problems under the headings of the bank's capital adequacy, the poor quality of the bank's assets, your low profits and the fact that your liquidity is very much out of line and is mismatched. We have a problem, Mr Gardener. This cannot go on.

It was as bad as I had anticipated. I sat forward and took some time to offer tea – which was declined – and to pour myself a fresh cup.

–I think you may be exaggerating the situation, I suggested.

–We are supervisors, Mr Gardener, said the very young Mr Kelly. –Our prime responsibility is for the safety of depositors' funds.

–And do you believe them to be at risk here? I asked, with frank disbelief.

–We know exactly what you're doing, Mr Gardener, said Mr Argo. –We know that, shall we say, tax-sensitive money comes in here and goes on deposit with Solinberg's in Bermuda. We suspect, but because we lack the information cannot yet prove, that this happens in breach of currency regulations. But we will, in time, get both information and proof, believe me. And we are aware that you are making loans to these depositors on the security of their deposits.

–Is it the tax aspect that worries you fellows?

–The tax is a secondary issue for us. Revenue do their job, we do ours. No, what worries us is that despite your previous specific assurances, none of the activities mentioned has been run down or even curtailed. They've been increased, in fact, as the latest returns show. We have regretfully had to come to the conclusion that you are not a fit and proper person to be in charge of a bank.

I sat back, impressed that a man so young could be so tough. But how tough? –And you propose . . . ?

–Your immediate resignation. We'll come in here and wind things down. No one will know, apart from ourselves, that's a guarantee. It's finished, Mr Gardener. This is a golden opportunity for you.

–And if I decline this . . . golden opportunity?

–We'll revoke your licence, said Mr Kelly, with a sudden rush of aggression.

I smiled, but not outwardly, for I knew that the revocation of a bank's licence by the Central Bank required the consent of the Minister for Finance, which in turn would mean the acquiescence of the government.

–Revoke it away, I said.

We sat in sudden silence. It was a feature of the boardroom, which overlooked a quiet garden, that no street noises ever reached this far.

–You won't resign? asked Mr Argo.

–Certainly not.

–Then we'll force you to.

–In theory, that is possible. In theory, you can request the resignation of the entire board. But we all know the effect that would have on Lipman's, don't we? A stampede of people at the door looking for their money back – which, of course, we, any more than any other bank, will not be able to give them. There will be a run. The bank will probably collapse. The depositors will lose their money. And as Mr Kelly has pointed out, your prime responsibility is for the safety of depositors' funds. So you will hardly take a course of action that will almost certainly result in your abrogating your prime responsibility.

–We've done it before, said Mr Argo. He seemed to have slipped down somewhat into his armchair.

–And caused consternation. Look, gentlemen, let us be men of the world here. I'm not someone who's going to do a midnight flit and surface in five years' time running a soccer club in England. This bank is not going to collapse – not unless you make it do so. But hear this: I accept your reservations and concerns. In fact, before this meeting was ever set up, I had resolved to take the action you are advocating.

–You mean resign? Mr Kelly asked.

–No. I mean wind down the deposits and the related activity. I'll resign in my own time and on my own terms, but not until I have finalised these matters. You have my word on that. By the end of this year, you will see a radical transformation, you can rely on it.

–We don't trust you, Mr Gardener, said Mr Argo. But the fight had gone out of him.

–You should, I said. –Hundreds of people have done so, and I've never yet let one of them down.

I turned on the television news just as the camera switched to Harry. He was dressed in a most impeccably cut dark double-breasted suit, a dark-blue shirt and deep-red tie, and his hair was moulded back just over the tips of his waxen ears. He smiled then and, as he did so, looked like a man whose sole fault in life was his own generosity. It was Friday evening. Even the stock market had fallen ahead of the vote the following week, which would decide Harry's fate.

–What is your reaction now, Taoiseach, to the events that have unfolded? asked the interviewer.

–One of surprise, the Taoiseach replied quietly. –I asked certain people to undertake certain tasks. This outcome is not what I expected.

–Do you feel betrayed?

–I prefer the word 'surprised'. You see, this is not about property deals or office rents or passports, this is about Ireland's amazing mineral resources potential, our oil and gas and riches that lie beneath the waves and under our mountains. Gold that has lain untouched since Celtic times. Our wealth and heritage. That is why my government set up the INRC – so as to manage this inheritance for the people of Ireland. This country of ours can be rich beyond our wildest dreams, but we must manage it properly. The INRC has the capacity to do that. Its establishment is something I am personally very proud of. But a lot of people, by the same token, are very jealous. That's politics.

–But with all due respect, Taoiseach, the INRC has hardly got off to the best of starts, has it? Instead of managing our riches, it seems to have spent every minute since it was set up in further enriching the people associated with it.

Harry rearranged his hands in his lap and began to speak. He had stonewalled a thousand interviews like this, hypnotising his questioners with wave after wave of statistics, mere points on the circumference of the issue, reshaping the conversation to one of his own making and somehow moving the entire infrastructure of the argument without anyone noticing.

–I'm sorry, Taoiseach, interrupted the interviewer, –but can you please tell us whether it is appropriate for a national organisation as important as the INRC to be chaired in the circumstances by Dr Brendan Broe?

Only if you knew Harry would you have seen his smile. Outwardly, he looked regretful, but I knew what he was going to say. He said that Dr Broe had done a wonderful job of bringing the INRC to the point it was now at. However, the media had made the situation unworkable for him. Groundless accusations had reached fever pitch. It was an impossible situation. –I think that he should consider his position as chairman until current matters are satisfactorily resolved.

–So Dr Broe should go, Taoiseach?

–Until such time as clarity has been achieved on these important issues, he should consider his position, yes.

Later that same evening, in a one-line statement, Dr Brendan Broe announced with regret his resignation from the INRC. And a snap telephone poll conducted next day found that over sixty per cent of voters thought that the Taoiseach had 'acted correctly' in the Dr Tobin's affair. Moreover, Harry's approval rating over other party leaders had widened by two percentage points. My instinct had been right, I felt, as I walked up to my office next morning and felt the sun on my back. And then, that same morning some time around noon, Mary Mates discovered that her telephone was being tapped.

–Bunny, have you heard what's happening?

It was three in the afternoon. Stan Sharkey sounded agitated.

–Yes.

–What do you think?

–It's bad, I said.

Stan spent about three days a month in Dublin, overseeing the transition of his property companies to his eldest son.

–You're dead right it's bad. I've just been in Leinster House and it's chaos in there. It's all over, Bunny. The end of the road. There are deputies who would, up to now, have given Harry their last remaining kidney but who are going to vote against him.

–Why?

–Why? Stan laughed, and I could imagine him rattling his bottom lip with his teeth like a chipmunk. –Because everyone knows this is a step too far. Up to this, he could have winged it, but this is blatant. Now you can't believe him even if you wanted to. Harry's been caught with his hand in the till.

I thought back to my cross-country flight at Easter to meet Larry Maher.

–Why does it have to be Harry? I asked.

–Ah, for fuck's sake, everyone knows that Larry Maher is a moron, said Stan, with uncharacteristic vehemence. –Look, I've got another call coming in. Let's keep in touch.

I tried to call Harry then, but I could not get through on his direct line. The evening papers were all running what amounted to political obituaries of Harry Messenger. That evening, Adi and I watched the nine o'clock news, which carried a brief interview with a manifestly agitated Larry Maher who announced he was setting up an inquiry under a Garda superintendent to discover how Mary Mates's telephone had come to be tapped.

–God, he looks wrecked, Adi said.

–He is, I said.

On the same news programme a statement from Harry was shown, saying that the Taoiseach had full confidence in his home affairs minister. The telephone tapping was 'deplorable', Harry said, and he hoped those responsible would be 'vigorously pursued'.

A type of hysteria had gripped the media, a frenzy that it seemed could only be satisfied by even more sensational developments. It got them. Larry Maher was rushed to hospital that night, suffering from 'exhaustion', although there were few who did not understand the real reason. A statement next morning issued by his wife, Primrose Maher, announced Larry's resignation as Minister for Home Affairs and his decision not to run in the next general election. Harry's words of regret for Larry's departure, issued through Big Mac, were less than effusive. At the same time 'sources close to the government' – in other words, Big Mac himself – were heavily briefing anyone who would listen that the telephone tapping had been Larry Maher's ham-fisted attempt to cover up his part in the Dr Tobin's controversy. Larry, because he was heavily sedated in Beaumont Hospital, made no immediate rebuttal of these charges. His resignation seemed to be all the proof that was needed to convict him.

Then I got a call from Milo Flood.

Da came in late one evening in January and said the reason he was late was he'd had to help carry Mrs Murphy's son home from Baggot Street. Simon Murphy had slipped on ice and hurt his ankle. He was roaring with pain and wouldn't let anyone near him.

No one went near the Murphys as a rule because of Mr Murphy's cross looks and the fact that the Murphys liked to keep to themselves. But in February Mam heard from Mrs O that in the month since he'd fallen Simon Murphy hadn't walked and that his mother was having a desperate time with him.

–He weighs more than two men, Mam said. –God help that poor woman.

The Germans were as good as done for and everyone was talking about rations coming to an end in the summer. In school it had gone from bad to worse for Harry Messenger with Mr Murphy. It was like every day was another battle day. Anyone who hung around with Harry was picked on too by Mr Murphy. He saw me with Harry at break one day and I wondered if he'd start picking on me when I moved up to his class.

–He brings his hell from home to school, said Rosemary, when Mr Murphy's name came up. –He brings the hell in his head.

–Simon fell on his mother two weeks ago, Mam said. –She was two hours lying underneath him.

–She has to try to carry him to the toilet, Rosemary said.

–They put in for a wheelchair but they were refused.

–She won't let Simon be put into Grangegorman, Mam said.

–When you go into the Gorman they never let you out.

Uncle Myles came over and said he'd been talking to one of the bosses in Clerys and they'd told him that Hitler'd be strung up by Easter. In school, Trundle said that his da'd said that England's misfortune was Ireland's opportunity and if the IRA didn't hurry up the war'd be over and the border'd still be there. Harry wasn't interested in the war: I heard at break that that morning he'd had the hands flogged off him by Mr Murphy on account of getting his Irish spellings wrong.

I'd been thinking a lot about Mr Murphy. It was actually Mam who'd said something that had stuck in my mind. She'd said, –There's good in everyone if you only look for it.

–You know Mr Murphy? I said to Harry, and they all looked at me. –Well, I was thinking about him and all.

–Bad thoughts is a sin, said Trundle.

–He's a b-bad b-bastard, said Jack O'Brien.

–There's good in everyone, I said.

–Ah, fuck off out of that! Maddocks cried. –What are you doing? Suckin' up to him? You don't even have him for anything.

–Let Gardener finish.

So I told them anyway what I'd been thinking about and when I'd finished Maddocks burst out laughing. –You're out of your mind! He'd go fuckin' mad!

–Especially if he saw Messenger, grinned Trundle.

But Harry wasn't laughing. –I think Gardener's idea is good. In fact, I think it's excellent.

–Murphy's a fucking header! Maddocks hissed. –He'd fuckin' brain you!

–Bunny knows Murphy, he knows the home situation, Harry said. –What's there to lose?

–Maybe your life, Maddocks said.

We talked about it all that day and the next. Trundle said, –I talked to me da and he said all right, provided it's only on loan.

–A loan's good, Harry said. –A loan's the best.

–You're all headers, just like Murphy! Maddocks cried.

–It can't get any worse, Harry said.

Dublin, May 1988

We met in a pub off O'Connell Street. Milo Flood looked as if he had not slept for a month. He was drinking Lucozade and attacking his cigarettes with murderous intent.

–What's the matter? I asked.

–You're to go out to Sutton and talk to Mrs Maher.

–To *Mrs* Maher?

–Larry's not allowed visitors. But the Taoiseach believes that Mrs Maher is winding up to something.

–How does he know that?

–I didn't ask.

I was put in mind briefly of a wildlife programme I had seen on television, which had focused on the ability of certain scavengers to discern prey, or danger, at a huge distance. –What have I got to do with this?

–This has to be a low-key approach, Milo said and rubbed his face vigorously. –To find out what's going on.

–So you do it.

–Ah, fuck it, Bunny, you know I can't. That's why the Taoiseach wants you to do it.

I felt massively weary, all of a sudden. –D'you want a drink? I asked. –I'm having one.

–I'm sick of drink, Milo said. –To be honest with you, I'm sick of everything. I'm sick of the tension, of the pain in my belly, of picking up the morning paper. The wife says I look shite. I feel shite. I'd never have come into this game if I'd known it was going to be like this. And do you know something? Your man is out there in his big house, and there's not a budge out of him. Jesus, I thought I'd met tough men, but he's got balls like conkers. It's unbelievable. He calls me out and there're front-page headlines that very morning saying that he'll go to the Park and resign by lunchtime, and I'm thinking, Jesus, he's brought me out to tell me he's going to the Park. I can barely breathe, I'm so fucking nervous. And he says, 'What's the matter with you, you little bollocks? You look as if you've seen a ghost.' 'Nothing, Chief, I'm just not sleeping great these days,' I says, and he says, 'Then you're a bigger eejit than I thought you were. When I start losing sleep over what these bastards are saying, then I'll really start to worry,' he says.

–What'll you have? I asked.

–I'll have one pint and then I'll go, Milo said, and sucked so deeply on a fag that its paper walls collapsed.

And although we had three before we went our separate ways, I was glad we had, for a sense of finality lay over us.

–He thinks you're going to fix everything up, you know, Milo had said, out on the street. –He told me, 'Bunny always does.'

–I'll see what I can do, I had said.

As I parked outside Larry Maher's house, I reflected on the last morning I had come here and the mess I had encountered – symbolic, it now seemed, of the much greater mess in which the government currently found itself.

Primrose Maher has not to date, I accept, had a profile of any substance in this recounting. A tiny woman in her mid-fifties, her hair still faithful to her name, she had never been politically active but had stayed at home for thirty years and reared her children. Her views on her husband's role in modern Irish politics were not on record. She had been in Dáil Éireann but once, on the day that her husband had taken his seat. If she had had to describe her occupation she would probably, like countless women before her, have put down 'housewife', or, at least, that is what I assumed.

I rang the doorbell. Primrose opened it. She was speaking to someone on a telephone and beckoned me in, pointing to the door of their large kitchen where, on my last visit, the minister had sat at the littered table and wept. This morning the room was fresh and clean, the windows ajar and puffs of early-summer air fluffing out the gingham curtains. Bluebells stood in a vase. Every hint of the previous misery had been swept away. I sat down and saw a heap of that morning's newspapers on a low stool. She'd been through them, by the look of them. The papers reported the demands that were being made from every quarter, or so it seemed, for an inquiry to establish what exactly Larry Maher had been up to in Dr Tobin's. Harry's terse comments implied that the Taoiseach held Larry Maher responsible for the entire débâcle. Primrose came in and I stood up. She was no taller than a ten-year-old child.

–That was our solicitor, she said. –Coffee?

–A cup of tea would be lovely, please.

She pressed a switch on the kettle and took out some white cups and saucers and a milk jug and sugar bowl. Her hands and wrists resembled sparrow claws.

–They say you're the man he sends when all other options have been exhausted, she said, not unpleasantly.

–I hadn't heard that, I said, and tried to laugh.

–It's interesting. Clearly he can't come out here himself, or even pick up the telephone. Too many people watching every move now. Waiting for him to put a foot wrong. Nor can he do anything through official channels for the same reason. And yet, because he's Harry Messenger, he knows he has to do something to try and keep the cork in the bottle. So I knew I'd get a call from someone, I didn't know from whom, but when you rang last night, it was just as I had imagined.

–It's sometimes like that in families.

–What – you think we're all related or something, Bunny? That politics is like blood, or even thicker, is that what you're saying?

–We've all known each other a long time, is what I'm saying.

–Look, I don't know you enough to dislike you, although the fact that you're Messenger's man speaks for itself, Primrose said, sitting opposite me and putting down the teapot between us. –Nor do you know me. Few do, in fact, which is the way I've always preferred it. But you and I have more in common than you may expect. For example, I worked as a bookkeeper for seven years before I married Larry, and since I married him I've kept the books for his business. I've a tidy mind, probably like yourself. Everything has its place. I don't say much, but I see everything and forget nothing.

–Very good, I said and drank tea, although I found it ominous the way the conversation was unfolding.

–My husband is in hospital with a gag in his mouth. Larry is a hopeless alcoholic. Earlier this week he would have drunk himself to death, literally, had he not gone into hospital. But he didn't and he won't now. His political career, as you know, is over. We're going to get through this. He's going to regain his self-respect and hold his head high again. Larry is going to learn how to live his life without Harry Messenger.

–The Taoiseach wants you and Larry to know that he deplores the remarks being currently attributed to him. He is genuinely very fond of Larry.

–I should actually throw you out right now for having said that. But I promised myself that I would see this through on my own terms and not allow myself to be provoked by any of the nauseous filth that Messenger specialises in.

The fact that she was so small and frail somehow made her words land like hammer blows.

–My husband has been criminally abused by that

monster. He has been bled to near death over thirty years. Messenger is like some appalling virus that has to devour every living thing that it comes in contact with. He has devoured Larry, I daresay he will devour you, or maybe he already has. He is a creature of unspeakable evil, a cancer in the gut of Ireland. It will be a great service to this nation to see him obliterated from the political landscape.

–You're upset, I said cautiously.

–I'm way, way beyond upset. Think of the most angry woman you've ever encountered, then multiply her by a thousand and you're getting close to my position. I've had to listen to Messenger's lies for years, but this week he reached new depths. I don't know if you are as loyal to him as Larry was, but if you are then one day you can expect the same treatment as Larry got this week – to be maligned in public, abandoned and disowned. Some friend. But I've promised myself I'm not going to let my emotions get in the way of doing what must be done. The fact that I'm sitting here talking to you, not raising my voice, tells me that I'm succeeding. And you know that, too, because you're scared of me now, Bunny, aren't you?

–I'm concerned for you, Primrose.

But she was right. I was terrified.

–There's a meeting in four days of the parliamentary party. Your friend Harry will go at that. For ever. And he'll go because the day after tomorrow, my husband is going to make a statement telling the world in exact and full detail precisely what went on in Dr Tobin's. I don't know the full picture, he has never told me. But I'd have had to be blind not to guess what's been happening. The deals, the bribes, the backhanders. The brown envelopes. I know Larry's no angel, but at least he's loyal. He's prepared to tell it all, everything. It's a litany of crime and Dr Tobin's is just the cherry on the cake. How much did Harry get out of that? Two million? Three? Larry will tell us. You probably counted it for him, Bunny. He probably brought it into your sordid little bank and you probably counted every note.

I made a disclaiming gesture, but the truth was, I could find no words.

–Harry Messenger has driven a wedge into the heart of our marriage, but the day after tomorrow, Larry is going to pull it out, she said.

Instead of driving home, I went on up the Hill of Howth, past St Fintan's Well, and up to the summit. I thought of other days in past times when I had taken this route. I felt myself briefly aroused by such memories of times that by comparison now seemed golden, although any honest analysis would have revealed that those days had been equally troubled. Age was the problem, I concluded, as I sat there and beheld the bay that had once filled me with such excitement and hope and from which I had often drawn such inspiration. My ability to deal with these crises had shrunk like everything else: my libido, my stamina and the days remaining before I died.

On a Saturday afternoon we headed out to Dun Laoghaire, myself and Harry and Frank Trundle and Jack O'Brien. The walk took us over two hours and when we got to the hospital we went round the back and Trundle went in. Five minutes later Trundle's da came out pushing an old wheelchair as if he was real busy. He didn't say anything, or even look at us, he just left the chair outside and went straight back in again.

We took the wheelchair and the four of us headed back for town.

We were all laughing and caught up in the excitement of what we were doing. At Monkstown, Trundle sat in and Harry pushed him. Trundle stuck his legs out and shouted at Harry to go faster. Jack O'Brien and I sat in on the hill down to Blackrock and Harry and Trundle pushed us but they let go and the chair hit a kerb and we pitched out. Jack O'Brien skinned both his knees.

–We'll break it and then we'll be fucked rightly, Trundle said.

Along the sea front, we raced all the way to Merrion, seeing if the pair with the chair could beat the pair running. Me pushing Harry was the fastest. Between Merrion and Ballsbridge, Harry stood up on the seat and waved to people. They were all staring at us.

–*God save Ireland!* Harry yelled.

The wheelchair veered sharply, and as Harry fell off, I lost my grip on the handles and the chair shot out into the road and nearly went under the wheels of the Dalkey tram.

–I'm tellin' you, you'll break the fuckin' thing! Trundle screamed.

We walked down Shelbourne Road with me in the chair. At the corner of Lansdowne Road two old women came over and asked what was the matter with me, and when Harry told them I was paralysed from birth, one gave me sixpence. The women went away blessing themselves and saying, –God preserve us from it, and we couldn't keep from laughing as we went down Bath Avenue. I got out and pointed out where Murphys lived, then I crossed the road and went home and watched the three lads go in Murphys' gate. We had agreed that if Mr Murphy told them to fuck off they would come up to my house and leave the chair there until we decided what to do with it, but otherwise we wouldn't meet until after Mass the next day. I went in and waited at the window for an hour, but no one came. And the next day, as arranged, we all went round the side of the church in Haddington Road, including Art Maddocks.

–It's fine, Harry said.

–What happened? Maddocks asked, and winked at me. He'd refused to come to Dun Laoghaire the day before on account of thinking that Murphy would come down on us all twice as bad.

–It's fine, Harry repeated. –We're not going to talk about it – all right?

–Ah, Jesus, Maddocks said. –Did he take the fuckin' wheelchair?

–He cried! Trundle whispered and his eyes were dancing. –He fucking cried!

Harry gave Trundle a sideways look.

–He *what*? Maddocks said.

–He c-c-cried like a ch-ch-child! hissed Jack O'Brien, and then burst out laughing.

Harry said, –There's good in everyone, all you have to do is find it. Things are rough at home for those people, so it's no wonder Mr Murphy loses his rag.

–He k-k-kissed M-M-Messenger!

–Ah, fuck off! Maddocks said.

–Gospel truth! Trundle cried. –Swear to God! He kissed him!

I stared at Harry. –Did he?

But Harry had turned his back on us and rejoined his parents.

I couldn't wait at break the next day to hear what had happened in class. Mr Murphy had been very quiet, Maddocks said, a different man altogether. But Harry just shrugged and said it was no big deal. I heard Mam saying how boys in Mr Murphy's class had got together and found a wheelchair for Simon. –It's changed Mrs Murphy's life, Mam said.

Simon Murphy got to like the chair more than walking. Sure enough, when the weather turned better, even though his ankle must have been better too, he'd hobble down their front path to the road and his mother would follow with the wheelchair. Then Simon would sit into it and off they'd go into town. Towards the end of May when Harry was just about to leave school, he took me to one side. –You're going to have Murphy yourself next year, he said. –Watch out for him.

–I thought he'd changed.

Harry shook his head. –He's a bastard, but it doesn't matter as long as you remember one thing.

–What's that?

–The wheelchair is just on loan. The hospital could ask for it back at any time. Never let him forget it.

It seems Mr Murphy knew as well, because I never had any trouble from him. And years later, when I'd forgotten all about Mr Murphy, I was walking down Herbert Terrace one day when a woman came up against me on the footpath pushing an old wheelchair with a big, bearded man in it. They had gone right past me before I realised who they were.

Dublin, early summer 1988

The news that the former Minister for Home Affairs was going to give a press conference in which details of the Dr Tobin's affair would be laid bare notched public interest in this débâcle almost to breaking point. As Larry Maher was driven home ahead of the scheduled event, two television outside broadcast units were set up beyond his front gate and a fair-sized crowd of onlookers had assembled. Photographers and television cameramen swarmed all over his car. Reporters shouted questions. Primrose could be seen next day on the front page of every paper, her teeth bared, manhandling her crouching husband inside. She then requested Garda protection, which arrived late, in the form of one uniformed man. The house was saturated in television arc lights.

I had, as I recall, just one telephone conversation with Harry at this time, and that was on the night that Larry came home to prepare himself for his press conference the next morning. We had not much to say to each other. We were like two people on a falling plane, braced for the impact, each with his own thoughts.

–You know, it mightn't be all that bad, the Taoiseach said. –You see, part of me believes that he doesn't have the bottle.

–Which bottle do you mean? I asked, and we both laughed.

–It'll all be the same in fifty years, Bunny, the Taoiseach said. –Try to get some sleep.

In her prize-winning book, *Dr Tobin's Hospital*, Mary Mates has already reconstructed in some detail what happened next; I will thus confine myself to a summary of her description.

Larry Maher had been put on an alcohol-replacement drug in Beaumont Hospital. Having needed stomach-pumping on his arrival there a week before, he had subsequently suffered severe withdrawal symptoms, necessitating the use of tranquillisers. None the less, he was ambulatory and conscious and aware of the actions being attributed to him in the outside world. It was he who suggested that he speak to the press and tell the true story. Primrose supported him.

They arrived home to Sutton at seven in the evening. When Primrose had left the house that day at noon, no media presence had existed; they came home to a circus. Inside the house, Larry made for the cupboard where the drink was kept, but found it empty. Primrose had thrown every bottle out. Larry had, however, been given pills for this contingency, which she now made him take. He calmed down a bit. She scrambled some eggs and brought them to him at the television, just as the nine o'clock news was coming on. He saw his own house. Primrose switched the television off. They spent the next hour or so discussing what he was going to say the next day, although he still insisted on maintaining the invisible barrier between them that had always existed, as if he could say it to the world of strangers but not to his wife; or, putting it more charitably, perhaps he did not wish to burden Primrose with the information. The final possibility, of course, was that he had no intention of revealing it to anyone.

They retired at about eleven. Larry took some further medication to make him sleep, but the arc lights of the television vans and news crews kept the room piercingly bright. There was a continual hum of conversation and the noise of cars coming and leaving. Primrose rang the guards but was told that nothing could be done. She hung some blankets over the curtains, but they made the room too hot. Somehow she went to sleep.

At around two, Primrose awoke. Larry was not in bed. This was not unusual, for he often got up during the night and spent hours in the bathroom. She went to the bathroom door. He was in there, as usual. He was crying. She went in to him and saw him, her husband of over thirty years, sitting athwart the bowl, every limb of him shaking, his unshaven face in his hands.

–It's all right, she said, and held him. –It's all right.

They stayed there for a good time. It was quiet, at least. He rambled on about what he saw in the tiles, about his life, his father. About death. Primrose soothed him, held him. She got him back into bed around four. He looked like a very old man, she said later. She didn't think he slept at all that night. For when she woke up again, the space in the bed beside her was cold.

The meeting of the Fianna Fáil parliamentary party was postponed because it would have clashed with Larry Maher's funeral and there were few deputies who did not want to be seen on television behind the hearse of their deceased colleague. Pat Smith alone tried to insist that the meeting and the vote should go ahead, but his stance came across as heartless and many said that the erosion of his support began from that moment.

Harry was magnanimous in his grief. At one point outside the church he wiped away a tear from his eye with the knuckle of his index finger, a gesture captured on all the television bulletins and on the front page of every national newspaper. Speaking to reporters, the Taoiseach blamed the 'pressures of work' for his old friend's tragic and premature death, saying that 'mischievous elements' in the media had a lot to answer for and that the recent comments attributed to him on Larry's position had been 'misconstrued, exaggerated and quoted completely out of context'. In reply to the question, 'What happens now?' the Taoiseach said, –I would urge everyone to put this sad business behind them and to let a dead man rest in peace. We have a great Ireland out there, waiting for all of us. Let's get on with the business of finding it. Let's honour Larry Maher's memory by ceasing this almost internecine feuding that we find ourselves in. Larry was a peaceful man. May he rest in peace.

And four weeks later, as everyone knows, at a meeting of the party called with the minimum of notice, Harry put his leadership to an open ballot and was re-elected, unopposed. It took place just before the summer recess. When it was all over, deputies fled the capital for the country lanes where monbretia was just budding, for coasts where dolphins kept pace with fishing trawlers, for lake counties heavy with the scent of woodbine and fern and the brilliance of dragonflies. These elected representatives would not return until the end of September, when the harvest was saved and the browning of the countryside was almost complete. When they did, few would ever mention Dr Tobin's again, for it had somehow acquired a taint of shame, like an indecent incident for which everyone held some responsibility. Dr Tobin's died with Larry Maher.

I never discussed it with Harry either. We had moved on. He, as if nothing had ever happened, or so it seemed; myself, newly determined to pick a moment of my own choosing to go quietly away.

Around six, or so it is calculated, as Primrose still slept, Larry Maher went downstairs to answer the telephone. The guard on duty outside the house said much later that he had heard the telephone ringing inside around this time. Primrose found Larry just before eight, curled up at the foot of the stairs, the telephone receiver in his hand.

Mates cited undisclosed sources for her assertion that the call had come from the Taoiseach's residence,

Oakwood, and that the Taoiseach himself had called Larry that morning in order to bully or cajole the former minister out of making his planned revelations. All Mates's attempts to obtain the relevant telephone records to prove her contention, however, were blocked, since the Taoiseach's calls came under the heading of national security. Harry refused to comment on the matter. The story fizzled out. After all, even if he had made the call, it was no crime to speak to someone on the telephone.

It was the old story, they said later, the way these things went in families. His father with the scissors in his hand; Larry with a telephone. No warning. There are, as everyone agreed, a lot worse ways to die.

PART II

7

Dublin, 1992

Chris put on a slick, tan-coloured raincoat with a check lining, no doubt from their spring fashion offerings, and we made our way together up North King Street. I had read that whilst she dressed only in clothes from Foy's, Barry had been heard to say that he wouldn't be found dead in them. Her hair bobbed at her neck and I felt a spring in my step. At the junction with the Green, we paused for traffic lights and she took my arm.

She had cancelled all her appointments for the morning, including lunch with the firm of auditors due to come in and scour the company's books on her behalf. The lights changed and we crossed. High clouds fluffed above us in lazy zephyrs. Chris linked me closer as we crossed the road again. Being with her armed me with a type of courage that, were I being honest – and I am being honest – I would have to say I had often lacked. The restaurant was in the basement of a nineteenth-century stone building. White tablecloths, silver-plated cutlery, chalice-sized wine glasses. A big, corner table with a curving banquette seat – Miss Foy's table.

–I'll have a glass of fizzy water, straight up, with a dash of bitters, and a bottle of the wine I had here the last time. Bunny?

–Whiskey, please.

–Back in a minute, she said.

I watched her make her way across the room and

towards the cloakrooms. I felt warm all of a sudden, glowing from my centre, a very pleasant spreading and self-sustaining incandescence. The waiter arrived and poured the wine; I gave it the nod. As I found myself looking forward to the sight of her coming back, I understood that the shape of the day had changed substantially.

Dublin, 1951

The practice of Seamus Long & Co, Chartered Accountants, was located in number twenty Herbert Place, on the first floor of a house that stood in a gaunt, unimpassioned terrace overlooking the canal not a stone's throw from Upper Mount Street. Mr Long had once been a famous rugby player and he spent much time – when he wasn't golfing out in Milltown – going to meetings of what he called 'the branch'. Rarely had a man and a name been so apposite, for at nearly six feet nine inches, with multi-jointed limbs that dangled and undulated and hands with fingers no less than simian, he had developed an irreversible stoop from having to incline to catch the gist of a conversation. His clients were a clutch of mostly small businesses – 'sole traders', as we referred to them – whose accounts we prepared once a year from cheque-book stubs, lodgement books, bank statements and the invoices and statements of suppliers. If the sole trader ran a garage, these documents came to us oil-smudged and smelling of engine grease; from the cheque-book stubs of confectioners rose little clouds of flour and wafts of vanilla and marzipan.

I think I always knew, even in my last two years in school, that I would follow Harry. How that would be I could not have said, for I had no overarching view of my career, or indeed of his; but in those days in school when we had hung around together, and afterwards, when we had met and talked about life – although now I could not tell you what we discussed – I knew that we would do special things together, that where he led I would follow and that when it came to the hard choices I would instinctively be on the side he had chosen. He had gone from university into a large auditing practice in central Dublin, and so although Uncle Myles could have got me into Clerys and Uncle John into Kimmage Manor to become a soldier for Christ, as he had put it, I became articled to Mr Long.

Seamus Long & Co dealt with a mixed bag of clients for whom we executed the basic functions of an annual report; but there existed, too, a more shadowy client category, individuals who did not require Mr Long to represent them in an official capacity, rather paid him to employ his considerable knowledge of offshore bank accounts, bogus companies, trusts of the flimsiest construction and the existence of tax anomalies and loopholes to their advantage. Mr Long himself was a hearty character who kept a street map of Douglas, Isle of Man, in the top right-hand drawer of his desk. Successions of Irishmen who had made it from the bottom up in England consulted Mr Long about the hitherto unforeseen benefits of dual nationality, multiple bank accounts, the use of their name as it was in the Irish language, the transfer of property to wives and children, the divestiture of assets to charitable and sometimes not-so-charitable trusts and the formation of companies using local solicitors in such exotic, to my mind, locations as St Helier, Jersey, and Douglas. This was all, as Mr Long explained, completely within the law. 'You join a club, you play hard by the rules' was a conviction he often aired, and apparently in the number-four jersey up to and including Leinster representation, he had been a ferocious competitor, staying just the right side of the referee, but lethal of boot and head-butt in the blind-side position.

That year Harry and I were both sitting accountancy exams in the hall of a school in Summerhill. I had heard that he had become involved in politics in university and that he had been one of a group that had gone into Trinity, torn down the Union Jack from the students' hall, and burnt it. Now, in the three intense hours that lay ahead, we had to answer questions mindless in their ambition, in which the proper accounting procedures for companies selling items in returnable containers were sought of us, and the principle of debit and credit was discussed on a par with philosophy.

–Still ticking and totting? he asked me.

I said I was but that I assumed he was too.

–Means to an end, Harry said, and winked at me. He had filled out and his nose had become more prominent. –Means to an end.

Then he told me that he was thinking of going forward for the corporation. –Crowd of old dossers in there, he said. –All that power going to waste. The committees are the key. All the action goes through the committees.

–D'you ever see any of the old gang? I asked.

–Frank Trundle's gone into the guards, Harry said. –Art Maddocks is working as a clerk in the corpo. I see Pat Smith every second day. He's got his head screwed on.

–He tells my sister that he'll be Taoiseach, I said, and laughed.

But Harry leaned forward and wagged his finger.

–Someone has to be, he said. Then he smiled. –Did you hear about Jack O'Brien?

–I heard he'd gone into Woolworths.

–Not at all, left after a month, Harry said. –Gone for the priesthood. G-g-god b-b-bless you, my s-s-son.

People began drifting into the exam hall.

–Listen, Harry said, –I want to ask you something. We're getting ready for an election. Dev'll be the next Taoiseach. I'm putting together a team, you know the stuff, handing out leaflets, putting up a few posters. There's three or four of the lads helping out. Pat Smith's on board. Could you give a hand?

–I'll see, I said. –There's a lot of work on in the office.

–Do what you can, Harry said.

Rosemary had become not just a woman but in many respects was the mam at home. She gave orders, even to Da. She'd always been smallish and fat to my eyes, but suddenly she was tall and slender. She made tea and cut cake and brought it on a tray into the front room for herself and Pat Smith. He was a quiet person and forever seemed to be taking in everything around him. I think Rosemary liked that in him, the fact that Smith wasn't always mouthing off. They spent hours in the front room. Rosemary used to giggle a lot, but from time to time she'd go very quiet as if Smith was doing something that really pleased her. I lay on my bed upstairs, aware of everything. I could hear Smith's low voice and Rosemary saying, 'Go on.' I could imagine me being there instead of him and her hands on me, where mine were, stroking me and me saying to her, 'Go on.' I could taste Rosemary's mouth. One evening she let out a cry and I brimmed over right then and saw everything white for a moment and my head spun and nearly burst.

Harry and his team were going flat out working the dusty streets of the north city. As well as Pat Smith, Harry had enlisted Aengus O'Reilly, a man older than the rest of us who had been trying to get a Fianna Fáil nomination for years, and Stan Sharkey whose father owned flats on the North Circular Road.

–Listen to this, Harry said one lunchtime.

We were gathered in the Old Shieling, the team's usual meeting-place, and Harry was shaking out the pages of that day's *Irish Times*.

–'Sir Archibald Jamieson has arrived from London and is staying in the Russell Hotel. Major and Mrs J.E.O. Walker have left Dublin for County Wicklow. Mrs Salesbury Craig has arrived in Dublin from Glasgow.' Did you ever in your life hear the like of it?

I saw the amusement in Pat Smith's eyes. He sat back a little from the group, following everything that was said, but seldom speaking.

Harry continued: –Who gives a monkey's about any of these people? Maybe down in Bally-go-shite they still doff their caps at the likes of them, but up here it's all changed. Sir Archibald Jamieson!

Just as he had been in school, he was the leader, even to a man like Aengus O'Reilly, ten years his senior. Harry seldom spoke about Derry, where he had grown up, or about his father, whom we understood had once been interned for subversive activities.

–Change takes time, Stan Sharkey said. He was small and hyperactive and his already partly bald head bobbed as he spoke. –It took my father thirty years to get where he is. But it won't take us as long.

–Why can you be so sure? I asked.

Stan frowned and sat forward and tugged out his shirt cuffs. I had never seen him wearing casual clothes.

–Because the change Harry is talking about is gathering pace. There's only so much wealth in the country, but it's being gradually redistributed. Mark my words, the time will come, and sooner than we think, when the fact that you're a Protestant in Ireland won't automatically mean that you've got money.

–Maybe we should just have taken their money in 1922, said Pat Smith, fishing for a reaction.

–That's what they do in jungles, Harry said. –We had that option, of course, but we realised it was beneath us. We now have a republic and our own constitution. Our own laws. We're law-abiding people, and law-abiding people don't take other people's money.

Pat Smith lowered his eyes.

–We'll do it our way, Harry said. –We've survived for centuries doing things our own way, the way we know best. Things will get better, bit by bit.

–Here's another one! laughed Aengus, reading from the paper. –'Prince Ferdinand d'Ardia Caracciolo has arrived in Dublin from Waterford'!

Harry looked sideways at him. –At least it sounds as if he might be a Catholic, he said drily.

Later, we set out on Collins Avenue East, then worked into the roads off it, fanning out in pairs, ringing the bells, getting the people to come out to their doorsteps. I stayed with Harry. We turned the corner and another twin row of promises to be made regarding social welfare entitlements, housing grants and precious local-authority jobs stretched into the haze of the late afternoon.

–You know what people want? Harry asked, as we

straddled the railings between houses. –They want to know that somebody cares about them. They want twopence off the price of a tin of baked beans, they want to be sure that their children can be vaccinated against whooping cough. They want to be able to buy a decent pair of shoes for under a quid.

A woman, smiling, stood waiting on her doorstep. Harry completed the passage from one property to another and was already shaking her hand and listening gravely to, for all I knew, her dissatisfaction with her household plumbing.

–Thanks, and God bless you, I heard him call out, as he left by way of the gate and crossed the road.

–At the same time, they don't want a lot of fuss about it. That's where the other crowd went wrong this year, mouthin' off about mother and child, something that's guaranteed to drive the Church into a lather. No wonder we'll get in. You have to respect the Church in this country, you have to be respectable. How are you? Great to see you! I'm Harry Messenger and I've come here to ask you for your vote for Fianna Fáil.

We turned into a short cul-de-sac.

–People couldn't give a monkey's about Truman, or the Korean War or where Burgess and Maclean are or what secrets they sold to whom. People are interested in the price of bacon. They want to know if they can buy chickens under three shillings a pound and how much the price of ray is. They want to be able to go down the country in a train on their day off and visit the old home place and come back with a sack of rabbits and eat like kings for a week.

–Rabbits?

We were poised at the entrance to another house

where a man in a cardigan, smoking a pipe, was being chatted up by Stan and Aengus.

Harry chuckled. –I'll tell you a queer one about rabbits I came across the other day. Have a guess at the value of the rabbits we exported to England last January alone.

–I haven't a clue.

–Three hundred thousand quid's worth, he said. –That's nearly forty thousand hundredweight of rabbits. I didn't think there were forty thousand fuckin' hundredweight of rabbits on the island of Ireland.

I got my finals eighteen months later and agreed to stay on with Mr Long. Among the clients on Mr Long's books were solicitors and chemists, dentists, surgeons and gynaecologists, professional men who, like the boss, had once played rugby but who now, in the case of the gynaecologists, at considerable financial benefit to themselves, delivered babies into the ruck and maul of life. These clients could regularly be heard climbing the wooden risers in Herbert Place and entering Mr Long's office. When they left, I was summoned in and entrusted with bundles of cash amounting to thousands of pounds, which over the succeeding weeks I then lodged in a variety of post office and savings accounts in the names of fictitious investors picked at random by Mr Long from the pages of Dickens.

–I have discussed this matter with my confessor, Mr Long once responded, his face grave, in response to a question of mine in which legality had been raised. –He has assured me, and I cannot put it in any stronger terms, that as long as I have a clear conscience about the manner which I believe to be the most expeditious for my clients' savings, then mere revenue regulations, contrivances of a mismanaged exchequer, cannot stain my actions with any suggestion of sin.

I met Harry one evening just before Christmas, coming out of the Shelbourne with a girl in a ballgown on his arm. I had been working flat out on jobs of Mr Long's and had lost touch with Harry for six months or more.

–This is my dear friend, Bunny Gardener, Harry proclaimed. –This man can fix anything.

–Can he fix my heel? the girl asked, supporting herself on Harry's shoulder and bending down to take off her shoe.

I had a glimpse of a white neck diving into the mysteries of a long back.

–If Bunny was a cobbler he'd be the best one in Dublin, Harry said.

His girl suddenly straightened up and kissed me on the mouth. I could smell drink. I later learned that her father was a senior politician.

–Did you hear I got elected? he asked.

I hadn't and I congratulated him.

–It's all there waiting for us, Bunny, he said and clapped his hands together. –We're going to transform this country. We're going to go places that the men in 1916 and 1922 could never have dreamed of.

–Let's go home, the girl said, and hiccuped.

Harry was looking at me. –There's only one obstacle in front of any of us, he said, –and that's the limit of our own imaginations.

The girl shivered and Harry stuck his hand up for a taxi. –Let's have lunch! he shouted.

I had no money for taxis let alone lunch; apart from their wedding breakfast in the Clarence Hotel, I don't think either of my parents had ever eaten in a restaurant. But that night, at home in bed in Upper Grand Canal Street, I embraced the scent and feel and image of Harry's girl until I slept.

Dublin, 1958

Mr Long sent word one day that he wished to see me for lunch in Milltown Golf Club. I drove out through Ranelagh in the Morris Minor I had acquired the year before and parked beside the first tee. I had sometimes delivered documents here for my employer, but this was the first time that lunch had been suggested. In the lobby of the clubhouse, beneath the rolls of honour of the winners of important competitions, I announced my arrival and was told that Mr Long would be with me shortly.

Harry, now a manager in a big Dublin accountancy practice, had two years before married Brigid Wall, the girl I had met that Christmas night outside the Shelbourne. I had been a guest at their wedding. Then Harry had been elected to Dáil Eireann. His effortless progress, in matters of the heart, in business and in politics, seemed of a different order from mine. Harry and Brigid lived in a house in Santry, whereas I still lived in Upper Grand Canal Street with my parents, was in my eighth year of working for Mr Long and had never gone out with the same girl more than twice.

–Ah, Mr Gardener. Mr Long had appeared, buttoning his jacket. –They took us to the eighteenth, the monkeys! He chortled. –You know match play! Do you play golf? Of course not, I'd forgotten. Let's go straight through, shall we?

The dining room was entirely empty. Mr Long said,

–Morning, George, to the head waiter, even though it was one fifteen. –What's the special?

–Baked ham with Cumberland sauce, Mr Long.

–I recommend the baked ham. Yes? Two of those, George, and a bottle of the house red, he said, and arranged his excessively long limbs at the table. –I understand you know young Mr Harry Messenger, Mr Gardener.

Before I could reply, the wine was poured for Mr Long and he took a generous swig. –Ah, you can't beat France for wine, don't you agree?

–I actually don't drink at all.

Mr Long made an expression of puzzlement, then shrugged as if to say that nothing would really surprise him. –He's a quite remarkable young man, Mr Messenger, he continued, –he's the future of this country. Bright, articulate, not afraid to take risks. Married a nice girl – what's her name?

–Brigid.

–Brigid, of course, Brigid Wall, her father Bill was Minister for Agriculture – that's what I mean by smart and bright. You see, the world is changing. You can't keep on ploughing fields with horses in an age when the Russians have sputniks circling the earth. Harry Messenger knows that. He'll get things done, wait until he gets a ministry, they'll not be able to overlook talent like that.

He had that effect on everyone, Harry, I thought as the food arrived, he made us believe that the future would be sweet and that we would all be part of it.

–Oh, that looks good, that was quick, George. Would you like a mineral? Bring us a jug of water, George, if you wouldn't mind, no, just one glass. I rust easily.

Mr Long ate quickly and with determination, pausing

only to take gulps of wine, or to make little noises of gratification when sugared ham fat or Cumberland sauce made contact with a previously unconsidered tastebud.

–Ah, that's better, he said, leaning back and pushing his plate to one side. –This new fad of eating at night is a big mistake. Gives you nightmares. When I go home this evening, the missus will give me just a boiled egg or a kipper – are you married, Bunny? No? – I don't want to go to bed with a gut on me. How old are you, Bunny?

–I'm twenty-seven, Mr Long.

–A great age, a great age. But you need to get married – like Harry. I had two children when I was your age. Good for business, too, you know what I mean? Clients like doing business with people who are like themselves, which means married. Makes them comfortable. I'm not saying that bachelors can't get business, but what I am saying is that it's easier when you're married. Not to mention the fact that that's what we were designed for, eh? Marriage, children, domestic bliss. It's the natural order, despite the filth we hear coming out of England. Now, look, have you ever done a receivership before?

As we made our way out to the terrace for coffee, Mr Long described Schwartz Importers (Ireland) Ltd, a company in Harold's Cross that imported printing machines from Germany and had run its course with the bank. Receivership was the process by which the bank, by direction of the courts, installed their own agent, normally an accountant, to 'receive' a company's outstanding debts and to realise its assets on their behalf. Few companies survived the receivership process.

–Pretty straightforward job in this case, said Mr Long. –A bust flush if ever I saw one. Problem is that the main shareholder and managing director is a member here. Name of Hans Schwartz, a German who came over just before the war, plays off twelve, lovely striker of the ball.

My employer became thoughtful for a moment, no doubt summoning to mind the graceful flights of golf balls struck over the years by Mr Hans Schwartz.

–My first thought was to say no, it would be too embarrassing. But then I thought, Hold on, Mr Gardener is qualified now! So I said, 'Yes, we'll do it, by Jove!'

We were now walking out towards the hall again. He produced an envelope. –Here's your deed of receivership, it's very straightforward, you just show up and take charge. They'll try to rob you blind, of course, but I'm sure you know that. Don't be afraid to put in a good fee – don't forget that our fees come out even before the bank's money, so don't be fainthearted or under any illusions that they'll think more of you if you charge them less. My experience is that the more you sew it into them, the more they respect you for it. Good luck.

Mr Long's advice about marriage remained in my head that evening when I went home and up to my room. Da was downstairs in the kitchen, sitting by the range, reading the *Evening Press* racing page, or maybe just dozing. He did little any more other than sign on once a week or walk up to Haddington Road to the pub. It would be impossible for a stranger to think that he and Mam were husband and wife, I often reflected, for apart from looking twenty years older than her, Da seemed to lack the merest spark or drive, whereas Mam's life had been transformed since she went in to Clerys where she now worked in the lingerie department. She had arranged for a woman from Sandymount to come in every day and cook Da's midday meal. Mr Long was right, I concluded, I needed a wife – more, I needed my own life, my own place, like Harry.

In those days sex beset my mind with tortuous frequency. I had gone out with a variety of women, many of whose names I can now not recall, but whose faces alone remain arrayed like pendulous fruits on the branches of my memory. A more erotic punter might have remembered their breasts or thighs, but the truth is, I slept with none of them, not through want of trying but more to do with generations of rectitude and the supremacy of the Catholic Church.

Set pieces existed, of course, in the back of my Morris Minor and on the couches of dark front rooms – Rosemary territory – where Irish women managed the practice of the heavy court, sexual mimicry with clothes on during which my orgasm was invariably achieved and, surprisingly, in about one third of the cases I encountered, the woman's too. It was a groaning, gusset-busting business, and messy to a fault.

I was twenty-seven and deserved more than the back of a car, I decided. In my mind, as I went to sleep that night, I had already left home.

The next morning at nine thirty, I got the bus to Harold's Cross. Schwartz Importers (Ireland) Ltd suggested a company with operations in other jurisdictions, whereas the truth was that Hans Schwartz had come from Germany with his family just before the war and, after a brief spell of internment at the Curragh Camp, had set up business in the premises fifty yards from where I now stood. It was a shed with an A-roof, offices to the front and a goods-inward gate to one side leading to stores and a workshop. Fifteen people were employed, some of them since 1946. The company imported large printing machines of high capital value and sold them to the likes of newspapers and print-set companies. The bank was owed £237,566 15*s.* 11*d.* with interest accruing daily. Schwartz Importers (Ireland) Ltd was indeed bust.

As I stood there, going over in my mind the procedures I was about to implement, it came to me that far more than mere accountancy was involved here. Although I had technically to take control of the premises and all its assets, including changing all the locks – a locksmith proven in these situations was due to arrive within the hour – it was in reality the lives of people I was taking charge of. Receiving their souls. A mere glance at the balance sheet of this company was enough to understand that nothing would be salvaged from the cadaver when I had skinned away the prime cuts and, having eaten my fill, fed the balance to the bank. Men who had worked here since the Emergency – who had not had to emigrate – would receive a pittance in statutory compensation and would, within weeks, be on the Liverpool boat. Mr Schwartz might even have to surrender his membership at Milltown – for how could he continue to play golf with his peers when his life's work lay in ruins? Inside men toiled, unaware of the fate that awaited them or that their lives would soon be changed for ever. What a pitiless business, I thought, how clinical and final.

I entered the tiled foyer and a middle-aged woman looked at me with suspicion from behind a small glass window.

–Mr Schwartz, please, I said.

With an expression of reluctance, she slid the window open six inches. –Mr Schwartz is holding a board meeting. He'll be busy all morning, she said.

–I'm afraid I have to interrupt him.

She blinked. She wore spectacles with blue lenses. –You *can't* interrupt him, he's holding a board meeting, she said, and made to slide the window closed, but I positioned the corner of my briefcase so that this manoeuvre could not be accomplished.

–This is not something that can wait, I said.

–Listen, you pup, Mr Schwartz is not seeing anyone this morning! she cried. –Do you want me to call the guards?

Resisting the impulse to take pleasure from the fate I knew awaited this unwitting woman – for she was nothing if not loyal and had probably spent years facing down creditors – I removed my briefcase and paused for a moment to consider my next move. As I did so, a nearby door opened and a lovely-faced young woman emerged. Her hair was almost white-blonde and tied back severely, which made her cheeks seem on the plump side. She was beautiful. I stared at her.

–May I help you? she asked coolly, for I had become momentarily dislocated from my grave mission.

–I must see Mr Schwartz, I said, –it's important.

–And you are?

–Andrew Gardener, Seamus Long & Co, chartered accountants, I said and realised how inappropriate I must have looked to her, my mouth open, my briefcase held across my midriff.

–That's the longest name I ever heard, she said. –And why is it so important that you see my father?

I winced, because even then, as ever after, I could not

bear the thought of hurting her. –I've been sent, I said. –By the bank.

Her eyes narrowed and I saw in them the love she had for her father.

I said, –I'm sorry.

–Just wait here, please.

I heard men's voices as a door was opened and closed behind her. I hated what would happen next. One could read all day and not find a word about compassion in the textbooks of the accountancy profession.

A silence seemed to fall on this building of German printing machines and overpledged assets, as if it were all at once three in the morning and the grand possibilities and brave hopes that had come blazing out of pre-war Germany were finally guttering. Behind the glass window the eyes of the receptionist feasted vindictively on me.

–*Vere is he?*

I heard a door wrenched open and then the corridor seemed filled by a single man. Mr Schwartz was immense. Steel-grey hair was swept straight back from a ruddy face. He had a spiked, ink-black moustache. The bottom part of his mouth jutted forward, showing a row of uneven teeth. I was aware of a huge chest and red hands with black hairs on the backs of the fingers. But even at that early moment I knew that this was all for show, that inside Mr Hans Schwartz there had to be another, gentler person – there had to be, for the man he was pretending to be could never have had a daughter like the one I had just met.

–You're the person who couldn't vait for a board meeting to end! he thundered. –So vat's so bloody vell important?

–Could I see you privately, Mr Schwartz? I asked.

–See me? Are you blind? You're seeing me! I've just left six people in there! Now say vatever it is you have to say so and get out!

I knew his daughter was standing behind him, although I could not actually see her. Never again did I want to do this, I knew, although I could understand, even as I stood there, how there must be people who would enjoy this moment, the feeling of absolute power, the demolition that would in seconds commence – that had already commenced – the reduction of this big, proud, blustering man to nothing. Because all he stood for, the building, board of directors, halting business, his standing, income, prospects, pension – everything that had been at least technically intact when he had awoken this morning would be meaningless by noon.

–Vell? he shouted and his eyes popped. –Have you lost your tongue?

–Are you Mr Hans Schwartz?

He rocked back in outraged disbelief, then took a step forward and for a moment I thought he was going to strike. –Who the hell else do you think I am?

–Mr Schwartz, I have here an order of the High Court in favour of the Bank of Ireland, appointing me receiver over all the assets of Schwartz Importers (Ireland) Ltd, I need first to secure the premises and then to carry out a detailed inventory. I would be most grateful if you could give me every assistance in my task.

Again, the only outcome that seemed possible from his outrage was for him to attack. But then, in a moment that I would later know to be as ephemeral as that of childbirth, in a beat of time individual and suspended from any other, Hans Schwartz metamorphosed. As if inner pillars were crumbling Ozymandias-like before my eyes, this big, barrel-chested man began to shrink.

His eyes alone clung to the beliefs that had brought him thus far, but his whole body, even the rest of his face, was now at the mercy of the dread I represented. Abruptly, his legs went. His kneecaps hit the tiled floor with a loud, pistol-like crack. I was terrified. I saw this lovely striker of the ball turn to his daughter, imploring her. She went to him and cradled his head, and then he began to sob, a low, gulping sound, and she held him closely and said, –It's going to be all right, Papa, it's going to be all right.

I cursed Mr Long then, for I knew why he had palmed off this job on me, and at the same time, there in that blighted foyer, I felt a totally inappropriate surge of desire for the daughter of the man whose business career I had just ended, a quite shameful feeling that the power I possessed was limitless and extended into areas way beyond the crystallisation of assets. The front door opened and a man walked in by the stricken tableau of father and daughter.

–Mr Gardener? he asked cheerily. –I'm your locksmith. I take it from what I see here that we're ready to begin?

By six that first evening, the premises of Schwartz Importers (Ireland) Ltd (In Receivership) were sealed drum-tight. I had already begun the task of devouring the records and regurgitating them into a comprehensive format, key debtors had been identified and would, over the coming days, have the fear of God put across them by Mr Long, and a security man with a nightstick and a dog was installed to patrol the premises during the hours of darkness.

How extraordinary the process of transformation, I thought, how unforgiving and lacking in respect. For over a dozen years this place had represented the dreams of at least one man and had filled the daily lives of many. They had all gone without a raised voice, as if my arrival had been long expected. Even my antagonist behind the window in Reception had packed her things into a couple of cardboard boxes, and when one of our clerks carried them for her out to the bus stop, she had thanked him.

The man who filled the position of company secretary and accountant, an elderly individual who at all times presented himself with a pipe jutting from his mouth, took me on a tour of the premises, beginning with the storeroom, which was the first place to be sealed, and then into the warehouse where a couple of mint-new printing machines had been in the process of being commissioned and now squatted like disconsolate animals in a zoo. I was obliged to ask that Mr Schwartz's car – the only one on the balance sheet – be brought into the warehouse and parked there. The tobacco-impregnated company secretary then walked me through the offices, and boardroom, scene of the final meeting, where there was a safe and some art on the walls and ten upholstered chairs set at a large teak table shaped like a coffin. The company secretary informed me that only Mr Schwartz held a key to the safe but that all that was in it anyway was the company seal, and some statutory books, and the petty-cash box. It was a big safe with a heavy door. I made a note to have it opened in my presence next morning.

I went around turning off lights, for the security guard would be confined to the stores and warehouse area. Everything here would be dealt with by way of quick sale by a liquidator when the bank had been seen to. If we played our cards properly, Seamus Long & Co could be in for that job too. The Schwartzes lived, I gathered, in a fine house in Mount Merrion. It struck me as ironic, if not symbolic, that someone of my age from Upper Grand Canal Street could wield such power over people whose lives it might be assumed I envied. I went out to the empty foyer and stopped as I smelt scent in the darkness. That was an instant before I saw her. She stepped out from beside the street door where she had been waiting.

–Mr Gardener?

–Ah, Miss Schwartz. I . . . I was just locking up.

–I know. You must do this a lot.

–Well, in fact, this is my first time, I said and wondered if she could hear the moidered thrumming of my pixillated heart.

–That explains how Papa upset you, she said.

I had not realised that I had looked upset. –Look, would you care for a cup of tea? I asked. –I saw a place in Harold's Cross earlier . . .

–I'd love one, she said.

We walked the couple of hundred yards. I had never before been so intensely aware of another human being. The café had lace curtains and was heated by a one-bar electric fire. I brought over a pot of tea and she poured. She was no more than twenty.

–One lump or two? she asked.

I sipped the hot tea and saw over the cup's rim how fathomless were her irises. –I'm very sorry about all this, I said.

–I understand. You have a job to do.

–How is your father?

–Beyond consoling, she said. –He's been let down so often, by customers, by people who reneged on promises. He's a good man.

–I'm sure he is.

–I feel so sorry for him, she said. –I don't remember Germany, we came here when I was an infant, but I grew up with all the stories of the horror and the fear, the persecutions. My father took us out in 1938. You see, my mother is Jewish.

My reaction was of surprise: the Irish see Jews as being confined mainly to Scripture.

–Papa was brave and clever to do what he did, when you look at all those who could not believe the evidence of their eyes and who stayed put and did nothing, poor things. He had worked in Frankfurt for a printing-machinery company so when he came here he knew little else than that business. Now it is his compassion as much as anything that has brought about this tragedy – debtors ringing up and saying, 'Please, Mr Schwartz, business is bad, my wife has had a stroke, my children must eat, the cheque will be sent next week,' and the week after, and the week after that. For all his shouting, he's not a man who can put another man to the wall. He saw too much of that before the war.

I wondered what she thought of me, a man little more than her own age, who had just put a score of people to the wall.

–I hope he finds something else, I said.

–I doubt it. He's not in good health. Mama wants us to sell the house and move down to Kerry. May I ask you something, Mr Gardener? I know it's all signed and sealed, but hypothetically: if the bank you represent had not sent you in and if Papa's business had, for argument's sake, evaporated and the bank had lost all its money, would one employee of the bank, let alone a director, have lost their job? Would any one of them have eaten less, or have had to sell their house?

Would it amount to anything but a tiny reduction in their overall profits for the year?

She was so composed.

I said, –I suppose no is the answer but, as I'm sure you know, that's not the point and if the bank took that attitude with every debt, they'd soon be in the same position as your father.

–But from what you've already seen today, will the bank recover the money it loaned to Papa? she asked.

–Yes, I think so. Yes, the debts and machines will cover the bank, I said.

–Then I'm going to take a big risk and tell you something, Mr Gardener. There is a safe in the boardroom which I'm sure you've seen. It's the company safe, but for years Papa has been using it as, shall we say, his personal bank. He sees banks as being there to borrow from, but he grew up in the worst days of German inflation in the early 1920s and doesn't trust banks to put his money into. Every week for the last dozen years he's put a little money in that safe.

–The company secretary told me the safe was empty except for a few books and the company seal, I said.

–That's what Papa told him to say, she said, and then she smiled.

I felt my breath shorten, for I knew and I knew she knew that whatever was in that safe belonged to Schwartz Importers (Ireland) Ltd (In Receivership).

–Does he have proof that it's his and not the company's? I mumbled.

–Of course not, she said, still smiling.

–There would have to be exceptional circumstances, then, I said.

–But there are always exceptions, aren't there? Life would be so dull if there weren't exceptions, don't you think, Mr Gardener? I think Papa is an exception.

All at once to swallow would have been to signify weakness; I made an elaborate pretence of coughing.

–All I'm asking is that he be given the opportunity to remove what's rightly his, she said.

–I can't let him do that.

–You don't have to. All you have to do is to tell the security guard that Papa will be dropping by to pick up some personal things.

–He won't be able to get in.

–He will if you give me a key, she said.

I stared at her. The complicity in her lovely face, the sudden vulnerability which in turn emphasised her bravery and the humanity of her motives succeeded in mere seconds in demolishing my years of training and indoctrination in the merits of probity.

–Tell him to leave it in the safe when he's finished, I said, passing over the key.

–You're a good man, Mr Gardener, she said softly.

–It's Bunny, I croaked.

–My name is Adi, she said.

That was the moment which would be the sweetest of all, because all I was ever truly to value flowed from it, memories too numerous to recount, the kind of man I would eventually become, my love and my children, everything, in fact, began at that instant when I first heard her name.

That night I slept in distracted snatches. Lying on my bed, waves of guilt washed over me. Nothing is more seductive, of course, than power and its abuse, but this seemed to have been all one-sided. Adi Schwartz had taken advantage of me. If the bank ever discovered that

I had given over the key to a safe where, for all I knew, lay thousands of the bank's pounds, Seamus Long & Co would never be given another receivership.

I awoke with a start and jumped out of bed, panting. It was three in the morning. I dressed hurriedly, ran outside and drove at speed to Harold's Cross.

Dublin slept sensibly. The smell of coal smoke from thousands of hearths and ranges mixed not unpleasantly with the dank night. I would reverse my earlier instructions to the security guard, inventing some technicality to tell him that Mr Schwartz should not now be admitted to the premises after all. For some reason, I imagined the founder of Schwartz Importers (Ireland) Ltd arriving with my key a little before dawn and removing his stash. I flew up past Mount Jerome and pulled in before the building. There was a car parked there already. As I fingered my bunch of keys, out from the shadows walked the broad-shouldered security man.

–No problems here, Mr Gardener, he said, and at that moment I saw that there was a light on in the office.

–Who's in there? I asked, and felt my chest tighten.

–Just Mr Schwartz, the guard replied, nodding towards the Mercedes. –Came in about an hour ago like you said he would.

I realised the extent of my stupidity and took a step back. –Very well, no problem, I'll go in and see how he's getting on, I said.

An hour? How much money did he have in there that he needed an hour? The earlier sense that Mr Schwartz, all six and a half feet of him, could well take a swipe at me if I threatened his survival strategy made me break out in sweat. I considered bringing in the security man, but to provide an independent witness to what I had stage-managed seemed even less preferable than getting beaten up. I eased my key into the new lock and let myself in.

The only light in the hall was coming through the door to the boardroom, which was ajar. I stood and listened for sounds of packing or sorting. My breath alone rasped, menacingly I hoped. He had to be in here, since he had not emerged through the front; nor could he gain access from here to the back of the premises without the new keys. Suddenly I crawled with renewed fear, for I imagined how he, desperate and cornered, might have concealed himself and be waiting to spring out at me.

–Mr Schwartz? MR SCHWARTZ!

My voice gave me confidence. I edged towards the boardroom, keeping a glance to my rear, put a toe to the door and nudged it in. Light was white and momentarily dislocating.

–Mr Schwartz?

I could not make out what he was doing down there. An unzipped grip was clutched in one outstretched hand. Taking another step, I saw how curled up he was on the floor by the open safe, embryo-like, knees drawn up towards his chest, hands crossed at his throat beneath his blue face, teeth bared.

I took a step towards the hall and almost shouted for the guard. Something made me stop. I came back into the room and saw what it had been: stacks of banknotes lining the shelf of the open safe. I bent and made myself pick up his wrist. Not only dead but cooling. I looked to the phone. I would have to call an ambulance. The time of my call would be recorded. If I hesitated any longer, someone might notice a discrepancy between the time I came in here and the time I raised the alarm.

Why did I not shout? Why did I not call? Because

I had already made up my mind, because I realised then that everything she had said was right, that there was a way, albeit insubstantial now, of salvaging something from the wreck of this man's life, of dignifying everything he had tried to achieve and of respecting the sacrifices he had made. Unclenching his big dead fingers, one by one, I freed the grip, then I scooped the money into it. I don't know how much it was, but they were bundles of tenners, mostly, and I had to squash in the last of them.

Adi would later say, in no disparaging sense, that that night I had discovered compassion. And I knew, even as I dialled 999, that I would marry her.

8

Dublin, 1992

As Chris came back across the restaurant, I could see men at several other tables glancing at her, then whispering to one another when they realised who she was. She must have been aware of them, but she walked with her chin high and her eyes ahead.

–You look thoughtful, Bunny, she said, as she sat down.

–And you look beautiful.

The words were out even before I knew it.

–Oh, Bunny. She laughed, settling into the leather seat.

–I mean it.

–I know, thank you. She touched my hand briefly. –It's a mess, this whole thing – for both of us – isn't it?

–It's what happened. History is a mess, I said.

She put her elbows on the table and looked at a point somewhere very far away. –I wonder will they remember us when it comes to be written? she asked.

Dublin, 1969

It was the summer that America put a man on the moon. At the end of that July it was all anyone could speak of, the wonder of it, and the fact that we could watch it at home on television.

–An old one came into my clinic and said it's all a

hoax, that they did it in a film studio in California, Harry said, and laughed.

He sometimes dropped into the office like this, as much to get away from the Dáil as anything. The ministerial Mercedes left him off at the corner of Wellington Road and he walked up beneath the cherry trees, savouring the calmness and, in season, the scent and blossom. It was eight years since we had rented these premises and put our plate up: Gardener Messenger & Co, Chartered Accountants. We employed a secretary, Violet, two clerks and a qualified accountant like ourselves, a man a few years older than us and with experience as a practitioner.

–How is Adi?

–Good. She's expecting.

–We're finished in that department. How's the new house coming along?

–Adi is at it night and day.

At Christmas and occasionally at other times we socialised together, but Brigid Messenger was a private, withdrawn woman who always gave the impression that she could not wait for us to leave. Earlier that year the Messengers had acquired a substantial house and lands at Oakwood in north County Dublin; Brigid could now withdraw into her estate and see only whom she pleased.

–What about that problem we discussed? Harry asked. –Your old fella?

–I've made enquiries. Trouble is, I can't talk to him. No one can.

–That's hard.

–It's been that way for years. My mother's a saint.

–You have to forgive. After what they went through, Harry said.

I felt closest to him at such times as then, when his understanding of ordinary people and their problems made everything else secondary.

–Da used to be happy. He'd cycle seventy miles a day for Findlater's, did so right through the War of Independence, then the Civil War. Swore he never heard a shot fired in either.

–Makes a change, Harry said. –Every other old bollocks I meet swears he got a bullet in the arse outside the GPO.

–Grief is pernicious, I said. –There was a time that Da'd cycle out as far as Howth, into the wind, then pray to God it wouldn't change so's he could freewheel all the way back into Fairview. We used all sit at home together at nights. No television then, of course. We'd take turns at doing things. Mine was reciting the Eucharistic Congress.

Harry was thoughtful. –We knew about it in Derry, of course, although the papers up there ignored it. People spoke about the South like a promised land. I was six or seven. One night shortly after that, there was a raid on the Bogside and the Bs took my father on suspicion. I didn't see him for another six months. That's my first memory.

I remembered a small furtive man in the Dodder Cottages. He'd died almost twenty years before. I'd gone to the funeral Mass, then the cortège had set out for Derry.

–If you want to get him in some place and you'd like me to put in a word . . . Harry was now saying.

–I know. Thank you.

–You don't have to thank me, that's what friends are for, he said, and crossed his legs and dangled one dark-stockinged foot in its highly polished shoe in a patch of sunlight.

He looked fit and well. Ever since he had become a parliamentary secretary six years before, he had taken no part in the business of our practice, and now, as Minister for Finance in the Gillespie government, I saw him even less. Moreover, our office now looked after the day-to-day running of his personal expenses, the payment of his bills and the reconciliation of his bank accounts, although Harry himself continued to handle his investments and loans. And although I discussed every new development with Harry, seeking his advice before I proceeded, it never troubled me that his own decisions were invariably made and executed before I had even heard of them.

–Did I tell you I've joined the Howth Yacht Club? I asked.

–How in the name of Jesus did they let you in there?

–Old Dennis Foy proposed me.

Harry made a face to say, I'm impressed. –I'll be expecting an invitation to crew some afternoon, gin and tonics by the Kish and all that.

–I've only sailed once. Haven't the time. It's more a place to meet people, have a jar.

–The Irish Sea is tame stuff compared to what we do in the west, a fucking millpond compared to the Atlantic.

–Have you come across Jamey Clinch in your travels?

Harry screwed his face up. –A West Brit? Runs a miserable little bank?

–Lipman Brothers.

–Is he a member out there too?

I said he was.

–I met him a couple of years ago at the Horse Show, was introduced to him in the judging ring, wearing a big Panama hat, you'd think bejasus he owned the place. 'So very *naice* to see you here,' he says, and I'm the fucking Minister for Agriculture at the time, I could close the fucking show down with a pen-stroke. 'So very *naice* to meet you both.' An hour later myself and Brigid are coming out of the stand after looking at the jumping and he's coming in with a county crowd, women with hats, men talking at the top of their voices. I was as near to him as you are to me. 'Goodbye now,' I says to him. Do you know what he did? He looked through me as if I was a pane of glass. Bollocks.

–He wants me to go on the board of the bank.

Harry's eyes slid sideways. –Interesting.

–Might be. I'm meeting him to discuss it.

–Banks. They're all right as long as everything is going their way. Once that stops, you're the enemy.

The door opened and Violet, my secretary, brought in a tray with tea things. She was wearing a skirt that allowed you to see her knees. Harry smiled at her and Violet shone for the minister.

–Didn't Foys have a tragedy a few years back? Harry asked, sipping, inspecting Violet's legs as she departed.

–A daughter died from meningitis. Fifteen or sixteen, I think.

–You can have all the money in the world, but in the end of the day it's no good to you. I think I could recover from anything but that. Does it affect the old fella?

–I don't know. I didn't know him beforehand, not that I really know him now. Made of tough stuff, I'd say. Do you want to meet him?

–Not at the moment. To be honest with you, there's

a lot more than landing on the moon on my mind at present.

I didn't respond. Harry could say anything to me, he knew. It was his choice.

–Ah, nothing you want to be bothered with. A lot of tension building up in the North, that's all, and Gillespie hasn't a fucking clue what to do. He's a ditherer, has no feel for the people up there, how could he have? Big stupid Munster gob on him. Anyway.

He stood up and clapped both his hands to his stomach. –What do you think, Bunny? Eight pounds off in the last three months. No butter or cream or eggs, just a few glasses of wine with dinner and out at seven every morning on one of my eventers, riding out on my own land or on Dollymount. God, you know, I feel if I put my mind to it, I can do anything. Anything on this earth.

I walked with him towards Baggot Street, the black car trailing us along the kerb.

–I mean, when I say your man Clinch is a bollocks that doesn't mean he can't be a useful bollocks. Jesus, when I think of all the wealth he and his kind still control. Hundreds of millions. All that land. Who's made it from our side of the fence in terms of real money? You could count them on one hand – old Dennis Foy, Stan Sharkey, the Sweepstake people. Listen, see what the bastard wants. At the end of the day, you're twice the man he'll ever be, remember that.

He winked and got into the car. A couple of people were coming towards us, two women in their forties, and one of them nudged the other and then waved at the departing Mercedes.

–Wasn't that Harry Messenger? she asked me.

I smiled, Yes.

–I *told* you that was Harry, the woman said to her friend.

As I made my way along the sea wall, a warm, almost exotic mist crept inexorably over the Hill of Howth. Right beside me on the foreshore was where King Brian Boru had beaten the Vikings, Harry had reminded me. 'This was where we first became a nation,' he had said. Adi had bought me a red setter, Murphy, for my thirty-eighth birthday and I took him down for walks along the sea, imagining the ancient battle, the desperate struggle for power and the old king in his tent, slain even in his moment of victory.

I had come across the Liffey with a sense of unease and trepidation, for nothing divides Dublin more than its river and the people on one shore sense that they are of a different race from those on the other. And yet, because Harry was over here, it seemed as if this was my destiny. Our house was big and stood in an acre and a half of gardens. The Howth Road, especially the Raheny end, was long and tree-lined and dignified and its fine residences bore names that evoked the country origins of their owners – Dunmanway, Kilronan, Skibbereen.

We had two boys, Andrew and Hans; the child Adi was expecting would be our third. When the Messengers' last child, a girl, had been born a few years before, I had accepted Harry's invitation to be her godfather. In 1966, Harry had been made minister for finance by Bob Gillespie, Taoiseach and leader of Fianna Fáil. Gillespie was a ponderous, indecisive man whose main appeal to the electorate was that it seemed he could be trusted. There were few who doubted who the next leader would be.

I sometimes thought that the past was something I had simply dreamed up, for the forces of success that were pulling us along seemed unstoppable and each new achievement made the old days become more and more blurred. Harry embodied the urgency and sudden supremacy of our generation. His ministry, after that of Taoiseach, was the most powerful; Gardener Messenger now employed nearly thirty people; Ireland had all at once realised the possibility of her own potential. And everyone in politics who was close to Harry had done well: Pat Smith, representing our old parish, was Minister for Defence; even Aengus O'Reilly, in the Dáil for a midlands constituency, was the Minister for Local Government. Ten years older than Harry, a man whose ability to recall the names of his constituents was legendary, Aengus's otherwise woolly head was ever a jumble of old wrongs awaiting justice and visions of Ireland green and united.

Although I kept my distance from politics, occasions arose where Adi and I had to become involved, such as at fund-raising dinners. One evening we drove in from our new house to the Gresham where Aengus was rolling out the carpet at a hundred pounds a head. Fianna Fáil had succeeded in becoming the party both of the peasant farmer and of big business, an acrobatic feat of considerable distinction. As we came in along Dorset Street, I was aware of Adi's presence, the way she turned men's heads, the way her gentian-blue silk dress moulded her lightly pregnant body. And yet, although I loved and admired her, lately my own attention had been ever more drawn to women with half her looks, vixen-like creatures with a certain expression across the eyes that could arouse me to the brink of murder.

At the Gresham, a porter came over to take the car. A small crowd had formed, probably in the hope of seeing Harry. If you put the whole cabinet on parade, Harry was the one they – the women especially – wanted to see. He had sex appeal, Adi had once said, then added, 'So have you.' I got out and handed the man the keys and walked around the car to Adi.

–You look the bee's knees, she said, and dusted off the shoulders of my dinner jacket.

I stopped. A knife-like pain divided my head. On the footpath, an elderly man was begging from the crowd, one cupped hand held out, the other hand supporting it. He was unshaven. His clothes were respectable, though.

–Come on, I said, and grabbed Adi's arm.

–What's wrong with you?

I was steering her roughly through the doors and then stopped in the lobby, my breath gone, hands on my knees, sucking in breath.

–Bunny?

–I'm all right.

–You look as if you've seen a ghost.

I had, in a way, I reflected, as we made for the bar. The man outside on the footpath was Da.

I watched the August sun wallow redly on the corrugated sea. The rattle of sail pulleys and cables on aluminium masts ceased only on dead days of no wind. I let my pint settle and watched Stan Sharkey as he came back from the bar with a bowl of peanuts. He had joined the yacht club around the same time as I had, except that in Stan's case he was the owner of a vessel and knew how to sail. Different parts of him reflected the evening sun: his bald head, his scrupulously crisp shirt cuffs, his gold cufflinks. With money had come the ability to hide most of his burning energy behind a grave and deliberate demeanour. He still looked like a rat.

–All well?

Stan was referring to things at home when he popped this invariable question.

–Fine, thanks. All yours?

–Not a bother.

He had spent the last twenty-five years turning his father's straggling flats and bedsits into a multi-million-pound property empire. Stan bought real estate like others bought rosebuds for their lapels. Sharkey Developments Ltd was a gilt-edged proposition as far as financiers were concerned: no sooner was a building completed than a government department of one kind or another became the tenant.

–Will you miss all this? I asked.

We handled Stan's tax affairs. He had decided a month before to become domiciled for tax reasons in Spain.

–I don't think so, Stan replied. –I'm not the sentimental kind. Spain will do fine. He crunched some peanuts. –Besides, he said, –things are hotting up here. Or in the North, I should say.

–So I see.

Derry's burning houses and shattered windows were on the front of every paper. I knew that Stan had relatives up there.

–It could get serious. I was talking to Aengus yesterday. He's upset that we're not doing more.

–What more can we do? Invade?

Stan's head tried out a number of different positions. –An old Fianna Fáiler like Aengus wouldn't bat an eyelid. This is our country, these are our people up there. Now that they're being murdered in their beds by unionists, are we going to stand by?

–I know that Harry's sympathetic.

–But he's not going to put on a Sam Browne belt and march over the bloody border. Stan leaned back, blinking rapidly. –I was out in Oakwood last night.

We were never all together any more, the old crowd; it was as if we were all now satellites, in separate orbits around Harry's mass. Stan's orbit was property and money and fund-raising duties when the need arose. I suspected, but hadn't been told, that when Harry had purchased Oakwood earlier that year he had done so with bank loans guaranteed by Stan.

–Harry was mentioning that you'd had an approach here from our banker friend. I was just wondering whether or not you'd pursued it.

–I'm still thinking about it.

–It's just that I happen to know that his bank, Lipman's, has a certain relationship with a bank based in Bermuda called Solinberg Brothers. Might be some opportunities there – not that I need to point them out to you.

–Clinch is away until next week. I'll let you know.

Stan inspected his fingernails, each one. –It's a funny old world. Just when we thought we were done with wars and fighting, when we were looking forward to taking our place at the banquet of the world, a place none of us would give twopence for jumps up out of nowhere and threatens to flatten everything we've worked our whole lives to achieve.

–Do you have many lawnmowers? Last time I dared count, which was at the beginning of this summer, I was up to seven.

We were driving in Jamey Clinch's car up the avenue to his home in Howth. A grand old property, its shrubberies overgrown, its lawns – despite so many mowers – untended, on a good day the views south extended as far as North Wexford. Clinch's father, a brewer from Kent, had bought himself a knighthood in the 1920s and had moved to Ireland – not a bad strategy, since Irish property was on the floor and the country still reeling from its wars. The old man bought his way into Lipman Brothers Bank for half nothing and died nine years later of cirrhosis.

–I just seem to accumulate them. Geraghty, my man, is meant to know his machines, but after fifteen years I now accept he couldn't mend a puncture. So irritating to have so much grass and not to have it cut.

Big-boned, still fair-haired, he was the sort of Englishman one saw photographs of playing county cricket. He couldn't have been much more than fifty, but he looked older, a gone-to-seed appearance like the grounds of his house. He spoke with the blithe, unconcerned manner of the Anglo–Irish, or those few I had met, a knack of gliding along without pauses in a conversation, though matters of substance were seldom visited.

–We play tennis over there. My wife was a junior at Wimbledon. Tennis costs me a fortune. Someone hits a ball over the hedge, it goes into the sea.

His house was single-level, or so it seemed when we pulled up at the front door that sunny day; but then as we went in through a hall cluttered with bags of golf clubs, tennis racquets and riding boots with wooden trees inset and past a round hall table carrying a most bountiful flower arrangement, and down steps into a large sitting room with windows on three sides through which the bay and its tiny criss-crossing traffic were majestically presented, I could see that the house was on a number of levels and hung limpet-like over Dublin Bay. The walls of the sitting room were adorned with pictures of dogs and horses and in one corner beneath a sagging portion of mildew-spotted ceiling stood a bucket.

–You have a wonderful view, I said, and watched him pour me a Guinness.

–You think so? Wonderful today, yah, but half the time we're covered in mist, might as well be living down a bloody coal mine. You pay a price for a view. *Sláinte.*

The accounts for Lipman Brothers Bank showed that, although the bank had access to capital from its other shareholders in London, it had achieved little success in attracting any meaningful volume of business in Ireland. Operations were carried out from a building in Hatch Street. Every morning, about eleven, Clinch rolled in there, accompanied by Geraghty in full morning dress, and conducted business for a few hours – mainly over in-house lunches – as if banking were part of a game being played at a very long-running house party.

–How is my good friend Harry Messenger?

–Oh, he's well. I didn't realise you knew each other.

–Just casually, but I admire him hugely. He's very good for Ireland.

He pronounced it 'Ah-land'.

–Very clever of you to have got in there, Clinch said.

–How do you mean?

–I mean, you know, into partnership with the country's Minister for Finance. Come on, Bunny! You'd think butter wouldn't melt!

–We've known each other for over twenty-five years, I said, and didn't smile.

–Oh, God, it was a joke, Bunny! He's been to supper here, you know.

–I didn't.

–Got quite a bit of style about him, old Harry. I can see how he gets the votes.

I wondered if Harry had been here since he'd come to my office and we'd discussed Clinch, or if it had happened before that but it had slipped his mind. Every day now there were marches in the North, and the front pages of the daily newspapers showed the blackened shells of burnt-out buses and people building tribal barricades at the mouths of their narrow streets.

–Solinberg's in Bermuda is part-owned by Lipman's in London, as are we, Clinch said, in answer to my question. –Excellent people, we must arrange a trip, there's a chap out there, my counterpart, called George Trout, absolutely A-1 man, would lay down his life for you. Of course, any business is absolutely ring-fenced confidentiality-wise by local regulations – as tight as Switzerland if not tighter.

–And yet the level of business you do there is modest.

Clinch gestured languidly around him, then glanced somewhat despondently towards Dublin. –That's where you come in, dear boy.

I had some further questions, but at that moment Clinch's big face hinged in a smile and he said, –Now, here's the best investment decision I ever made.

A golden woman had appeared outside. Wearing a sleeveless shirt that allowed the feast of her rippling brown arms to be savoured, her blonde hair was woven into a luscious single plait. As she came in, pulling off a sun visor, her short white tennis skirt was revealed and her long golden legs. Oil gleamed from her face. She was ten years his junior, at least.

–Heather, darling, this is Mr Messenger's partner, Bunny Gardener, the man who's going to make us our fortune in Lipman's.

She cocked her cheek for Clinch to kiss, then almost managed to look interested as she turned to me and said in an English accent, –Very pleased to meet you.

–Bunny and I were just discussing business. Would you like a drink?

–Of water. We're going to play another set.

Three other women had appeared outside and Clinch went out and kissed each of them as his wife poured glasses of water from a jug.

–Partner in what? she said, without looking at me or raising her voice.

–We're both accountants.

–*Accountants*?

–Yes.

She was slicing a lemon and I was drawn to the race of blonde hairs across her firm wrist and the way her sinews moved. She popped a lemon piece into her mouth. Outside, one of the women was bending forward so that Clinch could light her cigarette.

–Jamey says Mr Messenger's going to be the Tea-shop, or whatever you call it. That means you're very important, doesn't it?

–Not really. I'm just someone who adds up rows of figures.

–I suppose someone's got to do it, she said, a little bulge inside her cheek where she'd tucked the fruit. –Are you married?

–My wife's expecting our third.

–We've none. Never think about it any more. Jamey's not well.

–Oh, I didn't know.

–It's called Menière's disease. He can be walking along quite normally and he just collapses. Ghastly thing. Says it's like someone has strapped him upside down on a spinning top. Please don't say you know, he still thinks he looks thirty.

–Of course not.

–And say hello to Mr Messenger when you see him.

She smiled at me. Then as she turned to leave the room, she leaned over and rubbed the calf of her right leg with the heel of her hand. I had never seen anyone so graceful or so perfectly proportioned. Then out across the lawn she walked swinging her racquet, golden and untouchable, with all the sea behind her, as if no background could ever do her justice. It seemed impossible that this world could have been up here always, that years ago when we were kids playing up and down the train line or when everyone was on the lookout for the glimmer man, or when we had no tea, or even now, this minute, when my sister was in the kitchen of a house in Dolphin's Barn, children pulling out of her, wondering if she was going to get a slap that night – all the time this world was here and we didn't know it. Da must have. He'd cycled and driven out here often enough, and yet what he saw must have meant nothing to him; he must never have tried to connect the two. I saw all at once then, in the woman's hair as the sun caught it, in the pistillary scents tumbling in the open door, in the easy laughter and the blue vastness of the sea, what Harry often spoke about. It made me flush. There really was no limit. Only the one you laid down in your mind.

9

Dublin, 1969

One night in August the phone rang and when I picked it up I was surprised to hear Mickey O's voice on the other end. –I have a scrapbook for you, he said, when we had established each other's good health.

I was perplexed.

He said, –I was cleaning out the ma's place, God rest her, and I came across these old books we pasted up together with Tonto and the Lone Ranger and all the others from the old days – remember?

Mickey O was someone I now met only at the funerals of the people we both knew from the old neighbourhood, like Mrs Murphy down the street, the year before, or Mickey O's own mother. Mickey O had gone from school not to Arsenal Football Club but straight into the civil service and was now a high-grade clerk in the Department of Justice. He had a smooth, unflappable manner and at his mother's funeral in Haddington Road had gone to the altar and read the lesson: a tall, fit-looking, well-dressed man who spoke in a cultured voice and whose long, silent gazes embodied authority.

Derry was in flames and nationalists' houses were being looted and torched most evenings that week. Dublin knew these people only as strangers, for few of us had ever been north of the border. They were different up there with their generations-old feuds, they were still tortured by the questions we had resolved fifty years before.

Many people were on holidays and the office was quiet. I was spending every other morning in Hatch Street, getting to know the inner workings of Lipman Brothers Bank. One lunchtime I walked into Weir's on impulse and purchased Adi a thick gold neckpiece for a thousand pounds.

It was noon when I reached Bewley's in Grafton Street and found Mickey O at the back under the Harry Clarke windows. He sat there as if he was the owner, legs crossed, surveying the movements around him with an expression of disdain. His hair was a well-greased, black mat. I had heard he ate only fish and green vegetables and ran each day for an hour in an athletics ground.

–Do you remember the night your father died? I asked. –Da brought me over to the window to see Dev leaving your house. It was like looking at God.

Mickey O smiled knowingly. –He gave me a pound note that night. I couldn't believe it. A pound was a fortune. I gave it to my mother, but she made me keep it. I found out years later that Dev had given her twenty – to pay for the funeral. And then when I left school, my mother wrote to him about getting me into the civil service and he replied by return. He asked to see me and I went out to Blackrock one afternoon and his wife had the tea all set out and sandwiches and cakes. He was in opposition at the time. All he wanted to do was to talk about the old days, about Da, about the laughs they had. I realised for the first time that Dev had once been young.

Mickey O took out a gunmetal cigarette case on whose lid I could see a faded inscription, and a matching lighter. Bluish plumes rose between us as he opened his mouth wide and swallowed down the tinted smoke.

–He asked me did I want Justice or External Affairs and since I'd never heard of External Affairs I said Justice. That was a long time ago. I still get a call now and then to say I'm wanted up in the Park. I go up and we walk in the gardens.

–What does he think about what's going on up North?

Mickey O looked slowly around him with barely concealed contempt. –Dev's getting old, he's almost blind, but his brain is as sharp as a knife. He knew he was never going to get a thirty-two-county Ireland in 1922, that that would only happen in the context of a gradual, historical evolution.

–And what does he think of the roofs being burned over the people's heads up there? What does Dev say to that?

Mickey O smiled. –I would never presume to speak for anyone, least of all for the President of Ireland, he murmured, and carefully tamped the end of another cigarette.

A man came around the corner from the front, sat at an adjacent table and shook open his *Irish Times*.

–So you found one of the old scrapbooks, I said, for it seemed about time to find out what this was all about.

–Ah, yes, indeed, Mickey O said, and took a square brown paper bag from his briefcase and put it on the table. –Just to be safe.

I looked at him.

Mickey O glanced around the busy room of high ceilings. –You never quite know who's taking an interest nowadays.

He opened the scrapbook and the distance to the deep

past was eliminated for a moment as Ray Corrigan, Tim Holt and Audie Murphy made their appearance.

Mickey O spoke: –A climate of distrust, you might say. Flower, our department secretary, is a child of the conspiracy theory, has been in the job too long, sees trouble behind every door. Doesn't like Harry, not one little bit, goes back to the time when Harry had Justice and appointed political hacks regardless of the public interest over the heads of more able men. Shit on Flower from a height whenever he could. Shit sticks.

I had to leap to keep abreast.

–Certain Northern persons have been making the highway hot between Newry and Oakwood of late. Sure of getting a good hearing, is the word, can't bring their problems directly to the government even though Gillespie professes himself to be sympathetic. Problem with Gillespie is that he will always look to stand on firmer ground than where he is at any given moment. A weak man, and weak men are the most dangerous.

As Mickey O spoke his eyes patrolled the café.

–How do we know about Harry's visitors? Well, it's like a cosy club, despite what you may hear. Scramblers switched on three or four times a day between Stephen's Green and Whitehall. The Brits have tabs on certain people up there twenty-four hours. We share. If the truth were known, and of course it never will be, we depend on the Brits for almost all our information. Where else are we going to get it? Garda intelligence? Army intelligence? Our people know more about what's going on in the Belgian Congo than they do in Belfast.

–Surely our army has its spies up there too.

Mickey O smiled as if I'd attempted to raise an interesting point.

–No doubt, but government departments are sovereign entities, they jealously guard their powers, and knowledge is power, so to share knowledge is to lessen power. There is no collegial forum. They don't co-operate, they compete.

–Extraordinary.

–The two ministers remain as far apart as Mars and Pluto. Our poor man is a dipsomaniac whose only value to Gillespie is that he holds a marginal constituency. Pat Smith in Defence, on the other hand, is widely seen as an ambitious intellectual who, although an ally of Harry's, is never going to let matters as trivial as lifelong friendship come between him and the leadership of Fianna Fáil.

I had often wondered how people as bright as Mickey O stayed sane in the civil service and now I had the answer: they sat athwart the system, buttocks bared, and shit on everyone.

–Who are these Northern people in touch with Harry?

–Not the old Easter-lily dinosaurs, which is what's worrying. At least they were predictable. No, these are young people, much better adapted. Ambitious. They want arms. Grenades. Explosives. They intend to kill.

The word 'kill' hung in the air between us.

–Does Gillespie know all this? I asked, trying to be casual.

–Flower tells him everything. Our own minister's rarely sober enough to be briefed, so Flower goes direct. This is very dangerous stuff, Bunny. Gillespie may seem like he wants to help people in Derry or the Falls, but if there's the remotest chance of his being tainted by it, he'll not lift a finger. He's a realist. He knows that there are certain people in his cabinet such as Aengus O'Reilly who want us to send the army in. O'Reilly is so stupid he actually believes that will accomplish something.

I began to regret having come to this meeting.

–What does Gillespie think of Harry?

–Despises him with a passion. Believes that one day he'll bring the party into the mire. Gillespie's an old-fashioned politician, full of envy for the people coming up, especially people like Harry who flash their money around. Where Gillespie came from it was all patch, patch and keep the shillings in a jar under the bed.

Sudden sunlight illuminated hitherto unnoticed hues in the stained-glass windows behind us. I wondered if I was imagining it or if the man at the next table had been reading the same page of the *Irish Times* for ten minutes. Intrigue was addictive.

–Now, the only reason we've met, of course, is for me to give you this touching memento of our innocent youth, said Mickey O, looking at his watch. –You will not mention our discussion to anyone and when you tip Harry off, if he presses you for a source, which he probably won't, you will refuse to give it. I'm far more use to you lads operational than under suspicion or sacked.

We went out and I paid the bill.

Mickey O said, –Harry is that strange combination. He's both a pragmatist and an idealist, a position which, of course, is ultimately contradictory and untenable – as I'm sure he's just about to discover. You're lucky you're not in politics, Bunny. So am I. Cheerio.

I looked once more at Howth before I turned back for home. It was raining lightly, but still the dog whined to go further. He was guided by nothing more than instinct, I thought, whereas I, a man, had to consider so much more.

In the weeks since I had been up in Howth with Jamey Clinch, my mind had more than once strayed back to the image of his golden wife. I was ashamed of myself. And yet, when I tried to analyse my feelings, I had to conclude that they arose less from the fact that my wife was pregnant and that we had not been intimate for over two months than from the suspicion that Heather Clinch was available. The way she had tucked the lemon wedge into her cheek. Her assumption that I could share a secret about her husband's state of health and the betrayal, however small, implied therein.

Murphy, the red setter, looked up at me, panting.

As well as ashamed I was surprised, because during the course of Adi's two previous confinements, I had never once felt the gnaw of desire that now troubled me almost without cease. I had felt blessed and contented then within my family; now I seemed to want to put everything at risk in the cause of a shameless adultery. It was her cool sophistication, the way that sex lay on her casually that engorged me each time I thought of her. I could only calm myself by thinking it was all a front, that women who seemed outwardly to smoulder were inwardly cold and ungiving. Adi, cool and composed, could be volcanic in passion. Heather Clinch, for all her apparent availability, was probably a frigid, lonely woman.

The dog whined and pulled.

–You're looking at a big eejit, Murphy, I said, and we went home.

When I rang Harry's office and suggested he come down to mine, he seemed irritated. –I'm up to my neck here, Bunny. Whatever you want to do, do it.

–Well, I do need you for ten minutes, I said and left it at that.

I'd let Mickey O's warning sit for twenty-four hours: as much to judge it the better, as to bring myself up to date with events north of the border. 'Flames' was the word most used by the newspapers – the whole province, its cars and buses, houses, cinemas and shops, was going up in flames. Taoiseach Gillespie had formed an aid committee to deal with distress and appointed Harry and Pat Smith to run it. The day before, a march in support of besieged Northern Catholics had taken place down O'Connell Street to the GPO and a number of Northerners, who apparently had been driving by on their way to meet sympathisers in Dáil Eireann, had climbed on to the makeshift stage and appealed in emotional language for the Republic to give them the means to defend themselves.

I watched the black car pull up on Wellington Road. It was noon, the office windows were open and the air was thick with the scents from neighbouring gardens. I wished I knew more about flowers and shrubs, about the cycle of colours and the secrets of pollination. With a stab of panic that came utterly unannounced, I feared I would go to my grave leaving behind crucial, unlearned secrets.

Harry was shown in by Violet and the tea was presented and served with much mutual enquiry and flirting.

–How is your husband's game? Harry asked, with a smile.

Violet was married to a golf professional and Harry forgot nothing.

–He was third in the East of Ireland last month, Violet said, and went the colour of bright paint.

Harry really looked like the Minister for Finance. His suit, dark and expensive, was set off by his crisp, cream shirt, his dark-red tie and his black, gleaming shoes with intricate scrolls on the toecaps.

–Sorry I was short on the phone. I'm sure you've seen the news, he said.

–How bad is it?

–Bad up there, very bad. The trick is to keep it up there. I've spent the last twenty-four hours persuading that eejit Aengus that he shouldn't resign.

I poured tea for us both.

–God help him. We're in cabinet and we've agreed that the situation is serious but that there's little or nothing we can really do except channel a few quid to the victims and cry blue murder to London, and Gillespie is looking around him with eyes like gobstoppers and he says, 'Any other business? Yes, Aengus?' And O'Reilly says, 'I resign.' For the love of Jesus. 'What's the matter, Aengus?' asks Gillespie, as if he didn't know. And Aengus starts talking about the Fenian Brotherhood, I'm not joking, and O'Donovan Rossa and his own uncle, Jack, who got a bullet between the eyes in Dundalk in 1922 and whose name is up on a plaque in Arbour fucking Hill. 'I'm not going to abandon these people, Taoiseach,' he says. 'If this is the Fianna Fáil I joined and was elected for then I'm finished with it. I'm resigning from cabinet.' And up he gets and out he goes, and we're looking at a by-election that we're going to lose. 'He hasn't resigned,' Gillespie says to me outside. 'You have to resign in writing from the cabinet.' So I have to think of a way of keeping him in or we could lose a division. So I told Gillespie to ring the Park and to get Dev to ring Aengus. The end result of that was that at eight o'clock last night the two of us are being driven up to Áras an Uachtaráin.

I couldn't help laughing.

–You think losing power is funny? Harry scowled.

–You haven't lost it yet, I said.

–Anyway. Dev should be in bed by the look of him – I mean, all the time. We go in and Aengus starts up about the people in Derry being burned out by the B-Specials and the moral responsibility we have to march over the border, at whatever cost, and to try to save them. Dev has wrinkled up his face as if Aengus is a schoolboy who is reciting his homework all wrong. 'Look, Aengus, those people are the Brits' problem,' Dev says, in a voice like an old melodeon. 'The Brits' problem. The Brits wanted them and now they have them. We have enough problems down here, like what'll happen if you resign and Fine Gael win your seat in the by-election. So go home and do your job and don't be bothering yourself with things that have nothing to do with you.' And that was that. We drove home and Aengus is still on board, although I'd say he got some shock to hear one of the fathers of Irish freedom putting a by-election before the lives of people in Derry.

I felt a rush of excitement that I was playing a supporting, albeit very minor role in history as it was being written. –And what do you think should be done? I asked.

Harry made a gesture of partial indifference. –Unlike Dev, they *are* my people up there, I grew up with them. But unlike Aengus, I have a brain.

–So, some of the people up there could look to you for help, I said cautiously.

Harry narrowed his eyes. –Yes, they could look to anyone down here, and who could blame them?

–Yet you'd be an obvious choice.

–What's this all about, Bunny? he asked very quietly.

As I told him, without mentioning the source of my information, Harry's eyes contracted into small, hard pinheads.

I concluded, –I just felt I should pass it on.

Harry shifted slightly in his chair and although his eyes were on the window, he was blinking rapidly. –Well, yes, there was some contact, but it was of a completely casual nature. Just because there's a situation in the North doesn't mean that I can't meet people and discuss their problems. I mean, there's been a procession in and out of Gillespie's office since this thing started, so the fact that I may have received people at my residence as opposed to meeting them in Government Buildings is completely without significance.

We went together out through the hall and to the door. The day was abundantly glorious.

–How are you getting on with Clinch?

–I've joined the board of the bank. I understand you've been out to his house.

–Oh, just for supper. What a setting, eh?

–Beautiful wife.

Harry's eyes flickered at me. –Very charming, yes.

The image of her limbs surged at me.

Harry turned. –What we were talking about in there – it's all just politics at the end of the day. I don't want you to worry about it, any more than I worry about what you do – and I've complete confidence in what you do.

–Likewise, I said, and we shook hands, somewhat

formally, and then Harry made his way back up the lane to his waiting car, walking jauntily.

I sat on the boards of a few companies owned by Stan Sharkey, all of them involved in property. No one I knew worked longer hours, or was the master of so much detail where it concerned his own interest. His wife, Eileen, was rarely seen. They had three children and lived in Portmarnock.

–I want to drop in with something, Stan said on the phone. –Is an hour's time all right?

I had been feeling my way into Lipman's since my appointment: many of the files had been copied and brought over to Gardener Messenger & Co. The mechanisms of banking fascinated me. Inside the banking loop, particularly in a country like Ireland whose currency was tied to that of another country, England, and whose exchange controls were relaxed, you could go wherever your inclination took you. The banking network was like an enormous web: there was no part of it to which any other part was not connected. Mainly self-regulatory, banks reported their activities to authority only after the event. Jamey Clinch had made me a signatory of Lipman's and encouraged me to make loans and transact business without reference to him.

Stan was shown in and we shook hands, a Stan thing, something he did even if you met him every day.

–All well?

–Never better.

He was dressed in snowy linen and a double-breasted dark suit. Two fat commas of hair sat above each of his ears. He placed a canvas holdall on my desk so that I had to look over it to see him.

–You'd better count it.

–Is this yours? I asked, in some surprise. Stan was normally scrupulous when it came to tax.

–Not at all. There's been a whip-round for the nationalists in the North. This is what we collected.

Together we unloaded wads of cash bound with rubber bands and a number of large brown envelopes. Some of the wads were filthy and some mint-clean. Large denominations, mostly. I worked through them, noting each one as I went, and Stan returned each counted bundle to the holdall. The Six Counties were fixating the whole world. On the outskirts of 'Free Derry' with its defiant tricolour and in the no-go area between Belfast's Falls and Shankill, British troops patrolled in full combat gear.

–Where did all this come from? I asked, when I reached a hundred thousand.

–Oh, various sources, Stan said, and began to scratch his ear with unsettling rapidity. –Business mainly. One young fella starting out on his own, name of Broe, gave five grand, for example. There's a few more like that. There's a lot of sympathy for the people up there.

I shook out further envelopes. In the top right-hand corner of two in bold print was the name IRISH RED CROSS SOCIETY. I looked at Stan. He shrugged. From another envelope fell money bound by paper stapled at the joint and stamped with the harp, the emblem of the Irish State.

–This is government money.

–I know.

–Why am I sitting here counting government money?

–There's an aid fund. There's nothing wrong with that, you know.

–I'm just not clear why it's here on my desk.

–We have to figure out the best way of getting the

money to the people. Who to give it to. What to spend it on. We decided first of all to get as much money together in one place, then to use it.

Stan had got up and was standing over me, twirling his thumbs like someone trying to set a world record in that activity.

–So this is all sanctioned? I asked.

–You have my word. Ring Harry, if you like. Ring him.

–Did Harry sanction this?

–Gillespie has put Harry and Pat Smith in charge of alleviating distress up there. I've been asked to act in an informal capacity, shake a few trees, get a few quid together. I'm parking this cash with your bank until it's decided what's the best way to alleviate the distress that the cash was collected to alleviate. Okay?

I finished counting. The sum was £205,000.

–I'll write you a receipt, I said.

–Get lost! Stan said, and his head bobbed. –Just bury it.

–It's too much to chance like that, I said.

–The Brits can't learn about this, Stan said.

–Then I'll put it offshore. When you want to use it, I'll open a loan account for an equivalent amount here. Charge a small margin to cover the bank's costs.

–You're a genius, Bunny, Stan said. But he was thinking. –If that was a personal transaction, could I claim the interest on the Dublin loan against my income tax?

–I don't see why not.

Stan checked that his shirt cuffs were properly aligned, twice for each cuff. –I'll be in touch, he said.

Lipman's held accounts with the major Irish clearing banks and it was to such an account that the Northern

Ireland aid money was lodged. The funds were then transferred on my instruction to the Bermuda account of Solinberg's in London. Lacking a name, I spotted my missal in the drawer of my desk and opened it at the Feasts of the Saints. I assigned Abacus to the account for relief of distress in Northern Ireland. Abacus had been accused of devoting himself to the cause of imprisoned Christians. 'First he was scourged and then burnt with red-hot irons, then flayed alive. His hands were cut off. Finally, bound by the neck, he was led outside the city and beheaded.'

Harry rang me at home early one morning and asked to meet me. Said he was in need of fresh air and suggested we go for a walk down the Bull Wall in Dollymount. It was ten by the time his ministerial car pulled up at my house; I drove behind him for the short distance. As I was putting on my coat and scarf, a biting wind from Lambay made my eyes weep, but not so much that I could not take in Harry's appearance. His puffed face, his red eyes and the stale drink fumes from his mouth all did battle with the stiff easterly. I knew he drank, sometimes too much, and over the past months there had been jibes in certain newspapers about his lunching habits. I wound a scarf round my neck and pulled down a cap over my eyes, but Harry did not even put on a topcoat.

–I need to get cleansed, Bunny.

He grimaced as we set out and the cold air whistled into us.

–There must be penance after sin. It's what we're conditioned to accept. God, but that's a cold wind. I sometimes think of Parnell on mornings like this. The Chief. Forward and back to Westminster on a boat, the cabins dripping with damp, the cold eating into his bones. What a man! What men they were back then! It wasn't the sex scandal that killed Parnell, it was the fucking weather, mark my words.

His head was down and he was burrowing into the easterly.

–But if he hadn't died, he'd surely have achieved Home Rule and if that had happened then it's most unlikely I'd be Minister for Finance today – don't you agree?

–Hard to say.

–Think about it. I'm here today because Parnell died and Redmond got the job. Poor Redmond. Country squire. Clongowes Wood. When he put Ireland into the war in 1915 at Woodenbridge, a thankful Member of Parliament cried out, 'God save Ireland!' and Redmond replied, 'God save England!' He must have thought he was still playing cricket in Clongowes Wood.

The cold was boring into my chestplate, and I was wearing a heavy coat.

–I love Ireland for all its seasons, though, Harry continued. –I sail in the summer, fish in the spring, hunt and shoot in the winter. What better life for a man, eh, Bunny? What about you?

–Adi likes the sun. After she has the baby, we're thinking of going to Spain.

–Spain, Harry repeated. –Horses for courses, I suppose.

The tide was full, and the further out we went, the more we seemed to be walking into the bowels of the Irish Sea.

–It's a pressure cooker in there in Merrion Street. Most of the other government departments aren't even potty-trained when it comes to money. Giving money to Health is like giving it to the missions. You'd do more good tearing it up and throwing it out the window of your car.

As the intensity of the cold pierced him, he gasped with shock.

–As for cabinet, no one knows what way it's going to go. Who was it who fiddled while Rome burned? Nero, was it? Then we should call our man Nero Gillespie. He doesn't know what he wants to do. These people up North aren't going to let us turn our backs on them, I guarantee you that. Any three of them are tougher than ten of ours. It's like family. You may think you can get away with ignoring them but at the end of the day you're stuck with your own blood.

We passed the Bull Wall cottages and came into the comparative shelter of the links of Royal Dublin.

–There's something been on my mind for some time, Harry said, –and I thought this would be as good a time as any to discuss it with you. I want you to take complete control of my personal finances.

Our office already discharged most of his utilities bills, and all insurance matters relating to Oakwood, and items such as the taxation on Brigid's car and on a jeep they had recently acquired to pull a horse trailer.

–Vision is a funny thing, Bunny. It possesses you. I'm not an over-religious man, but I imagine the saints must have been caught up in a similar fashion, where their own lives were secondary, absolutely secondary, to the great cause they believed in. You don't get anywhere in politics unless you really believe in what you're about – again, I'd call it the same as religious belief, if that's not being sacrilegious, you know what I mean, a burning desire to give your whole life to your country. You have to see way beyond the trivial. That's where someone like Gillespie is doomed, he can't see beyond this afternoon, has no feel for history or his place in it – which will be almost invisible – he's terrified that he'll lose a by-election, end of story. I'm not like that, Bunny.

As the limits of Royal Dublin were passed, wind bowled us back on our heels. The tips of Harry's nose and ears had gone blue. We turned, the wind at our backs making it difficult not to break into a trot.

–The detail of my day-to-day personal finances has no place in such circumstances. I can't concentrate on Ireland's role in Europe, or the world, if I'm worrying that some little fool of a bank clerk is going to return a cheque. Not that that has happened or ever will, but I simply use the illustration. The greatest threat to philosophy is trivia. Napoleon understood that. So, in his own way, did Dev. The little men will always try to bring you down to their level. You know the expression '*L'état, c'est moi*'? I *am* the country. That's what I'm getting at, Bunny. That's what I need from you.

–What exactly would you like me to do? I asked. We were within sight of the cars and I could see exhaust pouring out the back of Harry's as his driver kept the heater going.

–Take over everything, all the income and expenditure, mortgages, health insurance, pension payments, every single thing. All the bills. I'm afraid I may have taken my eye off some of them for the reasons I've just given you. Tax is another thing, there may be some arrears. I've two or three different bank accounts, they're probably screwing the bejasus out of me with charges and interest, I haven't had time to check – I'm meant to be *setting* the fucking interest rates, not paying them!

Icy wind drilled into our backs.

–I had a letter the other week from someone in Customs and Excise about wine I'm importing, the pettiness is extraordinary, dressed up in 'entirely at your convenience' and 'yours respectfully' et cetera, et cetera, but it just diverts energy and time. You have a genius for systems, Bunny, for dealing with the nuts and bolts of these situations. It'll be a good day for Ireland when I can wake up and know that I've passed all that stuff over to you.

–Send it over, I'll look after it.

–I should have mentioned, there's quite a lot of it.

–Send it all over. We'll have it straightened out in a week.

–I knew I could depend on you.

We reached the cars and Harry's driver got out and held the door, but Harry stood there, jumping from one foot to the other and rubbing his hands as if a few inches of penance still remained to be dealt.

–You'll probably find a bit of strain on the overdraft situations, Harry said. –They've been asking me to come in, but I simply haven't had the time. It's either been the North or Brussels, I'm up to my neck, as you can imagine.

–I'll have a look at the overall picture and get back to you.

–I had a quick look at it yesterday myself and I reckon that about twenty-five grand would bring everything comfortably into line and up to date. Which is what I meant to say to you earlier. I'd like to open a temporary loan account with your new outfit, purely short-term. I realise it will have to be secured and I've spoken to Stan and he's expecting a call from you in that regard. He has the security, just ring him.

Harry had now sat into the rear seat of the Mercedes.

–If you could call me when you've set the account up. Some of these bankers have been on to me and I just want to be able to look them in the eye.

I watched the car drive on to the Clontarf Road and head towards Dublin. Back in here, on the land as opposed to where we had been, out at sea, a sudden fog had risen and the traffic moving up and down the coast had switched their lights on. It was afternoon before I reached Stan.

–Oh, yes, we did touch on it. How much does he want? he asked.

–Twenty-five thousand.

–Oh. He told me between ten and fifteen. What does he spend the money on?

–I don't know. Pension payments, mortgages.

–He spends fuck-all on mortgage payments since the loan to buy Oakwood came from me, Stan said. –I was out there the other night and I found out that he's employed a chef.

I had not known either of these things. I said, –We're taking over the running of all his personal stuff, as of now. But I assume that he wouldn't have asked for twenty-five unless it was needed.

I could hear Stan sighing. –All right, give him the money, transfer it into his accounts or whatever, but then hive off twenty-five grand of that cash I gave you recently. All right?

It was on the tip of my tongue to point out that at least part of the aid account was made up of Irish Red Cross funds and money from Harry's own government department; but then I realised that this was no longer the case, that the account had passed from whatsoever it had been originally designated for into the technical control of the martyr, St Abacus, on whose behalf I was now, technically, acting.

–Anything else I can do for you? Stan asked.

It occurred to me later that a line of sorts had been crossed that day; but then, we cross lines the whole time, we continually modify and compromise, we are like sailing boats between points on a dark sea, forever transcending the secrets of the deep.

10

Dublin, 1969

Little Rosemary was born in the Rotunda Hospital on the third day of November. Adi was enraptured, and so was I, cuddling and nuzzling the infant whom we had decided to call after my sister.

The feeling of boundless life and opportunity that had recently seized me returned with renewed force as I looked at my lovely wife and my daughter. As I sat there, just happy being in the presence of such a miracle, as nurses came and went with cups of tea, the recent thoughts about Heather Clinch that I had indulged in seemed like bouts of madness.

For the next few days there was a procession of visitors to Adi's bedside; Harry was one of the first and when he had walked into the Rotunda with a flower bouquet as big as himself, nurses had flocked out of the wards to get a glimpse of him.

I picked Rosemary up and looked into her tiny, almost formless face and let my index finger nudge open her exquisite little hands. She would never know what it took to make the world that she was about to inherit – for which of us ever does? I drove home as the lights of the Hill of Howth winked brightly at me, as curlews called along the sea front, as Dublin tucked itself up for another night, and far out to sea the warning light of the Kish lighthouse stabbed at predetermined intervals.

* * *

Stan left word that he wanted to meet me the next evening in the Gresham. I sent Andrew three doors up for the girl who babysat and half an hour later I was driving into town. I would visit Adi and the baby, having seen Stan. I found him in the little bar off the hall, fidgeting with peanuts.

–Adi well?

We talked about each other's family and children, briefly, and Stan professed confidence in the traditional way about my fertility still being in its inauguration.

–That few quid you're looking after, he began, all bases covered on the domestic front.

–Abacus, I said, then: –It's just the name I put on the account.

–Abacus, grand. Grand. We need a hundred thousand dollars. A banker's draft. Is that a problem?

I said I didn't think so.

–I have a name, Stan said, and took out an envelope. He read, –Seydlitz. S-E-Y-D-L-I-T-Z. Anton Seydlitz. That's the name to go on it.

I wrote it into my pocket diary. –Sounds Dutch.

–Flemish, I believe, Stan said, and jerked his throat loose of his shirt collar.

–What's he do?

–I don't ask. International Red Cross, probably. Thcy know how to get relief to people in crisis. You know, blankets and biscuits.

–You'd buy some biscuits for a hundred grand.

Stan raised his eyebrows as if this was no time to be frivolous. –I wouldn't know.

–I'll drop it over to you tomorrow.

–Look, I don't want it at all, Bunny. I want you to deliver it to someone.

–To . . . I looked at what I'd written. –To Mr Seydlitz?

–Actually to a man called McGrath. He'll be in Brussels on Friday. Can you manage that?

–You want me to go to Brussels?

–I know Adi's just had the baby, but this is important.

A loss of bearings made me flounder for a moment. –Is Harry involved in this? I asked.

Stan winced. –Is there some sort of ritual I don't understand where every time we meet you ask me the same question about Harry?

–Is he?

–If he is, I've not been told, that's on my oath. I'm a businessman like you and this sort of thing is way over my head. I was asked to put together a few quid and I did. Now I've been asked to deliver it.

Stan drummed his fingers against each other and regarded me from a number of different angles.

–By whom? I asked.

Little whistling noises came from Stan, halfway to impatience. –Someone very high up, but not Harry. All right?

–Gillespie?

Stan burrowed forward. –Why involve yourself more than you need? If I asked you to go to an auction and bid up to half a million on a property for me, would you question me? Would you ask to see the money first? Of course you wouldn't. Now I'm asking you to meet someone and hand them a draft for a hundred grand. Okay? It'll be done in two minutes.

–Why don't you go? I asked and felt my chest go tight.

Stan sat back and smiled faintly, but his eyes lacked

any humour. –McGrath will be in the Hôtel Royal in Brussels at six o'clock on Friday evening. He'll be expecting you.

–Who is he? I asked.

Stan made a face. –I don't ask. A businessman, a patriot, an Irishman, a friend of a friend, someone who has answered the call – who cares who he is?

–And does he have a first name?

Stan frowned, a process that began at the bridge of his nose and concluded on the crown of his almost-bald head. –He must have, I suppose, but you know, I haven't a fucking clue what it is.

As I sat that evening with Adi and we chatted about the two lads at home and their homework, I wondered how well I knew Stan really. Did an acquaintance of nearly twenty years mean I knew him – any more than did my familiarity with his family, his companies, his considerable net worth, the unveering way in which he operated or his ability time and again to succeed in a business where thousands failed every year? I could say that I knew a lot of things about Stan, even that I knew everything, but still I could sit with him for half an hour and realise that much of this hyperactive man remained in shadow to me. It was always so when politics overspilled into the street, for nothing in politics was subject to the normal rules of the day-to-day. Politics was mostly shadow and when one touched politics, as Stan was now doing, one became partly lost in the intricate mesh of deceit and self-interest that lay at the heart of the political system.

I flew to London, then to Brussels. A train took me into the city and I emerged on to a street of cobblestones surrounded by high buildings, some modern and one illuminated with a neon sign for Martini. I was booked for the night into the Hôtel Royal near the Grande Place where it had been arranged I would meet Mr McGrath. It was still only five, even allowing for the hour change, when I checked in. I rang Adi whose homecoming had been delayed by two days because of this trip; when I heard her voice I felt strong love coursing through me. I rang home and spoke to the babysitter, who was staying overnight, and to Andrew and Hans. A message had been left by Harry saying that he was having boxes with further personal documents delivered to the office.

Over in the Grande Place the windows of cafés glowed in their almost make-believe buildings. Coat collar turned up, I went downstairs and strolled for twenty minutes, across the Place and along a wide street on which traffic roared alongside trams and cars shot from an underpass. I made my way in a loop and on the way back stopped at a shop and bought cartridges, a gun, a dagger, a bomb and a sack of gold coins, all made from chocolate. Beside the shop I found a beer-house, a place whose internal size could not be guessed at from its narrow street front. It was packed, mainly with businessmen on their way home from work, it appeared, their noses in foaming steins, briefcases at their feet. Standing at the counter, I asked for a beer and looked around, and as I did so a man at a table by the window turned his pale face away. He had been observing me. Two other men, one with his back to me, sat at the same table. I finished my beer and went back to the Hôtel Royal. Thirty minutes later, I came downstairs and entered the small lounge off the lobby.

–Mr Gardener? McGrath.

He was positioned inside the door, to the right, and

now rose and we shook hands. He was my size, with a round face, thinning hair, very steady blue eyes and a mouth that seemed to be on the verge of breaking into a smile, but which I somehow knew would not.

–Room OK?

–Fine, fine.

–Nice people, the Belgians, nicer than the French for my money. Colonial past and a royal family, sure, but those apart they seem to be quite like us. Good Catholics, two languages, a historical divide through the heart of their country, a liking for dark beer, used to being invaded by bigger neighbours. And a bit of fun, too, you know?

His hands were large and the fingers long with square, blunt tips. The hands of a gym instructor, I thought for some reason. He spoke with the kind of accent that Dublin people call 'from down the country'.

–It is all at the end of the day about justice, Mr McGrath said reflectively, and crossed his ankles. –That is the way of our world. See it everywhere. Algeria, the Congo. The old order trying to hang on to what they know they shouldn't have in the first place. Same at home. Justice. People crying out for it, the little lad up on the Lagan playing his *fadóg stán*, a culture that goes back a thousand years. You can't take that from people. History.

A young woman in a pinafore appeared with glasses of beer and Mr McGrath raised his glass and said, –*Sláinte.*

I said, –I have a letter to give you.

–More than a letter, I hope.

Again, a smile would have helped.

–Of course. Mind me asking who Seydlitz is?

–Not at all. Arms dealer in Antwerp, or Antwerpen,

as they call it here, although the French-speakers call it Anvers. A detail, take your pick. But, yes, he's reputable, I've come across him before, you needn't worry about Seydlitz.

–An arms dealer?

–Yes. Surely you've been told.

So much for biscuits and blankets, I thought. Yet I remained impassive and asked, –What's the consignment?

–Worried about value for money?

–More curious.

–You could have ten million there in your pocket and it still wouldn't make a dent of a difference. We're talking about basic defence capability, the means to stop other people murdering your wife and children, that's what we're talking about. Justice again, Mr Gardener. History. You can't get away from it.

That, I thought, was as much as I was going to get, but then he sat forward, twitching up the creases of his trousers as he did so.

–Initially we're talking two hundred submachine-guns, one hundred light machine-guns and fifty general-purpose machine-guns. These are mainly Czech. Two hundred and fifty rifles, a couple of hundred percussion grenades, a hundred flak jackets, a quarter of a million rounds of ammunition and three hundred pistols. Now you may say, 'I want change from my hundred grand,' but bear in mind the chain of command here, the numbers of people who will have to be looked after. You'd be surprised how many it takes to organise a humanitarian gesture of this kind.

Surprise was hardly an adequate portrayal of my circumstances. And yet I had to concede that it was possible Stan had not known who Seydlitz was or the real purpose of the money – the problem was, who did?

–Is this all legal, Mr McGrath?

–Legal? he repeated, as if I'd used a word he wasn't familiar with.

–Legal in Ireland.

–You'd have to be more precise there, Mr Gardener, since the term 'Ireland' embraces two jurisdictions, each with its own laws, albeit one of them based on spurious legitimacy.

–On the island of Ireland, then.

–Of what concern to the laws of the island of Ireland could it possibly be that you and I are drinking a beer in a hotel in Brussels?

Which was surely the cue for him to unleash that long-gestated smile, but no, he simply frowned and waited for my reaction.

I said: –With a view to buying hundreds of guns and grenades for import to Northern Ireland.

Mr McGrath leaned back, steepled his competent fingers and looked at me intently. –Obviously buying arms in itself is not an *il*legal activity – the arms and munitions business is established worldwide and is an important employer in many countries, no less in the country we find ourselves in at this moment. Arms are bought and sold the whole time, frequently through reputable dealers. The man in Antwerp – Antwerpen, Anvers – Mr Seydlitz is licensed and reputable. Now we come to the movement of arms. The sovereign governments of countries have always given themselves the right to import arms for their defence forces and for their police. The Republic of Ireland – Éire, Ireland – has extensive rules, procedures and cross-checks for such importations. Unless the sovereign government of

Ireland wishes these arms to enter Ireland, I have no doubt they will not do so. But if they do do so, then it will be following the express wish of the sovereign government and will therefore be legal. Lastly, and the island of Ireland was mentioned, we come to the issue of the destination of the arms following their legal importation. We both accept that these guns will go to people in Derry and Belfast so that they can defend themselves against attack. Now, it is the unambiguous position of successive Irish governments that 'Ireland' means the island of Ireland. The very first free and democratic elections won by Sinn Féin were won on that basis. A war and a civil war followed, but the position as to Northern Ireland – Ulster, as they call it up there, although the Six Counties is also well understood – being an integral part of Ireland has remained constant. The Northern Ireland, Six Counties, so-called government is in fact *illegal* since it represents the continuing occupation of part of sovereign Ireland, Éire. So, once the elected government of Ireland allows importation of these arms, their destination anywhere within the island of Ireland is completely legal. Is that all right?

He was looking at his watch now and finishing his beer. I suddenly hated this hotel and whatever it was that I had been landed in. I just wanted to be at home with my family. I wondered were there flights that night.

–Would you like a receipt? he asked, as he examined the draft.

–Indeed I would.

He went to a desk across the room and brought back some notepaper. Very carefully he wrote out the acknowledgement of the transaction and signed and dated it. I realised, if somewhat abstractedly, that he might be a confidence trickster and that if so this cash would go straight into his private bank account. Part of me wished this would be the case.

–You should try some of the restaurants around here, Mr Gardener, Mr McGrath was saying as we moved out to the lobby. –They eat more than gee-gees here in Belgium, you know.

And there at last was a smile, or at least an expression that allowed a glimpse of his teeth.

–Might see you in Dublin some time, Mr Gardener, he said, as we shook hands.

He went out the revolving doors without a backward glance.

Lacking an appetite, disliking the idea of drinking alone, having asked the hall porter to check the flights and having ascertained I was stuck in Brussels for the night, I was seized by an insistent restlessness. Not just the feeling that I was involved in something wrong, or even the straightforward pressure of fear for the consequences of what I had done, but a feeling that unresolved matters awaited my attention. Without the slightest conscious grasp of what such matters might be, I put on my overcoat and set out to walk.

A Dickensian vapour now shimmied over the cobblestones and along the empty footpaths of Brussels. Way up in high buildings, a few windows glowed like kites. It came to me within a hundred yards: of all the evening's events, the one that stood out now most was the moment earlier in the bar or café when the man who had been watching me had turned his face away. Who was he? Or by what right had he taken that interest in me? Who, apart from Mr McGrath, knew I was in Brussels? I was angry about that – itself a mystery. Like an item or amount sidelined into a suspense account, it represented a gap in knowledge, however temporary, and with it, a loss of control.

It took me twenty minutes to find the bar. Half its lights were out, they were shutting up, but still no one objected when I went to the counter and ordered brandy. Standing there, in the same spot as earlier, I tried to re-create in my mind the people who had been by the window, at the table on which chairs were now upturned: three men, one with his back to me, the one who had turned away sitting to one side, his hand to the side of his face.

A white face was all I could drag up. Yet somehow familiar. I finished the drink and asked for another. Here and there sat a few people still, stragglers, but the staff seemed happy to sweep and wipe around them. What long-forgotten match in my memory had the white-faced man's profile, seen only in a fraction of time, sparked? And what about the long back of the second person, resolute and unmoving? McGrath's? Perhaps. Tall enough. Of the third figure, I could remember nothing. Swallowing the brandy, mildly heady, I paid and left.

Brussels had a middle-aged feel about it, a solid if slightly dull respectability, streets of substantial but begrimed buildings, shuttered shops that during the day sold furs, gold and leather, well-kept brass plates with bells inset. I wanted to clear my head before retiring, to come to terms with the fact that I had been used, and to put down markers so that none of this would happen again. It would have been one thing for Harry to have asked me to make this trip – he was a government minister – but to be a puppet of some faction on the edge was not acceptable.

But what if, I wondered as I turned into another

empty street, Harry was really behind it, but for reasons best known to himself wanted his association to remain concealed? Was it that unspoken possibility that had driven me to accept Stan's assignment in the first place? As the street narrowed before opening out into a small square, I heard the echo of my own feet, as if this was an empty church rather than a sleeping city; or I imagined it was my echo, a sharp footstep, for it took me another dozen strides to recognise that I was wearing rubber soles. I looked round, but could see only the mouth of the street I had left, like a coal hole. On a lamppost was pasted a poster advertising a dance troupe of touring Aboriginals, soon to perform in Brussels. Their half-naked bodies, glinting in the yellow street-lights, were oddly comforting.

The square had at its centre a statue of some kind, there were a few street-lights, but my interest of a sudden was now the route back to the Hôtel Royal. At least three exits presented themselves, replicas of the street I had left. Choosing the right-hand option, I proceeded at a brisk pace, my feet squelching occasionally on the cobblestones, my internal system of navigation awry. Why does one sweat in such situations? Why does the body understand the obvious long before the mind? The chosen street was uphill and winding. A few cars were parked along the kerb, there was a bus stop with a sign: I stopped to see if I could make out where I was. The footsteps behind me became suspended. Carrying on uphill, into a long bend, I began to run, praying now that I would meet another person. I had not run for years, and although I would not have thought that running is something one can forget, I seemed to have managed it. Perhaps it was because of the gradient, but my knees were not participating in this nocturnal frolic.

At the top of the street, I stopped, heaving. A figure ran into view fifty yards back, then melted into shadows.

I walked on, shaking as I did so, or rather, jiggling up and down as if a barrel of sloppy liquid took up the space between my groin and throat. And fumes of brandy mingled painfully with tight fear in my ears and nostrils. I could not see my pursuer now, but knew he was edging after me, from doorway to doorway, brass plate to brass plate. The street was endless, its lampposts widely spaced.

–Who's back there? I shouted, but my voice rolled downhill like a cartwheel.

Knees notwithstanding, I ran again. Fancied I could smell him behind me, scent of fear, or maybe it was myself, for I had broken out over every inch of my body, a panic of glands. The curling street. I could not keep this up much longer, shameful for a man not yet reached forty, but I would soon throw up. Found in a pool of his own making. Scuffling at my rear, I closed my eyes, braced forward against the blow, or the garrotte. Then a man's roar burst from the darkness back there. Never before had I heard such a sound, but knew it instantly: the stark precursor of a life's violent end.

I ran blindly. Traffic noises. I opened my eyes to horns blaring and realised I had run into the centre of a major traffic artery. I backed across it, eyes never leaving the street I'd left. No one emerged. Bells behind me made me leap. A tram clanged to a stop and its doors opened. I boarded. Only an old man as the other passenger. I said hello and he stared at me from rheumy Flemish eyes. I stayed on until the terminus, thirty minutes later. And there waited for a taxi to come and take me home. I never went to bed, just sat all night in a chair in my room, sipping brandy. Drunkenness, like so much else, was beyond me. At dawn I showered and shaved and was the first man up at the airport desk to check in for the flight to London.

Two weeks later

At seven on a Saturday evening I drove in with Adi along the Clontarf Road, over the Liffey and up by way of Holles Street into Merrion Square and Upper Leeson Street to the Burlington Hotel. Warm and close. Everyone was going on about how the seasons were becoming inverted, how the weather now in November was warmer than it had been last May. Mícheál Mac Liammóir was appearing in his one-man show, a gala performance for the Children's Hospital. Our first outing of this kind since Rosemary's birth.

–They say this will be his last show, Adi said.

–We're all getting old, I said.

She had been downcast since she had come home, not unusual according to the doctors, although I wondered if she had sensed from me, the way only women can, the unease that had gripped me since my return from Brussels. Twice I had awoken from a nightmare, a bottomless black gully of terror from whose depths a man was always screaming. Two days back in Dublin, in the foreign-news columns of an English newspaper, I saw a paragraph about a man's body having been found in Brussels not far from the Palais de Justice. He was described as a criminal figure. His name was not given. But I was sure that, whoever he was, I had heard his voice in its final aria.

–*Watch out*! Adi screamed.

Awash in my own thoughts, gripped by my fears, I had wandered across the median of the road and now the headlights from an approaching car were dead ahead of us. I swung the wheel and over-corrected. Our wheels bumped up on the left kerb, hard. I righted the car again.

–Jesus, Bunny! What's the matter with you? Adi gasped.

–Nothing, sorry. My mind was elsewhere.

–You almost killed us there!

–Sorry, I took my eyes off the road.

We drove for a minute or so in recuperative silence.

–There's a problem, isn't there? she asked. –You've been like this since you came back from Brussels. What is it?

–There's just a lot going on – in the practice. In the bank, I said. –I've a lot on my mind.

–And what about me and your children, are we not on your mind too? Adi asked. –Or is making money more important?

–That's not fair, I said.

–I'll tell you something that's not fair, Adi said, –and that's the change I see in you, Bunny. You've become a different man since you began to move in the circles you now move in. Cabinet ministers, property developers. The yacht club. I know it's all business and I know it's important, but so are you important. Don't let yourself become swallowed up.

–What do you mean?

–I mean that I married a lovely lad from Upper Grand Canal Street and I don't want to lose him, Adi said.

I parked and we walked into the Burlington. At this time most evenings the fact that I had not slept the night before heaved over me like a thick blanket and I had to fight to stay awake. Adi had brightened up when I had produced the tickets for Mac Liammóir. I hadn't told her that they had been sent to my office by Mickey O.

People thronged the lobby and were shuffling towards the ballroom at the back. I'd spoken twice with Stan, but he'd not wished to dwell on Brussels, just said, 'Very good,' when I'd reported the job done, then, before I could elaborate, was picking my brains on medium-term interest-rate prospects. Harry, too, had called me on several occasions but each time Brussels had been on my tongue's tip, I'd bitten it. The need to protect him was my best estimation of my own reaction, the need to build a wall around him, impregnable even to myself.

We were seated on upright chairs midway up the room when I saw Mickey O enter on the far side, preceded by his wife. Her face in profile took on the curve of her nose, which in turn made her top half resemble a ship's prow. Mickey O was dressed in a dinner jacket. He was on the board of trustees of the hospital, one of several such appointments. He found me and signalled back towards the lobby, then made a chopping motion with his flattened hands. At the interval. The house lights went down and when the temporary stage was illuminated, Mac Liammóir was seated on a *chaise longue*, an old man now, all rouge and mascara and a crow-black toupée.

I must have dozed, for I was being confronted by an Aboriginal with white-streaked genitals, which a gaping throng was loudly applauding, when Adi nudged me. I was awake in an instant, and sweating. Adi made her way towards the ladies' room and I headed for the lobby.

–You obviously don't take what I say very seriously,

hissed Mickey O, in one movement putting a glass of whiskey into my hand and steering me by the elbow into a corner beside the telephones. –Just act as if we're having a drink together.

–That's what we are doing.

–This thing is threatening to get out of control, my friend. You've become a problem.

–I'm sorry, but I have no idea what you're talking about.

He scowled deeply, slipped his hand inside the silk roll of his dinner jacket, then checking briefly to his right, opened his palm beneath my nose. A familiar face stared up at me from a passport-sized photograph. –Recognise him?

I cleared my throat. –Yes.

–Thought you might. Has he a name?

–McGrath.

Mickey O sniffed and looked around him again, this time with his usual unconcealed disdain. –This gent – Mickey O stabbed his tuxedo – is Colonel Rufus McGrath, military intelligence, which description the people I work with consider an oxymoron, but never mind. This gobshite has run away with himself. He's in with people in Belfast and Derry that we've been watching for the last twelve months – new people.

I had the strangest impression that I was still asleep. –He's army. Irish army.

–The coin drops.

–And the army know about him?

–Everyone knows about him except you and your pal Stan Sharkey. How much did you give him? Mickey O asked.

–So McGrath's acting on authority?

–How much?

–Is he legitimate?

–Not in a million years. Not while Flower is department secretary. This is a civilised country with laws that have taken two generations to lay down and have accepted. We don't run guns to subversives in a neighbouring friendly jurisdiction. We don't run guns, full fucking stop.

–Then arrest him.

–Easier said than done when we have people in authority who owe their position to the days when our old friend Harry Messenger was Minister for Justice.

It was at times such as this that I always thanked God for the cool equilibrium of accountancy.

I said, –I was followed over there, Mick. I don't know by whom, but something happened to whoever was following me, I'm sure of it. Something bad.

Mickey O rested his hand on my shoulder. –This is not a game for decent people, he said, in a voice that was attempting to be gentle.

This was how it felt to be foreclosed upon, I realised, this was the shit I spent my life dealing out. I asked, –Does Gillespie know what's going on?

–Flower has briefed him, yes. Look, have you any idea how serious this is? We have a Taoiseach peering over the brink of anarchy, yet he won't even let it be discussed in his cabinet. We have people like this McGrath character running loose, attempting to arm criminals, subversives. Flower is at this moment the only person who stands between this country and chaos. He won't let arms come in – and be very clear about this, he has the weight of the Gardaí behind him. To a man. Now, how much did you give McGrath?

Over Mickey O's shoulder I could see Adi out in the

corridor, looking for me. –Answer me one question first. Does Harry know all this?

–Oh, Jesus, said Mickey O and rolled his eyes. –Of course he fucking knows. But it's nothing to do with his loyalty to the nationalists or wanting to help people in Derry or historic considerations or any of the rest of that woolly shit – this is Harry's bid for power, can't you see? This is his move against Gillespie.

I could scarcely breathe. –A hundred grand. Dollars.

–I'll give you a call, Mickey O said and his face opened in a big smile for Adi.

Adi drove us home that night, back over the Liffey. It was half eleven, but the first editions of the Sunday papers were being sold on O'Connell Bridge. Adi pulled in and I bought the *Sunday Press*. It always gave me a little thrill to be reading tomorrow's newspaper today, as if this was one of the few instances in which time could be defied. On the front page was a scene from a riot 'yesterday' in Derry, taken from behind the helmeted heads of riot police with the assorted faces of the nationalists confronting them in sharp focus.

–You're very quiet, Adi said, as we drove out past Fairview.

–I'm just tired.

–You go to bed and I'll bring you up something nice and hot.

I wouldn't sleep that night either, I knew. However, this time it would not be the sound of a man's last cry that kept me awake, but the image from the paper of a man's distinctive white face in the Derry crowd.

11

Dublin, 1969

–McGrath, McGrath.

Harry pondered and turned his profile to me so that he could gaze out the window of his office. Pigeons scuffled their way up and down the green dome of the nearby College of Science.

–Don't know him, Harry said eventually. –And you say you met him in Brussels and you think he's going to try to import arms?

–Through Dublin port, then either park them for a while and send them north later, or send them north straight away.

–A bit crude to say the least. Any other details?

–No. I was followed, probably during my whole time in Brussels.

–By whom?

–I'm not sure, maybe someone from the North, but I think a man was killed in the process. It's horrible, all of it.

Harry's office was very spacious and calm. In an anteroom, three delegations whom I had leapfrogged awaited their turns to see the minister: a group of farmers, some trade unionists, and priests representing the financial-management section of the Catholic Church. A number of departmental officials were also standing by outside with briefing papers.

–Who do you think was killed?

–I don't know, Harry. Maybe someone working for Flower, a detective of some kind, maybe even McGrath, I don't know.

–Or maybe no one, Harry said, and got up. His suit was one I had not seen before, a beautifully cut pin-stripe that accentuated his slim figure. He turned to me, biting his lip. –You shouldn't have made the trip, Bunny. It was unwise. Unlike you, if I may say so.

–It's done now.

–Why exactly did you agree to go?

–To be honest, I thought that Stan was speaking for you. I went because I thought you wanted the money delivered.

–Why in God's name would I want that?

I thought of Mickey O rolling his eyes. –I don't know, Harry.

Harry looked at me for almost half a minute, as if trying to decide whether aspects of my physiognomy had mutated since our last encounter. –So you think I set you up to make that trip, he said at last.

–I'm sure you would never set me up for anything. And, of course, I accept your word completely that you didn't. But where, then, did the money come from? Some of it from this very department, I know for a fact.

–That doesn't mean anything, Bunny.

–I counted the money. Stan brought it to my office.

–Stan is a businessman. He's good with money.

–So who's behind it all if you're not? I asked and heard my own exasperation.

Harry sighed. He got up, emerged from behind his desk and began to pace, hands stuck in his pockets. –It's a very good question. It's not me, all right?

He halted and looked at me sharply from the corners

of his eyes. Sometimes I felt I was with someone I barely knew.

–All right?

–All right.

He said, –I wouldn't do that, you should know that. But I'll see Smith and find out what he knows about this McGrath, or whatever his name is – that's if he knows anything. It's not impossible that the Minister for Defence is not briefed on some aspects of operations in his own department – but let me try and find out.

He took his hands from his pockets, unified them behind his back and resumed pacing the sizeable room. –Smith and I are on a committee that's meant to help the victims up there. Funds have been allocated, yes. In other words, I allocated some funds. Smith's job is to use them. He's meant to know the score up there. Yes, he does have agents, that's their job, they're meant to slip in and out of the Bogside and the Falls and report to Dublin on the mood up there and so on. And, yes, the picture is very bad. People fighting for their existence. I can sympathise with those people. I was once one of them.

–So, you give the money to Pat Smith's department, I persisted. –Where does Stan fit in?

Harry scowled across twenty feet at me. –You think I'm going to ask Stan that? If Stan wants to come and tell me something, he knows where to find me, but I'm fucked if I'm going to start interfering in his business any more than he does in mine.

–So he must have got the money from Defence. Smith must have given it to him.

–Which is what I told you I'd find out.

–But why would the Minister for Defence distance himself from giving money to one of his own officers if the operation is legal in the first place? Why all the subterfuge?

–Look . . . Harry came and perched on my side of his substantial desk. –I'm sorry about this, Bunny, but politics doesn't run like a limited company. There's no balance sheet. All the assets and liabilities are people. They seethe and move the whole time, some going up, others down. What's going on here at the moment is like a political version of the turmoil happening in the Six Counties. No one knows how or where it will end. No one knows what is the right thing to do, least of all the Taoiseach of Ireland. These are dangerous times.

–There's a lot more contact between the IRA and Dublin than is being reported in the papers, isn't there? I asked.

Harry twisted up one corner of his mouth and laughed. –The papers! he said. –History is being written in front of their eyes but they're blind. You know the funny thing? The funny thing is that in a situation like this, there's no knowing who may win. Even Aengus O'Reilly with his old O'Donovan Rossa republicanism could be in with a chance. Now, that's not something you're going to read in the papers!

A knock sounded on the outside of the panelled door and a department official wearing glasses and clutching files entered. He smiled at me, placed down the files on Harry's desk, then left again, completing, I guessed, a much-choreographed intervention.

–I have the Irish Farmers Association waiting to see me, Harry said, pulling down the bottom wings of his waistcoat. –Talk about revolutions. You should see them in full cry when they're on about suckler calves and ragwort. Give me the Bogside any day.

My elbow in his hand, he piloted me across the room.

He had the ability to make me calm, to be assured by his omnipotence.

–How's Clinch's bank? he asked.

–It's . . . very interesting.

–It's an awful thing to say, you know, but money is what really matters at the end of the day. Look at the great families of England, the dukedoms and earldoms, look at the Europeans who began life under the Holy Roman Empire and are still on the go. How many wars have there been? How many changes in allegiance, how many governments and monarchs have come and gone? And yet money endured all that. Money is the rock. And patriotism? Hah! More like a shower of rain.

Lipman Brothers Bank occupied the top two floors of a building in Hatch Street. Brown linoleum, highly polished, was the order on stairs and in the general office. However, upstairs, in what was more chambers than an office, Jamey Clinch presided in a manner that suggested he considered offices were for other people: a good-sized dining-room appointed with valuable Georgian furniture was where customers dined, attended on by Geraghty, Jamey's butler, a rotund man with an upturned nose who had taken on most of his employer's more objectionable attitudes. A fire always glowed in the adjoining drawing room, its coals reflected in the polished walnut surface of a long sideboard. The deep chairs arranged round the fireplace were finished in floral-patterned covers that Jamey told me had been chosen by his wife. I wondered why he had told me that, or if he could possibly know the effect that the mere mention of his wife could have on me. For although my fantasies about her had seemed to disappear with the birth of my daughter, they had, since my return from Brussels, begun to resurface.

–You're working wonders, he said.

It was the Friday of Hallowe'en and following lunch we were sitting at the fire, a pot of coffee between us. In the adjoining room I could hear Geraghty clearing off.

Jamey said, –You must be paid. You can't work like you do for the bank and not get paid.

I had examined over thirty loan proposals since becoming associated with Lipman's, in nearly all cases from companies that had been turned down by one or more of the big, clearing banks. Some of them were last-gasp affairs that would soon be in the financial morgue – which was, from the point of view of the accountancy practice, an excellent source of new business – but others rode the thin line of acceptable risk. Some had raised their eyebrows when I told them that Lipman's would be advancing some of the cash required only if it was in the form of equity in their enterprises. And we required a seat on the board. No one is more open to a new suggestion than a businessman starved of cash. The volume of corporate-loan business had increased substantially. In a more modest improvement, I had acquainted some of my firm's more cash-flush clients with the existence of Lipman's associated bank in Bermuda, Solinberg's. None of them needed the concept explained twice.

–I'll mark you down for a thousand a month, does that sound fair? Jamey enquired.

–It's very generous.

A thousand a month, I knew, was the sum he drew as chairman.

–Not a bit of it, consider it done. I'm not blind, you know, Bunny. I realise that the tide is going out for us lot.

–What do you mean?

–Well, I'm a fraud for a start, I'm not *Anglo* in the way it's defined over here – horses and land for two hundred years and all that – I'm the son of a rather pushy brewer from Kent who threw his weight around until he got a knighthood, then came over here and reinvented himself. Sent my brother and myself to English public schools, insisted everyone bowed and scraped to us. Sir Horace and Lady Clinch. Of course, they were good actors, and the Irish are the most gullible audience you can find. Just shout at them with an English accent and they go at the knees.

Jamey leaned forward. –But Ireland is changing. Why? Because us lot no longer have political influence. The people I socialise with haven't a clue what's going on here, who's minister for what or where the power lies. But they know about every little by-election in England and they can talk until the cows come home about Harold Wilson and give you the latest gossip about George Brown and how he turned up last weekend pissed as an owl to a hundred-pounds-a-plate dinner at the Grosvenor House. Some use that is to them – they that haven't lived in England for two hundred years. We haven't yet grasped the basic fact that the Brits left this part of Ireland in 1922 and that the show here is being run by you chaps.

He was a man who wasn't afraid to acknowledge his own faults, even as he admitted there was little he could do about them.

–A little brandy to go with the coffee? he said, making his way to the sideboard and peering at the decanters. –I see Minister Messenger has opened an account with us.

–Yes, I set it up.

–Not one for half-measures, is he? Jamey held a brandy goblet in his left hand and the lip of the decanter poised over it. He said, –I gather he has already exhausted the hospitality of some of our larger competitors around town.

I watched the brandy oil its way into the snifter. Jamey might not have been mainstream, but he'd been in banking in Dublin long enough to know the current gossip. –I hadn't heard, I said, and cursed myself for not having yet made the time to become familiar with Harry's very heavy boxes of personal papers that had been left in and were being dealt with by the office.

–It's quite hard for a bank to foreclose on the Minister for Finance, you know, Jamey was observing. –It's a bit like sawing off the branch you're perched on.

–We're fully secured with a cash deposit, I said, and took the snifter.

–Oh, I'm not unhappy with the business, far from it. I know in the circumstances you had a difficult decision to make but that your professional judgement would have remained uppermost. I just think it's quite unusual that a man in his position would be into banks around town for quite so much. Frankly, I don't understand what he does with it.

–Harry doesn't play by the normal rules, I said.

–Well, indeed, that much is obvious. Look at his achievements. Good luck to him, I say. Who cares what he does with the money, eh? He's good for Ireland, and that's what counts.

So saying, Jamey raised his drink to toast the sentiments he had just offered, but then he put down the glass on the sideboard so sharply that it broke, and he was blinking, and shaking his head roughly.

–Jamey . . . ?

–Oh, no . . .

He took three steps backward, then simply fell, face to the ceiling, striking a small, antique table in his uncontrolled descent and smashing it into matchwood. I hurried over to him. He was lying, feet stuck out, breathing rapidly and blinking.

–Get . . . Geraghty . . .

I found the butler in a small pantry, washing up. –I think the chairman has had a heart attack!

–Ah, Jesus, not at all, it's the fucking vertigo! Geraghty cried. –Is he down?

–Yes.

–Go back in and put a cushion under his head, for Christ's sake. I'll get his pills.

I went back in and did as I had been told.

–One day this will kill me, Jamey gasped.

From my desk I could see, over the nearby rooftops, the luminosity of the Christmas lights from Baggot Street. Mickey O had phoned just as I was about to leave.

–Do you know one of the issues historians will comment on when they look back on all this? he asked. –How big a part alcohol played in the Irish *coup d'état*. I'm being serious. Start at the very top, the man from Munster. Flower says that when he goes to brief him, a full bottle of Paddy is always brought out and, as you know, there's a little map of Ireland on the label. The man from Munster always pours out two glasses and won't let my man out of the room until they've reached Cashel.

–That should loosen Flower up.

–He says the man in question can't function without it. Which I suppose is preferable to the position of our own minister who can't function with it.

–Why isn't he replaced?

–Up to last week he was drunk for three months. He is the first justice minister who has ever failed to turn up at a Garda passing-out parade in Templemore. Then last week the man from Munster called him in and ate the arse off him. Our man collapsed on the way out and now he's out in John of God's where they're trying to wean him off it. Your own man has been hitting it a lash too, by the way, although his style is to do it in full view of everyone at lunchtime. And, in fairness, it seems his liver is still pretty much intact.

I knew Mickey O hadn't called to discuss Harry's liver.

I said, –What other news?

–Hah!

I could imagine Mickey O's face curling in contempt as he looked out from his office across St Stephen's Green. He said, –You remember I told you about the new people up north?

–Yes.

–Well, they've split from the old crowd. Broken away and set up their own organisation. All the old socialist James Connolly shit has gone out the window. These people are young and ruthless and they have a taste for blood. And they're recruiting big-time – how? Because they have weapons to give their volunteers. The old crowd have fuck-all, but the new crowd have weapons. Where did they get the weapons? I think you know the answer to that one as well as I do.

Headiness and a feeling that this might all, ultimately, turn out to be a long-running hoax were my predominant feelings. –You mean . . . ?

–The very man. He set out to arm them and he's partially succeeded, has your Colonel McGrath. Without his intervention, there would be no Provisionals.

–Provisionals.

–Their name. Our information is that a further arms consignment for them is coming in. A very large one. When? How? Where? We don't know. All we do know is that both the army and the Gardaí are set against it. They've seen what a few guns and grenades have done up there already. They won't stand by this time and let it happen.

–What does that mean?

–They want it nabbed. And if people in the government have other ideas and want to let it in, then there's a good chance that you'll wake up here one morning soon and find the country is ruled by a military administration.

I was beginning to think that Mickey O was prone to exaggeration. –I'm not getting any hint of a problem of this scale, I said. –Are you sure?

A silence, which was meant as a reprimand, followed.

–Bunny, can I give you one piece of advice?

–Sure.

–If you're still in this, then get out. Now. This is not cowboys and Indians any more, my old friend. I can no longer protect you.

Merry lights had been strung all the way along the avenue of Oakwood, from the gate lodge to the house. In the dark paddocks beside the avenue, two-hundred-year-old trees brooded like enormous sentries. At least twenty-five cars were lined up on the gravelled sweep at the front door by the time we arrived: a man in a cap directed my parking. I could see the drivers of ministerial Mercedes chatting quietly to one side, the smoke from their cigarettes drifting piquantly through the damp December night. I had in my pockets a sum of eight thousand in cash that Harry had requested I bring out to him. He was entertaining guests at Leopardstown races over Christmas, he told me. The cash had come from his Lipman's loan account and a further ten thousand of St Abacus's funds had been diverted to secure it.

Adi rang the bell beside an enormous holly wreath and immediately the door was opened by Malcolm, Harry's butler. He took our coats and indicated an open door along the broad hall from which heat and light and noise were pouring out. I had been here a dozen times but each new time I was struck anew by, on the one hand, the feeling of substantiality, and on the other, by the magnitude of the gap between here and the Dodder Cottages.

Adi enjoyed parties and relished the attention of men like Harry, and they in turn were attracted by her looks and the flair for clothes that she always showed when we went out. The room that night was full of familiar faces and she plunged in. I saw Pat Smith smile as she approached him. She flicked back her hair with her hand and I wondered how I could ever have thought of myself with another woman. Smith kissed Adi's cheek. He seemed utterly at ease and I tried to imagine how this was possible, given the events of the past few months and the intrigues as described by Mickey O. Then I stared beyond Smith. In a corner of the big room, as if only the two of them existed, Harry stood with Heather Clinch. He was telling her something and she was shining for him. Her dress was black with a low neck and the rope of gold that lay there set off her skin most deliciously. She laughed, mouth open, teeth a-sparkle. Harry was making delving motions, part of the story, whatever it was, and she caught her breath in a second of disbelief, then threw back her head and laughed with gusto. To one side, a little removed and alone, stood Jamey Clinch, a champagne glass in hand, a fixed smile on his face but his eyes on his wife, as were mine.

–Happy Christmas, I said, as I went up to him.

–Oh, hello, Bunny. Yes, funny how quickly it all comes round again, isn't it?

–Good crowd here. The Messengers do things in style.

–They certainly do, Jamey said, and his eyes drifted back to the corner. –I see in the paper that Mr Messenger was in London last week, trying to ensure that Britain keeps us up to date on their efforts to join the Common Market.

–It's vital we get in.

–Well, yes and no. I mean, if Britain goes in, clearly we must too. But I personally don't think they will. I mean, English people may have fought on the side of France in the war, but apart from that I can't imagine that one would want to have very much more to do with thc French. By the way, who's that chap talking to Minister O'Reilly?

In the centre of the room Aengus O'Reilly was in conversation with a man whose hair was mostly grey and whose face looked swollen. It took me a moment to reconcile the old image with the new reality. –That's Art Maddocks. We were all in school together. He's a planner now with Dublin Corporation.

–Wrong. He's moved to the county council, said Harry, suddenly behind us. –The county is where the action will be from now on. Mr Clinch, I'm delivering you back your very lovely wife. Look after her. Happy Christmas, Bunny.

His eyes were alight and it seemed as if he was trying but failing to keep a smile from his face. In his hand was what looked like a small chalice containing red wine.

–Everyone wants Bunny, Harry was saying and I realised that he was quite drunk. –I want him, Jamey wants him. Why? Because Bunny makes the world go round, that's why. Always did. Even as a little boy, Bunny made things happen. Didn't you, my old friend? You sure did. Sugar – d'you remember the sugar? God, I remember it and that bastard of a teacher – forgive me, darling – Murphy was his name, little fair-haired Corkman and his father had been with Michael Collins. Hated me. But Bunny sorted him out. By God, you did. What are you drinking?

–Whatever's going.

–Come over here with me.

He steered me into a little space beside the table where a barman was pouring champagne and I handed him the bundles of cash.

–Well done, he said, and trousered them. –Look, this is not the place, of course, but I told my old friend Pat Smith over there what you had told me about this McGrath or McCarthy character or whatever he is called. And d'you know his reaction? A-1. McGrath is a top-notch man and he's acting completely with the approval of the Department of Defence. Pat knows him personally. He's his boss, for fuck's sake. And Gillespie has been briefed about what's going on and he's one hundred thousand per cent behind it. So there is no problem, Bunny, d'you understand? Even Gillespie now agrees that we can't stand by and abandon the

Catholics up there. So McCarthy, or McGrath or whoever he is, is just someone doing his job. Like me and you. Just doing our jobs.

Harry put a glass of champagne into my hand. –Can I tell you something? I was in London last week, trying to make sure that the Brits don't pull a fast one on us with Brussels, and we were meant to fly home that night, but there was fog. So I had to spend the night in the Irish embassy, bored out of my mind but with a lot of time to think. And I thought about you, Bunny. I'm absolutely serious. I thought about what a loyal friend you've been to me over the years.

–Thank you.

–We can do such great things together, you and me. Massive. But I think if anything happened to you – even more than if it happened to Brigid, no kidding – I don't think I could go on. I depend on your friendship more than anything I can think of. The only thing that means more to me than you do is Ireland. That's saying something, eh? Because Ireland is what I live for, and what I'm saying to you is, Bunny, that you're not too far behind.

Jamey Clinch left at nine to go on to another party, which was being given by a client of Lipman's; and I assumed his wife had gone with him. Adi tired easily since the baby's birth, so we said our good-nights and went looking for our coats. As Malcolm led the way through the hall, I saw Heather Clinch on the phone.

–An hour and a half? she said, in disbelief. –Forget it.

She could walk home in the hour and a half it would take a taxi to get there, we all agreed, as Malcolm helped her into her coat and she got into the back of my car.

The lights along the rim of Dublin Bay swayed prettily in the mist. Once or twice I glanced in the rear-view mirror and saw her profile: she was looking out into the night, lost in her thoughts. When we reached our house in Raheny, I got out and saw Adi to the front door. When I got back to the car, Heather had transferred to the front. –Are you sure? she asked.

–It's only a ten-minute drive.

It had begun to rain and the road ahead was slick and black.

–Jamey's depending on you to turn things round, she said, as we neared Sutton Cross. –I'm sure you will. After all, Bunny makes things happen, isn't that right?

Her hair was tied up on top of her head, allowing an uninterrupted golden sweep from high up on her neck to the flat collar of her coat.

–I do my best.

–He gives me nothing.

My breath caught. –Sorry?

–Everything is done on accounts – my clothes, the groceries, our petrol, everything. He's paranoid about money, says we're running out. It's crazy. One minute he's flying first class to Bermuda and staying in a place that costs a fortune, the next I'm at home wondering if I can afford to have one boiled egg or two for my supper.

We had lost sight of the sea for a moment and the yellow street-lights stood out forlornly in the rain.

–This may be out of order, but do you need some money?

She turned to me. –Yes, I do.

–I mean, do you need some tonight?

She giggled. –Not tonight, silly.

We were climbing past the cemetery and the golf course.

She said, –Couldn't I have my own account? There must be hundreds of them and mine would be very, very tiny. Jamey wouldn't have to know, would he? After all, from what I can gather, half the people who have accounts in Lipman's use other names.

–I'll see to it. I'll think of a name and I'll mark a loan on it. Would a thousand be enough?

–A thousand would be wonderful.

We had reached the driveway to her house.

–Oh, Bunny, thank you so much, she said.

She gave me her cheek to kiss, but as I leaned across, she turned her face to me. Her lips were moist and salty and the tip of her tongue as quick and supple as a fish.

Dublin, 1970

The damp greyness of January seemed to emphasise everything we lacked in Ireland, a backdrop to the absence of riches, to constant struggle, to the marginalisation of a small, thinly populated island on the edge of Europe, and a reminder of the wisdom of those who had left to make their fortunes elsewhere. It appeared that at a national level we were always waiting for just one more event in order that everything become possible: that had once been independence, then the end of wars, then the realisation of our own republic. All these had come to pass and still we in the present struggled: curse of centuries, burden of shameful want, gaping lack, we heaved onward. Now it was membership of the Common Market that would liberate us. People need something to believe in.

I could not shake off the dismay that had entered my bones like ice since Brussels; not even the birth of my daughter succeeded in lightening my mood. And with prolonged dismay came disorientation together with a feeling that the world in which I lived was somehow different from the one I had recently inhabited. The phrase 'parallel universe', which I had read about somewhere, was apt. And although I went about my daily routines with no less conscientiousness than usual, I was operating like a sleepwalker, just going through the motions.

I began to think of Heather Clinch more and more, reliving the moment when she had kissed me. It had, of course, followed a Christmas party where much champagne had been drunk and to remember such happenings as more than just momentary indiscretion seemed unwise. Images of her lovely body, of its rippling golden plains and contours, cropped up regularly in my mind. It was outrageous that I should so imagine the wife of a fellow director. And I loved Adi, whose affection I was not prepared to risk. And yet whenever I thought of Heather and tried to relegate her in my mind to the status of just another managerial problem, it was the memory of her tongue that swamped all else, the tiny moment in which I had tasted her, for that had been no fantasy, that had happened outside her house and had been my reward for agreeing to help.

Which I had, meeting her once in Arnott's in the first week of January and handing her a thousand pounds from the new loan account opened in my mother's name – itself a matter that alternately shamed and titillated me – for which she had simply thanked me, this time just in so many words since the perfume section of Arnott's was hardly the appropriate place for another clandestine kiss; but, none the less, we both knew that we had created a secret between us and that a secret is like a key into another world. At home with the two boys, aged nine and six, and Adi and Rosemary, I looked out each evening at the distant lights of the slender causeway that connected where I lived to Howth, and imagined her up there in her mist-shrouded house, clad usually in silks, moving from point to point like a beautiful, dissatisfied cat. Jamey spent most evenings in the yacht club. He drank heavily. I would swoop up to the summit on dark, silent wings.

I was glad that the holiday break was over and that I was back at work. On the day after New Year, I left the office at lunchtime and walked into Baggot Street, then up towards the canal. An east wind bit into the herringbone of my topcoat. I pulled down my hat and dug my hands deep into my pockets. Ducks in the lock gates waddled about on a sheen of thin, litter-covered ice. It was the kind of day when the sun had almost not bothered to rise.

I was struggling with a weight whose nature I could not easily articulate, a daily immersion of my guts in a strange dread, as if everything I lived for stood on the lip of destruction. As if my mind was in a brace of someone else's choosing, I could not get back to the point of ease and harmony with Adi – and myself – that had existed a few months before.

The grey canal banks were like a symbol of the life that lay ahead of me. Grease-smeared fish-and-chip bags tumbled along the tow-path on the brim of a giddy breeze. At Baggot Street Bridge I sank down and prayed to Dick's soul to come to my rescue, knowing even as I did so that it was unworthy to evoke the dead only in times of trouble.

–Not the best time of the year, Mr Gardener.

A man wearing a hooded anorak had fallen into step with me. I had noticed him ten yards back on a bench, his scuffed running shoes, and had assumed he was a vagrant.

He said, –But you seem to be doing well, which is the main thing. And that's the way we want to keep it. Family pride, you know.

I felt a start. Something about his face.

–Who are you? I asked.

–I'm your cousin, Bunny, he said. –I'm Mooney.

Now the face was poked out a little more from the hood and I could see a grizzled chin and a small but smiling mouth. Aunt Nancy. He offered me a cigarette.

–No, thanks, I said. –How do you know me?

–We always knew that we had these respectable cousins in Upper Grand Canal Street, he said. –I've watched your career, Bunny. You're a star. You're what I could have been. Same blood, after all.

Briefly, an ancient fear of someone I had never met but whose name lingered in the shadows of conversations jumped in me. *Your man is mixed up in something.*

Mooney said, –We are what we are, Bunny. But blood is what it is, too, and that's why we're walking along here together. By the way, I'm sorry about your brother.

–My . . . ?

–He was drowned here, wasn't he? Your brother Dick. We went to the funeral, you know, me father brought us. We stayed at the back of the church. We didn't go out to Deansgrange, but we lit a candle for him in Haddington Road.

–Thank you, I said. –I always liked Aunt Nancy. I remember her very well.

–More than I do, Bunny, more than I do. I often wonder what it would be like to have a mother. You see, my oul' fella fecked off to Liverpool with me when I was two.

The past reared in me again. We were approaching Leeson Street Bridge, the planned limit of my constitutional. He must have been waiting for me. He must have known where my office was.

I said, –Do you need a few quid?

Mooney laughed. –Tip-top for asking, but no thanks, Bunny, I'm well sorted, believe me, despite appearances. Happy, even. No, I didn't bump into you to make a touch, mate, I bumped into you because you're my cousin and I want to give you a bit of advice.

–Go ahead.

Mooney drew hard on his cigarette and his two cheeks sank.

–I'd be in the way of knowing what's moving down on the North Wall, you understand? Coming in and out of the port, like. Well, over the last three months, I know about some special bits and pieces, Bunny. I think you know what I mean. The ones with 'machinery' on the manifest. Machinery, me bollocks. I don't give a monkey's what they do to each other up there, but that's dangerous stuff that's coming in.

–What are you talking about?

Only the smoke streaming from his hood was evidence that Mooney was still in there. He said, –And I thought yous were the respectable side of the family.

He broke into high-pitched laughter, more yelps than laughs.

–I haven't a clue what you're on about, I said.

–Bunny, this is your cousin Mooney, not the beak

down in Morgan Place. I know all about your connection with the great Harry Messenger – right? That's why I'm tipping you off. This is his deal, his problem, the dogs in the street know that. But you're in business with the great Harry, so his problem is yours, too, right? If he falls, so do you.

–Maybe.

–This stuff is coming in and going up to Drumcondra. To the Most Reverend John O'Brien. 'Most Reverend', you know! Machine-guns and fucking hand grenades!

I stared at the dishevelled figure. My parallel universe was taking over. I said, –Are you telling me that . . . arms have been coming in through the docks and are being sent to Jack, to Father O'Brien's house in Drumcondra – is that right?

–Dead on. 'Lawnmower parts'.

–Then what?

–Then a certain element from the North comes down to Drumcondra and removes them at their leisure.

–And how often has this happened?

–Two shipments that I know of for certain, although there may well have been a third.

–Quantity?

–Small. A couple of boxes in each case. Nothing that the powers that be down there are going to get too upset about, not with high-up people involved. But that's what I'm warning you about, Bunny. Word is that there's a much bigger quantity about to arrive but that it won't be let in. You see, everyone knows what's going on, not just the likes of me but the Garda Siochána, the Customs, everyone. There could be shooting on the North Wall, especially if that dirt from the North are there at the same time. Dangerous, Bunny, very dangerous.

I reeled under a weight of fear and confusion. –When? I asked, sounding very calm, just the way I would be were I everything that Mooney suspected.

–In the next three weeks. I can keep you informed.

–Is there any danger to you personally?

–Naw, tip-top, Bunny. I'm just like vermin to the powers that be, they know I'm there, but they tolerate me. D'you ever see a dock rat? He's always well fed and looks after his family, but he's that small he can go in places no one else can. The trick is not to be too important.

–I appreciate the warning.

Mooney grinned and I saw yellow, crooked teeth.

–Can I tell you something? I always wanted to meet you. You see, I'm proud of you, Bunny. I see your office here, your house in Raheny, your name in the papers – and it makes me feel good. I may be scum, but now I'm scum with good connections – d'you understand?

–Here's my numbers, I said, and gave him my card. –You can ring me anytime.

–No problem. I'll keep you up to date with what's happening.

–Just one question. What's Father O'Brien's role in all this?

Mooney made a disparaging shape with his mouth. –All I know is the stuff goes in and out of his place dead handy. But look – no surprise, that, the Church have been fooling the people for years. I better head home now or I'll be missed. Cheers, Bunny, nice to meet you.

Instead of driving out Amiens Street, I turned into Gardiner Street and made my way via Dorset Street into Drumcondra. I could feel the shift of circumstances, for in the thickets of half-truths and concealed purposes the one person I recognised who had no motive for being a liar was my cousin Mooney. I thought of Aunt Nancy, who had died young. Now her son had come to warn me, just because he and I were related. I turned in the gates, drove up the short drive and parked.

I had not met Jack O'Brien since we'd left school. Not even seen him. A small boy with a stutter, but one who had always managed to hold his place in the gang. Now a parish priest living in this very comfortable house in Drumcondra. I rang the bell. I'd thought about telephoning first, but had feared he might not see me.

–Yes? A thickset man wearing a cardigan and an open-necked shirt had come to the door. He was holding a pair of spectacles.

–I'm looking for Father O'Brien.

–Well, you've found him.

–Jack? I'm Bunny Gardener.

He walked back in ahead of me, chuckling. –Ah, merciful heavens, what a surprise. I was just thinking of you the other day. I was saying Mass and out of the blue I had this image of us riding our horses along the railway line. Maybe it was St Paul brought it all to mind. He was never off a horse, St Paul, you know, except when he fell off one on his way to Damascus. How are you at all, Bunny?

–I'm well, Jack, thanks. Or is Jack gone?

–You hardly think my mother calls me John. Mind you, I have aunts in Dun Laoghaire and they never call me anything else but Father now. Tea?

–No thanks, Jack.

–Or something stronger? he asked slyly.

–I'd rather not, if you don't mind. I'm on my way home.

The room was over-warm by virtue of a fire of bulging red coals. Jack sank into a deep, worn leather armchair and I sat the other side of the fireplace on a more upright chair with tweed covering. Was this his life, I wondered, nothing done in pairs, all plans made in a single and solitary dimension?

Jack said, –How is your da at all?

–Poor Da. He has it hard.

–The Lord has strange ways. He never got over Dick, did he?

–He often says he wishes it had been him.

–To me he always seemed a countryman at heart. I'd see him on the bike with the red cheeks and the pedals going and I'd shout out, 'Good morning, Mr Gardener!' – you know, half cheeky – and he'd wave back, 'Well, young fella!' I imagined him on a country lane somewhere with no traffic. Why, I don't know, because he came from the Coombe, didn't he?

–The Liberties.

–Funny the way we get ideas about people and even though we know we're wrong we cling to them. You're married, of course, Bunny.

–With three children. Two boys and a girl.

–Thank God, and living in Raheny, I hear, don't ask me how I know – I do know, I do. I met Frank Trundle somewhere – Frank went into the guards – and he was telling me you'd moved over here. I hope it means we'll see more of each other.

Although his face was unlined, the way he sat, or rather slumped, the way his shoulders curved inwards and the rise of his stomach through his unbuttoned cardigan somehow reminded me of a much older person.

Jack popped on his spectacles and said, –I think you're troubled, Bunny.

I wondered was it that obvious or if it was simply the safe assumption that a parish priest could make about a nocturnal visitor. –I do have some concerns, yes, Jack.

–Of a personal nature?

–Yes.

–You have a confessor?

–I do.

Jack sat up and looked at me with a mixture of kindness and apprehension. –If this is something you cannot discuss with him, perhaps you'd like me to hear your confession. I mean, it may be the safest approach.

–This is not something I have done or need to confess, Jack. It's something I think you're involved in.

–Me?

–I'm afraid so.

He sat back again, clasping and reclasping his hands and switching his gaze from me to the fire and back again.

I said, –I have been approached by someone who says he knows what's going on here. He thought I should know.

Jack looked at me defiantly. –What business is this of yours?

–I'm concerned for you as an old friend.

–I haven't seen you for twenty years.

–I'm still your friend.

His face had drained to white and all at once sagged to one side, as if some elemental underpinning had come undone. His breath was coming in gasps. –There's been a full investigation carried out by the archdiocese, which took th-three years to complete, and I have been cleared totally of any wrongdoing. Wh-who has sent you here? I l-love children. I resent you coming in here like this and opening it all up again.

I began to sweat, as if I were a vector for fever.

Jack was trembling. –The Lord said, 'Suffer the little children to come unto me, and forbid them not: for of such is the kingdom of heaven.' St M-Mark ten, fourteen. I don't know who your informant is, but there are p-p-people out there with evil in their minds, pure, unadulterated evil.

The man was weeping.

–Do you not think I have already suffered enough? Accusations, innuendo. What did I do, Bunny? I brought a boy to the pictures. To the pictures. He hadn't the price of it himself. 'Why did you bring him to the pictures?' they asked me. 'Was it to get him into the dark?' God forgive them. I forgive them. I forgive you. But I will prevail and my c-conscience is clear. God will keep a place in His kingdom for the meek and the innocent, that I know to be t-t-true.

I closed my eyes as if I had stumbled into someone else's bedroom and seen what I had not been meant to. –Jack, stop. Please.

He stared at me, eyes wet, mouth agape.

I said, –I'm sorry, but I think we're at cross purposes. What I'm talking about is the fact that this house has apparently been used as a transshipment point for certain goods in recent months. That's why I'm here. That's all.

The priest stared and as he did so his face enjoyed a visible improvement. He even managed, at the end of this process, to smile. –Ah, that old stuff! he cried. –Sure that was only a few old lawnmower parts going up to Newry. I never even saw them!

–Lawnmower parts – in the middle of winter.

–They're probably stocking up, what's wrong with that?

–Can you tell me who asked you to take in these lawnmower parts?

–No problem. A man who's been very good to the Church here in Drumcondra, a businessman. Stan Sharkey. You must know him, he's a great pal of Harry Messenger's. He has a brother or a cousin, I can't remember which, who does one of these van runs up and down from Newry to here, right past the door, and Stan asked could he have these parts left here for your man to collect. Of course, I said, yes. I left the garage door open. I never even heard him driving in.

I yearned for the taste of sea air.

Jack was looking at me from narrowed eyes. –Don't tell me they're stolen parts.

–No, they're not.

–Well, thank God for that, he said, and we stood up. –Bunny, that business I mentioned, the archdiocese . . .

–I've forgotten it already, Jack.

–It was nothing.

–I know.

–I did nothing. I never would.

–It's gone. I don't even know what you're talking about.

–That's good.

We went outside and stood for a moment.

He said, –I suppose, just in case it's as long again, I should say goodbye.

–Goodbye, Jack. Sorry to disturb you.

We shook hands and I got into the car. He remained there, watching me as I drove out. I longed for the past, for the warm embrace of old times, for the words of comfort that I still craved. I longed, too, for the cheeky boy by the railway line who stumbled over his words but knew his Injuns and horses. He was gone now, that boy, lost for ever, and in his place was a lonely, tortured man for whom I would, on those rare occasions when I did, say a prayer. Up to a few minutes before when I had seen what I had not been meant to, the past – or the selected moments of the past that I had chosen – had been somehow alive, places I could visit and enjoy, like a house just down the road, another place than where I lived, the years that had elapsed since inconsequential. Now that was gone. That house was demolished. I did not even want to think about it again. I drove home slowly, pity and sorrow, but not for myself, welling within me. I parked the car and breathed in the nearby sea's night tang.

Adi was in the hall, her face split in two with worry. It was only half past eight. –Oh, Bunny, where were you?

My legs did not want to bear my weight. –What's wrong?

–Terrible news.

–Is it one of the children?

–Oh, Bunny, Jamey Clinch has fallen down the cliff in Howth. He's dead.

12

Dublin, 1970

I must have passed by the Church of Ireland in Howth on countless occasions without noticing it tucked away up from the road behind its trees, a sandstone building with a generous belltower and a pleasing aspect out to Ireland's Eye. Adi and I sat with Harry and Brigid in the mid-body of the nave. Dublin businessmen, and in particular bankers, were there in numbers. Jamey had fallen to his death while out walking his dog, presumably having suffered one of his dizzy spells. His body had been recovered from the water by a prawn man.

I had watched Heather come into the church, her chin high beneath a short black veil. The night before, I had been asked by Lipman's shareholders in London to step in as temporary chairman of the bank, and I had accepted.

There was none of the incense or candles that we were used to. A great many hymns. Ruddy-faced, big-handed men from the harbour shouldered the coffin and brought it out for the journey to the cemetery on the other side of the hill. The men in the congregation were to walk behind the hearse as far as the waterfront; as we left the church, photographers ran forward and let off their flashbulbs at Harry as he did the rounds, shaking hands with the people who made up this part of his constituency.

–She's a remarkable woman, isn't she? Harry said, as we fell into step to the beat of the tolling bell.

He was dressed in an ankle-length black cashmere coat with a satin collar. Black leather gloves on his hands. He was allowing his fair hair to grow so that it already licked over the tips of his ears and curled at his neck.

–Very composed, very dignified, I said.

–They're different from us like that, the Anglos and the Brits, or at least the upper-class ones are. They have this emotional toughness. I think it came from being a ruling class, from never being able to show weakness to the people they had conquered – to people like us. It gave them a sense of unyielding authority.

–Heather seems very much in control.

–In a woman like that it's extremely attractive, Harry said.

The cortège left the spur road to the church and we were now making our sombre way beneath the cliff and into the harbour.

–The bank could be very interesting, Harry said.

–Yes, a challenge.

–But one you'll take up, I've no doubt.

–Depends. Running a bank is a full-time job. So is running an accountancy practice.

–A monkey can tick and tot when it comes to it, but you need talent for finance. We're still in a very relaxed environment here when it comes to such things as exchange control. I look at the regimes in other countries I visit from time to time and you'd think Hitler had won the fucking war in some of them. And I meet bankers here at functions, Irish bankers sitting on committees of this and that making pre-budget submissions to my department. They're still in the last century, the majority of them. You can say a lot of generous things about the man we're walking behind, but not even his best friends could claim that he was a financial genius.

The window-blinds of shops were pulled down, and where a few trawlers were offloading a catch, men paused and removed their caps. Jamey Clinch had been important in Howth.

–You, on the other hand, have this fantastic talent for money, Harry continued. –It's the reason men want you on the boards of their companies. They've discovered what I knew twenty years ago, that you have a way of making things happen. That's very rare, Bunny. This is an opportunity from heaven.

–I'm reluctant to leave what we've taken so long to build up in the practice. What I'd like to do is to try and run the two things together for a while. It would mean moving most of the bank stuff into Wellington Place.

Harry spread out his black-gloved hands. –Look, you're making the decisions, I'm just a sounding-board. But I do think this is an exciting time, not just because of what has happened here, but generally. It's 1970 and, you know, this is probably the first time ever, I mean in two thousand years, that we're beginning to have the confidence to be as good as anyone else. I mentioned bankers a moment ago. They're all like your man here, they're Prods, they live in Howth or Killiney, they talk as if they have boils on their tongues, and they're all absolutely and completely fucking useless. Had it easy too long. Never in their lives imagined they'd have to make a decision that involved imagination. Or balls. Fifteen years ago, ten even, it would have been unthinkable that a lad from Upper Grand Canal Street could be mixing with the likes of them. But here you are, the new chairman of a bank, walking behind the hearse of the old order. Your time has come, Bunny.

The ensigns outside the yacht club were at half-mast. When we reached the other side of the harbour, we would regain our cars and drive up and over Howth Hill to the cemetery of St Fintan.

–I had an encounter the other day on the canal, I said, not changing the tone of the conversation.

–Oh, yes?

–The person involved is known to me from the old days, someone who has a knowledge of criminal activity, especially on the docks.

–A guard.

–Not exactly, I said, and smiled to myself as I thought of Mooney. –It doesn't really matter who he is. But he tipped me off that there have been at least a couple of shipments of arms and ammunition that have come in over recent months labelled as machine parts – lawnmower parts, to be precise – and that these have been consigned care of Jack O'Brien, who as we know is the parish priest in Drumcondra.

–Go on.

–It all follows from this McGrath man and my trip to Brussels. The items in question were picked up by someone connected to Stan Sharkey and brought to Newry.

–You saw Jack?

I nodded.

Harry said, –How is he?

–Changed. All right, though.

Little clicking sounds came from Harry's mouth. –He's had his own problems, you know.

–I gathered.

–His mental state may not be the best at the moment,

I'd take anything he says with a grain of salt, Harry said, –but having said that, I'll talk to Smith.

I sensed that I had surprised him and that he was trying to recover his composure. –So you know all about this? I asked.

Harry half-turned his head and looked at me from the corners of his eyes, as if a forbidden line had been crossed. –I know absolutely nothing about it. But I'll try to find out what's going on. All right?

–Sure.

–For all I know what you've described is a load of rubbish – it certainly sounds as much. Did you personally see any of these alleged items?

–No.

–Did Jack?

–No. He just left his garage open.

Harry shook his head dismissively. –A lot of people know our relationship. A lot of people, probably including this character you met on the canal, would like to get at me through you. This is a hate call, Bunny. This has begrudgery written all over it.

Up ahead the hearse had halted and people were regaining their cars. Behind us, seagulls wheeled and screeched all of a sudden as boxes of fish were brought up from a boat.

I said, –I doubt it. His main purpose was to tell me that the next consignment will be nabbed. I understand that Gillespie has come down hard against what's going on in the North, and so any more attempts to bring in further lawnmower parts will result in their being seized. That's all. I thought you should know.

–Well, thanks very much for giving me the inside story on what's happening in cabinet, Bunny. It must be fascinating to be so well briefed.

Harry turned away, thumping the palm of one gloved hand with the fist of the other and searching now for his Mercedes.

–However, I fail to see the relevance this has for me, he went on, –and so if I was you, I'd forget everything you've heard and that you've just told me. My advice is, don't let anything ruin the opportunities you and I were discussing a few minutes ago. They're limitless. Parnell said, 'No man can set the boundary to the march of a nation.' We've been hemmed in too long, Bunny. Now our time has come.

I walked back to where Adi had driven up, feeling as if I'd been run through a mangle by an expert. Harry had got into his car and the driver was already turning and driving back to Dublin on the lower road. He was not going over the hill to the burial. The heat of the car made my face flush. We drove slowly uphill, past the Catholic church. Each time I strayed across the boundary between business and politics, if that was what had just happened, I saw a side of Harry that I would never otherwise have known. I should have had the same confidence in him doing his job as he manifestly had in me doing mine, I realised. I would pass no further warnings.

–Bunny?

I looked at Adi.

She said, –Well, you're a man. Are you not going to answer me?

–I'm sorry, my mind was elsewhere.

–It often is nowadays, Adi said, and looked away.

–What was the question? I asked.

Adi sighed. –Don't you think that Mrs Clinch is the most attractive widow you've ever seen?

–I'm sorry, I said, –I didn't get a good look at her.

* * *

It was a spring of silver fish, of white caps dancing beyond the sea wall, of gorse scent eddying down from the Hill of Howth. I transferred all the key files of Lipman Brothers Bank to my office, then flew to London for a day of meetings with the City men whose support was needed to keep the little bank capitalised. They were delighted with the job I was doing in Dublin, they told me. Whatever I wanted, just ask, they said. They particularly liked the margin on the risk-free business that I was beginning to introduce to an ever-widening market: lending money in Dublin to companies and wealthy individuals secured against their own deposits in Bermuda. You simply could not find a better banking proposition, as one of my London directors observed.

With the coming of spring, too, the spectre of arms and ammunition, of political upheaval and dark plots seemed to melt away like the short cold days of winter. I saw little of Harry, although we spoke on the phone every other day. All his expenditures and monthly bills were being discharged by our chief clerk. One morning he came in and told me that apparently Harry had bought an island in the west. He was going to build a house on it, the clerk said, adding with considerable awe, 'He'll be like a king.' I replied, 'He already is.'

I met him one glorious, God-gifted Saturday morning when I took our dog for a walk on Dollymount Strand. The dog had been Adi's present to me, a red setter, a demented, perpetually anxious beast whose reservoirs of energy were inexhaustible. The plan was that Murphy would get me out and force me to take exercise – a requirement that I should seriously heed, according to our new doctor, Dr Ward, who lived just up the road in Raheny. He had listened to my chest and back and then tut-tutted at my expanse of flab. He prescribed daily walks, then asked me if I would mind looking after some money for him in Lipman's. I came home with a holdall; Violet counted the contents next day and told me it amounted to twenty-three thousand pounds. I told Adi about the medical side of the consultation and a week later she gave me this red dog.

Murphy ran in a series of wide, frantic arcs, spray rising behind his paws when he skirted the tide-line, disappearing into the haze of the morning, reappearing from another direction, his pink, vivid tongue draping from his frothing mouth like a jagged wound. As he ranged and closed in spurts and dashes without logic or purpose, stopping occasionally for a smell as if his nose was all at once stitched to the ground, marking patches of sand with squirts of piss, connected via nose and kidneys to the entire universe of dog-kind, I saw vehicles out on the strand ahead: a jeep and horse trailer and another car. A horse was being unloaded. Murphy hurtled crazily for this new curiosity, yelping, making the horse skittish. A girl held it on a head-collar. I saw two men, one of whom I somehow knew was a guard. Then Harry emerged from the car. He was bareheaded and held a riding crop in his hand. He made a threatening gesture to Murphy, then saw me. –I don't believe it, he said, with a big smile.

–Doctor's orders, I said.

–Ah, God, I sometimes think of my poor father at times like this, Harry said, and spread his arms. –If he hadn't come down here I'd still be up in Derry, probably in charge of a Provo battalion, for all I know. But he had the vision, he got out. Could see the whole island rather than just a street or two in the Bogside. That's why I can enjoy being out here this morning, because of him. God bless him.

We stood for a moment in the silence that seemed appropriate to Harry's sentiments. Then I said, –I hear you've bought an island.

–You and Adi will be my first guests. It's the real Ireland down there, Bunny, no telephones or delegations. No pressures. No cabinet colleagues trying to put a knife between my shoulder-blades.

We'd walked a dozen yards away from the horse and yapping Murphy.

I asked, –How is it?

Harry looked out to sea. –Difficult.

–I thought as much.

–It's hard to stand here and imagine that events are unfolding that could bring this country back to 1922.

–I'm sorry to hear that.

–We'll all be sorry, believe me. He slapped the crop against his riding boot. Then he smiled. –But nobody asked me to do this job, you know – did they? How's Adi?

–This dog is her idea, I said, as Murphy, bored with the horse, had begun a fresh series of circumnavigations out on the wide strand.

–Let's all have a night out together soon, Harry said, walking back to his horse. –Just the four of us. Like the old times.

I stood there and watched him mount and then ride out, a lone figure, the sea before him and gulls rising from the sand in a dense cloud. He was like one of our cowboys from years ago, I thought, except that he had a real horse. He was the only one of us who had.

* * *

I got home an hour later and there was a note to ring a number.

–A man. He wouldn't leave his name, Hans said.

–Hello, this is Bunny Gardener, I said, when the phone was answered.

–Bunny, look, I just want to tell you that they're not going to use the docks for that business, said my cousin Mooney. –It's too dangerous. But my information is that they'll try and use the airport.

–When?

–Soon.

–Look, I appreciate the call, but I'm out of all that now. I don't want to talk about it again.

–I understand.

–If I can ever do you a favour . . .

–Thanks, Bunny. Cheers.

I put the phone down and stood there, listening to the radio in the kitchen and the voice of a newsreader warning listeners about an impending bank strike.

A week later, on another bountiful day, I felt strangely detached as I drove out the Clontarf Road, passing within mere yards of where I lived, of where my wife and small child were probably in the garden. I never discussed clients with Adi: my training had been hammered into me. Mrs Heather Clinch was my client and this meeting had been called by me for her affairs needed to be regularised, and part of the inheritance she would receive from her husband's estate would discharge her indebtedness to the bank. I had suggested she come to town; she had suggested lunch in Howth.

–Seems a shame not to enjoy this weather, Bunny. The garden is heaven at this time of year.

I parked, then, briefcase in hand, walked up to the

warm front door where roses awaited bloom, and rang the bell.

–It's open!

The tennis racquets, croquet mallets and leather saddles jumbled with one another in the porch as formerly. I stepped down into the big living room, alert to the impossible: that her husband would suddenly appear, a glass of gin in hand, drawling on about the bank and Ah-land.

–Bunny, I'll be with you just as soon as I've finished here.

She was watering plants out in the conservatory. Her hair was tied back at her neck, she was wearing a pair of baggy corduroys and a jacket with a suede collar. I sat at a large table whose top was done in faded tiles.

–I've got an appointment in Sutton at three with the solicitor, she said, brushing her hands against her jacket and sitting. –This won't take long, will it?

–Not long at all.

I wondered had she forgotten lunch. She had her own files relating to the monies she owed the bank, and her husband's estate; we ran through the items and she suggested that her indebtedness to Lipman's would be cleared by the summer. When reading she wore spectacles perched on the tip of her nose, although twice at least they threatened to slide off, at which point she nudged them back up again with her middle finger, a gesture I began to relish, wondering even as I did so what it was about it that warmed me. She looked sideways once and saw me, and I must have been smiling for she, too, smiled, as if the files and the money were things that neither of us much appreciated but that we were nonetheless obliged to toil through.

–Is that all? Well, then, while I get lunch, why don't you pour us a drink? You know your way around.

She went down further steps and I found the drinks tray that Jamey had used in the living room. I poured two gins, found ice in a tub, skinned zesty pieces from a lemon and carried the frothing glasses out. She'd taken off the jacket and had put on an apron.

–Well done, she said, and took the drink from me by reaching across the table on which she was setting out place-mats and cutlery. –Hmmm, that's strong! Cheers.

I sipped and watched her coming and going. Although she was indisputably the same woman who had kissed me in her driveway, she was different, as if widowhood and inheritance had tilted the balance between us. We ate some sort of fish stew and shared a bottle of wine that had already been one-quarter drunk before we got to it. She chatted on about life without Jamey, which, by the sound of it, she was taking to, and things to be done to the house now, and life as a project to be got on with. She was forty, she told me, and asked me my age, and made a little face of being pleasantly surprised when I said I was thirty-nine. We spoke of the bank and business in general. The yacht club. Sailing. Her garden. Walks she took on the Hill of Howth, although she had not done so since Jamey's final walk but had gone instead over to Sutton. I told her I walked on Dollymount with my dog, and she asked was it as crazy as all red setters, and when I said yes, she laughed and told me that she had once had a Kerry Blue that was quite mad and that one day it had killed eleven cats in the neighbourhood.

I saw the sweep of her neck as she rested her hand there, and the way such a lovely pool of flesh was formed at her collarbone. Never once in an hour and fifteen minutes did either of us ever cross the line and allude, other than to my dog, to my personal circumstances, or to how many children I had, or to Adi. I realised that the appointment she had mentioned for three o'clock and her businesslike approach were all stages along a way, points at which she was inviting me to step off, making it easy for both of us, releasing us in the absence of unanimity from the destiny of our single Christmas kiss. So that when she said, 'Leave the dishes,' and got up, as did I, and on a small landing of whose existence I had been unaware but which was on yet another level on the way to the bedrooms I gently caught her shoulders and turned her to me, we had covered all the ground between Christmas and spring.

The bedroom must have been for guests, for it lacked personal effects, a neutering I was glad of; although Heather might have cared less, such was the quickness of her undressing, stepping as she did from the corduroys and leaving them on the floor, upright, like two amputated stumps, and making her way naked to the window to pull the curtains in a movement of such grace and loveliness that it made my legs give way. She undressed me in that position, which is to say, she stood and I knelt, and I clung to her as if to be subsumed into her might be the only way to quench my passion.

She came before I did, which I would have bet long odds against, but her ardour was quick and somehow efficient, a rapid burst of very quick gasps, her own hand in on the hastening, and then an arching of her body so that at the climax only her head, shoulders and heels touched the bed. Mine was lingering, for I had never had access to a body like hers, and my finish perfunctory. She asked me later if I could give her a lift and let her off at Sutton Cross, which I did. I was, of course, burning with desire again before we got there and asked if we might do it again; but she simply laughed and said, 'Give me a ring first,' and got out, and without looking back walked along the footpath in the black skirt and top she had put on, saying hello to several people, as might any attractive woman of forty whose husband has recently met a very tragic end.

In the aftermath of my subsequent visits to Howth, I tried to reason that this was the path to ruin, that as much as this woman was available to me, we had little in common, that nothing lasting could ever come from this affair. But when I thought I had found a way of taming myself, of sneering at my own folly, without warning, perhaps in the midst of a meeting with a potential depositor, or on the way home, or even on the way to work, the image of her body blotted out all else and an hour or so later I was driving out the Clontarf Road.

It was, I realise now, all part of my general dislocation, my removal from the world I had been brought up in. Such a small step: one day, a family man whose highest preoccupation was a client's trial balance, the next, an intermediary in gun-running and an adulterer. Rationality did not come into it.

Blessed with limbs that begged for my tongue's attention, with an attitude that paid no heed to consequences and a single-minded desire to secure her own sexual gratification, she bewitched me. I brought her flowers on the second occasion, having telephoned in advance; but when I presented them to her she burst out laughing, as if I had been naïve enough to think that flowers might be needed. On my third or fourth visit,

I cannot remember which, the telephone rang shortly after my arrival and she undressed in the hall where the instrument was installed and we copulated beside it as she continued her conversation with a cousin in Devon.

We had baths together in the ancient Victorian fixture beside her bedroom, and she sat in my lap and made me enter her in the water. Once when she had her period, or said she had, she brought me into the kitchen and, overlooking the bay where yachts from my club sailed, relieved me into the sink. I would have imagined that activity on this scale would have subdued my want. I was dismayed to find that the opposite was the case: the more I got, the more I craved.

During this time, I must have been like a stranger to Adi. I often slept in the spare room, pleading insomnia, but thinking of Howth. And guilt? Guilt was like a tiny cymbal beating in the guard's van of the train, always there but scarcely audible from where I was, astride the roaring engine.

At Mass on Sundays I made special vows that in the week ahead I would not weaken, that I would not make the call. And although one week I got as far as Saturday, by noon that day it was call and go or burst, that simple. Some days in Howth I found myself almost running in from the car. She saw me, breathless, and often laughed. I liked it best, and I think she did too, when I sank to my knees in want, as I had on the very first occasion.

Her body, and by extension the house in which she lived, exuded unique scents, a layering in which I became an authority, a complex signal system transmitted entirely through the sense of smell. For example, except when she had showered, her golden hair harboured the same fragrance as her bed linen, a warm, sleepy, but at the same time urgent redolence whose mere inhaling made me weak with want. Her skin had the tang of salt to it, a freshness I associated ever after with tennis, except that when she undressed and began forging for her delivery, this freshness transmuted into a pithy, musk-like sweetness, which, the lower I bent to savour it, the sweeter and more overpowering it became. And when she climaxed with great gasps of gratitude, her former essences became instantly dissolved in the omnipotent pollen of her release.

The house itself, perhaps now that she was its sole resident, seemed to ooze Heather at every turn: the chaotic porch, the cushions and curtains, the kitchen and bathroom, even the garden – although I cannot imagine how that was possible – all reeked of her at various stages of the lovemaking process. The house, like Heather, became my intimate. From the moment I entered it – the first stage of my entry, as it were – the swollen river that carried me became a flood; and she, too, I think, savoured the ever shorter periods between my arrival and our copulating as copulation in another key, a delicious overture to the opera – if that's not stretching too far the lyrical side of what was, plainly, a most wonderful fuck.

We had no rules as to what could or could not happen – beyond, that is, her repeated insistence that I should telephone before I appeared, which I always did – nor were any parts of her body off limits, nor did she ever express even the mildest surprise at my at first shy but increasingly bold suggestions. No expectation of any obligations beyond the carnal ever surfaced, such as hints – I awaited these in the early days with dread – that I should leave my wife and come to live there, or a variation on this theme. Loneliness did not seem to be a problem either: if I arrived at, say, ten in the evening and got dressed to leave at midnight, she never pleaded with me then to stay the night, or even a minute longer.

Apart from our inaugural lunch, we never ate another meal together – that is, if you don't count sitting up in bed with cheese and crackers, which she often did post-coitus, claiming that sex made her ravenous. Once, on the way back down the Hill of Howth, my desire resurged so powerfully that I executed a U-turn and crashed back in to find her eating chocolate liqueurs and watching television. That was the sole occasion on which she showed annoyance, pointing out that I had, however technically, deviated from the rule of telephoning in advance. I told her she was being pedantic, which she eventually accepted, and we had sex on the rug as she continued to watch *I Love Lucy*.

The call came through at mid-morning. As soon as Violet said, 'Mrs Messenger on the line,' I knew that although something bad had happened it was not very bad. The wife doesn't ring if it's very bad.

–Brigid, how are you? I said, keeping my voice light.

–Bunny, Harry's had an accident. He's in Mount Carmel.

She told me how that morning Harry's horse had shied just as he had been mounting it in the yard in Oakwood. His face was badly bruised and he had a suspected fracture of the skull. The doctor had insisted on tests and X-rays.

–That's terrible, Brigid, I said.

–I was over in Balbriggan last night, staying with my mother, Brigid Messenger said. –They rang me when it happened. Harry wants you to go and see him, Bunny. He's agitated.

I told Violet to cancel my appointments for the rest of the day, but before I set out for the ten-minute drive to Mount Carmel nursing home, from nothing more than instinct – or incorrigible suspicion – I made a call on my private line. It was picked up almost before it had rung once.

–It's me, I said.

–I thought it might be, said Mickey O.

–Any news?

–None that you want to hear.

–That bad.

–Worse, worse.

I was getting the impression that Mickey O thrived on worse. –Go on. I'm under pressure, I said.

–You don't know what pressure is, my friend. Ask your partner this morning.

–He's discommoded.

Mickey O's dry laugh. –How well put. Listen, I bet you a thousand pounds to a farthing that they'll put a double spin on what you're referring to. The first part of the spin will say that he fell off a skittish horse, which then kicked him. Fine. That appeals to the broad majority of Irishmen who all accept without question the myth that they're descended if not from Cuchulainn himself then at least from one of his charioteers. Horses are acceptable. But then comes the second part of the spin, which will appear to arise from a completely different source: it wasn't his horse that kicked him, but the husband of the woman he was caught out riding with. Within twenty-four hours my forecast is that every jackass in every pub in Ireland will have a theory as to the real cause of our old friend's accident. It's brilliant, because it's exactly the kind of thing they expect of him and that they love him for. And it's brilliant because it diverts everyone from the truth.

–Which is what exactly? I said, without entirely managing to suppress my irritation. Mickey O had always been a know-all. I added, –That's if you know.

–Oh, I know all right. Let's just say that he met some of his Northern cousins late last night about matters on which you and I are acutely informed. Your army friend you met in Brussels was there. And when your partner was, in their view, less than helpful in facilitating their plans for certain importations, one of them, or perhaps several of them, beat the shit out of him.

–Jesus Christ.

–I told you things were bad.

–He's a senior minister in our democracy, for Christ's sake. What you've told me is a disgrace.

–We may like to believe we're a democracy, but we've still got the blood from 1922 on the soles of our boots, Mickey O said.

–And where were your fucking people? I asked, my temper up and having a rare outing.

–What happened happened in a pub between Drogheda and Dundalk. He likes to play the sly boy and give us the slip.

–At least he stood up to them.

–What now remains to be seen is whether he continues to do so, Mickey O said, so smugly that I just put down the phone.

My thoughts as I drove along by the Dodder were all for Harry, not so much for what he had obviously suffered but for what, as Mickey O had implied, he was about to face. The likelihood was that Harry had lied to me over six months where the importation of arms was concerned. However, there were lies and there were the exigencies of politics. In Ireland we had survived as a separate people to those who ruled us for seven hundred years by creating a shadow world in which we could exist. This world, which had the law and authority as its adversaries, had its own rules and ways of operating. The truth, as commonly defined, was negotiable in this shadow world. Harry was popular because people knew instinctively that when it came to the shadow world he was its embodiment.

At the gates to Mount Carmel cars blocked the road and I saw a television crew and Gardaí trying to regulate the flow of traffic. I parked on the Dodder and when I got back up to the gates, Harry's press spokesman from Finance was reading a prepared statement. It was brief and confirmed the story as told to me by Brigid. The spokesman didn't take any questions from the media, but as he was turning to go back in, he spotted me. –He wants to see you, he said, guiding me through the barricade and nodding to the guard that I was acceptable.

I asked, –Is he all right?

–Meant to be resting, but he's been on the telephone since he got here, the man said.

Instead of entering the hospital by the main doors, I was escorted round the side of the building, through the gardens. The grass had had its first cut that morning and the fresh scent of it rinsed my face as I ducked under the branches of birch trees. Around this side, I could see that several rooms opened directly on to the garden. A uniformed guard was smoking a cigarette but concealed it when he saw us. The double doors to one room stood open. My guide spoke to the guard, then made his way back to the front by the route we had come in.

–That's his room, the guard said to me.

Although the doors were open, as I got nearer I could see that the position of the bed meant that its occupant faced away from where I was coming. The toecaps of my shoes shone wetly. I could hear Harry's unmistakable voice. I paused outside the room to wipe the grass from my feet.

–Look, you know me to be a man of my word, Harry was saying. –If I personally guarantee that they go straight north, can you let them through?

I could hear the static but not the substance of the voice of the man on the other end. Harry said, –I see.

Fifty yards away, an old man in a dressing-gown was being brought walking by a nurse.

Harry said, –I'd better have it called off so.

I heard the phone being put down. I went in.

As I sat at my desk, preparing, as I recall, an interim report on the activities of the bank for the shareholders in London, Violet entered. If I have not to this point done other than refer to Violet O'Shaughnessy in a most general way – taking her for granted, as it were, as secretaries tend to be taken – let me now allow her her well-deserved place. She had been *our* secretary – our sole employee – when Gardener Messenger & Co, Chartered Accountants, had commenced business. How old was she? Marginally older than either of us, if I am to be accurate, and that at a time in life when such margins seemed significant. She ever presented an air of crispness and capability that was seldom less than matched by the way she discharged her duties. Tall, her hair flat, short and fair, her eyes light blue, she was married to a golf professional, someone I only twice heard her refer to. Violet's unflappable personality – she never objected, for example, when, in business associated with Lipman's, I asked her to count deposits of money that sometimes exceeded half a million pounds – was an asset I had grown used to and had come to depend on.

Such safe assumptions made Violet's entry that morning in late April 1970 all the more disorientating. She was flushed, her hair dishevelled by virtue of the fact that one hand was caught up in it making a bird's nest of her head, and her mouth was open, although she had not yet spoken. Violet's mouth was never open.

–Violet?

–Mr Messenger's after being arrested! she cried.

A small battery-powered radio was on in the basement where teas were made, a part of the building I was not too familiar with but to which, in keeping with the sense of emergency, I now hurried down with Violet. It was only later it occurred to me that it would have been much easier for her to have brought the radio, the size of a pound of butter, up; but then, too, I realised that confining it down there, underground, was Violet's way of trying to suppress all the vile news emanating from the apparatus. Not just Harry, but Pat Smith, Minister for Defence, along with a Colonel Rufus McGrath, and a man called Pope, described as a leading republican figure from Derry, had all been brought to Dublin's Bridewell and charged with a criminal conspiracy to import arms into the state. I knew, somehow, that Mr Pope would be pale of face.

–It's the end of him, isn't it? Violet sniffled, meaning Harry.

–It's not good, I agreed.

Having settled my secretary down, I drove to the Bridewell. The opposition was in full cry, calling for

Gillespie to come clean about the whole affair, which, it claimed, was threatening the foundations of the country. A *coup d'état* by the army was now a distinct possibility, the leader of Fine Gael, a small man grappling with a large political inheritance, had said. As I was about to park at the Garda station, noting the absence of media, a further news bulletin gave the information that the ministers for finance and defence had both been relieved of their posts by Taoiseach Gillespie and that Aengus O'Reilly, minister for agriculture, had resigned in protest. Statements from both Harry and Pat Smith denied categorically that they had had any part whatsoever in a plot to import arms. Harry's statement added that Gillespie's sacking of him and his arrest were politically motivated.

The lack of media presence outside the Bridewell, I now discovered, was accounted for by the fact that all the accused, having been charged and brought before a special sitting of the district court, had then been released on bail. From a public telephone, I rang Harry's private number in Finance. No reply. The phone in Oakwood was engaged. I rang Violet, but there had been no contact from Harry. I told her I would not be back in the office that day. Then I rang Mickey O on his direct line; a series of rapid pips indicated that the number was no longer in use. I rang home. Adi was out but Andrew picked up the phone. No calls for me. No, Uncle Harry had not been on. Was I coming home to bring Murphy for a walk? the child enquired. The animal had spent the whole morning running in circles round the garden and Mammy had said that unless Murphy stopped we would have to give him away.

As I headed slowly for home, dismay engulfed me, although it was trimmed with a little zest of craziness, the way I had heard that people in England, for example, had gone out and drunk champagne on the day that war with Germany had been announced. One era had well and truly ended and the future, so recently assured, was now dangerous and unclear. Not that the accountancy practice would necessarily suffer, or the bank for that matter, although I had to concede that doing business divorced for the first time ever from politics would be new territory. I think what hurt most was the knowledge that in the end I knew so little, that I was just one of very many who thought that they were central to Harry's life as he was the fulcrum of theirs, that events of great magnitude had taken place but neither he nor anyone associated with him had bothered to pick up the phone and reassure me. I hadn't been consulted because this was out of my league. This was more than a few tea leaves could patch up.

I parked the car on James Larkin Road beside St Anne's Park. Harry out of politics would be a different Harry from the one I had known for twenty-five years, someone hard to imagine; or, put otherwise, the old Harry who had effortlessly risen through the ranks of party and cabinet and whom everyone saw as a Taoiseach in waiting was now gone, or so it seemed. That indeed was similar to a bereavement: the end of the man I knew. He had been ravenous for politics from the first day we had met, had gorged on it; now politics had consumed him. He and I were like a prize pair that had long been driven together in harness, our complementary strengths and needs polished and refined. Now one had fallen, leaving the other's position askew.

A great yearning to excise somehow the negative aspects of the day over a long and wanton session with Heather Clinch possessed me. I started the car and drove out the sea road, passing the crucial junction to my own home as I had on so many other occasions. It began to rain heavily. I considered stopping at a public telephone to make the call, as I had always done, but I did not want to get wet in the now monsoon-like rain shower and so I reasoned that today was an exception: war had broken out on all fronts and the answer was champagne. She would, of course, want to gossip, as would everyone today, about unfolding events and the once powerful we both knew now fallen. We could gossip afterwards, I decided, as a large dark car, coming down the hill against me, sent a slick of rainwater across my windscreen. The relatively enduring power of money compared to that of politics was so potent that it made me see her house blurred for a moment as I came into her driveway. I prayed, aware of how inappropriate my action, that she would be at home; the sight of her car, a Mini, at the hall door was on a par with that of an apparition. Making myself breathe slowly and deliberately, I depressed the latch of the porch and let myself in.

I smelt her first. Extraordinary, the human body, and hers was, but the coded scents to which I have already alluded now came powerfully into play, as if she had written down her whereabouts and pinned the result to the porch door: the essence of her body, the fragrances enlarged when she stepped from her clothes, drew the curtains and came to bed now swam like invisible, seductive fish around my head. What a wonder, I thought smilingly as I tiptoed down the several steps that led to the sleeping quarters, that a beautiful body could have its own code to ride out on the still air of an early afternoon, to guide me in, as it were, to its centre.

The scent swamped my senses, or did almost, for my hearing, although distorted, was still somewhat functional and I could hear her voice. Noises, half-words, pleasurable gurglings slipping like starlings from her throat, for of course I then realised that she must be asleep, that she had undressed after a solitary lunch and had gone to lie down. But why not in her own bedroom? I wondered, as the doorway approached. I smiled again, for I could believe if I wished – and I wished more than I wished for life – that she had chosen the spare room because there she could more easily summon me to mind before she slept. Awash in such assumptions, I removed my shoes, sank to my hands and knees and in this position completed the journey along the corridor, a mere two yards, so that I could then enter the room from the least expected angle and, being honest, see her naked and asleep, her hands perhaps in union with her womanhood and the reason for her pleasurable groans. The room was dim, as usual. At the point where the different carpets were married together by a metallic strip, I paused, doggy-like, and peeped. Gradually the room and my pupils swam into unison. And I saw.

Shock is a peculiar condition. It allows execution of the functional present within a frozen framework in which neither thought nor analysis is possible. I was thus able to regain the upper level of the house in an upright position, put on and tie my shoes, leave by the porch as I had come in and drive my car back down the Hill of Howth with clinical but unthinking efficiency. The heavy rain had ceased. Beyond St Fintan's Well, I pulled in. My hands trembled. I saw the two sweeps of sea either side of Sutton, the one inland, the other running north, both like the slopes of a lovely neck. If I searched hard enough towards Dublin I might be able to discern my own home. Small spits of fresh rain appeared on the windscreen and players on the nearby golf course put up their umbrellas. I was sure of only two things in life at that moment, leaving out the third, which was that I loved my wife: that I would never make love to Heather Clinch again. And that Harry had not seen me.

PART III

13

Dublin, 1992

I was considering the light when it happened. Chris had been called to the phone and I was studying – more, I was absorbed in – the texture of light coming through the French windows of the restaurant. The light's weave, the way it was ever changing, the many layers of lightness and the continual metamorphosis it wrought on fabric acted on me virtually as hypnosis; and as I beheld this fluctuating miracle I could summon up a range of memories in which light had also played a central part, whether on sea water so far out that only the glint of it made you keep faith, or in tiny yet crucially isolated moments such as the reflection from the windscreen of a car as I had been crossing a busy street on the way to a meeting, or the light on the gasworks on a summer's evening when I was so young I had been brought up to bed even as the day still barrelled on in the street; light abundant, I was thinking, yet it comes from infinities of darkness, the pictures they took nowadays seemed to prove it, the pitch and vastness of outer space like a gigantic filter through which the light I was now savouring had first to flow.

The pain then struck from nowhere. It was a stab so intense it made me gasp. My first thought was: How unfair! Just when we seemed to be getting somewhere. How unjust! Stiletto-like, the pain sucked away my breath, a hope-swallowing intrusion into a place so profound it did not bear thinking of. Deep in my back, yes, but more: this was as if plates had moved in the seabed of my constitution.

Chris was returning from the phone, her face tight. –Never have I been subjected to such abuse, she began, sliding in beside me. –That was Barry. Do you know . . . ?

She saw me. –Bunny? You're in pain.

–I'm all right. I'm fine.

–You don't look fine to me. What's the matter?

–Nothing, it's my back. It comes against me at funny times.

–You should have it seen to.

–I know. Adi keeps telling me.

–It's these damn seats here, they should provide cushions, Chris said, and raised her hand. –Excuse me, we need cushions for my guest. Lots of them.

–Right away, Miss Foy, said the head waiter who, despite the late hour, was clinging gamely to his post.

Chris leaned back, started a cigarette, then poured herself coffee. She fixed me with a look. –How long has this been going on?

–It started about a month ago. I was on a flight from Bermuda to London that was delayed. All the sitting. When I got out and was able to move around I was fine.

The head waiter reappeared, his arms clutching bright cushions, which he began to wedge round me. Chris stubbed out her cigarette, then made squiggling motions in the air. –You need some fresh air. Let's get out of here and drive up to the Park. Are you up to it?

–I think so.

–Then we can go back to my house and have some tea.

We walked up the Green together in the warm sunshine.

–That was Barry on the phone?

–Back as if nothing had ever happened. His language! What he's not going to do to me and my family!

–Is it worth it trying to get rid of him?

–I have to do it. For me. Life is too short.

–I know.

–You and me, we should write all this down. Or you should. You have the ability, Bunny. Who else knows all these things? What happens if we get hit by a bus this afternoon?

–Plenty of speculation. 'Is it true they were seeing each other for all those years?'

She smiled. –You haven't changed, have you?

It was the first evening of the spring with any length to it. In the Foy's basement car park we got into her red Mercedes and drove in light traffic down the south quays, across Kingsbridge and up into the Phoenix Park where she nosed in from the road on to grass and parked beside a wood.

–Where are your family? I asked.

–I sent them off to the Canaries. Couldn't bear to have them here with all this filth coming out every day and their uncle's big, stupid face on the front of every paper.

It was four thirty. Deer grazed fifty yards away and, as we got out, looked up at us, then glided off. The trees, although bare, had a sheen of coiled energy, thousands of tiny furled pennants waiting to burst, and green pinheads scattered throughout the brown crinkling undergrowth. We walked arm in arm, and I relished her closeness and her perfume and the way when I looked down I could linger on her slim neck.

–Any better?

–Much better, thank you.

–I'm glad. I hated it back there to see you in pain, she said, and squeezed my arm. She paused. –Do you realise that if we hadn't done what we did eleven years ago, we wouldn't be in this position today?

She had not brought that up before, nor had I; neither was it something I had ever spoken of.

I said, –Someone else would have done it. Your father would have found someone else.

–But he didn't, he found you. Or I did.

She stopped and turned to me. –Tell me exactly what happened.

–You were there.

–I know, but I want to hear it from you.

A thick bough from a tree had come down in the recent storms. I leaned against it. –I remember your father telling me to tell Harry that if it all worked out okay, he would be extremely grateful. He used those words several times.

–He did? Chris bit her lower lip. –I don't remember him saying that.

–That's what he said. And he said it in a voice that put the heart across me.

–I remember that voice.

–He was tough. He was down on the floor then, laid out, but he could still command.

Chris looked, unseeing, into the dark depths beneath the trees. –Fuck it, she said with venom. –We should have left the little shit up there.

Dublin, 1981

The 1970s was when we really made our fortunes, I often reflected: it was the decade in which Harry constructed the power base that would eventually give him all he desired, and in which I consolidated, then expanded all aspects of my business. The 1970s began with us appearing to have no future and ended with us as kings.

No one who was informed, myself least of all, expected Harry to go to jail for the charges of conspiracy to import arms brought against him in 1970; we were not disappointed. Acquitted in a sensational trial in which the State's case collapsed for lack of evidence, he walked free from the courtroom along with Pat Smith and an army intelligence officer, Colonel Rufus McGrath. Over a thousand people cheered when they emerged, although it was clear for whom their main cheers were intended. However, hard words and bitter accusations had been traded between the two lifelong friends and now former cabinet ministers. Pat Smith soon found refuge within the Gillespie camp in Fianna Fáil; but Harry was out in the cold.

I had worried then that if he came back into our accountancy practice, as he was entitled to, our supply of clients would begin to ebb. I also fretted that Lipman's might now be avoided by those seeking to distance themselves from Harry – and, by association, myself – and that Gillespie's government might even try to make business difficult for the tiny merchant bank. I need not have feared. Harry never had the slightest intention of quitting politics, but instead launched himself into a grassroots political cultivation that would take seven years to bear fruit. No retrenchment was necessary for Gardener Messenger & Co either. Our client list continued to burgeon happily, and at Lipman's by early 1972 I needed to lay down an entry threshold for deposit business of five thousand pounds.

It was a time of great happiness for, out of office but continuing his usual way of life with never a dropped beat, Harry was more available to me than he had ever been. I channelled funds to him, either from bank loans guaranteed by those in business who continued to believe in him, or from their outright donations. It was a given that Harry had certain cash requirements to support the *modus vivendi* for which he had become famous and on which his reputation, now more than ever, depended; my job, as I saw it, was to make sure that reputation stayed intact.

Adi, the kids and I spent Christmases at Oakwood. The murky business of 1970 had receded and Adi and I had long been easy again with each other. I no longer had nightmares or heard voices in my sleep.

I told her once, a couple of years after the event, what had happened in Brussels. She looked at me as if suddenly seeing a stranger. –Why did you do it? she asked.

–It was just another business transaction, or that's what I thought at the time, I replied.

But I knew, and so did she, that Brussels had been no ordinary business transaction, for my welfare had not been a concern of whoever it really was who had sent me there. Of course, by then Harry had long been acquitted so it was easier not to confront the possibility that he, my best friend, had been the guiding hand behind my mission.

Adi, with time, was able to assuage her doubts about Harry's role; a political crisis that no one had been able to control or take ultimate responsibility for had occurred. She criticised him less, for out of power and favour Harry was softer, more accessible, less devious.

Adi would have been happy, I think, for Harry to have always remained in that position: easy-going, happy with his old friends, a man as normal as the next, or nearly so.

She and I took the kids on a fishing trawler out to Inis Breadáin where they were taught the art of periwinkling by the future Taoiseach of Ireland. Nothing is so uniting as a cause awaiting its moment; we never had any doubt as to our victory, although we would never really believe it until the moment took place.

Harry's readmission to the cabinet as Minister for Health in 1977 was a cause for great celebration. And in 1979 when he shunted Gillespie from power and was sworn in as Taoiseach, not just we but the whole country seemed to be dancing. We had come back full circle to the point of unlimited horizons that we had left ten years earlier. Any rational analysis of that earlier time, however, would have had to concede that it was exactly at such a moment that we had been in greatest danger.

The boardroom in Upper Mount Street, which I now occupied, was comprised of two gracefully interconnecting rooms on the first floor with stupendous ceilings by Robert Adam. Fifteen years before, a big west-of-Ireland man with a face like a shovel had come into my office and put up a canvas bag on my desk and told me to open it. The bag contained eighty thousand pounds. He wanted to open a bank account and didn't know how to go about it. He was F.X. Delaney, a house-builder, and in the decades that followed, he learned politics, formed companies – or I did on his behalf – purchased a number of sand-and-gravel merchants countrywide and in England, invited me to join his board as chairman, which I did, devolved the day-to-day running of his company to his eldest son, Frank, purchased a villa not far from Málaga, transferred there for tax reasons and within six months had died of heart disease. Frank, as good as his father and a qualified engineer, changed the name to FXD and moved the whole show to Upper Mount Street.

Now, a meeting was held once a month in my office of the board of FXD, whose ever-growing business required unending flows of information, a requirement catered to by Gardener Messenger & Co. And although Lipman Brothers Bank still operated from its original premises in Hatch Street, it was in the boardroom in FXD that the nub of the bank's business was to be found.

I believe I was in the throes of completing documentation in relation to exchange-control procedures for Lipman's when my telephone rang and the telephonist said, –Dennis Foy on one.

It occurred to me at the time that she could not have known who Dennis Foy was, otherwise she would surely have said 'Mr Foy'; I made a mental note to have a word with her.

–Hello?

–Bunny? This is Dennis Foy.

–Yes, Dennis.

–They've got Barry, he said.

Although I had not spoken to Dennis Foy in all a dozen times, and never by phone, the meaning of his words now was immediately and appallingly clear. It was his voice, of course. It quivered with anguish.

–Somewhere on the border, he said. –If we don't pay,

they're going to kill him. He faltered, gulped. The man was crying.

–When did this happen, Dennis? I asked.

–This morning. He was on his way to Belfast to a new store. When he didn't turn up by noon, we started to get worried. The RUC found the car near Newry. Oh, Jesus, Bunny, he's . . . He choked and someone else was there with him at the other end. –. . . he's my son.

–Mr Gardener?

A woman had taken over the phone.

–This is Chris Foy. My father just wants a moment.

–Would he like me to call him back?

I heard her asking.

–No, no, he'll speak to you in a moment.

I hadn't met her, the daughter, but had heard that she was made of cooler stuff than her brother. –Chris, tell me what you know, I said. I could imagine her looking at her stricken father, then making a decision to confide in me.

–Barry's been kidnapped, probably by republican subversives, she said, with calm authority. –They've contacted the store manager in Newry and demanded half a million, saying that otherwise they'll kill him. The money's not a problem, but the guards and the RUC know what's happened and the guards are insisting we do things their way.

–What about the media? I asked.

–It's probably on the news as we speak, she said.

I knew why Dennis had rung me, of course, and what he now wanted of me; what did come as a surprise was my own late grasp of why it was this very wealthy man had years ago gone out of his way to put forward the name of an accountant he barely knew for membership of his yacht club.

–Here he is now, Mr Gardener, she said.

–Bunny, I said.

She passed the phone.

–Look, said Dennis, his voice shaky, –the guards aren't going to let us make this payment. We need help. Do you think you could talk to Messenger?

–I'm sure I can.

–Thank you. Thank you. He'll understand the position. All I want is my boy back.

–I'll make the call, I said.

–Messenger's got contacts up there. If he put the word out that this is a friend of his, I'm sure it would help poor Barry's chances, Dennis said.

–Harry will know what to do, I said.

–There's no time to lose. And we want the guards to back off, Dennis said.

–I'll try to talk to him as soon as I put down the phone, I said.

–And, Bunny . . . Now the old man's voice was suddenly the low one that I was sure made his suppliers go cold. –Tell him Dennis Foy will be extremely grateful, do you understand?

–Yes.

–You're to use those words. Extremely grateful.

–I've got it.

–Thank you with all my heart, Dennis said.

I went out and sat in my car and listened to the news bulletin, as much to give myself time to think as to verify what had taken place. The news led with the Foy story. Barry's car, which had been found in a field in South Armagh, was being forensically examined. Republican paramilitaries were thought to be involved. The commissioner of the guards described the kidnapping as cowardly and stated that, whilst everything possible was being done, no ransom would be paid to terrorists.

I wondered why Dennis Foy, a very wealthy businessman with extensive contacts, felt he needed to go through me to get to Harry. Just because Dennis did not channel funds through me to Harry or to Fianna Fáil did not mean that he wasn't a contributor – in fact, the likelihood of him not being a contributor, given the way things worked, was very small.

The Taoiseach was at a meeting, I was told when I called. Ten minutes later my private phone rang. –Sorry, but I've been busy, he said.

–Busy times, I said.

–I hope you are.

–Certainly am, I said. –FXD are flying.

–House-building has got to be a winner, Harry said. –If we don't continue to build houses in the tens of thousands over the next few years, we won't be re-elected, it's that simple.

–I agree, I said.

–They're reasonable people too, the Delaneys, he said.

–I've always found them reasonable, I said.

–Unlike some others, the Taoiseach said drily, and I immediately grasped why Dennis Foy had called me instead of going direct to Harry.

–Did you hear the news? I asked.

–Fuckin' eejit of a young fella, Harry said.

–The father has been on to me, I said.

–Hah!

–He's up in a heap, as you might expect. Wanted you to know that anything you did for them would be appreciated. He said to tell you that Foy's would be extremely grateful.

I could hear Harry's breathing. –Barry Foy will be lucky not to end up with a bullet in his forehead, and that's the reality, he said. –Can you imagine anything more brain-dead than allowing yourself to be a mark like that?

–Dennis wants to pay the ransom. Five hundred thousand, I said.

–If he pays the asking price, they'll want more, Harry said.

I said, –I'm hardly going to tell Dennis Foy how to negotiate.

We both laughed.

–I've been briefed, Harry then said. –The situation is a mess because of the location. Although they took him on the Northern side, it's believed they then brought him back south. He could be in either Louth or South Armagh. Our lads obviously can't cross the border and the RUC won't go near South Armagh. Then there are the overlying national implications. It's a mess, believe me.

–Any message for Dennis Foy? I asked.

–Message? Harry said, and I could hear the displeasure in his voice. –No message. The forces of law and order are doing their job. It would be highly inappropriate for me to interfere.

It was part of our shorthand, long developed, that both of us knew when not to ask a question.

–How's Adi? he said.

–She's due next week, I said.

–Give her my best. Your other lads well?

–The best. How're your gang?

–Growing up too fast, Harry said. –We'll do something in the next few weeks, we'll all get together and have a family day. A barbecue.

–It's November, Harry.

–I love barbecues, the Taoiseach said.

That night I felt sorry for Dennis Foy. It was a huge story by then and the lead picture in the evening papers was of Barry's young wife, her face a picture of dread, at the front door to their house. But there was a deeper story, I suspected, between Harry and Dennis Foy. Had the old man been approached for funds and refused to give? I wondered. Judging by Harry's reaction to Barry Foy's predicament, it seemed likely. But Harry, I also knew, would see a crisis like this as an opportunity.

–They say he's dead already, said Adi, as she sat on her side of the bed, taking off her rings. Pregnancy made her very beautiful. –They say they always shoot them straight away.

–Please God they haven't, I said.

–Sometimes I think this country is the Wild West, Adi said, and opened the evening paper. –Listen to this. 'The border is criss-crossed by many roads and footpaths. The main Dublin–Belfast road follows a narrow salient of County Louth which bites into South Armagh and consequently Northern Ireland for a distance of four or five miles. The road is flanked on both sides by mountains and forest land – perfect cover for any getaway. It was in this same area that Captain Nairac of British intelligence was abducted six years ago. His body was never found.' God Almighty, can you imagine his poor wife or his parents reading that? They must all be in a bad way.

–They are, I said.

She leaned over and kissed me. –I'll say a prayer for him, Adi said.

* * *

Next evening I drove across town through sheeting rain and out the Galway road to a pub. When the telephone call had come through at five that evening to my office, I had not been surprised. I had known that Harry would make a move, but just which move I had not been able to say. On television, a young priest had been interviewed, appealing to the kidnappers. He had an earnest face and spoke of compassion. There was little else on the news.

I'd been in this pub before, a dimly lighted men's drinking-place where people met when they didn't want their meeting to be seen. The publican saw me and made a sideways motion with his head. I went to the side of the bar and the little door to a snug swung open. I smiled. –I was wondering would I recognise you, I said.

–Well, by the look of you, I obviously went into the wrong business, Frank Trundle said. –What'll you have?

His hair had gone grey and he had cut it almost to the scalp, but otherwise I could see the boy from St Peter's in the man's face, as perhaps he could in mine. He wore a business suit and a white shirt and red tie, but nothing could hide the fact that he was a cop. Two pints appeared like a trick through a tiny hatch. We nudged our glasses towards each other.

–Ahh, Frank said, and leaned back. –Tell us everything. I know you're married – family?

–Three, I said, –plus one on the way any day. And you?

–Seven.

–Seven?

–And another due for Christmas.

–God bless you, I said.

–I love them, Frank said. –I was one of eight, you know. You get used to big families. Da would come home from work and we'd be crawling all over him. Sometimes he'd be asleep in the chair but he never minded. We were a comfort to him.

I had a fleeting memory of a man with furtive eyes pushing a wheelchair out through the rear doors of the hospital in Dun Laoghaire.

–Is he still . . . ? I asked.

–Da? No, poor Da died eighteen years ago, Frank said. –Had it bad for his last six months, but never complained. He was a great warrior.

–How well I remember that, I said. –Holles Street and his Browning revolver.

Frank frowned. –Da?

–He shot a Tommy in Holles Street, I said. –Didn't he?

Frank studied his pint. –Da? No, I don't think so. I mean, he was certainly around, but I don't think he was involved or he would have said. He actually hated violence.

We sat for a moment in respect for another man's life and the vagaries of memory.

–Our mutual friend was on to me, Frank said. –He told me you're close to the Foy family.

–I know them, yes, I said, –or Dennis, I know him.

–Tough old bollocks, they say, Frank said, and I wondered what Harry had told him.

–You don't get to be that wealthy and not be tough, or so I hear, I said.

–He's going to want to be tough for the next while, I can tell you, Frank said, –because this is a right fuck-up and if anyone so much as twitches when they shouldn't it'll all be over.

Outside in the bar I could hear the barmen taking orders and levering the beer taps. –Any leads? I asked.

Frank shook his head. –Difficult is not the word. We have fifty men in Dundalk, listening to phones, drinking in pubs. We have a mobile chip van on the street, a refuse-collection outfit. The information will come in, but it's slow.

–Some people think he's dead already.

–He's not. Not yet.

Frank's eyes were of the lightest blue; I wondered how I had never noticed that before.

–He's okay, he said. –But the problem is he's on the other side. We can't reach him.

–Can't the Brits?

–They have no penetration in that part and they're afraid of their shite of sending men into South Armagh, Frank said, –although I hear they have SAS waiting for the word. They're using helicopters, but they don't really know where to start. This is going to take time.

I drank the stout and leaned back. –If the money was paid, would he be released?

–The question is hypothetical, Frank replied. –No ransom will be paid. Two attempts have been made already, by the way. On Saturday we intercepted a manager from Foy's with half a million in cash trying to go over near Crossmaglen, and yesterday afternoon the RUC picked up a fool of a priest with a couple of hundred grand on him hiding in a shed outside Jonesborough. There was a gun battle. He's lucky he didn't get shot.

–Why not let them pay it?

–Policy, Bunny. Start paying these bastards, the next thing is you'll be negotiating with every criminal on the street.

–You already do.

–Not with terrorists.

–Who makes this policy? Is there a law which says you can't pay a ransom?

Frank scratched his bristly head. –Policies evolve within organisations. They're driven by people.

–Who drives this one? I asked.

–A senior man.

–Who has a name.

Frank looked at me long and hard. –Paul Neilly.

Paul Neilly was the Garda commissioner.

–He won't be breached on this one, Frank was saying, –it doesn't matter who's involved. He's a cold fish, doesn't think like you or me. No kids, maybe that's the difference.

From time to time media stories had suggested differences between Ministers for Justice and the commissioner of the guards, a solitary, priest-like man, a bachelor with unwavering standards whose support within his own organisation was at best mixed.

–Dennis Foy has the money ready, I said. –He doesn't give a damn about policy, just about his son.

–Forget it. With Neilly, it's like an article of faith, Frank said.

–And are you a believer?

Frank stuck out his long legs and joined both hands behind his head.

–Not that it matters, but I'd be less attached to principles, he said. –Men who don't bend usually break. Call these people who did the kidnap all the names you want, but at the end of the day they believe they're fighting a war to get rid of an occupying army and a kidnapping like this is just a means to an end. I may be wrong, but I'd say that one day we're going to be sitting down and talking across a table to these people, man to man. So my view would be that there's little point in looking back, from whenever that day will be, and saying, 'It's a shame we didn't pay them a few quid all those years ago and stop them shooting young Barry Foy.'

–But in the meantime . . .

–We wait for a breakthrough, we slog along.

We drank another pair of pints.

–We were a good team in the old days, Frank said. –It's funny to look back and see what everyone has done.

–You mean Harry?

–I think I could have told you thirty years ago that Harry was going to be Taoiseach, almost from the first minutes I met him, although I probably didn't even know what Taoiseach meant.

Frank looked at his watch and we both went out to the car park.

–Any advice on what to say to Dennis Foy? I asked.

Frank's eyes glinted in the yellow lights. He said, –To be quite honest, if I was you I'd tell him to prepare for the worst.

It was dark when I reached Castleknock. The Foys lived in a big house at the bottom of a cul-de-sac, a detached residence on five acres, built by the developer for himself when he had constructed this estate of houses, then sold to Dennis Foy. A Garda squad car at the top of the road was admitting residents only.

–I'm expected, I said.

I wondered why I was coming up here in person instead of relaying Frank's information by phone. At one level, of course, I saw the opportunity to get Dennis

Foy in as a Harry contributor. Over the years I had floated out hints to Dennis but he had ignored them; and Harry himself, I was now certain, had approached the old man directly, but with no success. Now Dennis's only son's life was on the line and perhaps Harry could save him. But something deeper was drawing me up to this house of anguish outside the Phoenix Park. I admired Dennis Foy, and if there was a chance that I could fix the dire situation his son was in, I wanted to do so.

I drove in through gates and down the short drive. A number of cars were already parked in there. The door was opened by a man I did not recognise but who I later learned was one of Dennis's senior executives. –How is he? I asked.

The man shook his head. –Hasn't closed his eyes in three days.

The hall was dark and smelt of furniture polish. A group of people stood whispering; as I came in they all turned to me and stared. I had no idea who they were, but at that moment the bulk of my years melted away and I was a boy at the front door of the house in Upper Grand Canal Street again, looking out at the group of people in our garden who had been whispering but who, as soon as I appeared, all turned to me and stared. This was how death announced itself, I had known then, and now. The man knocked on an inner door and opened it for me. I went in.

They had been praying. Three people on their knees: Dennis, a priest with ginger hair and a young woman. They all got up, the priest dusting his knees. The woman looked at me coolly.

–We were just saying a rosary for Barry, the priest said and smiled. We shook hands. –I'm Father Little.

Dennis Foy looked like someone who couldn't see properly. He came over, jaw hanging, his arms out as if to receive something. –Well, Bunny?

I realised that, perhaps by virtue of the rosary they had just said, he thought my presence meant that I had brought some positive news. I wished I had. –I have no good news, I'm afraid, Dennis. I'm sorry, I said.

I knew as soon as I spoke that my words were ill chosen and sounded as if I had come to deliver the news of Barry's death; for Dennis Foy staggered backwards and fell heavily into a chair, hands to his face, crying.

–Is he dead? the woman asked quietly. She had an elfin, intelligent face. –I'm Chris, we spoke on the phone.

–No, I'm assured he's not, I said.

–It's all right, Daddy, she said, and went down on her knees beside Dennis. –Barry's not dead, he's alive.

But having surrendered to grief, it seemed that Dennis could not now escape its grip and he continued to weep unstoppably, a spluttering, wet business, not helped by the fact that he continued to keep both hands pressed to his face. Once I, too, had been in the midst of similar parental fragmentation, when my whole life had depended on being calm and functional even as the world around me was disintegrating. I knelt down beside Chris Foy at Dennis's chair. –It's Bunny, Dennis, I said. –Barry is safe. We'll get him home.

He was gasping. –Do you promise, Bunny?

Chris turned and looked at me. Her eyes were very deep and brown. As I held her gaze, right then I felt a sudden arc of connection form between us, a powerful fusion of common interest and experience. She was me in another era, and I for her was someone older to whom she could anchor in this storm of grief.

–Do you? Dennis repeated.

–Yes, I promise, I said, still looking at Chris.

The priest had joined us and now he began to speak to Dennis. Chris Foy stood up. –Would you like to come through here? she asked.

She led the way through glass double doors into a dining room and we both sat at one end of a long, polished table. She was small and slim, and the splay of bones going from her chest to her shoulders stood out beneath her sweater.

She said, –He's definitely alive?

–As far as they know, yes.

She put her head back, closed her eyes and breathed deeply. Her father was already lost to her, I could see. She had taken control.

–How do we get him back? she asked, her eyes still closed.

Although I'm sure she knew anyway, I related Frank Trundle's caution about the problems of trying to find someone in the border counties, of the dilemma posed by uncertain jurisdiction. As I spoke, I could see her observing me with her wise young eyes, and I could feel again the connection that had taken place in the other room.

–This is about money, she said, when I had finished. –They want it, we have it, we want to give it to them. That's all.

–There's a problem with the Garda commissioner, I said. –He's dead set against ransom.

–We know all that, she said sharply, –we've been stopped three times already.

–But the problem remains, I said.

–So get rid of the Garda commissioner, she said.

The glass double doors opened and the priest popped

his head in. I could hear the old man still sobbing. –Tea, anyone?

Chris sliced her hand through the air. The priest disappeared.

–Let me ask you something straight up, she said. –Is Messenger going to help us?

–I'm sure he will, I replied, although all I had to go on was the fact that Frank Trundle had been sent to meet me.

–I'm not, Chris said, and set her jaw. –He's been here more than a few times over the last ten years with his hand out and gone away with nothing. When my father contributes money, he does so to the party, not to individuals. Because of that, Messenger doesn't like us and now I have no doubt he'll try and leverage the position to his own advantage. She looked at me grimly. –But as you know, Mr Gardener, sometimes events change everything and this is such an event.

I felt a rush of affection that she, like myself at an even younger age, already knew the many compromises that must be met and accepted on the road to success and how not to confuse the leaving aside of principle with weakness.

–It's Bunny, I said.

She sagged, all of a sudden, both hands on the table, her first sign of weakness.

–All right? I asked.

She looked up at me and smiled faintly, a suddenly very personal look. Friendships gel like that, from the air we breathe, from the essences we send out from deep within ourselves.

–I want you to speak to me from now on, Chris said, getting up. –My father is not able for this. Here's my private office number. Call me.

I could hear the telephone ringing outside. –Will you be all right? I asked.

–I'll be fine, I'm young, she said. –Thanks. And thanks for coming up here. I appreciate it.

I spoke to Harry that night.

–She said that? he cried. –That's bollocks! I helped those people when they needed me, and you know what I mean, Bunny. Money never came into it. The way I feel now, Dennis Foy can go and fuck himself.

–Those remarks weren't made by Dennis, I said, and thought of Chris's vulnerability, which I had seen below the surface of her toughness, and how I had seen myself, thirty years before, weeping inside but unable to show it. I said, –And, anyway, I think this is a good time to show compassion.

We chatted then about the main obstacles to Barry Foy's release.

–Neilly is a disaster, Harry said thoughtfully, referring to the Garda commissioner. –You can't talk to people whose god is principle.

I thought about how Chris had been able to detach her personal feelings for Harry from the imperatives of the situation.

–I mean, why shouldn't someone be allowed to do what they want with their own money? Harry asked. –It's Dennis Foy's money, he made it. A lot of people in the force would agree with that attitude.

–If Neilly could be made see the compassionate aspect of the case, rather than dwell on the dimensional aspects of dealing with terrorists, then maybe he could be turned, I suggested.

–Let me think about it, Harry said. –I've got a lot of

other things on my mind. The least those Foys might do, though, is to show me a little respect.

Late sun picked out the white of headstones in the cemetery on the flanks of Howth as I drove out the sea road. Strong memories were attached to this journey for me, no matter how many times I made it. At Sutton Cross I turned left, then, a couple of hundred yards further on, right, into a narrow lane, Lauder's Lane, which led to a railway crossing and on to Burrow Road.

I had spoken to her three hours before.

–Not on the phone, she said, before I could even begin. –Look, both my parents are in bed under heavy sedation and the place is crawling with priests. Can we meet some place?

–Wherever you like.

–I'd like some fresh air, she said.

I turned right and drove slowly along by the boundary of the links course. She was pulled in by the hedge and got out when I parked. –You don't mind? she asked.

–Of course not.

Clouds had come in from the north-east on a sudden wind and it had become chilly. We walked down a lane by the golf-course and an Alsatian dog appeared at the door of a cottage and began to bark. The tide was out and a wide band of shells lay in an unbroken crust along the high-water mark. We walked towards Howth.

–Harry is on the case, but he needs time, I said. –He feels very personally involved in what happens to Barry.

–What is he doing? she asked.

–I don't know, but he understands the obstacles in the way to paying the ransom. He understands the problems.

–The problem is getting the money to the Provos. The problem is not up there, it's down here.

–Harry knows that, I said. –Give him time.

–Oh, Jesus, time is agony at the moment, she said. –It's second by second. You wait for – anything! A phone call, a knock at the door. Every time the clock chimes I jump. Death is not as bad as this, I know that.

Rain spits began to sting our faces. She swung her arms as she walked and I could see her hips beneath her jacket. She took out a headscarf and tied it on. –If they kill Barry, they'll kill my father, she said. –Maybe they already have. He adores Barry, never could see his defects. This, of course, is all Barry's fault, because no one has ever been able to tell him anything, not his teachers in school, nor my parents, nor his wife. Not me either, that's for sure. He thinks all women are like our mother, people in support operations. He's been warned a dozen times about going up there in the present climate, he's been told to take the train, he's been told not to tell the people in the stores up there when he is going, he's been told not to go at all – that there's no need for him to be up there. But he had to do it, he had to be the big fella – I'm not afraid of the Provos, I'm Barry Foy, no one can touch me.

The rain had thickened in a squall behind us. A concrete lean-to, an old shed or summer-house in ruins, stood behind the sand dunes to our right and we hurried to it.

–He's the same in the business, Chris said, and took off her scarf and shook out her dark hair. –Heedless. It's like he grew up beside my father for thirty years but learned nothing. I'm meant to be in charge of the fashion end, I work as hard as I can learning and listening and travelling to shows. I try to work out a plan with people who know about these things, I try to co-ordinate ranges of clothes for spring and summer. I spend a fortune on trying to get it right – and what happens? Barry'll be in Indonesia or Hong Kong and he'll come across what he considers to be the bargain of all time in men's leather jackets or chinos or women's casuals and he'll buy six container-loads of this shit and everything I've planned for months will be out the window.

The squall had become a storm and was churning up the sea in front of us like a scene from the Old Testament. Sand blew inwards over our shoes. I heard a sob and realised she was weeping.

–This has been the worst week of my life, not just because my brother may be found with a bullet through his head, but because this is the first time I ever really grasped that I'm not a child any more, she said. –I'm grieving for all that now, you know?

I did know, and I wanted to protect her.

–My parents are old people all of a sudden. This has made my father an old man, he'll never get over it, whatever the outcome, and I'm suddenly the responsible adult. Perhaps the only responsible adult in the family. It's very hard.

–We'll work this out, I said.

–I'm sorry, she said, and blew her nose. –I'm not a tough bitch, you know.

–I know, I said. –None of us is, deep down, we're just kids trying to keep the world on its axis.

–I thought life would be very different, despite everything, although I should have known better. I thought as long as I pleased my father life would be smooth. So I've pleased him, best I can. I went to college, I got married. I had kids – and all those things pleased him. But what about me? Who ever thought about the things that pleased me?

The wind whipped viciously outside and she cried inconsolably. I was her only connection left to a world that had abruptly vanished. I stroked her sweet-smelling hair and brought the warmth of my hand to her cheek. –It's all right, I said. –It'll be fine.

I could feel her racing heart. I held her, and she cried as if crying was not something she had been able to indulge in recently.

–I have no one to turn to, she said.

–I know.

Outside, the rain and wind ceased. We set out then for the cars, the last of the sun now in our faces.

Chris said, –I'm sorry about my behaviour back there. It won't happen again.

–I think you're fantastic, I said.

–I lost control. I'm sorry, she said.

–I mean it.

–Do you? Really?

–Absolutely. Fantastic beyond words.

She grinned. –No one has said anything like that to me for years.

The dog started up its barking again as soon as we came within range.

–You're not like Messenger, are you? she said, at her car. –You wouldn't try and trade someone's life for your own advantage, would you?

I don't think she expected a reply, because she got into her car then and drove off, and I was left there, praying on her behalf that Harry would come up with something.

14

Dublin, 1981

Three days later I was walking from my house in Raheny when Adi called me back. It was a Saturday morning and I had been on my way out to buy the papers.

–Oakwood, Adi said, covering the receiver with her hand.

I took the phone. One of the Taoiseach's personal secretaries was on the line. –It's urgent, the woman said. –He asks can you come out immediately.

I went upstairs and changed from my weekend clothes into a suit, shirt and tie, not just because I was going to see the Taoiseach but because, based on past experience, anyone from a visiting head of state to European royalty could be staying as a house guest in Oakwood and I knew that Harry always liked to present me as a professional functionary.

The morning was cold and bright, and the low sun seemed more like a ball of luminous ice than the source of all heat. I wondered what matter of great urgency required my presence on a Saturday morning. The night before in Dublin's Pro-Cathedral, several hundred people had gathered for Mass, after which impassioned pleas had been made from the altar to the kidnappers of Barry Foy; but the cold reality of the options open to paramilitaries in such situations was already setting in. I had no way of knowing if

Harry was prepared to use the contacts he was fabled to have in order to try and have Barry released, or if he was first reconciling his differences with Dennis Foy. Even had we spoken, I would not have asked. Politics is a business of ever dividing and re-forming cells, an endless metastasis that only the very few can understand, let alone control.

A guard outside Oakwood squinted at my number-plate, then ushered me through the gates. Eleven o'clock had just passed. The avenue curled round two ponderous trees, then straightened out, paddocks with cattle to the right, dense stands of rhododendron on the other side. Almost at once I became aware of a sharp, loud noise, as if hammering were taking place in the middle distance. It ceased as I pulled up at the hall door.

–Mr Gardener. Malcolm was attired in his standard green apron. He looked at my suit and shoes. –The Taoiseach asked that you be taken out to him as soon as you got here, the manservant said. –Can I suggest you wear these? He placed a pair of green rubber boots beside me.

–Where is he, Malcolm?

–Out on the estate, Mr Gardener. It's the Oakwood shoot today.

I exchanged my shoes for the wellingtons, as Malcolm removed his green apron and put on an anorak and a deerstalker hat. Together we walked round the side of the house to a battered old jeep. It lacked windscreen or glass in its side windows. Malcolm started the engine and we lurched out by the back of the house on an internal road. Although wearing my ankle-length, black cashmere coat, made for me by Louis Copeland – my funeral coat, Adi called it – I was already numb from cold.

–Not a bad sort of a day at all for the shoot, Malcolm said cheerfully.

I knew nothing of the mechanics or protocol of shooting or hunting, activities that the Taoiseach had embraced with great enthusiasm. –Who is here? I asked.

–The ambassadors of France and Italy, Malcolm replied, –Mr Stanley Sharkey and our own Minister for Finance, a group of the horse-breeding people from the south. Dr Brendan Broe, the businessman. A lovely group of gentlemen altogether, he concluded, with some satisfaction.

–And what do they shoot? I asked.

Malcolm looked over at me anxiously. –Pheasants, Mr Gardener. Last year the total bag was three hundred and sixty-six, but this year the Taoiseach hopes we'll top the five hundred.

Although the front gates of Oakwood lay within a stone's throw of a north Dublin suburb, the interior of the estate itself seemed to widen into the boundless vistas of woods and tillage land and bare horizons that I associated with countryside hundreds of miles to the west. The jeep rattled along and the cold intensified. Now we were driving across a field of stubble. Several hundred yards distant, beside a wood, a pair of tractors were pulled up with trailers on which rows of straw bales were set out. Two distinct groupings stood in the bright morning: to one side, keeping in check what seemed like dozens of spaniels, men were wearing rough clothes and wool-knit caps, holding sticks and smoking cigarettes. Nearer the trailers a further bunch were attired in tweed jackets, leggings or plus-fours. Silver cups were being passed around. The Taoiseach was holding court, coming to the end of a story. All the heads went back heartily as he delivered. He stood up and wiped his eyes. –Bunny.

He came over and put his hand on my shoulder. –I was telling them about the first time I met Maggie, he said, bringing me over. 'I'm told you think that what I need is "a rub of the relic", Taoiseach. What exactly do you mean?' says she. 'Oh, it's just a religious term, Prime Minister,' says I. 'Religion is exactly what we should be trying to take out of Irish politics, is it not, Taoiseach?' 'Absolutely, Prime Minister, absolutely.'

Everyone laughed again. I shook hands with the ambassadors, and with Stan, and with men with the clever eyes of horse-tanglers, and with Dr Brendan Broe on whose yacht Harry had recently holidayed. The men with the dogs began to troop along the top side of the wood.

–Isn't this the most natural thing in the world to be doing on an Irish winter's morning, Bunny? Harry asked, steering me downhill.

I agreed, although I felt self-conscious in my citified clothes, in my long coat trailing the ground almost, the ridiculous spectacle I must have presented in the setting. Walking beside the Taoiseach was a country-looking man with what looked like guns in leather cases slung over both his shoulders. Behind us came Stan Sharkey and Dr Broe.

–We've reared fifteen thousand pheasant this season alone, Harry explained. –The man who lived here two centuries ago would have been doing exactly the same thing this morning.

I saw Stan halt thirty yards back and uphill of us, then, after another fifty yards or so, Broe. We continued down a steep hill and into a corner of the field beside a gurgling stream.

–My father, God rest him, used to beat on a shoot like this on an estate near Limavady. Harry chuckled. –He used to slip a few birds into his jacket and bring them home for dinner and tell us they were Chinese chickens. Which I suppose they are, in a queer sort of way.

Broken veins stood out in the Taoiseach's nose and cheeks, but his eyes were quick and dangerous. The attendant began to unsleeve the shotguns. I had seen a cheque for over fifteen thousand go through for these weapons.

A whistle blew at the far side of the wood and there was an eruption of shouts and of sticks being banged against trees. Uphill to our right I saw Dr Broe bring his gun up to his shoulder, as if he was taking aim, and remain in that position.

–Stand immediately behind me, Bunny.

A frantic cluck-cluck-clucking swung my attention to the tops of the trees. A long-tailed, screeching pheasant flailed out, midway between Broe and the Taoiseach. I saw Broe's shoulder recoil as he fired twice. The shrieking pheasant continued. Harry pivoted and fired. The flying bird became a tumbling, airborne ball and hit the field twenty yards behind us with a loud thump.

–I wanted to let you know that there may be a window of opportunity about to open in the Foy case, the Taoiseach said, as he exchanged guns smoothly with the man attending him. –But it needs to be taken advantage of straight away.

I stuck my fingers in my ears as another pheasant appeared, straining its neck in a bid to escape. Harry shot it directly above us. As the bird hit the frozen ground beside me, I heard its wind punch out.

–You need to be ready to act, possibly as soon as tomorrow, the Taoiseach said.

Birds were now pouring out the length of the wood, their squawks almost drowned by the gunfire. Harry shot in an unbroken rhythm, one gun, then the other. I wondered why he thought that I should be ready to act, and in what capacity.

–This needs to be handled very carefully, he said. –Trust is essential. We're dealing with very volatile people.

A bird burst from trees fifty yards away and flew along the face of the wood. Uphill I saw Broe's gun-barrels swing towards us.

–Watch out! the Taoiseach cried and we all ducked.

Two explosions were followed by a light peppering of shot. Harry stood up and took the bird just before it disappeared. –I don't want to be within firing range of Dr Broe again today, or ever – understood? he said to his attendant.

–Sorry about that, Taoiseach.

–Just because he gives thirty grand a year to the party doesn't mean he's entitled to fucking shoot me, Harry muttered to me.

I could hear the shouts of the beaters much nearer now, and the yelps of their excited dogs. My ears rang.

–I've communicated the fact that I am personally concerned about young Foy, Harry said. –That this is personal to me. And the best way for me to demonstrate my personal involvement is for me to send my closest friend and adviser to deliver the money.

It took me some seconds to grasp what was being suggested.

–Me?

–You'll be up and down in a couple of hours, the Taoiseach said, taking a high bird with his second barrel.

I actually wondered was he being humorous. –I don't think I'd be much good as a bagman, Harry, I said, and forced a smile.

Two whistle blasts sounded and the Taoiseach handed over his gun. –You're the only man for the job, he said. –My man. Everyone will be comfortable that there's no trap if they see my man involved.

–You're serious, aren't you? I asked.

–You're the guarantee that everything is above board, the Taoiseach said, and we began to walk back uphill. –It's a win-win situation. Young Foy gets off, old Foy is suddenly free to express his gratitude.

I thought of Chris and how she now depended on me. –Adi's due to have the baby tomorrow, I said.

–Bunny, Bunny, said the Taoiseach, with a smile to show that he could not believe I might disappoint him, –we're talking about a drive, probably to Dundalk. Less than an hour. First thing in the morning. It's nothing. You'll be back and Adi won't even know you were gone. You won't be harmed.

–Can you guarantee that?

–Absolutely, Harry said, and put his arm around my shoulder. –Do you imagine for a moment I'd send you up there if there was any risk attached? Look, you spoke to me about compassion the other night and I thought about what you said. You were right, as usual. I said to myself, 'For God's sake, listen to Bunny.' I did. I've set it all up now and we're ready to go.

–Has Dennis Foy been told that I'll do this? I asked.

–Of course, Harry said. –I spoke to the daughter. You obviously made an impression there. When I told her what was going to happen, she said, 'I knew Bunny would keep his promise.'

Dogs were now trotting back to their keepers, their mouths stuffed with head-drooping birds.

The Taoiseach smiled. –Doesn't it do your heart good, Bunny? We're all part of a team. The lads rear the birds and beat them out, I shoot them, the dogs retrieve them. We'll all eat them. It's the cycle of creation.

I drove home slowly. And that evening, on the fifth day of the Foy kidnapping, the media became convulsed with the news that Paul Neilly, the Garda commissioner, had abruptly resigned.

The man was in his forties and looked as if he counted money for a living. His fingers, shod with rubber thimbles, flew through the stacks of hundreds. Dennis Foy was slumped to one side of a coal fire, his eyes locked on the cash. Chris sat on a stool beside him and in a chair in the corner sat Father Little, whose face had been on television a lot in recent days. I had not met the mother, but understood she had been in bed, sedated, since the abduction. Each time the teller got to ten thousand, he snapped rubber bands round the wad and added it, brick-like, to the mound. It was six o'clock in the morning.

I had told Adi that I was going to supervise a major stocktaking at a hotel group and that I would be back at eleven. I looked at Chris once or twice and she smiled at me, but otherwise her attention was all for her father. The gap between misery and happiness was often just waiting to be bridged, I thought, as in this case, with money. The teller was now loading the cash into a sports holdall. He zipped it shut and everyone stood up. If the situation begged for silence, then it had got it. But now the priest had spread his arms and Dennis and Chris and even the teller had dropped to their knees; I did likewise. I heard the word *'Benedicamus'* as if from the bottom of a well. Then we were outside and I was placing the sports bag on the front passenger seat of my car – the instructions had been specific – and it was six twenty a.m. I closed the passenger-side door and turned back to the house, but all I saw was the front door closing. The guards in the unmarked car didn't seem very interested as I drove out.

–Advice? Frank Trundle had asked. –Just give them the money and come home. What's the place and time?

–Tomorrow morning, eight o'clock in the car park of the Fairways Hotel in Dundalk, I said.

I could hear children playing in the background in Frank's house.

–All right, here's exactly what you'll do, he said. –Get there no more than five minutes early. Put the money outside the car. Leave your engine running and when they come for it, just back away gently so that they can see the bag or whatever. Let them pick it up and fuck off with it. Under no circumstances get out of your car – d'you understand that?

–I think so.

–We'll pull back tomorrow morning until ten, he said. –You won't get hassle, that's a promise.

–Thank you.

A child screamed and I could hear Frank make a soothing noise. –You'll have nothing to worry about, he told me, –it's all set up. It'll be like making a lodgement in the bank.

I drove across the north city and thought of all the years that had led up to this morning. I wondered briefly had I become hostage to them. A milk float was working the main street in Balbriggan. I turned on the car radio.

It was approaching half seven as I drove through Dunleer. Traffic was light and, as far as I could see, I was not being followed. The fact that I was, albeit in an unusual way, cheating on Adi again at a time when she was pregnant occurred to me, for I should really have been at home with her, waiting to drive her to the Rotunda, rather than trying to fix the problems of people I barely knew. I turned up the radio for the news bulletin. Commentators were falling over one another trying to suggest the reason for former Garda Commissioner Neilly's resignation from the force. It was truly wondrous. Less than a week ago, it had been assumed that this man would be the country's number-one law-enforcement officer until his retirement, half a dozen years hence. Now he was nothing. Death must be like failure, I thought, as I met the outskirts of Dundalk: open-ended disappointment. I felt happy, all at once, to be part of such awesome power. And I felt slightly ashamed of myself that I had worried on my own account in what was clearly a very straightforward transaction. It was seven fifty-seven a.m. as I turned off the main road into the car park of the hotel. The forecourt was empty. I manoeuvred into a central position, pulled up the handbrake but kept the engine running, as Frank had instructed. I was about to get out and place the holdall outside the car when another vehicle, a blue van, popped into my rear-view mirror. Better to wait until it had parked, I decided. I saw it pause about twenty yards back, directly behind me. Then I heard its engine revving and saw – without really believing what I was seeing – the van hurtle straight for my boot.

The steering-wheel reared up and slammed the bridge of my nose. I felt my head whip back and tasted blood and gristle. A rush of cold air meant my door had been dragged open. Then I was manhandled, one man to each shoulder, round the back and flung head-first through the open side door of the van. As I began to shout I saw a blanket, framed as it were by the open van door, plunging on top of me and, as it did so, the merest glimpse of slit eyes in head woollens; but not for long, since the door clanged shut on rollers, the weight of several men punched the wind from me and the van was travelling at speed.

–I can't breathe! I shouted into the blanket, and tried to spit blood. –I'm smothering!

–You feel this, Bunny? asked a voice. –This is a wee shooter in your ear. Now scream or shout again or give us hassle and I'll have to blow a hole in your fucking head!

I remembered Harry's accent the first time we'd met, but that was so many years ago it seemed ridiculous.

The man was continuing in a reasonable tone: –I don't want to, of course, all we want to do is drive nice and quiet across the border with the money. But you're our insurance that nothing goes wrong, d'you understand me? Then we'll let you out and you'll be home in time for the dinner.

I tried to imagine the map and to remember how far it was to the meandering procession of black dots that divided Ireland. I had to talk to them, I had to ascertain that their intentions for me were really as they stated. I had lost control of my tongue as well as my bladder.

–I'm Harry Messenger's business partner! We've been in business together for thirty years! D'you know Harry?

–Shut the fuck up.

–Harry's been in touch with your side, he's made a lot of things happen down south this week, the Garda commissioner has resigned . . .

–Sorry, Bunny.

He must have hit me very hard, because the next thing I knew, apart from a headache worse than any I could ever remember, someone was helping me into a sitting position. I had been sick.

–Just sit up, Bunny, but keep the blanket over your head, someone said.

–I'm sick.

–Just keep the blanket over your head.

I retched again and explosions behind my eyes made me see white.

–Is Barry Foy safe? I asked.

–Ach, he's in the best of form.

I drew in my breath, for that had been a different, deeper and more authoritative voice. I guessed that we had crossed the border.

–Are you going to kill me?

–Why would we do that and you Harry's partner?

–Do you know him?

The man laughed. –Me daddy grew up in Derry in the same street as the Messengers. About six doors up from them. Harry's daddy was good to us when my mother's first husband died, got her her entitlements where she could get none. Cyril Messenger was always on the side of the people and he had to take up a gun in the end to try to get what he wanted. They'd long gone south by the time I was born, but I remember my mother saying, 'However far Cyril goes, that young lad Harry will go further.' How right she was.

–He promised me I wouldn't be harmed, I said.

–And neither were you, save for a wee bump on the head. Harry's a good man, he put himself on the line for us once – that was ten years ago, before my time, but that doesn't mean I don't know the story. I mean, the man went on trial and all and him a minister in the government. So I don't care what they say about him, Harry Messenger's all right.

–What do they say about him? I asked. I didn't think they'd kill me as long as we were talking to one another.

–Ach, it's not for me to say, and if you're his friend you know it already. But great men are human like the rest of us. That's why they always fall in the end, or are brought down. It's as if people can't believe that they really are human. But that doesn't mean they haven't been great.

The van was lurching from side to side, consistent with negotiating sharp bends. I felt the urge to vomit again and a renewed, powerful headache, both strangely welcome since they seemed to lessen the space available to my fear. All at once we stopped, I heard the sliding door trundle back and saw daylight again through the blanket.

–Just don't try to look, Bunny.

They helped me out, almost gently.

–Lie face-down, there's the good man. Try not to worry, the voice said.

It was then, feeling wet grass, that the images of a dozen roadside figures with entry wounds in the backs of their heads made me consider Adi powerfully. Adi and only Adi, her sweet face, now sad, her warmth, the divide I had sometimes created from her, the massive nature of loss and the truly insignificant place I would be seen to have occupied in her eyes in this whole mediocre scheme. I shook and could find no words. I pressed down, face to the dew, and wept for my insubstantiality. The blanket was plucked off. The van sped away. I lay there for fifteen minutes, unable to rise. And when I did, it was to yellow the green roadside with the bile of decades.

I drove home so slowly that cars behind made angry gestures when they eventually passed my U-shaped boot. A man in a lorry out delivering coal had picked me up on the outskirts of Forkhill and had driven me all the way in to the Fairways Hotel. I think he thought at first that I was Barry Foy. He had a blackened face, as if he had awoken so begrimed, and spoke in a throaty, chuckling voice about 'the lads' and people who had things coming to them. He shook my hand on our parting, but I didn't wipe his coal-dust grime off: rather, I wanted to inhale its sootiness that boasted so powerfully of robust, uncomplicated life.

That was a myth, too, of course, I knew, as I came in through Swords, for we all simply elevate to one degree or another the complications that are part of life, and some of us to high art. Harry, with his wealth and his grandeur, was probably the most complicated man I knew, although he had always been elected on platforms of almost childish simplicity. Help the sick. Build more houses. Give people a fair deal. With his estate and his island and his vintage wines, he performed an ongoing balancing act that incorporated the highest risks, that depended on political and other networks of labyrinthine proportions, that operated equally on fear as on love, on loyalty and on a skewed and sometimes monstrous interpretation of the concept of honour.

Passing the airport at noon, I heard the Angelus and then the news. My voiding had left me cleansed and clear-headed, not to mention buoyant. The lead item was that kidnap victim Barry Foy had been found near Crossmaglen and had been rushed to an undisclosed location in Dublin where his condition was said to be comfortable. His father said there would be no interviews and thanked people for their prayers and support. He denied absolutely that any ransom had been paid.

I would go first to Upper Mount Street, where I would change my clothes and then go home, praying that Adi had not yet made the trip to the hospital. I crawled, aware with every mile of the decisive nature of the day and of the fact that few of us are ever given the opportunity to dwell so starkly on the details of the lives we have led or to look so clearly into the future. Because I seemed to have got where I was without any pause for reflection, or audit, as it were, of why or how or whence, I needed that time now. When the baby was born and settled down, Adi and I would go away somewhere for a week, to West Cork, maybe, away from phones and telexes, and I would take long walks and try to figure out, by virtue of where I had come from, where I was going. For nothing really had changed in a decade, I then knew: Harry was back in power and I had been sent on a mission in which my welfare had been of no more concern than it had been in Brussels. How could I ever tell Adi what I had been through without reopening a gulf between us? One day that gulf would swallow both of us, if I didn't get out first and take her with me. I would do so, I swore to myself, I would change, cut my ties to Harry and save my marriage. That was my plan. But in the meantime all I really wanted was to sleep.

My part in Barry's release never became public knowledge, a fact that I was in no hurry to change; neither did I discuss it much, if at all, with Harry, as I remember, and never with Dennis Foy. In fact, I never saw Dennis Foy again, and when he died a couple of years later, as Chris had said he might, he had not played an active part in the business since the time of the kidnap. Nor did I ever tell Adi what I had done; three days later our baby boy, Dick, was born and my happiness made the darkness of Dundalk and the border seem like a bitter dream.

It took me a few weeks to settle down again, to stop jumping every time someone tapped me on the shoulder. But in the early dark days of December I telephoned Chris in her office one evening.

–I was wondering if I'd ever hear from you, she said.

I had hesitated to ring her beforehand, not wishing to crowd her in the aftermath of the kidnap; but the experience had left me scarred and I had no one else to share it with.

–Are you all right? she asked me on the phone.

–Okay now, but at the time it was bad, I said.

–I should have called to thank you, she said.

We agreed then to meet for a drink, and three days before Christmas found ourselves together in the hotel at the airport. In a booth of the bar, I told her what had happened in Dundalk and as I did so, without any understanding of what was going on, I began to cry. It was as if our former roles had been reversed, me now weeping unstoppably, Chris holding both my hands in hers.

–I have no one to turn to, I said.

–I know.

She got up and came round to sit beside me and then, as I wept – for myself, my pathetic life, for all my deeply buried and now excavated fears – she put her arms around me and said, –It will all work out for the best, believe me.

It was as if I had stepped through an unseen portal into a reverse world abrim with sorrow and disconsolation, for I had not appreciated the depths of my wounding. We stayed there for an hour or more and I dried up and went and bought us another drink. I felt better for my tears, that I had been able to let out some of what had been trapped inside me and had been able to cry on the shoulder of a friend.

Later, outside, in the car park, we had a last hug. I took away a taste of sweetness that I kept with me for years, and I felt sure that Chris did too. Although we saw each other again here and there over the next decade, as one has to do in Dublin, we didn't ever meet again, because to do so with our respective spouses would have meant involving them in the events of Barry's kidnap and release; and to meet otherwise seemed somehow inappropriate. That didn't mean we weren't friends, of course: once a friend, always.

Events have a funny way of turning out, as if forces quite beyond us are responsible for our interactions. For if I had never met Chris in 1980, then twelve years later when her brother, Barry, was sensationally arrested in Florida on charges involving drugs, I would not have been the person hurrying to see her that morning, distracted by unfolding events, worried that I was late.

PART IV

15

Dublin, 1992
One week before Bunny's meeting with Chris

I awoke at six thirty drenched with sweat, breath short and a weight on my chest as if someone had crept in as I had slept and laid a car battery there. Adi was beside me, lying on her side, turned away from me, her shoulder gently rising and falling. I have always had the ability to think calmly in a crisis; and thus I could even at that moment rail off a tiny area of stillness in which I could project forward what would happen if I cried out for help. Dr Ward and a visit to the Mater at minimum. Detained then for observation, with Adi to the fore in batting away my protestations. I lay, quilt and blankets peeled back, willing the weight away.

I remember thinking, These things always happen in threes, which was perversely optimistic since if I was in the throes of a coronary I was unlikely to be around for the remaining two items. Or maybe pain was two and death three. Flexing toes and fingers, moving hands, arms and legs, my breathing slowly relaxed and my chest loosened. I went to the bathroom, light-headed, and sat on the toilet's cool porcelain rim.

When, some time in the mid-1940s, in Upper Grand Canal Street, the toilet came inside, a seat had not been part of the arrangements. My first toilet seat had been in Mr Long's, a butt-nosed, wooden contraption that squeaked whenever it was raised or lowered, and which I considered a bizarre option when the alternative was the shoulder-like roundness of Mr Long's speckled-hen enamel. (The measurement of the fitting plumbed into Upper Grand Canal Street was one half that of Mr Long's and its edges thin and not designed for prolonged straddling.) The habits acquired in youth are not easily prised away. I sat, grateful for the unscheduled space, glad to be still alive but suddenly mindful that time was running out.

I tried to analyse what had happened to me back in the bedroom. I felt I knew. Like everyone else in Ireland, I had read three days before of the sensational circumstances in which Foy's boss, Barry Foy, had been arrested in Florida. I knew the likely consequences of those developments, but had not dared dwell on them. Then, as I slept, the dark realities slithered out from the cellars of my mind, crawled up through the vapours and entwined my chest and my reason.

Morning was glad that March day, full of the song of birds whose names I only vaguely knew, warm already outside, scents accumulating around the summer-house should I decide to go out there and avail myself of them. I did. Dew damped my ankles and the hems of my pyjamas as I strode out on the lawn, dressing-gown untied and billowing modestly in my wake. I opened the summer-house doors and dragged a cushioned chair out on to the porch. Sun was coming up behind chimney-pots from the Howth direction, spotlighting seagulls on ridge-tiles, illuminating television aerials and working its way into the foliage of my sycamore trees. What a shame it would have been, I thought, to have died in bed on a morning like this.

Barry Foy had been installed in a $1500-a-night suite of a hotel in West Palm Beach, a four-hundred-bed monument to knowing overstatement upon which Irish newspaper reporters had descended in numbers and whose extravagant setting they had vied with one another to describe. Some spoke of how the hotel, built on a former mangrove swamp, glittered at night like a jewel; how it could be spotted from as far south as Fort Worth, or from Juno Beach to the north if you were travelling the coast in darkness; how local yachting men on night voyages used it as a landmark; how the pilots of aircraft making the descent into Miami cross-checked their ETAs when they passed over the hotel's intense luminescence. Others gorged on the details of the main atrium: thirty floors capped by a soaring dome, with fronds and herbage, vines and deep-green, glossy-leafed plants of jungle origin plunging from balconies and down sixty feet either side of an unceasing waterfall. They described spume rising in fine clouds from the surface of the hotel-lobby pond, home to eleven different species of ornamental fish.

At two in the morning, following repeated complaints from the adjoining suite, the assistant night porter, Dee Dee Robb, having failed to get an answer to the buzzer, had let herself into suite 2908 with her master key. Robb – blonde, pony-tailed, thirty-three and a single mother, as all reports faithfully recounted – had been confronted by a scene of devastation: shredded cushions, curtains pulled down, tables and chairs overturned. The light fittings on the near wall had been pulled out. In the centre of the room stood a naked man. Big-framed, his stomach bulged massively. The white flesh of his chest, back, arms and legs was covered in fuzzy, wire-wool-like reddish hair. The way he now cocked his head, the way he slowly revolved his eyes, reminded Dee Dee of a bear she had once seen in a circus in Jacksonville, she told reporters later. Goaded, terrified and dangerous, she described him as. The man saw Dee Dee, gasped, put his hands to the sides of his head and opened his mouth.

–AhhhhhHHHHH!

–Jesus, Dee Dee muttered into her hand-held to the desk twenty-nine floors below. –D'you guys hear that?

Beside the windows, a young olive-skinned woman was pulling on her knickers. A prostitute from Miami well known to the night staff of the hotel, her head of curls resembled black squid. She clipped on a skirt, pulled a sweater over her head, stepped into her shoes, picked up a shoulder bag and walked out past Dee Dee. –You should get this guy a doctor or somethin', she said.

–*NO!* The man lurched to grab the girl but Dee Dee spread her arms.

–It's okay, sir, it's okay, Mr Foy. Let her go.

Barry Foy swung wildly at Dee Dee. As Dee Dee dived to one side, she could see, as she would later tell the world, Mr Barry Foy, the occupant of suite 2908, lurch out past her and climb the balcony of the atrium. Dee Dee gasped. –Hey, shit, he's goin' to jump! she yelled into the hand-held.

–Grab him! a voice on the radio said.

Breath gone, struck deaf, Dee Dee approached. Perched above the abyss, the naked man's mouth was open. Dee Dee walked as if on eggs. At different levels underneath, a few people had come out and were looking up.

–It's okay, Mr Foy. Just tell me what you want and I'll get it right away. Just tell me, honey.

Barry Foy turned. His face was that of a man who has seen his own death – not unreasonable, in the circumstances. –I want my father.

–We'll get him, honey, just give me your hand. Dee Dee reached. –We'll get him.

I drove into Dublin, unable to quiet the swirling sense of foreboding that I felt attending my every moment. At a deeper level than I could articulate I could foretell the events that would follow Barry's disgrace, as if he had been the first domino to fall. I had last met him a year before in the Foy's headquarters just off the top of Grafton Street. Barry's office was enormous. He was swinging a golf club.

–Jesus, Bunny, you have a right gut on you. He smirked.

–Cost a lot to put there, I retorted.

He looked me up and down and I could see in him how every bully was simply passing on the treatment that he himself had received.

–The old man used to talk a lot about you, he said, putting down the club. –Said you'd fix anything. I suppose that's why he went to you about me, the time I had the trouble.

–It all worked out for the best.

–All the fuckers wanted was money.

–Common complaint.

He looked at me as if perhaps I had cracked a joke that he should respond to. –I tried to thank you for what you did, to show my appreciation by inviting you to come on the board. But you wouldn't. What was the matter? Were we not grand enough for you? Or was it something else? Or some*one* else? Was that it? Am I getting close there, Bunny, or what?

I ignored the oafish leer. –I didn't have the time to do justice to a place on your board, Barry. Still don't. I'm trying to scale back.

–Well, I'm not fucking scaling back, he said, and walked to a filing cabinet and pulled out the top drawer.

–I have another good twenty years left in me, maybe more, and I'm going to take this business places my old man would never have dreamed of.

–That's fantastic.

–Work hard, play hard, that's me. And fuck the begrudgers. Here, this is for your man.

He had handed me an envelope.

–Thanks, Barry. Much appreciated.

–Like I told you before, I don't want that man ever going begging – ever, d'you get it? Not as long as Barry Foy is in town.

I joined the flow of traffic around the Custom House and found myself – not for the first time – moving my lips in a silent prayer of thanks for the treasure of my wife and my family. They would, in the end, be all I was left with, I knew with stark comfort; which made me no different, I accepted, from the great majority of men. What was intensely dismaying was that it had taken me so long to realise this fact. And yet, at a deeper level than I could even claim to be aware of, I knew that events were moving to a conclusion and that someone was watching over me.

Only Dick, aged ten, was still at home with us. Rosemary, a secretary in the Department of Finance, owned her own apartment in Ballsbridge, Hans had just married and was a partner in Gardener Messenger and Andrew, now nearly thirty years old and unmarried, worked in Brussels for the European Commission. At Christmas when they came home, we still went to Mass together in Raheny.

I'd had an extension built on to the garden side of the house, two bedrooms and a bathroom upstairs, and below a study for me, making it, by my own estimate, five times larger than the house in Upper Grand Canal Street. Why did I bother with such calculations, I often wondered. A month before, the old house had been sold and I had given my portion of the proceeds to my sister. It was a year to the day since Mam had died.

I had two meetings scheduled for that morning, the first with Stan Sharkey, arranged the day before, the next with inspectors from the Central Bank. The inspectors I could deal with, we had met regularly over the years when they had come to express their reservations about Lipman's activities; decent men but lacking in imagination – which in the end was why they were civil servants – guided by the barely flickering beacon of an Ireland that had once existed only in the mind of de Valera, God rest him. Dead nearly fifteen years now, hard to believe. I still smiled when I thought of the way Harry used to take him off. The short-sighted, peering face, the whining voice. *The Catholics up there are the Brits' problem.* Poor Aengus, living on a tiny minister's pension down in the midlands somewhere, still writing his memoirs about what really had happened back in 1969. Now and again some inattentive newspaper editor let a piece slip by in which Aengus was referred to as either dead or, worse, disgraced. A solicitor's letter always followed and the eventual out-of-court settlements, although minuscule, had paid some of the heating bills over twenty-three winters.

Harry had never once acknowledged him, the man who had resigned in protest at Harry's sacking from office and arrest. Not long afterwards I'd been present when Aengus's name had come up. Harry had turned his head a fraction and the hoods of his eyes had closed them into small, unforgiving slits. 'Old fool,' was all he'd said.

The front pages of the papers were preoccupied with Barry Foy. The Miami prostitute had acquired an agent and was telling it as it really happened for ten thousand US a shot. Barry, meanwhile, was in full confessional mode. I felt a fresh and unpleasant surge of premonition as I passed by the Huguenot cemetery where a beggarman sat on the ground playing a tin whistle. 'Carrickfergus' rode the sweet morning in uneven, halting, yet strangely pleasing notes. A piper had played the same air as they'd hand-strapped Gillespie down into his Munster soil half a dozen years back. Pat Smith had given the funeral oration. Although he and Harry had stood either side of the open grave, there had been no eye contact between the two former political allies, one newspaper had reported.

There are marble stones as black as ink. Under the musician's hopeful eyes I fumbled for a coin, found nothing, took out my wallet and dropped a fiver in his upturned cap. The inner lining, gleaming with grease, still bore the name 'Callaghan's'. I hurried on, checking my watch. Ten fifty-eight a.m. I have always liked to be on time.

Stan had commandeered a back corner of the lounge and was looking down his short nose through reading glasses at a plate of biscuits alongside coffee jugs and crockery on the linen-covered table. He looked tanned and fit. Apart from the one occasion when he had arrived with a sack of money and put it on my desk, he had never set foot in my office but had always held the meetings of his companies either in the penthouse boardroom of a building he owned on O'Connell Street or out in the yacht club or here in the Shelbourne.

–All well?

–Great, thanks. And yours?

–Not a bother. Did you read the other day what they put into these fucking biscuits?

–I must have missed it.

–Enzymes and hormones and enough shit to kill a bullock. Stan nudged the plate away with his knuckles. Sitting back, he crossed his legs and fidgeted with his cream double shirt cuffs, tugging them out; he sat up again, picked the smallest biscuit from the plate and bit on it. –You can never believe what you read in the papers, he said.

When he shifted and twitched the way he was now doing, he was, without much need of imagination, exactly the same person I had met with Harry nearly forty years before.

–How old are you, Bunny?

–A year younger than you.

–I'll be sixty-three next year. Sixty-three is a desperate fucking age when you're young. Old fellas are all sixty-something. Old Mr So-and-so is in his sixties – Jesus, you'd see him and you'd think they'd taken the poor old divil out of the fridge for the afternoon. And then one day, you're Mr So-and-so, you're sixty-three.

–Sixty-three is not too bad. It's better than not reaching it.

And many didn't. Who comes to mind straight away for you? Stan asked.

–Larry Maher is one.

–God be merciful to him, but he was some piss artist. I'd say there wasn't a house built in north County Dublin in the twenty-five years before he died that Larry didn't get a screw out of.

–He was killed, though. He just didn't die.

–By whom?

–By the system.

Stan looked at me coolly. –That's your opinion, Bunny.

I held his gaze. Stan dropped his eyes to the teapot, topped his own cup. –Who else comes to mind? he asked.

–Jamey Clinch, the man who got me into Lipman's.

–Ah, yes.

–And my own brother, Dick, of course.

–That must have been dreadful to lose a brother like that, dreadful.

–Then there was a fella my age I grew up beside. Mickey O'Connor, went into Justice, made assistant secretary. His father had been wounded in 1916, died when we were all young, I remember Dev coming to the house. But Mickey O was thin as a lath, jogged, ate fish and lettuce. Dropped dead one day at an interdepartmental meeting. Just like that. He was forty-three.

–Flower, Stan said, and narrowed his eyes.

–Yes, he would have been under Flower.

–Never knew you knew him, Stan said, and strayed with his eyes back to the biscuits.

We sat for a moment, both dealing with one of life's central mysteries, which is that you can know someone very well but at the same time not know them at all.

–My father comes to mind for me, Stan said, chewing again. –Problems and worry. Never really made the leap out of the pre-war era, never trusted the fact that a bank statement meant what it said. Came down here about three years before the Messengers. In fact I think it was he that encouraged them to leave the North. He'd been a caddie-master. Saved every shilling, then came down here and bought property. Died when I was twenty-five, he was forty-seven. 'Have all your problems solved before you're fifty,' he used to tell me. Now I'm nearly sixty-three.

–Do you have problems, Stan?

Stan's head bobbed in a way I once remembered it had when he was up for something.

–It's the problems I see down the road, Bunny. Problems no one wants, whatever their age, never mind a man of sixty-three.

I said nothing. Behind me, over my shoulder and out through thc big windows, I could hear the hotel porter whistling for a taxi. Stan leaned in closer. –I want to live in this country, by which I suppose I mean I want to die here. Last year when Eileen had to have her hip done I was told that the best place in the world for hips is in Florida. D'you think she'd go to Florida? No way. Nowhere but Ireland would do her. That got me thinking. What's the point of having all this money if you can't live in your own country?

–There are tax issues, I said.

–The issues were once about tax, Stan agreed. –I've saved a fortune living abroad. But that's elective, you can make the decision any time you want – all right, I'll pay the tax, I'll come home. What I'm worried about is that the time may come when I *can't* come home.

Again, I did not respond, even though I had a growing sense of where all this might be leading.

Stan continued, in his low, intense voice, –Look at Broe, for God's sake. Transferred everything offshore and now lives in Andorra. Fucking Andorra. You think he did that for tax reasons? I know you don't, but in case you do, let me clue you in. The great Dr Broe lives in Andorra because he's afraid of his shite that if anyone ever finds out what really happened in the Dr Tobin's business he'll end up doing a stretch in

Mountjoy where the best bedsheets are rubber ones, or so I'm told.

Stan sat back, nodding like a puppet. He ate another biscuit, his jaws working rapidly.

–So, here we are this morning, I said. –Still here.

–But suddenly in a different ball game, said Stan, and threw down the *Irish Times* on the table between us. The girl from Miami in the front-page photograph had coarse, unattractive features. –I met Milo last night, Stan was saying. –He sees this as a very negative development.

Milo Flood had been elevated to cabinet by Harry the previous November. He was now the Taoiseach's closest political confidant.

Stan said, –Milo says that Chris Foy has become hysterical. There's no reasoning with her. Apparently she's insisting that Barry resigns from the company and sells her his shares. It'll be in all the papers tomorrow.

–How can she insist?

–She's begun to dig, Stan whispered. –She's already found some stuff. She's talking about getting in an independent firm of auditors to unravel the whole thing, stupid cunt.

I winced, inwardly.

Stan said, –Look, what's done is done. I always had an idea that some day something like this would pop up. Don't get me wrong, I've been in this from the beginning and I've done very well, but there was a time when I could keep Harry going on my own. Loans that I knew were never coming back. I bought him his house, for God's sake. He rang me one day and said there was an island for sale off Connemara and he was thinking of buying it. 'How much'll buy it?' I asked, and he said, 'Forty grand.' I told him to go ahead and buy it if he wanted to and he did so that afternoon. He didn't even have enough money for the fucking deposit. I had to send round a cheque there and then for four grand.

–He's himself, I said.

Stan crossed his legs and sighed. –I know that, and nothing I've said means that I still wouldn't walk the length of Ireland for him. But now we're into injury time and the last thing anyone wants to do is to let in a goal in injury time. Look, if this starts, no one knows where it will end. Do you think the Brits aren't just waiting for their chance to get Harry? They know all about the money, about you, about your bank and Bermuda.

I must have looked surprised.

–Oh, yes, Stan said. –Ever hear of MI6? Well, MI6 knows what Harry had for his breakfast this morning, believe me. And this crisis is playing straight into their hands.

Was this the end, I wondered dismally. Had it all petered out in this sordid conclusion?

–Milo has made some approaches, Stan was saying.

I knew by the way Stan wasn't meeting my eye any more that something bad was coming.

–He's got on to Chris Foy's top financial people. Foy's may have tax problems. Milo has conveyed the information that the government will do all it can to mitigate any problems that may exist in exchange for Chris shutting her mouth and letting Barry come back quietly.

–And?

–And she more or less told him to fuck off, Stan said.

That heartened me, for I could imagine just how she would have said that to a cabinet minister and how two spots of colour would have come into her cheeks as she did so.

–We've all been here before, I said. –We're just that bit older.

–You're referring to Dr Tobin's, of course, Stan said. –Somehow that was never going to be the threat this is. Harry would have ridden it out. But this is different. This is a woman who's completely independent of the political system and who just happens to be one of the wealthiest people in Ireland. She may well have suspected over the years that Barry was dropping to Harry, but I don't think until now she realised the full extent of it.

I knew how Harry's mind worked, in these circumstances, and how only survival held any meaning for him.

Stan said: –For decades everyone has known that Harry's lifestyle costs twenty grand a week to sustain, but they've never really focused on how such a thing could be possible. If Chris pushes Barry far enough and he comes out and tells his side of the story, there'll be trouble like we've never seen it. Intense pressure from all sides to find the truth. Where's that going to lead? Very possibly to a formal tribunal of inquiry, set up under statute. Everything that ever moved spilled out on the record down in Dublin Castle or some place similar. People like Art Maddocks on the witness stand. Have you seen him lately? Probably not. Lives in a six-bed detached in Malahide. He's got a villa in Marbella that must have cost three hundred grand. He's got a boat down there. He owns three racehorses, none of which can run out of its own way. The man is on a salary of twenty-five grand a year, max. Twenty-five grand. How is that going to sound in Dublin Castle? And all for what? All because Chris fucking Foy is thrashing around her office like a mad cow with a sharp stick up her arse.

A woman removed the plates and teapot from the table. Stan's body was now curled into a ball away from me. –Milo rang me yesterday, he said, speaking more at the window than to me. –She can't be persuaded so she has to be stopped. And quick. Milo suggested that there might be a way to stop her – but I said I'd talk to you first.

I felt strangely detached. –Go on, Stan.

–Frank Trundle is another one who should have been on our list, Stan said quietly. –I mean, the list of those who aren't around any more. Car crash, the Navan Road, 1985 or '86. I saw you at the funeral. A desperate sight, all those little children. Garda intelligence, of course. An able man, Frank. Knew a lot more than he let on.

–I know. Set up the whole business in 1981 when Barry Foy's ransom was paid.

–So I understand. And apparently in an operation like that you keep tabs on everyone – for their own protection, of course. The family, friends of the family. You need to get the overall picture. In fact, apparently they took pictures. A lot of them. And for a while after Barry was released too, Bunny.

Stan was looking at me, his small eyes cold and distant. He said: –Milo is a bit of a hothead. He wanted to go right in and confront her with this stuff, but I said, 'Hold on a second, there's more than Chris Foy involved in this. What about Bunny? His marriage is involved here as well.' So Milo agreed that I should get your reaction and see what you wanted to do.

As the sheer crassness of the threat sank in, I looked at Stan in disbelief. Then I laughed. –You're out of your fucking mind, I said. –That was nothing.

–Of course not, said Stan, nodding soberly, –and of

course I believe you when you say that. But it may not look that way to everyone.

I slapped my head with my hand. –This is crazy! I cried. –I was upset at the time and I hadn't told Adi I'd delivered the ransom. It was completely innocent.

–As I said, I know that, Stan said, without a break, –but what will her husband think? Or Adi?

I sat back, feeling light-headed. –This is all Harry, isn't it? I asked.

–Oh, I don't think so, Stan said and made a dubious face. –No way. This is something Milo is running with. And Big Mac, too. He's got everything ready to feed out to the papers.

–You mean, these pictures . . . ?

–Haven't seen them and don't want to. But I understand they were taken in and around that hotel out at the airport, or so I'm told. Of course they were totally innocent but, still, you know newspapers and the way people talk. No one wants this kind of hassle, Bunny, no one.

That such a business, initiated in the wake of the Foy kidnapping, could have been continued only with official connivance should have pierced me. A clock chimed. I stood up. –I've got to go now, Stan.

–I'm sorry, Bunny.

–So am I.

–Remember, this town is like a battlefield. Everywhere you sink your pick you'll find a body.

–I know.

–What'll I tell Milo?

–Tell him, hold off for the moment.

–I knew you'd do the right thing, Stan said, and he smiled.

* * *

I telephoned Violet from the Shelbourne and instructed her to cancel my meeting with the Central Bank on the grounds that I was indisposed, which was as near the truth as I was prepared to go. Then I walked along Merrion Row and by way of Government Buildings to Upper Mount Street. I had always liked the fact that our places of work were connected by some of Dublin's most elegant thoroughfares.

In the 1980s Harry had seized the old College of Science with its magnificent façade and domed roof and had it turned into his office, a move that at the time his critics had called 'Napoleonic'. Harry had smiled when he heard that, the same way he smiled when people referred to him on his Atlantic island as being 'kingly'. Because he was a king for many, or, more accurately, the chieftain they had so admired, who had been laid low by cowardly forces but who then, having braved years in the wilderness, had returned to his people. I smiled as I recalled Mam's old stories, her link to her father and her father's to his mythical past. Recently the chieftain from his domed palace had told his people that these were hard times, that they all, him included, would have to face the realities of a fragile economy and accept grim and austere measures. Swingeing cuts to the budgets of health and education. Higher taxes. Scale-backs in the public services. The people accepted it. They would have accepted anything, many of them, as long as they could have their chieftain.

The sun, now triumphant, bathed my face as I walked along the top of Merrion Square. We would never again, I knew, go down to the island together and sit out on the cliffs watching dolphins. Whenever I thought of the island, it was always warm and the air was heavy with scent. No noise except sea and gulls. And every now and then, Harry would look over at me in the mischievous way he used to years and years ago, and we'd both lie back on the heather, laughing.

At one that afternoon I drove out to Oakwood. Schoolchildren were playing in wired-off enclosures in the sunshine; if I opened the car window I could hear their heartening voices. Although not likely, it was possible that Milo Flood was acting alone. Or Stan and Milo together. Although not likely, it was possible that Harry knew nothing of Milo's blunt proposals. If so, Harry would be outraged. It was possible. I had tried to ring him for over an hour. His private line was diverted to his secretary. Malcolm had answered the phone in Oakwood and had sounded vague. He was expecting the Taoiseach, yes, but he could not say when for sure. 'You know the Taoiseach, Mr Gardener,' Malcolm said. I did, and that was what bothered me. I had to hear him say it himself.

I saw the bare treetops of Oakwood in the distance. If Milo was advising Harry, as he now seemed to be, then his strategy was crude and plainly stupid. I did not believe that a woman like Chris Foy would buckle under a threat as ridiculous and base as the one that had been outlined to me that morning; but of course that did not mean that Milo would not persist. His political career had been notable for his ability to bludgeon his way through problems, and this was what he was now endeavouring to do again. The fact that the lives of four people might be lamed or ruined in the process would not intrude on his decision.

I had made this journey so often, I felt myself quickening with the pleasure it always brought, the sense of privilege, however shared, that possessed me as soon as I drove through the great gates. I would open the car's windows and smell cut grass, and remark one further time on the quietness, and savour the beauty of shining horses wandering the paddocks and of speckled cattle munching beneath ancient trees. I was as much a part of this setting as Harry was, I thought, and as I did so I felt my old faith rise.

There was the usual squad car parked across the closed gates. As I pulled up, a guard got out, putting on his cap. He came over to my side. A time was when I had known them all out here, that when I appeared I'd be waved straight through.

–Bunny Gardener, I replied to the guard's question.

He wrote my name down on a clipboard and the registration number of my car. –Are you expected?

–No, but he'll see me.

The young man's thick, black eyebrows went up sceptically. –Hold on a second.

He said something to his companion and made his way with almost derisory slowness to a wooden hut outside the gates. I saw him lift a telephone. I could hear his words at first – saying my name, 'a Bunny Gardener' – but then his voice was entombed as if we were in the sudden path of an avalanche. An immense shadow swallowed up the sun, then the long and ugly shape of the helicopter swooped in over the walls of Oakwood and settled somewhere beyond the trees. The guard was walking back. I expected the gates to swing inwards.

–You have to have an appointment, the guard said.

–I beg your pardon?

–You need an appointment.

–I've never had to have an appointment in forty years, I said.

–Would you move on now, please? You can't park here.

I got out of the car and found myself panting. –Guard, who did you speak to?

–It's none of your business. Now, move the car, please. Now.

–Did you speak to Malcolm?

I could see the flicker of doubt that Malcolm's name gave rise to, as if someone with no business here might not have such information.

I said, –Listen, Guard, I'm the Taoiseach's oldest friend and business partner. Now, I'd like to speak to Malcolm on the phone.

The guard looked at me belligerently, then he seemed to give in. –Ring him, so, he said, and stood aside. –You dial nine.

I tried to keep my back to him so that he would not see the shake in my hand as I picked up the receiver. I dialled nine. It rang once.

–*What?*

It was Harry.

–Harry, this is Bunny.

I could hear other voices in the background.

–Bunny.

–I'm out at the gate.

There was a muffled sound as he put his hand over the telephone. Then: –Yeah, Bunny, I'm just about to go down to the island. There's a helicopter waiting here. We'll have to talk another time.

–This is most important.

–Look, you'll have to talk to somebody else – all right? Talk to Milo, will you?

–You know what Milo is proposing to do, don't you?

–Bunny, I have no fucking idea what you're talking about.

–Then you should open these gates and let me in so that I can tell you.

–I can't do that now, I've told you. I haven't got the time.

–There won't be another time, Harry. Open the gates!

A silence, a cold absence of sound.

–You're threatening me, aren't you? he asked, very quietly. –You're standing outside the gates to my residence, making threats. Do you know that I could have you arrested for that? All I'd have to do is raise my little finger and they'd take you off somewhere in a squad car and beat the living shit out of you – do you know that?

–I'm very, very sorry, Harry.

I could hear Malcolm's voice saying something.

Harry was breathing noisily. –Look, I'm sorry too, Bunny. It's the pressure, you know all about it, sometimes it becomes too much. Everyone competing for my time – you think I enjoy this? See what you can do to clean up this mess, would you? I don't know all the details, you know me and details, but I gather she can be persuaded. There doesn't have to be fallout, I think that's the message, although you know the score much better than I do. I mean, we helped those people out big-time before and now we're not asking too much, are we? We're actually offering some sort of a tax deal, I understand – what could be fairer? The father, if he was alive, he'd go for it in a shot. Tell her that. No point in her cutting off her own nose to get a dig in at Barry, he's suffered enough, he's just an overgrown eejit, we all know that, this is maybe the kick in the arse he needs. Tell her that her father would go for this deal. Tell her there's no point in her upsetting the whole applecart just to get rid of one fucking apple. Persuade her. You're the best man to do it. The only man. She'll listen to you, Bunny.

Explain what's at stake for everyone, you included. That should do the trick.

I held the phone out from me, then placed it on a rough table that bore the brown rings of a thousand coffee mugs. I could still hear Harry's voice as I walked out.

–When you sort it out, give me a ring, I'll tell them I'm expecting you, you'll be put straight through. Or, better still, come out here and we'll have a long walk together, I'd enjoy that. And when this is all behind us, we'll get together, just the four of us, how about that? How is Adi, anyway? And your lads? It must be ages since we've all seen each other . . .

I walked to my car and sat in. The guard was behind the wheel of the squad car, eating a sandwich. Sudden lightness overcame me and I saw the gates of Oakwood recede into the very far distance.

Time passed, how much I can't say, probably no more than a few minutes. Then my body went rigid as a great roar shook the trees, the gates, the ground I was parked on. And this time, the shadow seemed to grow outwards from Oakwood as the helicopter shuddered upwards and hung above me, terrifyingly, as if stays still held it to the earth. Then it banked, veered at an angle over the wall and was lost to sight.

I heard a knock on the glass. Two guards were outside this time. I rolled down the window.

–Are you all right? one of them asked.

–Just a bit short of breath. And I've got a pain in my back, I said.

–Where do you live? asked the guard I had met when I had arrived.

–Raheny.

–It's none of my business, he said, –but if I was you I'd go and see a doctor.

16

Dublin, 1992

Cars were heading north through the Phoenix Park, their headlights on, a procession of muted yellow beams forming a tunnel of light through the dusk. We'd been walking for nearly thirty minutes and the pain in my back had eased.

–You're very silent, Chris said, and linked me closer.

–Just thinking.

–About what's next?

–More about how bad I feel, how disappointed. Not by you – never by you. By events.

–I was just thinking, too – about Dennis. What he would do. Was Messenger right?

–Probably. Dennis would close ranks, milk the situation for all it was worth, extract the maximum from Harry, take Barry back quietly, carry on. Nothing would change.

Chris shivered. –I'd like to go home now.

As soon as we got back into the car and the headlights were switched on, the parkland disappeared. We joined the traffic leaving the Park. I felt as if the whole world had shifted between sunrise and sunset, as if movement towards change had been born this morning and had now, by the end of day, taken over. The feeling was both welcome and terrifying, like love that is long overdue. She switched on the radio. Some financial analyst was predicting that the Foy Group might have to be broken up and sold off in pieces in order to buy out Barry: –Chris Foy is an unknown, unproven entity and banks hate the unknown. Chris Foy may not therefore be able to finance the buy-out of her brother that she suddenly sees as a necessity and so, in the circumstances, might have been better advised to have sat tight and allowed this crisis to blow over.

–Moron, Chris said, and stabbed the on/off button. –Does he think I'm so stupid that I haven't the finance in place before I make my move?

–How much will he cost?

–Between a hundred and a hundred and twenty million. God knows what he'll do with it. But I reckon we can make it back in eighteen months with him out of the way.

Chris drove in the short driveway and pulled up. Four cars were parked there. She rang the bell and a woman opened the door and stood back to let us in.

–This is Mary; Mary, this is Mr Gardener.

–Bunny.

–Any messages? Chris asked.

–The phone has been going non-stop, Mary answered. –One man in particular.

Chris looked at a notebook beside the phone. –I'd better call him, she said. –It will only take a minute.

Mary showed me into a large sitting room where a log fire was blazing. On a sideboard were pictures of a man with short, sandy hair, and First Communion pictures of two girls and a boy. One of the girls was so like Chris when I first met her that I had to suck in my breath. In another frame was a family group in which the man had his arm protectively round Chris's shoulders. No pictures of Dennis Foy, or of Barry.

–That was the independent firm of auditors, said

Chris, as she came back in. –They're waiting for the word to come in tomorrow morning and tear the place asunder.

–Why are they waiting?

–I told them I'd call them back later this evening and give them the final word.

Mary knocked and entered, pushing a trolley heavily charged with tea things and dishes. She positioned it between us and left.

–You're lucky to have someone like that, I said.

Chris smiled. –Remember Mary I was telling you about? The lady from Phibsboro who used to look after us as kids years ago? Well, Mary's her daughter. She worked for us in town, then she came out here and is looking after our kids. And me. I need more looking after than they do.

She kicked off her shoes, flopped into a chair and put her feet on a stool. –Do you want to hear my decision? she asked.

–I think I know what it is.

She looked at me and for an instant I could see in her face the determination that was needed to keep great wealth intact.

She said, –I abhor what has happened and I am aghast at the depth to which Messenger is prepared to stoop to shut me up. And yet I shouldn't be surprised. I've grown up in this environment. We do pretty tough things ourselves in the business. I try to be fair, but we know what it takes to get a new store up and running, how to set our prices against local competitors. We come up against people who have been selling over the counter for three generations – we just shrug, cut our prices, wait for them to give up. We manage situations so that suppliers depend on our business – then we cut them back to the bone and tell them if they don't like it we'll go elsewhere. Meanwhile, we're earning hundreds of thousands of pounds' interest on money on deposit whilst they're paying a fortune on an overdraft. It's nauseating, if you think about it. I don't think much about it. I'm running a business. That's the way it works. I accept that it's much the same in politics.

She sat forward and looked into the fire.

–Yet I am committed to my business, she said, –and I understand, as perhaps I always have understood, that my brother will one day bring Foy's to its knees. What happened in Florida was just a graphic illustration of the sum total that Barry amounts to. That's Barry, and no matter how much he cries now, or confesses, or asks for forgiveness, he'll do something equally stupid again. It's the way he is.

Chris handed me a cup, sat back with her own. She looked at me intently. –I think of you often, Bunny, and never with anything but fondness. But you have to make up your own mind about Messenger and his regard for you and the depths he's prepared to go to in order to save his skin. It's disgusting. And yet today has brought home to me the reality of this country we live in.

I stared at her.

–You and I have spent the whole day talking about Messenger, she said. –He's the Taoiseach and anyone who has ever taken him on over the years has always lost. I don't want to lose. This is the business my father built up. I want to keep it, whatever it takes. So I'm going to back off. I'm going to cancel the independent audit.

–And Barry?

–It's a shame, but he can come back in – on my terms.

He will go, but not now. It's too expensive. He'll go another time.

I heard the phone ringing and Mary came in again, her face happy, and told Chris that Mr Price was calling from the Canaries. It took me some seconds to work out who Mr Price was.

–I might even join them, now that the crisis is over, Chris said, as she went out to take the call.

Perhaps I should have been elated by developments and yet I felt nothing. For what Chris had just decided meant that Harry had once again been victorious. He had defied the odds and neutralised the source of greatest danger. And despite what Chris's intentions were for the future, her opportunity to get rid of her brother would now pass and once he got back into Foy's Barry might never again be so vulnerable. He would regain his authority quickly, and within six months Chris would be back in spring fashions.

I tried to understand why I felt so dismayed at having achieved what I had set out to. Allowing Barry Foy to come back as if nothing had changed seemed so ignoble now. For nothing less than the outcome that Harry most feared was deserved by these events: not just a trawling through the political donations made by Barry Foy, but the convulsion of official scrutiny that would then follow, the microscopic examination of anything that Harry had been involved in over twenty years and of anyone who had ever been associated with him, me included. He would walk on, regal and untouched, controlling his court with mere turns of his head or the expression of his eyes whilst what he deserved was to be ruined. He had always known this, of course; and I had been foolish to think that our personal relationship might have given him pause to consider my own situation.

I had to admire him, too, for the way he was still feared, even by a brave and wealthy woman like Chris Foy. The reach of his power was truly terrifying and he used it reflexively. Nothing personal. In three weeks' or a month's time, when the days lengthened, I'd get a call suggesting that Adi and I join him down on the island.

–They're all learning to water-ski, Chris said, as she came back in. She sat down by the fire again. –Maybe it's time I took it up.

–Maybe.

She frowned. –You look sad. I thought you'd be jumping in the air. After all, the mad cow with the sharp stick up her arse has gone back to chewing the cud.

–Don't say things like that. Please.

Chris got up and came to sit beside me. –I'm sorry. Tell me what the matter is.

–I don't know. I feel different. It's hard to describe.

–Try.

–I've led my life in a certain way, but for some time now I've been convinced that I've let myself down. It's always been in the back of my mind that myself or my family shouldn't want for anything – that goal drove me. So I did certain things, supported certain people, one in particular, and I've got more money now than I'll ever need. I'm within the golden circle. It's so easy when you are.

–But there's been a big price.

–I've been the price – whoever I am. Hard to say, that, because I don't know who I am or what I stand for. I'm like a tool that everyone has used to their best advantage. Time and time again. I've spent over forty years prostituting myself on Harry's behalf, not caring what decent people must have thought of me – the bagman, here he comes again, look at him, and when he goes back to Messenger and empties out his bag, he probably gets a kick in the arse, and do you know something? He probably says, 'Thank you very much, Taoiseach.'

–You're being hard on yourself.

–Not really. I just wanted to please everyone from as far back as I can remember, and when I met Harry, I found the opportunity to please someone for the rest of my life. Why else would I have done all the things I did? Why would I put even my own life in danger? I suppose because he expected that of me. Nothing less. Still does. But it's not just me who's expendable now in his eyes, it's my marriage, my family. It doesn't matter that his threat is hollow. And, yes, that's a big price.

Chris got up, went to the mantelpiece, found a packet of cigarettes behind a picture.

–The kids and Tom don't know I smoke, she said, and looked at me as if to see if I might tell on her.

–Your secret is safe with me, I said. She hadn't mentioned him by name before.

–What does being in love mean, Bunny?

–I think, in the end, it means being true, I said, and felt a stab of surprise at myself.

–Go on.

–And that means being true to yourself first and then to those you love. True in everything. But you can't deliver what you haven't got. I never realised that before this week – I thought that my belief and trust in another man was all I needed to see me over. And it looked for a long time as if I was right. Adi and I are happy. We want for nothing. All the kids are set up for life. What more can a man achieve? Then out of the blue in a faraway place a man is arrested and within two days I realise that the cornerstone I built everything on is rotten. Always was, but I didn't see it. You see, I thought that was love.

–Is what I've decided not being true? Chris asked quietly. –Being true to what my father would have done?

–It's the right thing for all the wrong reasons, I replied. –And it's not being true to yourself. That's not good for you, Chris. Not good for Foy's in the long run, probably not good for your brother. Not even good for me any more. Just good for one person and we all know who that is.

–It's a huge risk, she said, and looked into the fire.

–I've spent my whole life making calls on risks, I said, –and I'm prepared to bet any money now that if you do what you should do, what you know is right, Harry Messenger will never bother you again.

She looked at me for a long time. –You're serious, aren't you? she said at last.

–More than I've ever been. Now, go out and make that call and tell that firm of auditors that they're to get started first thing tomorrow morning.

She smiled. –I should have known, really.

–Do it now, I said. –Do it for me.

She came out with me the short distance to the road. She had wanted to drive me back into town and had then tried to insist that I called a taxi; but I told her that I really wanted to walk. We hugged then, as once before, and I headed back towards the Phoenix Park, that great slab of fertile darkness that lies like a mirror sea on the north-west side of Dublin City.

I found a new spring in my step. I was headed into the

wildness in whose midst we had roamed over an hour before, where we had shared the feeling of being one with night creatures looking out at the cars' headlights and the russet glow of the city. I edged through the gates as traffic funnelled northwards, stepped off the road and within fifty strides could not see my hand before my face. I paused, breathing easily. Wind sang in the grass, and I could hear deer as they adapted to my presence and resumed their grazing. Gradually the outline of trees grew from the night. I began to walk.

My grandfather, too, had come up from the Liberties on such evenings as this, I thought, perhaps when the house had become too hot, or the children too boisterous, or his head had swarmed with thoughts and desires that he could not articulate. Beneath these trees, walking in these grasses, he had stood and listened. Smelt. Inhaled the land. Tried for perhaps the ten-thousandth time to come to terms with what he had left behind in exchange for what he now held. He must have raised his head, like a fox at this hour, probing the absolute limits of possibility, trying to discern in the laden air sweet molecules from west of the Shannon.

He had been hurt, I could tell even though I'd never met him. Uncle Myles had no sign of being so wounded by his separation from the west, from the land, but he had not been the eldest son. Uncle Myles had never stopped talking about Castlebar; Richard never mentioned it. If he had, then Gran Gardener would have cherished what he had held dear, passed it on and tried to keep the memory alive. But I was sure that he had known evenings like this up here for comfort, the sound of grass at night as it is being grazed, the shine moon makes on it, the soothing odour of animals and the urgent sense that if you stretch your hands far enough, you will feel the loam of the earth.

Da, too, must have come up here sometimes, perhaps on his bicycle or in Findlater's van. Maybe he had brought Dick.

When I thought of all of us together, as I did then, I always came back to thinking of Dick. After he died, all that was left of him in the house was a photograph that Uncle John had taken on the day of his First Communion. It didn't really look like Dick at all, with his hair so neat and a smile on him that'd make you swear he was a saint. The way I best remembered Dick was with his ten-gallon hat pushed back on his head and a good horse beneath him.

I had walked into the expanse of acres where by day racehorses galloped and beside which was the site on which the Pope had said Mass. So much greater this, up here, than I had ever imagined, and at night, vast beyond comprehension.

Up to that morning, I think I had believed that change was bad, that Ireland was really no more than one big parish – for if you asked anyone in a parish what it was they most feared, they would tell you it was change. The local postman got his job because his father was the postman, or his uncle was, and the family knew the people in the post office who gave out the jobs in that area. The local guard got into Templemore, too, most likely, because his father had a friend who was a superintendent in Garda headquarters. The same for the shop assistants in the town, the man who swept the streets. Parnell, and later Redmond, had spent their lives advocating change, but change within the existing order.

It was those few who caused real change who would

be remembered most by history. For one act, or one book, or one idea. Some did it as young men and died; others spent a lifetime and were confronted without warning by this extraordinary opportunity. What made them grasp the moment was a belief in themselves and a conviction in where their true destinies lay. The moment hung just long enough to grasp, like a sunset that you can catch in a net and bring home and have it light the rest of your life.

I knew then that because of what I had done the dam would rupture, that years of subterfuge and connivance would be washed away and that the uproar that would follow would never end. Yet none of it mattered to me because I had gained something far greater than the hounding and change that would come: I was free of Harry at last. If I had meant something to him, it would have been different; but I hadn't. That left me free, a most delicious feeling, for I had never been free before.

I had gone far enough in this darkness; I turned and headed for the lights. It would take me another half-hour to reach the city. I'd find a taxi at Heuston Station and I would be home with Adi by seven thirty. I had so much to tell her. I could just imagine her face when I did so.

That made me want to skip in the darkness; I skipped, perhaps for half a dozen paces before I got out of breath, and then I began to laugh. I threw back my head and laughed and saw the stars warmly, all the various clusters and groupings of which I understood nothing except that stars are the eyes of the dead and that all the old people could see me clearly now and could probably hear me laughing as well. That was good, for we were all in this together. I skipped, I laughed. My back no longer hurt. It didn't matter if I was late.

Author's Note

By 2003 in Ireland there were ten tribunals and public inquiries looking into the relationship between certain leading politicians and big business, corrupt payments to politicians, tax evasion on the part of leading Irish citizens and the use over many years by these same citizens of offshore bank accounts.

Apart from examining serious wrongdoing in public affairs and the perversion of the work of public institutions, these inquiries, some established in the mid-1990s, were also examining scandals relating to the Garda Siochána, the Blood Transfusion Service and the abuse of children in state institutions.

To date, the estimated cost of these inquiries to the Irish taxpayer has been over €60 million.

Although some of the key figures being investigated relating to corrupt payments to politicians are now deceased, recent estimates suggest that, based on progress to date, these public inquiries will continue until at least 2018.